Gustave Doré, Henry F. Cary

The Vision of Hell

Gustave Doré, Henry F. Cary

The Vision of Hell

ISBN/EAN: 9783337391102

Printed in Europe, USA, Canada, Australia, Japan

Cover: Foto ©Andreas Hilbeck / pixelio.de

More available books at **www.hansebooks.com**

PREFACE.

It is a somewhat remarkable circumstance that outside of his own country
Dante has nowhere been so much read as in England. Next to Italy,
England possesses by far the largest number of Manuscripts of his great
poem, many of which have, no doubt, been in the country from early times.
Our own poet, Chaucer, born seven years after Dante's death, quotes him
several times by name, and borrows from him frequently. Many instances of
this will be found duly recorded in the notes to the present work. One
of the most interesting of the early commentaries on the *Divine Comedy*
was written at the request of the English Bishops of Salisbury and Bath
and Wells, by the Italian Bishop of Rimini, whom they met at the Council
of Constance.* Spenser knew Dante, undoubtedly, and Milton was evidently
very familiar with his works. No actual translation into English, however,
appears to have existed till the end of the last century, when the Rev. Henry
Boyd produced a version which cannot be regarded as satisfactory. In
1805 the Rev. H. F. Cary, librarian at the British Museum, published a
translation in blank verse of the first seventeen Cantos of the *Inferno*,
following it up by other fragmentary issues until the whole appeared complete in three small volumes in 1814. Since then translations innumerable
of the whole poem, or portions, have appeared in every sort of metre and
in prose; but it is safe to say that Cary's holds its own. Its verse, if it
seldom rises much above mediocrity, never falls below it; as a translation

---

* See note 3, p. xiv. John of Serravalle is there wrongly called *Bishop* of Fermo. He
was Prince of that town, and Bishop of Rimini. A copy of his work is now in the British
Museum.

it is exceedingly accurate, while its notes, it is not too much to say, are
the most helpful to the student that have ever been appended to any
English edition. Since its first appearance it has been repeatedly reprinted
in almost every imaginable form, and must have found its way into almost
every English household, taking with it at least the opportunity of
acquaintance with one of the half-dozen greatest works in the world's
literature. Messrs. Cassell's large folio editions, accompanied by the popular
illustrations from the hand of Gustave Doré, are widely known. Doré's
work, though unequal, has, notably when he deals with the *Inferno*, merits
of its own ; while in nearly all cases he has succeeded, at any rate, in so
representing the scenes described in the poem as to arouse curiosity, and
thereby encourage the study of the text. It is hoped that this issue in
a more handy form will increase the acquaintance of English readers with
the excellent work of an Englishman, and lead them on to a closer study
of the great original.   A. J. B.

CONTENTS.

THE VISION OF HELL.

CANTO I.

The writer, having lost his way in a gloomy forest, and being hindered by certain wild beasts from ascending a mountain, is met by Virgil, who promises to show him the punishments of Hell, and afterwards of Purgatory; and that he shall then be conducted by Beatrice into Paradise. He follows the Roman poet 3

CANTO II.

After the invocation, which poets are used to prefix to their works, he shows that, on a consideration of his own strength, he doubted whether it sufficed for the journey proposed to him, but that, being comforted by Virgil, he at last took courage, and followed him as his guide and master 19

CANTO III.

Dante, following Virgil, comes to the gate of Hell; where, after having read the dreadful words that are written thereon, they both enter. Here, as he understands from Virgil, those were punished who had passed their time (for living it could not be called) in a state of apathy and indifference both to good and evil. Then pursuing their way, they arrive at the river Acheron; and there find the old ferryman Charon, who takes the spirits over to the opposite shore; which as soon as Dante reaches, he is seized with terror, and falls into a trance 26

CANTO IV.

The poet, being roused by a clap of thunder, and following his guide onwards, descends into Limbo, which is the first circle of Hell, where he finds the souls of those who, although they have lived virtuously, and have not to suffer for great sins, nevertheless, through lack of baptism, merit not the bliss of Paradise. Hence he is led on by Virgil to descend into the second circle 37

CANTO V.

Coming into the second circle of Hell, Dante at the entrance beholds Minos the Infernal Judge, by whom he is admonished to beware how he enters these regions. Here he witnesses the punishment of carnal sinners, who are lost about ceaselessly in the dark air by the most furious winds. Amongst these, he meets with Francesca of Rimini, through pity at whose sad tale he falls fainting to the ground 49

CANTO VI.

On his recovery, the poet finds himself in the third circle, where the gluttonous are punished. Their torment is, to lie in the mire, under a continual and heavy storm of hail, snow, and discoloured water; Cerberus meanwhile barking over them with his threefold throat, and rending them piecemeal. One of these, who on earth was named Ciacco, foretells the divisions with which Florence is about to be distracted. Dante proposes a question to his guide, who solves it; and they proceed towards the fourth circle 65

CANTO VII.

In the present canto Dante describes his descent into the fourth circle, at the beginning of which he sees Plutus stationed. Here one like doom awaits the prodigal and the avaricious; which is to meet in direful conflict, rolling great weights against each other with mutual upbraidings. From hence Virgil takes occasion to show how vain the goods that are committed into the charge of Fortune; and this moves our author to inquire what being that Fortune is, of whom he speaks: which question be'ng resolved, they go down into the fifth circle, where they find the wrathful and gloomy tormented in the Stygian lake. Having made a compass round great part of this lake, they come at last to the base of a lofty tower 74

CANTO VIII.

CANTO XXVII.

CANTO XXVIII.

CANTO XXIX.

CANTO XXX.

CANTO XXXI.

CANTO XXXII.

CANTO XXXIII

CANTO XXXIV.

LIST OF ILLUSTRATIONS.

LIFE OF DANTE.

DANTE,[1] a name abbreviated, as was the custom in those days, from Durante or Durando, was of a very ancient Florentine family. The first of his ancestors,[2] concerning whom anything certain is known, was Cacciaguida,[3] a Florentine knight, who died fighting in the holy war, under the Emperor Conrad III. Cacciaguida had two brothers, Moronto and Eliseo, the former of whom is not recorded to have left any posterity ; the latter is the head of the family of the Elisei, or perhaps (for it is doubtful which is the case) only transmitted to his descendants a name which he had himself inherited. From Cacciaguida himself were sprung the Alighieri, so called from one of his sons, who bore the appellation from his mother's family,[4] as is affirmed by the poet himself, under the person of Cacciaguida, in the fifteenth canto of the "Paradise." This name, Alighieri, is derived from the coat-of-arms,[5] a wing *or*, on a field *azure*, still borne by the descendants of our poet at Verona, in the days of Leonardo Aretino.

Dante was born at Florence in May, 1265. His mother's name was Bella, but of what family is no longer known. His father[6] he had the misfortune to lose in his childhood ; but by the advice of his surviving relations, and with the assistance of an able preceptor, Brunetto Latini, he applied himself closely to polite literature and other liberal studies, at the same time that he omitted no pursuit necessary for the accomplishment of a manly character, and mixed with the youth of his age in all honourable and noble exercises.

In the twenty-fourth year of his age he was present at the memorable battle of Campaldino,[7] where he served in the foremost troop of cavalry, and was exposed to imminent danger. Leonardo Aretino refers to a letter of Dante, in which he described the order of that battle, and mentioned his having been engaged in it. The cavalry of the Aretini at the first onset gained so great an advantage over the Florentine horse, as to compel them to retreat to their body of infantry. This circumstance in the event proved highly fortunate to the Florentines ; for their own cavalry being thus joined to their foot, while that of their enemies was led by the pursuit to a considerable distance from theirs, they were by these means enabled to defeat with ease their separate forces. In this battle the Uberti, Lamberti, and Abati, with all the other ex-citizens of Florence who adhered to the Ghibelline interest, were with the Aretini ; while those inhabitants of Arezzo who, owing to their attachment to the Guelph party, had been banished from their own city, were ranged on the side of the Florentines. In the following year Dante took part in another engagement between his countrymen and the citizens of Pisa, from whom they took the castle of Caprona,[8] situated not far from that city.

From what the poet has told us in his treatise entitled the "Vita Nuova," we learn that he was a lover long before he was a soldier, and that his passion for the Beatrice whom he has immortalised

---

[1] A note by Salvini, on Muratori, "Della Perfetta Poesia Italiana," lib. iii., cap. 8.

[2] Leonardo Aretino, "Vita di Dante."

[3] "Paradise," xv. He was born, as most have supposed, in 1106, and died about 1147. But Lombardi computes his birth to have happened about 1090.

[4] Vellutello, "Vita di Dante." There is reason to suppose that she was the daughter of Aldigerio, who was a lawyer of Verona, and brother of one of the same name, bishop of that city, and author of an epistle addressed to his mother, a religious recluse, with the title of "Tractatus Adalgeri Episc. ad Rosuvidam reclausam (or, ad Orismundam matrem inclusam) de Rebus moralibus." See Cancellieri, "Osservazioni," &c., Roma., 1818, p. 119.

[5] Pelli describes the arms differently; "Memorie per la Vita di Dante, Opere di Dante," ediz. Zatta, 1758, tom. iv., part ii., p. 16. The male line ended in Pietro, the sixth in descent from our poet, and father of Ginevra, married in 1549 to the Conte Marcantonio Sarego, of Verona.—*Pelli*, p. 19.

[6] His father Alighiero had been before married to Lapa, daughter of Chiarissimo Cialuffi ; and by her had a son named Francesco, who left two daughters and a son, whom he named Durante after his brother. Francesco appears to have been mistaken for a son of our poet's. Boccaccio mentions also a sister of Dante, who was married to Poggi, and was the mother of Andrea Poggi, Boccaccio's intimate. —*Pelli*, p. 267.

[7] G. Villani describes this engagement, lib. vii., cap. cxxx.

[8] "Hell," xxi. 92.

commenced[1] when she was at the beginning and he near the end of his ninth year. Their first meeting was at a banquet in the house of Folco Portinari,[2] her father; and the impression then made on the susceptible and constant heart of Dante was not obliterated by her death, which happened after an interval of sixteen years.

But neither war nor love prevented Dante from gratifying the earnest desire which he had of knowledge and mental improvement. By Benvenuto da Imola, one of the earliest of his commentators, it is stated that he studied in his youth at the universities of Bologna and Padua, as well as in that of his native city, and devoted himself to the pursuit of natural and moral philosophy. There is reason to believe that his eagerness for the acquisition of learning, at some time of his life, led him as far as Paris, and even Oxford;[3] in the former of which universities he is said to have taken the degree of a Bachelor, and distinguished himself in the theological disputations, but to have been hindered from commencing Master by a failure in his pecuniary resources. Francesco da Buti, another of his commentators in the fourteenth century, asserts that he entered the order of Frati Minori, but laid aside the habit before he was professed.

In his own city, domestic troubles, and yet more severe public calamities, awaited him. In 1291 he was induced, by the solicitation of his friends, to console himself for the loss of Beatrice by a matrimonial connection with Gemma, a lady of the noble family of the Donati, by whom he had a numerous offspring. But the violence of her temper proved a source of the bitterest suffering to him; and in that passage of the "Inferno," where one of the characters says—

> "La fiera moglie più ch' altro, mi nuoce,"
>
> *Canto* xvi.;

> "Me, my wife
> Of savage temper, more than aught beside,
> Hath to this evil brought "—

his own conjugal unhappiness must have recurred forcibly and painfully to his mind.[4] It is not improbable that political animosity might have had some share in these dissensions; for his wife was a kinswoman of Corso Donati, one of the most formidable as he was one of the most inveterate of his opponents.

---

[1] See also the beginning of the "Vita Nuova."

[2] Folco di Ricovero Portinari was the founder of the hospital of S. Maria Nuova, in 1280, and of other charitable institutions, and died in 1289, as appeared from his epitaph.—*Pell.*, p. 55.

[3] Giovanni Villani, who was his contemporary, and, as Villani himself says, his neighbour in Florence, informs us that "he went to study at Bologna, and then to Paris, and to many parts of the world" (an expression that may well include England), "subsequently to his banishment." *Hist.*, lib. ix., cap. cxxxv. Indeed, as we shall see, it is uncertain whether he might not have been more than once a student at Paris. But the fact of his having visited England rests on a passage alluding to it in the Latin poems of Boccaccio, and on the authority of Giovanni da Serravalle, Bishop of Fermo, who, as Tiraboschi observes, though he lived at the distance of a century from Dante, might have known those who were contemporaries with him. This writer, in an inedited commentary on the "Commedia," written while he was attending the Council of Constance, says of our poet: "Anagorice dilexit theologiam sacram, in quâ diu studuit tam in Oxoniis in regno Angliæ, quam Parisius in regno Franciæ," &c. And again: "Dantes se in juventute dedit omnibus artibus liberalibus, studens eas Paduæ, Bononiæ, demum Oxoniis et Parisius, ubi fecit multos actus mirabiles, intantum quod ab aliquibus dicebatur magnus philosophus, ab aliquibus magnus Theologus, ab aliquibus magnus poeta." *Tiraboschi, Storia della Poes. Ital.*, vol. ii., cap. iv., p. 14, as extracted from Tiraboschi's great work by Mathias, and edited by that gentleman, London, 1803. The bishop translated the poem itself into Latin prose, at the instance of Cardinal Amedeo di Saluzzo, and of two English bishops, Nicholas Bubwith, of Bath, and Robert Halam, of Salisbury, who attended the same council. One copy only of the version and commentary is known to be preserved, and that is in the Vatican. I would suggest the probability of others existing in this country. Stillingfleet, in the "Origines Sacræ," twice quotes passages from the "Paradiso," "rendered into Latin" (and it is Latin prose), as that learned bishop says, "by F. S."— *Origines Sacræ*, b. ii., chap. ix., sect. xviii., § 4; and chap. x., sect. v., edit. Cambridge, 1701. This work was begun in February, 1416, and finished in the same month of the following year. The word "anagorice" (into which the Italians altered "anagogice"), which occurs in the former of the above extracts, is explained by Dante in the "Convito" ("Opere di Dante," tom. i., p. 43, edit. Venez., 1793), and more briefly by Field, "Of the Church," b. iii., cap. 26; "The anagogicall" sense is, "when the things literally expressed unto us do signifie something in the state of heaven's happiness." It was used by the Greek Fathers to signify merely a more recondite sense in a text of Scripture than that which the plain words offered. See Origen in Routh's "Reliquiæ Sacræ," vol. iv., p. 323.

[4] Yet M. Artaud, in his "Histoire de Dante" (8vo, Paris, 1841, p. 85), represents Gemma as a tender, faithful, and affectionate wife. I certainly do not find any mention of her unhappy temper in the early biographers. Regard for her or for her children might have restrained them. But in the next century, Landino, though commending her good qualities, does not scruple to assert that in this respect she was more than a Xanthippe.

In 1300 he was chosen chief of the Priors, who at that time possessed the supreme authority in the state; his colleagues being Palmieri degli Altoviti and Neri di Jacopo degli Alberti. From this exaltation our poet dated the cause of all his subsequent misfortunes in life.[1]

In order to show the occasion of Dante's exile, it may be necessary to enter more particularly into the state of parties at Florence. The city, which had been disturbed by many divisions between the Guelphs and Ghibellines, at length remained in the power of the former; but after some time these were again split into two factions. This perverse occurrence originated with the inhabitants of Pistoia, who, from an unhappy quarrel between two powerful families in that city, were all separated into parties known by those denominations. With the intention of composing their differences, the principals on each side were summoned to the city of Florence; but this measure, instead of remedying the evil, only contributed to increase its virulence, by communicating it to the citizens of Florence themselves. For the contending parties were so far from being brought to a reconciliation, that each contrived to gain fresh partisans among the Florentines, with whom many of them were closely connected by the ties of blood and friendship; and who entered into the dispute with such acrimony and eagerness, that the whole city was soon engaged either on one part or the other, and even brothers of the same family were divided. It was not long before they passed, by the usual gradations, from contumely to violence. The factions were now known by the names of the Neri and the Bianchi, the former generally siding with the Guelphs or adherents of the Papal power, the latter with the Ghibellines or those who supported the authority of the emperor. The Neri assembled secretly in the church of the Holy Trinity, and determined on interceding with Pope Boniface VIII. to send Charles of Valois to pacify and reform the city. No sooner did this resolution come to the knowledge of the Bianchi, than, struck with apprehension at the consequences of such a measure, they took arms, and repaired to the Priors, demanding of them the punishment of their adversaries, for having thus entered into private deliberations concerning the state, which they represented to have been done with the view of expelling them from the city. Those who had met, being alarmed in their turn, had also recourse to arms, and made their complaints to the Priors. Accusing their opponents of having armed them- selves without any previous public discussion, and affirming that, under various pretexts, they had sought to drive them out of their country, they demanded that they might be punished as disturbers of the public tranquillity. The dread and danger became general, when, by the advice of Dante, the Priors called in the multitude to their protection and assistance, and then proceeded to banish the principals of the two factions, who were these: Corso Donati,[2] Geri Spini, Giachonotto de' Pazzi, Rosso della Tosa, and others of the Neri party, who were exiled to the Castello della Pieve, in Perugia; and of the Bianchi party, who were banished to Serrazana, Gentile and Torrigiano de' Cerchi, Guido Cavalcanti,[3] Baschiera della Tosa, Baldinaccio Adimari, Naldo, son of Lottino Gherardini, and others. On this occasion Dante was accused of favouring the Bianchi, though he appears to have conducted himself with impartiality; and the deliberation held by the Neri for introducing Charles of Valois[4] might, perhaps, have justified him in treating that party with yet greater rigour. The suspicion against him was increased, when those whom he was accused of favouring were soon after allowed to return from their banishment, while the sentence passed upon the other faction still remained in full force. To this Dante replied that when those who had been sent to Serrazana were recalled, he was no longer in office; and that their return had been permitted on account of the death of Guido Cavalcanti, which was attributed to the unwholesome air of that place. The partiality which had been shown, however, afforded a pretext to the Pope[5] for dispatching Charles of Valois to Florence, by whose influence a great reverse was soon produced in the public affairs; the ex-citizens being restored to their place, and the whole of the Bianchi party driven into exile. At this juncture Dante was not in Florence, but at Rome, whither he had a short time before been sent ambassador to the Pope, with the offer of a voluntary return to peace and amity among the citizens. His enemies had now an opportunity of revenge, and, during his absence on this pacific mission, proceeded to pass an iniquitous decree of

---

[1] Leonardo Aretino. A late biographer, on the authority of Marchionne Stefani, assigns different colleagues to Dante in his office of Prior. See Balbo, "Vita di Dante," vol. i., p. 219, ediz. Torino, 1839.

[2] Of this remarkable man, see more in the "Purgatory," xxiv. 81.

[3] See note to "Hell," x. 59.

[4] See "Purgatory," xx. 69.

[5] Boniface VIII. had before sent the Cardinal Matteo d'Acquasparta to Florence, with the view of supporting his own adherents in that city. The cardinal is supposed to be alluded to in the "Paradise," xii. 115.

banishment against him and Palmieri Altoviti; and at the same time confiscated his possessions, which, indeed, had been previously given up to pillage.[1]

On hearing the tidings of his ruin, Dante instantly quitted Rome, and passed with all possible expedition to Sienna. Here, being more fully apprised of the extent of the calamity, for which he could see no remedy, he came to the desperate resolution of joining himself to the other exiles. His first meeting with them was at a consultation which they had at Gorgonza, a small castle subject to the jurisdiction of Arezzo, in which city it was finally, after a long deliberation, resolved that they should take up their station.[2] Hither they accordingly repaired in a numerous body, made the Count Alessandro da Romena their leader, and appointed a council of twelve, of which number Dante was one. In the year 1304, having been joined by a very strong force, which was not only furnished them by Arezzo, but sent from Bologna and Pistoia, they made a sudden attack on the city of Florence, gained possession of one of the gates, and conquered part of the territory, but were finally compelled to retreat without retaining any of the advantages they had acquired.

Disappointed in this attempt to reinstate himself in his country, Dante quitted Arezzo; and his course is,[3] for the most part, afterwards to be traced only by notices casually dropped in his own writings, or discovered in documents, which either chance or the zeal of antiquaries may have brought to light. From an instrument[4] in the possession of the Marchesi Papafavi, of Padua, it has been ascertained that, in 1306, he was at that city and with that family. Similar proof[5] exists of his having been present in the following year at a congress of the Ghibellines and the Bianchi, held in the sacristy of the church belonging to the abbey of S. Gaudenzio in Mugello; and from a passage in the "Purgatory"[6] we collect, that before the expiration of 1307 he had found a refuge in Lunigiana, with the Marchese Morello or Marcello Malaspina, who, though formerly a supporter[7] of the opposite party, was now magnanimous enough to welcome a noble enemy in his misfortune.

---

[1] On the 27th of January, 1302, he was mulcted 8,000 lire, and condemned to two years' banishment; and in case the fine was not paid, his goods were to be confiscated. On the 16th of March, the same year, he was sentenced to a punishment due only to the most desperate of malefactors. The decree, that Dante and his associates in exile should be burned, if they fell into the hands of their enemies, was discovered in 1772, by the Conte Lodovico Savioli. See Tiraboschi, where the document is given at length.

[2] At Arezzo it was his fortune, in 1302, to meet with Busone da Gubbio, who two years before had been expelled from his country as a Ghibelline, in about the twentieth year of his age. Busone, himself a cultivator of the Italian poetry, here contracted a friendship with Dante, which was afterwards cemented by the reception afforded him under Busone's roof during a part of his exile. He was of the ancient and noble family of the Rafaelli of Gubbio; and to his banishment owed the honourable offices which he held of governor of Arezzo in 1316 and 1317: of governor of Viterbo in the latter of these years; then of captain of Pisa; of deputy to the Emperor in 1327; and finally of Roman senator in 1337. He died probably about 1350. The historian of Italian literature speaks slightly of his poetical productions, consisting chiefly of comments on the "Divina Commedia," which were written in *terza rima*. They have been published by Sig. Francesco Maria Rafaelli, who has collected all the information that could be obtained respecting them—*Deliciæ Eruditor.* v. xvii. He wrote also a romance, entitled "L'Avventuroso Ciciliano," which has never been printed.—*Tiraboschi Storia della Poes. Ital.*, v. ii., p. 56. In Allacci's Collection, Ediz. Napoli 1661, p. 112, is a sonnet by Busone, on the death of a lady and of Dante, which concludes—

    "Ma i mi conforto ch' io credo che Deo
    Dante abbia posto in glorioso scanno."

At the end of the "Divina Commedia," in No. 3,581 of the Harleian MSS. in the British Museum, are four poems, the first, beginning—

    "O voi che siete nel verace lume,"

is attributed as usual to Jacopo Dante. The second, which begins—

    "Acio che sia più frutto e più diletto
    A quei che si dilettan di sapere
    Dell' alta comedia vero intelletto,"

and proceeds with a brief explanation of the principal parts of the poem, is here attributed to Messer Busone d'Agobbio. It is also inserted in Nos. 3,459 and 3,460 of the same MSS. The third is a sonnet by Cino da Pistoia to Busone; and the fourth, Busone's answer. Since this Note was written, Busone's romance, above mentioned, has been edited at Florence in the year 1832, by the late Dr. Nott.

[3] A late writer has attempted a recital of his wanderings. For this purpose he assigns certain arbitrary dates to the completion of the several parts of the "Divina Commedia;" and selecting from each what he supposes to be reminiscences of particular places visited by Dante, together with allusions to events then passing, contrives, by the help of some questionable documents, to weave out of the whole a continued narrative, which, though it may pass for current with the unwary reader, will not satisfy a more diligent inquirer after the truth. See Troya's "Veltro Allegorico di Dante," Florence, 1826.

[4] "Millesimo trecentesimo sexto, die vigesimo septimo mensis Augusti, Paduae in contrata Sancti Martini in domo Domine Amate Domini Papafave, praesentibus Dantino quondam Alligerii de Florentia et nunc stat Paduae in contrata Sancti Laurentii," &c —*Pelli*, p. 83.

[5] *Pelli*, p. 85, where the document is given.

[6] Canto viii. 133.

[7] "Hell," xxiv. 144. Morello's wife Alagia is honourably mentioned in the "Purgatory," xix. 140.

The time at which he sought an asylum at Verona, under the hospitable roof of the Signori della Scala, is less distinctly marked. It would seem as if those verses in the " Paradise," where the shade of his ancestor declares to him

> " Lo primo tuo rifugio e'l primo ostello
> Sarà la cortesia del gran Lombardo,"

> " First[1] refuge thou must find, first place of rest,
> In the great Lombard's courtesy,"

should not be interpreted too strictly ; but whether he experienced that courtesy at a very early period of his banishment, or, as others have imagined, not till 1308, when he had quitted the Marchese Morello, it is believed that he left Verona in disgust at the flippant levity of that court, or at some slight which he conceived to have been shown him by his munificent patron, Can Grande, on whose liberality he has passed so high an encomium.[2] Supposing the latter to have been the cause of his departure, it must necessarily be placed at a date posterior to 1308 ; for Can Grande, though associated with his amiable brother Alboino[3] in the government of Verona, was then only seventeen years of age, and therefore incapable of giving the alleged offence to his guest.

The mortifications which he underwent during these wanderings will be best described in his own language. In his "Convito," he speaks of his banishment, and the poverty and distress which attended it, in very affecting terms. "Alas !"[4] said he ; "had it pleased the Dispenser of the Universe, that the occasion of this excuse had never existed ; that neither others had committed wrong against me, nor I suffered unjustly ; suffered, I say, the punishment of exile and poverty ; since it was the pleasure of the citizens of that fairest and most renowned daughter of Rome, Florence, to cast me forth out of her sweet bosom, in which I had my birth and nourishment even to the ripeness of my age ; and in which, with her good will, I desire, with all my heart, to rest this wearied spirit of mine, and to terminate the time allotted to me on earth. Wandering over almost every part to which this our language extends, I have gone about like a mendicant ; showing, against my will, the wound with which fortune has smitten me, and which is often imputed to his ill-deserving on whom it is inflicted. I have, indeed, been a vessel without sail and without steerage, carried about to divers ports, and roads, and shores, by the dry wind that springs out of sad poverty ; and have appeared before the eyes of many, who, perhaps, from some report that had reached them, had imagined me of a different form ; in whose sight not only my person was disparaged, but every action of mine became of less value, as well already performed as those which yet remained for me to attempt." It is no wonder that, with feelings like these, he was now willing to obtain, by humiliation and entreaty, what he had before been unable to effect by force.

He addressed several supplicatory epistles, not only to individuals who composed the government, but to the people at large ; particularly one letter, of considerable length, which Leonardo Aretino relates to have begun with this expostulation : " Popule mi, quid feci tibi ? "

While he anxiously waited the result of these endeavours to obtain his pardon, a different complexion was given to the face of public affairs by the exaltation of Henry of Luxemburgh[5] to the imperial throne ; and it was generally expected that the most important political changes would follow, on the arrival of the new sovereign in Italy. Another prospect, more suitable to the temper of Dante, now disclosed itself to his hopes ; he once more assumed a lofty tone of defiance ; and, as it should seem, without much regard either to consistency or prudence, broke out into bitter invectives against the rulers of Florence, threatening them with merited vengeance from the power of the emperor, which he declared that they had no adequate means of opposing. He now decidedly relinquished the party of the Guelphs, which had been espoused by his ancestors, and under whose banners he had served in the earlier part of his life on the plains of Campaldino, and attached himself to the cause of their opponents, the Ghibellines. Reverence for his country, says one of his biographers,[6] prevailed on him to absent

---

[1] Canto xvii. 68.

[2] "Hell," i. 98, and "Paradise," xvii. 75. A Latin epistle dedicatory of the "Paradise" to Can Grande is attributed to Dante. Without better proof than has been yet adduced, I cannot conclude it to be genuine. See the question discussed by Fraticelli, in the "Opere Minori di Dante," tom. iii., part ii., 12mo, Firenze, 1841.

[3] Alboino is spoken of in the "Convito," p. 179, in such a manner that it is not easy to say whether a compliment or a reflection is intended ; but I am inclined to think the latter.

[4] " Ahi piacciuto fosse al Dispensatore dell' Universo," &c., p. 11.

[5] " Paradise," xvii. 80, and xxx. 141.

[6] Leonardo Aretino.

himself from the hostile army, when Henry of Luxemburgh encamped before the gates of Florence; but it is difficult to give him credit for being now much influenced by a principle which had not formerly been sufficient to restrain him from similar violence. It is probable that he was actuated by some desire, however weak, of preserving appearances; for of his personal courage no question can be made. Dante was fated to disappointment. The emperor's campaign ended in nothing; the emperor himself died the following summer (in 1313), at Buonconvento; and, with him, all hopes of regaining his native city expired in the breast of the unhappy exile. Several of his biographers[1] affirm that he now made a second journey to Paris, where Boccaccio adds that he held a public disputation[2] on various questions of theology. To what other places[3] he might have roamed during his banishment is very uncertain. We are told that he was in Casentino, with the Conte Guido Salvatico,[4] at one time; and, at another, in the mountains near Urbino, with the Signori della Faggiola. At the monastery of Santa Croce di Fonte Avellana, a wild and solitary retreat in the territory of Gubbio, was shown a chamber, in which, as a Latin inscription[5] declared, it was believed that he had composed no small portion of his divine work. A tower,[6] belonging to the Conti Falcucci, in Gubbio, claims for itself a similar honour. In the castle of Colmollaro, near the river Saonda, and about six miles from the same city, he was courteously entertained by Busone da Gubbio,[7] whom he had formerly met at Arezzo. There are some traces of his having made a temporary abode at Udine, and particularly of his having been in the Friuli with Pagana della Torre, the patriarch of Aquileia, at the castle of Tolmino, where he is also said to have employed himself on the "Divina Commedia," and where a rock was pointed out that was called the "seat of Dante."[8] What is known with greater certainty is, that he at last found a refuge at

---

[1] Benvenuto da Imola, Filippo Villani, and Boccaccio.

[2] Another public philosoph.cal disputation at Verona, in 1320, published at Venice in 1508, seems to be regarded by Tiraboschi with some suspicion of its authenticity. It is entitled, "Quæstio florulenta et perutilis de duobus elementis aquæ et terræ tractans, nuper reperta, quæ olim Mantuæ auspicata, Veronæ vero disputata et deci-a ac manu propriâ scripta a Dante Florentino Poetâ clarissimo, quæ diligenter et accurate correcta fuit per Rev. Magistrum Joan. Benedictum Moncettum de Castilione Aretino Regentem Patavinum Ordinis Eremitarum Divi Augustini, sacræque Theologiæ Doctorem excellentissimum."

[3] Vellutello says that he was also in Germany. "Vita del Poeta."

[4] He was grandson to the valiant Guidoguerra.—*Pelli*, p. 95. See "Hell," xvi. 38.

[5]
   "Hocce cubiculum hospes
  In quo Dantes Aligherius habitasse
  In eoque non minimum præclari ac
   Pene divini operis partem com-
  posuisse dicitur undique fatiscens
   Ac tantum non solo æquatum
    Philippus Rodulphius
   Laurentii Nicolai Cardinalis
  Amplissimi Fratris Filius summus
   Collegii Præses pro eximia erga
  Civem suum pietate refici hancque
  Illius effigiem ad tanti viri memo-
  riam revocandam Antonio Petreio
   Canon. Floren. procurante
    Collocari mandavit
   Kal. Maii. M.D.L.VII." *Pelli*, p. 98.

[6] In this is inscribed,

   "Hic mansit Dantes
   Al-ghierius Poeta
   Et carmina scripsit." *Pelli*, p. 97.

[7] The following sonnet, said to be addressed to him by Dante, was published in the "Delitiæ Eruditorum," and is inserted in the Zatta edition of our poet's works, tom. iv., part ii., p. 264, in which alone I have seen it:—

  "Tu, che stampi lo colle ombroso e fresco,
   Ch' è co lo Fiume, che non è torrente,
   Linci molle lo chiama quella gente
   In nome Italiano e non Tedesco:
  Ponti, sera e mattin, contento al desro,
   Perchè del car figliuol vedi presente
   El frutto che sperassi, e si repente
   S' avaccia nello stil Greco e Francesco.
  Perchè cima d'ingegno non s'astalla
   In quella Italia di dolor ostello,
   Di cui si speri già cotanto frutto;
  Gavazzi pur el primo Raffaello,
   Che tra dotti vedrallo esser veduto,
   Come sopr' acqua si sostien la galla."

Translation.

 "Thou, who where Linci sends his stream to drench
  The valley, walk'st that fresh and shady hill
  (Soft Linci well they call the gentle rill,
  Nor smooth Italian name to German wrench)
 Evening and morning, seat thee on thy bench,
  Content; beholding fruit of knowledge fill
  So early thy son's branches, that grow still
  Enrich'd with dews of Grecian lore and French.
 Though genius, with like hopeful fruitage hung,
  Spread not aloft in recreant Italy,
  Where grief her home, and worth has made his grave;
 Yet may the elder Raffaello see,
  With joy, his offspring seen the learn'd among,
  Like buoyant thing that floats above the wave."

[8] The considerations which induced the Cavalier Vannetti to conclude that a part of the "Commedia," and the canzone beginning

  "Canzon, da che convien pur, ch' io mi doglia"

were written in the valley Lagarina, in the territory of Trento, do not appear entitled to much notice. Vannetti's letter is in the Zatta edition of Dante, tom. iv., part ii., p. 143. There may be better ground for concluding that he was, some time during his exile, with Lanteri Paratico, a man of ancient and noble family, at the castle of Paratico, near Brescia, and that he there employed himself on his

Ravenna, with Guido Novella da Polenta ;[1] a splendid protector of learning ; himself a poet ; and the kinsman of that unfortunate Francesca,[2] whose story has been told by Dante with such unrivalled pathos.

It would appear from one of his Epistles that about the year 1316 he had the option given him of returning to Florence, on the ignominious terms of paying a fine, and of making a public avowal of his offence. It may, perhaps, be in reference to this offer, which, for the same reason that Socrates refused to save his life on similar conditions, he indignantly rejected, that he promises himself he shall one day return "in other guise,"

> " And standing up
> At his baptismal font, shall claim the wreath
> Due to the poet's temples."—*Purgatory*, xxv.

Such, indeed, was the glory which his compositions in his native tongue had now gained him, that he declares, in the treatise, " De Vulgari Eloquentia,"[3] it had in some measure reconciled him even to his banishment.

In the service of his last patron, in whom he seems to have met with a more congenial mind than in any of the former, his talents were gratefully exerted, and his affections interested but too deeply ; for, having been sent by Guido on an embassy to the Venetians, and not being able even to obtain an audience, on account of the rancorous animosity with which they regarded that prince, Dante returned to Ravenna so overwhelmed with disappointment and grief, that he was seized by an illness which terminated fatally, either in July or September, 1321.[4] Guido testified his sorrow and respect by the sumptuousness of his obsequies, and by his intention to erect a monument, which he did not live to complete. His countrymen showed, too late, that they knew the value of what they had lost. At the beginning of the next century, their prosperity marked their regret by entreating that the mortal remains of their illustrious citizen might be restored to them, and deposited among the tombs of their fathers. But the people of Ravenna were unwilling to part with the sad and honourable memorial of their own hospitality. No better success attended the subsequent negotiations of the Florentines for the same purpose, though renewed under the auspices of Leo X., and conducted through the powerful mediation of Michael Angelo.[5]

The sepulchre, designed and commenced by Guido da Polenta, was, in 1483, erected by Bernardo Bembo, the father of the cardinal ; and, by him, decorated, besides other ornaments, with an effigy of the poet in bas-relief, the sculpture of Pietro Lombardo, and with the following epitaph :

> " Exiguâ tumuli, Danthes, hic sorte jacebas,
> Squalenti nulli cognite penè situ.
> At nunc marmoreo subnixus conderis arcu,
> Omnibus et cultu splendidiore nites.
> Nimirum Bembus Musis incensus Etruscis
> Hoc tibi, quem imprimis hæ coluere, dedit."

A yet more magnificent memorial was raised so lately as the year 1780, by the Cardinal Gonzaga.[6]

---

poems. The proof of this rests upon a communication made by the Abate Rodella to Dionisi, of an extract from a chronicle remaining at Brescia. See Cancellieri, " Osservazioni intorno alla questione sopra l'originalità della Divina Commedia," &c., Roma., 1814, p. 125.

[1] See " Hell," xxvii. 38.

[2] " Hell," v. 113, and Note. Former biographers of Dante have represented Guido, his last patron, as the father of Francesca. Troya asserts that he was her nephew. See his " Veltro Allegorico di Dante," ed. Florence, 1826, p. 176. It is to be regretted that, in this instance, as in others, he gives no authority for his assertion. He is, however, followed by Balbo, " Vita di Dante." Torino, 1839, v. ii., p. 315 ; and Artaud, " Histoire de Dante," Paris, 1841, p. 470.

[3] " Quantum vero suos familiares gloriosos efficiat, nos ipsi novimus, qui hujus dulcedine gloriæ nostrum exilium postergamus."—Lib. i., cap. 17.

[4] Filippo Villani, Domenico di Bandino d'Arezzo, and G. Villani, " Hist." lib. ix., cap. cxxxv. The last writer, whose authority is perhaps the best on this point, in the Giunti edition of 1559, mentions July as the month in which he died ; but there is a MS. of Villani's history, it is said, in the library of St. Mark, at Venice, in which his death is placed in September.

[5] Pelli, p. 104.

[6] Tiraboschi.—In the " Literary Journal," February 16, 1804, p. 192, is the following article :—" A subscription has been opened at Florence for erecting a monument in the cathedral there, to the memory of the great poet Dante. A drawing of this monument has been submitted to the Florentine Academy of the Fine Arts, and has met with universal approbation." A monument, executed by Stefano Ricci of Arezzo, has since been erected to him in the Santa Croce at Florence, which I had the gratification of seeing in the year 1833.

His children consisted of one daughter and five sons, two of whom, Pietro[1] and Jacopo,[2] inherited some portion of their father's abilities, which they employed chiefly in the pious task of illustrating his "Divina Commedia." The former of these possessed acquirements of a more profitable kind, and obtained considerable wealth at Verona, where he was settled, by the exercise of the legal profession. He was honoured with the friendship of Petrarch, by whom some verses were addressed to him[3] at Trevigi, in 1361.

His daughter Beatrice[4] (whom he is said to have named after the daughter of Folco Portinari) became a nun in the convent of S. Stefano dell' Uliva, at Ravenna; and, among the entries of expenditure by the Florentine Republic, appears a present of ten golden florins sent to her in 1350, by the hands of Boccaccio, from the state. The imagination can picture to itself few objects more interesting than the daughter of Dante, dedicated to the service of religion in the city where her father's ashes were deposited, and receiving from his countrymen this tardy tribute of their reverence for his divine genius, and her own virtues.

It is but justice to the wife of Dante not to omit what Boccaccio[5] relates of her; that after the banishment of her husband, she secured some share of his property from the popular fury, under the name of her dowry; that out of this she contrived to support their little family with exemplary discretion; and that she even removed from them the pressure of poverty, by such industrious efforts as in her former affluence she had never been called on to exert. Who does not regret, that with qualities so estimable, she wanted the sweetness of temper necessary for riveting the affections of her husband?

Dante was a man of middle stature and grave deportment; of a visage rather long; large eyes; an aquiline nose; dark complexion; large and prominent cheek-bones; black curling hair and beard; the under lip projecting beyond the upper. He mentions, in the "Convito," that his sight had been transiently impaired by intense application to books.[6] In his dress, he studied as much plainness as was suitable with his rank and station in life; and observed a strict temperance in his diet. He was at times extremely absent and abstracted; and appears to have indulged too much a disposition to sarcasm. At the table of Can Grande, when the company was amused by the conversation and tricks of a buffoon, he was asked by his patron why Can Grande himself, and the guests who were present, failed of receiving as much pleasure from the exertion of his talents as this man had been able to give them. "Because all creatures delight in their own resemblance," was the reply of Dante.[7] In other respects, his manners are said to have been dignified and polite. He was particularly careful not to make any

---

[1] Pietro was also a poet. His commentary on the "Divina Commedia," which is in Latin, has never been published.* Lionardo, the grandson of Pietro, came to Florence, with other young men of Verona, in the time of Leonardo Aretino, who tells us that he showed him there the house of Dante and of his ancestors.—*Vita di Dante.* To Pietro, the son of Lionardo, Mario Filelfo addressed his "Life" of our poet. The son of this Pietro, Dante III., was a man of letters, and an elegant poet. Some of his works are preserved in collections: he is commended by Valerianus, "De Infelicitate Literat," lib. i., and is, no doubt, the same whom Landino speaks of as living in his time at Ravenna, and calls "uomo molto literato ed eloquente e degno di tal sangue, e quale meritamente si dovrebbe rivocar nella sua antica patria e nostra republica." In 1495, the Florentines took Landino's advice, and invited him back to the city, offering to restore all they could of the property that had belonged to his ancestors; but he would not quit Verona, where he was established in much opulence.—*Vellutello, Vita.* He afterwards experienced a sad reverse of fortune. He had three sons, one of whom, Francesco, made a translation of Vitruvius, which is supposed to have perished. A better fate has befallen an elegant dialogue written by him, which was published, not many years ago, in the "Anecdota Literaria," edit. Roma, (no date), vol. ii., p. 207. It is entitled "Francisci Aligerii Dantis III. Filii Dialogus Alter de Antiquitatibus Valentinis ex Cod. MS. Membranaceo. Saec. xvi. nunc primum

* [Published in 1845 by Lord Vernon.]

in lucem editus." Pietro, another son of Dante III., who was also a scholar, and held the office of Proveditore of Verona in 1539, was the father of Ginevra, mentioned before, in Note 5, page vii. See Pelli, p. 28, &c. Vellutello, in his "Life" of the poet, acknowledges his obligations to this last Pietro for the information he had given him.

[2] Jacopo is mentioned by Bembo among the Rimatori, lib. ii., "Della Volg. Ling.," at the beginning; and some of his verses are preserved in MS. in the Vatican, and at Florence. He was living in 1342, and had children, of whom little is known. The names of our poet's other sons were Gabriello, Aligero, and Eliseo. The last two died in their childhood. Of Gabriello nothing certain is known.

[3] "Carm," lib. iii., ep. vii.

[4] Pelli, p. 33.

[5] "Vita di Dante," p. 57, ed. Firenze, 1576.

[6] "Per affaticare lo viso molto a studio di leggere, intanto debilitai gli spiriti visivi, che le stele mi pareano tutte d'alcuno albore ombrate: e per lunga riposanza in luoghi scuri, e freddi, e con affreddare lo corpo dell' occhio con acqua pura, rivinsi, la virtù disgregata, che tornai nel prima buono stato della vista."—*Convito.* p. 108.

[7] There is here a point of resemblance nor is it the only one) in the character of Milton. "I had rather," says the author of "Paradise Lost," "since the life of man is likened to a scene, that all my entrances and exits might mix with such persons only whose worth erects them and their actions to a grave and tragic deportment, and not to have to do with clowns and vices."—*Colasterion, Prose Works,* vol. i., p. 339, edit. London, 1753.

approaches to flattery, a vice which he justly held in the utmost abhorrence. He spoke seldom, and in a slow voice; but what he said derived authority from the subtileness of his observations, somewhat like his own poetical heroes, who

> " Parlavan rado con voci soavi."
> " Spake
> Seldom, but all their words were tuneful sweet."—*Hell*, iv.

He was connected in habits of intimacy and friendship with the most ingenious men of his time: with Guido Cavalcanti,[1] with Buonaggiunta da Lucca,[2] with Forese Donati,[3] with Cino da Pistoia,[4] with Giotto,[5] the celebrated painter, by whose hand his likeness[6] was preserved; with Oderigi da Gubbio,[7] the illuminator, and with an eminent musician[8]—

> " His Casella, whom he wooed to sing,
> Met in the milder shades of Purgatory."—*Milton's Sonnets.*

Besides these, his acquaintance extended to some others, whose names illustrate the first dawn of Italian literature: Lapo[9] degli Uberti, Dante da Majano,[10] Cecco Angiolieri,[11] Dino Fresco-

---

[1] See " Hell," x., and Notes.

[2] See " Purgatory," xxiv. Yet Tiraboschi observes, that though it is not improbable that Buonaggiunta was the contemporary and friend of Dante, it cannot be considered as certain. " Storia della Poes. Ital.," tom. i., p. 109, Mr. Mathias's edition.

[3] See " Purgatory," xxiii. 44.

[4] Guittoncino de' Sinibaldi, commonly called Cino da Pistoia (besides the passage that will be cited in a following Note from the " De Vulgari Eloquentia "), is again spoken of in the same treatise, lib. i., c. xvii., as a great master of the vernacular diction in his canzoni, and classed with our poet himself, who is termed " Amicus ejus ;" and likewise in lib. ii., c. ii., where he is said to have written of " Love." His verses are cited too in other chapters. He addressed and received sonnets from Dante ; and wrote a sonnet, or canzone, on Dante's death, which is preserved in the Library of St. Mark, at Venice.—*Tiraboschi, della Poes. Ital.*, v. i., p. 116, and v. ii., p. 65. The same honour was done to the memory of Cino by Petrarch, son. 71, part i. " Celebrated both as a lawyer and a poet, he is better known by the writings which he has left in the latter of these characters," insomuch that Tiraboschi has observed, that amongst those who preceded Petrarch, there is, perhaps, none who can be compared to him in elegance and sweetness. " There are many editions of his poems, the most copious being that published at Venice in 1589, by P. Faustino Tasso ; in which, however, the Padre degli Agostini, not without reason, suspects that the second book is by later hands."—*Tiraboschi, ibid.* There has been an edit on by Seb. Ciampi, at Pisa, in 1813, &c. ; but see the remarks on it in Gamba's " Testi di Lingua Ital.," 294. He was interred at Pistoia with this epitaph: " Cino eximio Juris interpreti Bartolique præceptori dignissimo populus Pistoriensis Civi suo D. M. fecit. Obiit anno 1336."—*Guidi Panziroli de Claris Legum Interpretibus*, lib. ii., cap. xxix., Lips. 4to, 1721. A Latin letter, supposed to be addressed by Dante to Cino, was published for the first time from a MS. in the Laurentian Library, by M. Witte.

[5] See " Purgatory," xi.

[6] Mr. Eastlake, in a Note to " Kugler's Hand-Book of Painting, translated by a Lady," Lond., 1842, p. 50, describes the recovery and restoration, in July, 1840, of Dante's portrait by Giotto, in the chapel of the Podestà, at Florence, where it had been covered with whitewash or plaster. But it could scarcely have been concealed so soon as our distinguished artist supposes, since Landino speaks

of it as remaining in his time, and Vasari says it was still to be seen when he wrote.

[7] See " Purgatory," xi.

[8] *Ibid.*, canto ii.

[9] Lapo is said to have been the son of Farinata degli Uberti (see " Hell," x. 32, and Tiraboschi, " Dello Poes. Ital.," v. i., p. 116), and the father of Fazio degli Uberti, author of the " Dittamondo," a poem, which is thought, in the energy of its style, to make some approaches to the " Divina Commedia," (*ibid.*, v. ii., p. 63), though Monti passes on it a much less favourable sentence (see his " Proposta," v. iii., part ii., p. 210, 8vo., 1824). He is probably the Lapo mentioned in the sonnet to Guido Cavalcanti, beginning

> " Guido vorrei, che tu e Lapo ed io,"

which Mr. Hayley has so happily translated (see " Hell," x. 62); and also in a passage that occurs in the " De Vulgari Eloquentia," v. i., p. 116: " Quanquam fere omnes Tusci in suo turpiloquio sint obtusi, nonnullos Vulgaris excellentiam cognovisse sentimus, scilicet Guidonem Lapum, et unum alium, Florentinos, et Cinum Pistoriensem, quem nunc indigne postponimus, non indigne coacti." " Although almost all the Tuscans are marred by the baseness of their dialect, yet I perceive that some have known the excellence of the vernacular tongue, namely, Guido Lapo " (I suspect Dante here means his two friends Cavalcanti and Uberti, though this has hitherto been taken for the name of one person), " and one other " (who is supposed to be the author himself), " Florentines ; and last, though not of least regard, Cino da Pistoia."

[10] Dante da Majano flourished about 1293. He was a Florentine, and composed many poems in praise of a Sicilian lady, who being herself a poetess, was insensible neither to his verses nor his love, so that she was called the Nina of Dante.—*Pelli*, p. 60. *and Tiraboschi, Storia della Poes. Ital.*, v. i., p. 137. There are several of his sonnets addressed to our poet, who declares, in his answer to one of them, that although he knows not the name of its author, he discovers in it the traces of a great mind.

[11] Of Cecco Angiolieri. Boccaccio relates a pleasant story in the " Decameron," Giorn. 9, Nov. 4. He lived towards the end of the thirteenth century, and wrote several sonnets to Dante, which are in Allacci's collection. In some of them he wears the semblance of a friend ; but in one the mask drops, and shows that he was well disposed to be a rival. See Crescimbeni, " Com alla Storia di Volgar Poesia," v. ii., par. ii., lib. ii., p. 103 ; Pelli, p. 61.

baldi,[1] Giovanni di Virgilio,[2] Giovanni Quirino,[3] and Francesco Stabili,[4] who is better known by the appellation of Cecco D'Ascoli; most of them either honestly declared their sense of his superiority, or betrayed it by their vain endeavours to detract from the estimation in which he was held.

He is said to have attained some excellence in the art of designing; which may easily be believed, when we consider that no poet has afforded more lessons to the statuary and the painter,[5] in the variety of objects which he represents, and in the accuracy and spirit with which they are brought before the eye. Indeed, on one occasion,[6] he mentions that he was employed in delineating the figure of an angel, on the first anniversary of Beatrice's death. It is not unlikely that the seed of the "Paradiso" was thus cast into his mind; and that he was now endeavouring to express by the pencil an idea of celestial beatitude, which could only be conveyed in its full perfection through the medium of song.

As nothing that related to such a man was thought unworthy of notice, one of his biographers,[7] who had seen his handwriting, has recorded that it was of a long and delicate character, and remarkable for neatness and accuracy.

Dante wrote in Latin a treatise "De Monarchiâ," and two books "De Vulgari Eloquio."[8] In the former he defends the imperial rights against the pretensions of the Pope, with arguments that are sometimes chimerical, and sometimes sound and conclusive. The latter, which he left unfinished, contains not only much information concerning the progress which the vernacular poetry of Italy had then made, but some reflections on the art itself, that prove him to have entertained large and philosophical principles respecting it.

His Latin style, however, is generally rude and unclassical. It is fortunate that he did not trust to it, as he once intended, for the work by which his name was to be perpetuated. In the use of his own language he was, beyond measure, more successful. The prose of his "Vita Nuova," and his "Convito," although five centuries have intervened since its composition, is probably, to an Italian eye, still devoid neither of freshness nor elegance. In the "Vita Nuova," which he appears to have written about his twenty-eighth year, he gives an account of his youthful attachment to Beatrice. It is, according to the taste of those times, somewhat mystical: yet there are some particulars in it which have not at all the air of a fiction, such as the death of Beatrice's father, Folco Portinari; her relation to the friend whom he esteemed next after Guido Cavalcanti; his own attempt to conceal his passion, by a pretended attachment to another lady; and the anguish he felt at the death of his mistress.[9] He

---

[1] Dino, son of Lambertuccio Frescobaldi. Crescimbeni (*ibid.*, lib. iii., p. 120) assures us that he was not inferior to Cino da Pistoia.—*Pelli*, p. 61. He is said to have been a friend of Dante's, in whose writings I have not observed any mention of him. Boccaccio, in his "Life of Dante," calls Dino "in que' tempi famosissimo dicitore in rima in Firenze."

[2] Giovanni di Virgilio addressed two Latin eclogues to Dante, which were answered in similar compositions; and is said to have been his friend and admirer. See Boccaccio. "Vita di Dante;" and Pelli, p. 137. Dante's poetical genius sometimes breaks through the rudeness of style in his two Latin eclogues.

[3] Muratori had seen several sonnets, addressed to Giovanni Quirino by Dante, in a MS. preserved in the Ambrosian Library. "Della Perfetta Poesia Ital.," ediz. Venezia, 1770, tom. i., lib. i., c. iii., p. 9.

[4] For the correction of many errors respecting this writer, see Tiraboschi, "Storia della Lett. Ital.," tom. v., lib. ii, cap. ii., § xv., &c. He was burned in 1317. In his "Acerba," a poem in *sesta rima*, he has taken several occasions of venting his spleen against his great contemporary.

[5] Beside Filippo Brunelleschi, who, as Vasari tells us, "diede molta opera alle cose di Dante," and Michael Angelo, whose "Last Judgment" is probably the mightiest effort of modern art, as the loss of his sketches on the margin of the "Divina Commedia" may be regarded as the severest loss the art has sustained; besides these, Andrea Orgagna, Gio. Angelico di Fiesole, Luca Signorelli, Spinello Aretino, Giacomo da Pontormo, and Aurelio Lomi have been recounted among the many artists who have worked on the same original. See Cancellieri, "Osservazioni," &c., p. 75. To these we may justly pride ourselves in being able to add the names of Reynolds, Fuseli, and Flaxman. The frescoes by Cornelius in the Villa Massimi at Rome, lately executed, entitle the Germans to a share in this distinction.

[6] "In quel giorno, nel quale si compieva l'anno, che questa donna era fatta delle cittadine di vita eterna, io mi sedeva in parte, nella quale, ricordandomi di lei, io disegnava uno Angelo sopra certe tavolette, e mentre io il disegnava, volsi gli occhi." *Vita Nuova*, p. 268.

[7] Leonardo Aretino. A specimen of it was believed to exist when Pelli wrote, about sixty years ago. and perhaps still exists in a MS. preserved in the archives at Gubbio, at the end of which was the sonnet to Busone, said to be in the handwriting of Dante.—*Pelli*, p. 51.

[8] The two were first published in an Italian translation, supposed to be Trissino's, and were not allowed to be genuine, till the Latin original was published at Paris in 1577.—*Tiraboschi*. A copy, written in the fourteenth century, is said to have been lately found in the public library at Grenoble. See Fraticelli's "Opere minori di Dante," 12mo, Firenze, 1840, v. iii., part ii., p. 16. A collation of this MS. is very desirable.

[9] Beatrice's marriage to Simone de' Bardi, which is collected from a clause in her father's will, dated January 15, 1287, would have been a fact too unsentimental to be introduced into the "Vita Nuova," and is not, I believe, noticed by any of the early biographers.

tells us, too, that at the time of her decease, he chanced to be composing a canzone in her praise, and that he was interrupted by that event at the conclusion of the first stanza ; a circumstance which we can scarcely suppose to have been a mere invention.

Of the poetry, with which the "Vita Nuova" is plentifully interspersed, the two sonnets that follow may be taken as a specimen. Near the beginning he relates a marvellous vision, which appeared to him in sleep, soon after his mistress had for the first time addressed her speech to him ; and of this dream he thus asks for an interpretation :—

> "To every heart that fee's the gentle flame,
>> To whom this present saying comes in sight,
>> In that to me their thoughts they may indite,
>> All health ! in Love, our lord and master's name.
> Now on its way the second quarter came
>> Of those twelve hours, wherein the stars are bright,
>> When Love was seen before me, in such might,
>> As to remember shakes with awe my frame.
> Suddenly came he, seeming glad, and keeping
>> My heart in hand ; and in his arms he had
>> My lady in a folded garment sleeping
> He waked her ; and that heart all burning bade
>> Her feed upon, in lowly guise and sad
>> Then from my view he turned ; and parted, weeping."

To this sonnet Guido Cavalcanti, amongst others, returned an answer in a composition of the same form, endeavouring to give a happy turn to the dream, by which the mind of the poet had been so deeply impressed. From the intercourse thus begun, when Dante was eighteen years of age, arose that friendship which terminated only with the death of Guido.

The other sonnet is one that was written after the death of Beatrice :—

> "Ah, pilgrims ! ye that, haply musing, go,
>> On aught save that which on your road ye meet,
>> From land so distant, tell me, I entreat,
>> Come ye, as by your mien and looks ye show?
> Why mourn ye not, as through these gates of woe
>> Ye wend along our city's midmost street,
>> Even like those who nothing seem to weet
>> What chance hath fall'n, why she is grieving so
> If ye to listen but a while would stay,
>> Well knows this heart, which inly sigheth sore,
>> That ye would then pass, weeping on your way.
> Oh, hear : her Beatrice is no more
>> And words there are a man of her might say,
>> Would make a stranger's eye that loss deplore."

In the "Convito,"[1] or Banquet, which did not follow till some time after his banishment, he explains very much at large the sense of three out of fourteen of his canzoni, the remainder of which he had intended to open in the same manner. "The viands at his banquet," he tells his readers, quaintly enough, "will be set out in fourteen different manners ; that is, will consist of fourteen canzoni, the materials of which are love and virtue. Without the present bread, they would not be free from some shade of obscurity, so as to be prized by many less for their usefulness than for their beauty ; but the bread will, in the form of the present exposition, be that light which will bring forth all their colours, and display their true meaning to the view. And if the present work, which is named a Banquet, and I wish may prove so, be handled after a more manly guise than the 'Vita Nuova,' I intend not, therefore, that the former should in any part derogate from the latter, but that the one should be a help to the other : seeing that it is fitting in reason for this to be fervid and impassioned ; that, temperate and manly. For it becomes us to act and speak otherwise at one age than at another ;

---

[1] Perticari ("Degli Scrittori del Trecento," lib. ii., c. v.), speaking of the "Convito," observes that Salviati himself has termed it the most ancient and principal of all excellent prose works in Italian. On the other hand, Balbo ("Vita di Dante," v. ii., p. 86) pronounces it to be certainly the lowest among Dante's writings. In this difference of opinion a foreigner may be permitted to judge for himself.

since at one age certain manners are suitable and praiseworthy, which at another become disproportionate and blameable." He then apologises for speaking of himself. "I fear the disgrace," says he, "of having been subject to so much passion as one, reading these canzoni, may conceive me to have been: a disgrace that is removed by my speaking thus unreservedly of myself, which shows not passion, but virtue, to have been the moving cause. I intend, moreover, to set forth their true meaning, which some may not perceive, if I declare it not." He next proceeds to give many reasons why his commentary was not written rather in Latin than in Italian; for which, if no excuse be now thought necessary, it must be recollected that the Italian language was then in its infancy, and scarce supposed to possess dignity enough for the purposes of instruction. "The Latin," he allows, "would have explained his canzoni better to foreigners, as to the Germans, the English, and others; but then it must have expounded their sense, without the power of, at the same time, transferring their beauty;" and he soon after tells us, that many noble persons of both sexes were ignorant of the learned language. The best cause, however, which he assigns for this preference, was his natural love of his native tongue, and the desire he felt to exalt it above the Provençal, which by many was said to be the more beautiful and perfect language; and against such of his countrymen as maintained so unpatriotic an opinion he inveighs with much warmth.

In his exposition of the first canzone of the three, he tells the reader that "the lady of whom he was enamoured after his first love was the most beauteous and honourable daughter of the Emperor of the Universe, to whom Pythagoras gave the name of Philosophy:" and he applies the same title to the object of his affections, when he is commenting on the other two.

The purport of his third canzone, which is less mysterious, and, therefore, perhaps more likely to please than the others, is to show that "virtue only is true nobility." Towards the conclusion, after having spoken of virtue itself, much as Pindar would have spoken of it, as being "the gift of God only"—

"Che solo Iddio all' anima la dona,"

he thus describes it as acting throughout the several stages of life:

"L' anima, cui adorna," &c.

> "The soul, that goodness like to this adorns,
> Holdeth it not conceal'd;
> But, from her first espousal to the frame,
> Shows it, till death, reveal'd.
> Obedient, sweet, and full of seemly shame,
> She, in the primal age,
> The person decks with beauty; moulding it
> Fitly through every part.
> In riper manhood, temperate, firm of heart
> With love replenish'd, and with courteous praise,
> In loyal deeds alone she hath delight.
> And, in her elder days,
> For prudent and just largeness is she known;
> Rejoicing with herself,
> That wisdom in her staid discourse be shown.
> Then, in life's fourth division, at the last
> She weds with God again.
> Contemplating the end she shall attain:
> And looketh back; and blesseth the time past.

His lyric poems, indeed, generally stand much in need of a comment to explain them; but the difficulty arises rather from the thoughts themselves, than from any imperfection of the language in which those thoughts are conveyed. Yet they abound not only in deep moral reflections, but in touches of tenderness and passion.

Some, it has been already intimated, have supposed that Beatrice was only a creature of Dante's imagination; and there can be no question but that he has invested her, in the "Divina Commedia," with the attributes of an allegorical being. But who can doubt of her having had a real existence, when she is spoken of in such a strain of passion as in these lines?

"Quel ch' el'a par, quando un poco sorride,
Non si può dicer ne tenere a mente,
Si è nuovo miracolo e gentile."—Vita Nuova.

> " Mira che quando ride
> Passa ben di dolcezza ogni altra cosa."—*Canz.* xv.

The canzone from which the last couplet is taken presents a portrait which might well supply a painter with a far more exalted idea of female beauty than he could form to himself from the celebrated Ode of Anacreon on a similar subject. After a minute description of those parts of her form which the garments of a modest woman would suffer to be seen, he raises the whole by the superaddition of a moral grace and dignity, such as the Christian religion alone could supply, and such as the pencil of Raphael afterwards aimed to represent :

> " Umile vergognosa e temperata,
> E sempre a vertù grata,
> Intra suoi be' costumi un atto regna,
> Che d' ogni riverenza la fa degna."[1]

One or two of the sonnets prove that he could at times condescend to sportiveness and pleasantry. The following, to Brunetto, I should conjecture to have been sent with his " Vita Nuova," which was written the year before Brunetto died :

> " Master Brunetto, this I send, entreating
>   Ye'll entertain this lass of mine at Easter;
>   She does not come among you as a feaster :
>   No: she has need of reading, not of eating.
> Nor let her find you at some merry meeting,
>   Laughing amidst buffoons and drollers, lest her
>   Wise sentence should escape a noisy jester:
>   She must be wooed, and is well worth the weeting.
> If in this sort you fail to make her out,
>   You have amongst you many sapient men,
>   All famous as was Albert of Cologne.
> I have been posed amid that learned rout,
>   And if they cannot spell her right, why then
>   Call Master Giano, and the deed is done."[2]

Another, though on a more serious subject, is yet remarkable for a fancifulness such as that with which Chaucer, by a few spirited touches, often conveys to us images more striking than others have done by repeated and elaborate efforts of skill :

> " Came Melancholy to my side one day,
>   And said, ' I must a little bide with thee :'
>   And brought along with her in company
>   Sorrow and Wrath.—Quoth I to her, ' Away :
> I will have none of you : make no delay.'
>   And, like a Greek, she gave me stou reply.
>   Then, as she talk'd, I look'd, and did espy
>   Where Love was coming onward on the way.
> A garment new of cloth of black he had,
>   And on his head a hat of mourning wore ;
>   And he, of truth, unfeignedly was crying.
> Forthwith I ask'd, ' What ails thee, caitiff lad ?'
>   And he rejoin'd, ' Sad thought and anguish sore
>   Sweet brother mine ! our lady lies a-dying.'"

For purity of diction, the *rime* of our author are, I think, on the whole, preferred by Muratori to his " Divina Commedia," though that also is allowed to be a model of the pure Tuscan idiom. To this singular production, which has not only stood the test of ages, but given a tone and colour to the

---

[1] I am aware that this canzone is not ascribed to Dante in the collection of "Sonetti e Canzoni," printed by the Giunti in 1527. Monti, in his " Proposta," under the word "Induare," remarks that it is quite in the style of Fazio degli Uberti ; and adds, that a very rare MS. possessed by Perticari restores it to that writer. On the other hand, Missirini, in a late treatise "On the Love of Dante and on the Portrait of Beatrice," printed at Florence in 1832, makes so little doubt of its being genuine, that he founds on it the chief argument to prove an old picture in his possession to be intended for a representation of Beatrice. See Fraticelli's "Opere Minori di Dante," tom. i., p. 203, 12mo, Firenze, 1834.

[2] Fraticelli (*ibid.*, pp. 302, 303) questions the genuineness of this sonnet, and decides on the spuriousness of that which follows. I do not, in either instance, feel the justness of his reasons.

poetry of modern Europe, and even animated the genius of Milton and of Michael Angelo, it would be difficult to assign its place according to the received rules of criticism. Some have termed it an epic poem, and others a satire; but it matters little by what name it is called. It suffices that the poem seizes on the heart by its two great holds, terror and pity; detains the fancy by an accurate and lively delineation of the objects it represents; and displays throughout such an originality of conception, as leaves to Homer and Shakespeare alone the power of challenging the pre-eminence or equality.[1] The fiction, it has been remarked,[2] is admirable, and the work of an inventive talent truly great. It comprises a description of the heavens and heavenly bodies; a description of men, their deserts and punishments, of supreme happiness and utter misery, and of the middle state between the two extremes: nor, perhaps, was there ever any one who chose a more ample and fertile subject, so as to afford scope for the expression of all his ideas, from the vast multitude of spirits that are introduced speaking on such different topics, who are of so many different countries and ages, and under circumstances of fortune so striking and so diversified, and who succeed one to another with such a rapidity as never suffers the attention for an instant to pall.

His solicitude, it is true, to define all his images in such a manner as to bring them distinctly within the circle of our vision, and to subject them to the power of the pencil, sometimes renders him

---

[1] Yet his pretensions to originality have not been wholly unquestioned. Dante, it has been supposed, was more immediately influenced in his choice of a subject by the "Vision" of Alberico, written in barbarous Latin prose about the beginning of the twelfth century. The incident which is said to have given birth to this composition is not a little marvellous. Alberico, the son of noble parents, and born at a castle in the neighbourhood of Alvito, in the diocese of Sora, in the year 1101, or soon after, when he had completed his ninth year, was seized with a violent fit of illness, which deprived him of his senses for the space of nine days. During the continuance of this trance he had a vision, in which he seemed to himself to be carried away by a dove, and conducted by St. Peter, in company with two angels, through Purgatory and Hell, to survey the torments of sinners, the saint giving him information, as they proceeded, respecting what he saw; after which they were transported together through the seven heavens, and taken up into Paradise to behold the glory of the blessed. As soon as he came to himself again, he was permitted to make profession of a religious life in the monastery of Monte Casino. As the account he gave of his vision was strangely altered in the reports that went abroad of it, Girardo, the abbot, employed one of the monks to take down a relation of it, dictated by the mouth of Alberico himself. Senioretto, who was chosen abbot in 1127, not contented with this narrative, although it seemed to have every chance of being authentic, ordered Alberico to revise and correct it, which he accordingly did, with the assistance of Pietro Diacono, who was his associate in the monastery, and a few years younger than himself; and whose testimony to his extreme and perpetual self-mortification, and to a certain abstractedness of demeanour, which showed him to converse with other thoughts than those of this life, is still on record. The time of Alberico's death is not known; but it is conjectured that he reached to a good old age. His "Vision," with a preface by the first editor, Guido, and preceded by a letter from Alberico himself, is preserved in a MS. numbered 257, in the archives of the monastery, which contains the works of Pietro Diacono, and which was written between the years 1159 and 1181. The probability of our poet's having been indebted to it was first remarked either by Giovanni Bottari in a letter inserted in the "Deca di Simladi," and printed at Rome in 1753; or, as F. Cancellieri conjectures, in the preceding year by Alessio Simmaco Mazzuchi. In 1814 extracts from Alberico's "Vision" were laid before the public in a quarto pamphlet, printed at Rome, with the title of "Lettera di Eustazio Dicearcheo ad Angelio Sidicino," under which appellations the writer, Giustino di Costanzo, concealed his own name and that of his friend, Luigi Anton. Sompano; and the whole has since, in 1814, been edited in the same city by Francesco Cancellieri, who has added to the original an Italian translation. Such parts of it as bear a marked resemblance to passages in the "Divina Commedia" will be found distributed in their proper places throughout the following Notes. The reader will in these probably see enough to convince him that our author had read this singular work, although nothing to detract from his claim to originality. Long before the public notice had been directed to this supposed imitation, Malatesta Porta, in the Dialogue entitled "Rossi," as referred to by Fontanini in his "Eloquenza Italiana," had suggested the probability that Dante had taken his plan from an ancient romance, called "Guerrino di Durazzo il Meschino." The above-mentioned Bottari, however, adduced reasons for concluding that this book was written originally in Provençal, and not translated into Italian till after the time of our poet, by one Andrea di Barberino, who embellished it with many images, and particularly with similes, borrowed from the "Divina Commedia." Mr. Warton, in one part of his "History of English Poetry," vol. i., § xviii., p. 463, has observed that a poem, entitled "Le Voye ou le Songe d'Enfer," was written by Raoul de Houdane, about the year 1180; and in another part (vol. ii., § x., p. 219) he has attributed the origin of Dante's poem to that "favourite apologue, the 'Somnium Scipionis' of Cicero, which, in Chaucer's words, treats

> 'Of heaven and hell
> And yearth and souls that therein dwell.'
>   *Assembly of Foules.*

It is likely that a little research might discover many other sources from which his invention might, with an equal appearance of truth, be derived. The method of conveying instruction or entertainment under the form of a vision, in which the living should be made to converse with the dead, was so obvious, that it would be, perhaps, difficult to mention any country in which it had not been employed. It is the scale of magnificence on which this conception was framed, and the wonderful development of it in all its parts, that may justly entitle our poet to rank among the few minds to whom the power of a great creative faculty can be ascribed.

[2] Leonardo Aretino, "Vita di Dante."

little better than grotesque, where Milton has since taught us to expect sublimity. But his faults, in general, were less those of the poet than of the age in which he lived. For his having adopted the popular creed in all its extravagance, we have no more right to blame him than we should have to blame Homer because he made use of the heathen deities, or Shakespeare on account of his witches and fairies. The supposed influence of the stars on the disposition of men at their nativity, was hardly separable from the distribution which he had made of the glorified spirits through the heavenly bodies, as the abodes of bliss suited to their several endowments. And whatever philosophers may think of the matter, it is certainly much better, for the ends of poetry, at least, that too much should be believed, rather than less, or even no more than can be proved to be true. Of what he considered the cause of civil and religious liberty, he is on all occasions the zealous and fearless advocate ; and of that higher freedom, which is seated in the will, he was an assertor equally strenuous and enlightened. The contemporary of Thomas Aquinas, it is not to be wondered if he has given his poem a tincture of the scholastic theology, which the writings of that extraordinary man had rendered so prevalent, and without which it could not perhaps have been made acceptable to the generality of his readers. The phraseology has been accused of being at times hard and uncouth ; but, if this is acknowledged, yet it must be remembered that he gave a permanent stamp and character to the language in which he wrote, and in which, before him, nothing great had been attempted ; that the diction is strictly vernacular, without any debasement of foreign idiom ; that his numbers have as much variety as the Italian tongue, at least in that kind of metre, could supply ; and that, although succeeding writers may have surpassed him in the lighter graces and embellishments of style, not one of them has equalled him in succinctness, vivacity, and strength.

Never did any poem rise so suddenly into notice after the death of its author, or engage the public attention more powerfully, than the " Divina Commedia." This cannot be attributed solely to its intrinsic excellence. The freedom with which the writer had treated the most distinguished characters of his time, gave it a further and stronger hold on the curiosity of the age : many saw in it their acquaintances, kinsmen, and friends, or, what scarcely touched them less nearly, their enemies, either consigned to infamy or recorded with honour, and represented in another world as tasting

> " Of heaven's sweet cup, or poisonous drug of hell ;'

so that not a page could be opened without exciting the strongest personal feelings in the mind of the reader. These sources of interest must certainly be taken into our account, when we consider the rapid diffusion of the work, and the unexampled pains that were taken to render it universally intelligible. Not only the profound and subtile allegory which pervaded it, the mysterious style of prophecy which the writer occasionally assumed, the bold and unusual metaphors which he everywhere employed, and the great variety of knowledge he displayed ; but his hasty allusions to passing events, and the description of persons by accidental circumstances, such as some peculiarity of form or feature, the place of their nativity or abode, some office they held, or the heraldic insignia they bore—all asked for the help of commentators and expounders, who were not long wanting to the task. Besides his two sons, to whom that labour most properly belonged, many others were found ready to engage in it. Before the century had expired, there appeared the commentaries of Accorso de' Bonfantini,[1] a Franciscan ; of Micchino da Mezzano, a canon of Ravenna ; of Fra. Riccardo, a Carmelite ; of Andrea, a Neapolitan ; of Guiniforte Bargigio, a Bergamese ; of Fra. Paola Albertino ; and of several writers whose names are unknown, and whose toils, when Pelli wrote, were concealed in the dust of private libraries.[2] About the year 1350, Giovanni Visconti, Archbishop of Milan, selected six of the most learned men in Italy—two divines, two philosophers, and two Florentines—and gave it them in charge to contribute their joint endeavours towards the compilation of an ample comment, a copy of which is preserved in the Laurentian library at Florence. Who these were is no longer known ; but Jacopo della Lana[3] and Petrarch are conjectured to have been among the number. At Florence a public

---

[1] Tiraboschi, " Storia della Poes. Ital.," vol. ii., p. 39 ; and Pelli, p. 119.

[2] The " Lettera di Eustazio Dicearcheo," &c., mentioned in Note 1 on p. xviii., contains many extracts from an early MS. of the " Divina Commedia," with marginal notes in Latin, preserved in the monastery of Monte Casino. To these extracts I shall have frequent occasion to refer.

[3] Pelli, p. 119, informs us that the writer—who is termed sometimes " the good," sometimes the " old commentator," by those deputed to correct the " Decameron," in the preface to their explanatory notes—and who began his work in 1334, is known to be Jacopo della Lana ; and that his commentary was translated into Latin by Alberigo da Rosada, Doctor of Laws at Bologna.

lecture was founded for the purpose of explaining a poem that was at the same time the boast and the disgrace of the city. The decree for this institution was passed in 1373; and in that year Boccaccio, the first of their writers in prose, was appointed, with an annual salary of 100 florins, to deliver lectures in one of the churches, on the first of their poets. On this occasion he wrote his comment, which extends only to a part of the "Inferno," and has been printed. In 1375 Boccaccio died; and among his successors in this honourable employment we find the names of Antonio Piovano in 1381, and of Filippo Villani in 1401.

The example of Florence was speedily followed by Bologna, by Pisa, by Piacenza, and by Venice. Benvenuto da Imola, on whom the office of lecturer devolved at Bologna, sustained it for the space of ten years. From the comment, which he composed for the purpose, and which he sent abroad in 1379, those passages which tend to illustrate the history of Italy have been published by Muratori.[1] At Pisa the same charge was committed to Francesco da Buti, about 1386.

On the invention of printing, in the succeeding century, Dante was one of those writers who were first and most frequently given to the press. But I do not mean to enter on an account of the numerous editions of our author which were then or have since been published, but shall content myself with adding such remarks as have occurred to me on reading the principal writers, by whose notes those editions have been accompanied.

Of the four chief commentators on Dante, namely, Landino, Vellutello, Venturi, and Lombardi, the first appears to enter most thoroughly into the mind of the poet. Within little more than a century of the time in which Dante had lived; himself a Florentine, while Florence was still free, and still retained something of her ancient simplicity; the associate of those great men who adorned the age of Lorenzo de' Medici; Landino[2] was the most capable of forming some estimate of the mighty stature of his compatriot, who was indeed greater than them all. His taste for the classics, which were then newly revived, and had become the principal objects of public curiosity, as it impaired his relish for what has not inaptly been termed the romantic literature, did not, it is true, improve him for a critic on the "Divina Commedia." The adventures of King Arthur, by which Dante had been delighted, appeared to Landino no better than a fabulous and inelegant book.[3] He is, besides, sometimes unnecessarily prolix; at others, silent, where a real difficulty asks for solution; and, now and then, a little visionary in his interpretation. The commentary of his successor, Vellutello,[4] is more evenly diffused over the text; and although without pretensions to the higher qualities, by which Landino is distinguished, he is generally under the influence of a sober good sense, which renders him a steady and useful guide. Venturi,[5] who followed after a long interval of time, was too much swayed by his principles or his prejudices, as a Jesuit, to suffer him to judge fairly of a Ghibelline poet; and either this bias or a real want of tact for the higher excellence of his author, or, perhaps, both these imperfections together, betray him into such impertinent and injudicious sallies, as dispose us to quarrel with our companion, though, in the main, a very attentive one, generally acute and lively, and at times even not devoid of a better understanding for the merits of his master. To him, and in our own times, has succeeded the Padre Lombardi.[6] This good Franciscan, no doubt, must have given himself much pains to pick out and separate those ears of grain which had escaped the flail of those who had gone before him in that labour. But his zeal to do something new often leads him to do something that is not over wise; and if on certain occasions we applaud his sagaciousness, on others we do not less wonder that his ingenuity should have been so strangely perverted. His manner of writing is awkward and tedious; his attention, more than is necessary, directed to grammatical niceties; and his attachment to one of the old editions so excessive, as to render him disingenuous or partial in his representation of the rest. But to compensate this, he is a good Ghibelline; and his opposition to Venturi seldom fails to awaken him into a perception of those beauties which had only exercised the spleen of the Jesuit.

---

[1] "Antiq. Ital.," v. i. The Italian comment published under the name of Benvenuto da Imola, at Milan, in 1473, and at Venice, in 1477, is altogether different from that which Muratori has brought to light, and appears to be the same as the Italian comment of Jacopo della Lana before mentioned. See Tiraboschi.

[2] Cristofforo Landino was born in 1424, and died in 1504 or 1508. See Bandini, "Specimen Litterat. Florent.," edit. Florence, 1751.

[3] "Il favoloso, e non molto elegante libro della Tavola Rotonda."—*Landino, in the Notes to the Paradise*, xvi.

[4] Allessandro Vellutello was born in 1519.

[5] Pompeo Venturi was born in 1693, and died in 1752.

[6] Baldassare Lombardi died January 2, 1802. See Cancellieri, "Osservazioni," &c., Roma., 1814, p. 112.

He who shall undertake another commentary on Dante[1] yet completer than any of those which have hitherto appeared, must make use of these four, but depend on none. To them he must add several others of minor note, whose diligence will nevertheless be found of some advantage, and among whom I can particularly distinguish Volpi. Besides this, many commentaries and marginal annotations, that are yet inedited, remain to be examined ; many editions and manuscripts[2] to be more carefully collated ; and many separate dissertations and works of criticism to be considered. But this is not all. That line of reading which the poet himself appears to have pursued (and there are many vestiges in his works by which we shall be enabled to discover it) must be diligently tracked ; and the search, I have little doubt, would lead to sources of information equally profitable and unexpected.

If there is anything of novelty in the Notes which accompany the following translation, it will be found to consist chiefly in a comparison of the poet with himself, that is, of the " Divina Commedia " with his other writings ;[3] a mode of illustration so obvious, that it is only to be wondered how others should happen to have made so little use of it. As to the imitations of my author by later poets, Italian and English, which I have collected in addition to those few that had been already remarked, they contribute little or nothing to the purposes of illustration, but must be considered merely as matter of curiosity, and as instances of the manner in which the great practitioners in art do not scruple to profit by their predecessors.

---

[1] Francesco Cionacci, a noble Florentine, projected an edition of the " Divina Commedia " in 100 volumes, each containing a single canto, followed by all the commentaries, according to the order of time in which they were written, and accompanied by a Latin translation for the use of foreigners."—*Cancellieri, Ibid.*, p. 64.

[2] The Count Mortara has lately shown me many various readings he has remarked on collating the numerous MSS. of Dante in the Canonici collection at the Bodleian.

[3] The edition which is referred to in the following Notes is that printed at Venice in 2 vols. 8vo, 1793.

THE AGE OF DANTE.

A.D.

1265 May.—DANTE, son of Alighieri degli Alighieri and Bella, is born at Florence. Of his own ancestry he speaks in the "Paradise," canto xv., xvi.

In the same year, Manfredi, King of Naples and Sicily, is defeated and slain by Charles of Anjou. "Hell," xxviii. 13; "Purgatory," iii. 110.

Guido Novello of Polenta obtains the sovereignty of Ravenna. "Hell," xxvii. 38.

Battle of Evesham. Simon de Montfort, leader of the barons, defeated and slain.

1266 Two of the Frati Godenti chosen arbitrators of the differences of Florence. "Hell," xxiii. 104.

Gianni de' Soldanieri heads the populace in that city. "Hell," xxxii. 118.

Roger Bacon sends a copy of his "Opus Majus" to Pope Clement IV.

1268 Charles of Anjou puts Conradine to death, and becomes King of Naples. "Hell," xxviii. 16; "Purgatory," xx. 66.

1270 Louis IX. of France dies before Tunis. His widow, Beatrice, daughter of Raymond Berenger, lived till 1295. "Purgatory," vii. 126; "Paradise," vi. 133.

1272 Henry III. of England is succeeded by Edward I. "Purgatory," vii. 129.

Guy de Montfort murders Prince Henry, son of Richard, King of the Romans, and nephew of Henry III. of England, at Viterbo. "Hell," xii. 116. Richard dies, as is supposed, of grief for this event.

Abulfeda, the Arabic writer, is born.

1274 Our poet first sees Beatrice, daughter of Folco Portinari.

Rodolph acknowledged Emperor.

Philip III. of France marries Mary of Brabant, who lived till 1321. "Purgatory," vi. 24.

Thomas Aquinas dies. "Purgatory," xx. 67; "Paradise," x. 96.

Buonaventura dies. "Paradise," xii. 25.

1275 Pierre de la Brosse, secretary to Philip III. of France, executed. "Purgatory," vi. 23.

1276 Giotto, the painter, is born. "Purgatory," xi. 95.

Pope Adrian V. dies. "Purgatory," xix. 97.

Guido Guinicelli, the poet, dies. "Purgatory," xi. 96, xxvi. 83.

A.D.

1277 Pope John XXI. dies. "Paradise," xii. 126.

1278 Ottocar, King of Bohemia, dies. "Purgatory," vii. 97. Robert of Gloucester is living at this time.

1279 Dionysius succeeds to the throne of Portugal. "Paradise," xix. 135.

1280 Albertus Magnus dies. "Paradise," x. 95.

Our poet's friend, Busone da Gubbio, is born about this time. See the life of Dante, prefixed.

William of Ockham is born about this time.

1281 Pope Nicholas III. dies. "Hell," xix. 71.

Dante studies at the Universities of Bologna and Padua.

About this time Ricordano Malaspina, the Florentine annalist, dies.

1282 The Sicilian vespers. "Paradise," viii. 80.

The French defeated by the people of Forli. "Hell," xxvii. 41.

Tribaldello de' Manfredi betrays the city of Faenza. "Hell," xxxii. 119.

1284 Prince Charles of Anjou is defeated and made prisoner by Rugier de Lauria, admiral to Peter III. of Arragon. "Purgatory," xx. 78.

Charles I., King of Naples, dies. "Purgatory," vii. 111.

Alonzo X. of Castile dies. He caused the Bible to be translated into Castilian, and all legal instruments to be drawn up in that language. Sancho IV. succeeds him.

Philip (next year IV. of France) marries Jane, daughter of Henry of Navarre. "Purgatory," vii. 102.

1285 Pope Martin IV. dies. "Purgatory," xxiv. 23.

Philip III. of France and Peter III. of Arragon die. "Purgatory," vii. 101, 110.

Henry II., King of Cyprus, comes to the throne. "Paradise," xix. 144.

Simon Memmi, the painter, celebrated by Petrarch, is born.

1287 Guido dalle Colonne (mentioned by Dante in his "De Vulgari Eloquentia") writes "The War of Troy."

Pope Honorius IV. dies.

1288 Haquin, King of Norway, makes war on Denmark. "Paradise," xix. 135.

Count Ugolino de' Gherardeschi dies of famine. "Hell," xxxiii. 14.

A.D.

1288 The Scottish poet, Thomas Learmouth, commonly called Thomas the Rhymer, is living at this time.

1289 Dante is in the battle of Campaldino, where the Florentines defeat the people of Arezzo, June 11. "Purgatory," v. 90.

1290 Beatrice dies. "Purgatory," xxxii. 2.
He serves in the war waged by the Florentines upon the Pisans, and is present at the surrender of Caprona in the Autumn. "Hell," xxi. 92.
Guido dalle Colonne dies.
William, Marquis of Montferrat, is made prisoner by his traitorous subjects at Alessandria, in Lombardy. "Purgatory," vii. 133.
Michael Scot dies. "Hell," xx. 115.

1291 Dante marries Gemma de' Donati, with whom he lives unhappily. By this marriage he had five sons and a daughter.
Can Grande della Scala is born, March 9. "Hell," i. 98; "Purgatory," xx. 16; "Paradise," xvii. 75, xxvii. 135.
The renegade Christians assist the Saracens to recover St. John D'Acre. "Hell," xxvii. 84.
The Emperor Rodolph dies. "Purgatory," vi. 104, vii. 91.
Alonzo III. of Arragon dies, and is succeeded by James II. "Purgatory," vii. 113; "Paradise," xix. 133.
Eleanor, widow of Henry III., dies. "Paradise." vi. 135.

1292 Pope Nicholas IV. dies.
Roger Bacon dies.
John Baliol, King of Scotland, crowned.

1294 Clement V. abdicates the Papal chair. "Hell," iii. 56.
Dante writes his "Vita Nuova."
Fra Guittone d'Arezzo, the poet, dies. "Purgatory," xxiv. 56.
Andrea Taffi, of Florence, the worker in mosaic, dies.

1295 Dante's preceptor, Brunetto Latini, dies. "Hell," xv. 28.
Charles Martel, King of Hungary, visits Florence. "Paradise," viii. 57, and dies in the same year.
Frederick, son of Peter III. of Arragon, becomes King of Sicily. "Purgatory," vii. 117, "Paradise," xix. 127.
Taddeo, the physician of Florence, called the Hippocratean, dies. "Paradise," xii. 77.
Marco Polo, the traveller, returns from the East to Venice.
Ferdinand IV. of Castile comes to the throne. "Paradise," xix. 122.

1296 Forese, the companion of Dante, dies. "Purgatory," xxxiii. 44.
Sadi, the most celebrated of the Persian writers, dies.

A.D.

1296 War between England and Scotland, which terminates in the submission of the Scots to Edward I.; but in the following year, Sir William Wallace attempts the deliverance of Scotland. "Paradise," xix. 121.

1298 The Emperor Adolphus falls in a battle with his rival, Albert I., who succeeds him in the empire. "Purgatory," vi. 98.
Jacopo da Varagine, Archbishop of Genoa, author of the "Legenda Aurea," dies.

1300 The Bianchi and Neri parties take their rise in Pistoia. "Hell," xxxii. 60.
This is the year in which Dante supposes himself to see his Vision. "Hell," i. 1; xxi. 109.
He is chosen chief magistrate, or first of the Priors of Florence, and continues in office from June 15 to August 15.
Cimabue, the painter, dies. "Purgatory," xi. 93.
Guido Cavalcanti, the most beloved of our poet's friends, dies. "Hell," x. 56; "Purgatory," xi. 96.

1301 The Bianchi party expels the Neri from Pistoia. "Hell," xxiv. 142.

1302 January 27. During his absence at Rome, Dante is mulcted by his fellow-citizens in the sum of 8,000 lire, and condemned to two years' banishment.
March 10. He is sentenced, if taken, to be burned.
Fulcieri de' Calboli commits great atrocities on certain of the Ghibelline party. "Purgatory," xiv. 61.
Carlino de' Pazzi betrays the castle di Piano Travigne, in Valdarno, to the Florentines. "Hell," xxxii. 67
The French vanquished in the battle of Courtrai. "Purgatory," xx. 47.
James, King of Majorca and Minorca, dies. "Paradise," xix. 133.

1303 Pope Boniface VIII. dies. "Hell." xix. 55: "Purgatory," xx. 86, xxxii. 146; "Paradise," xxvii. 20.
The other exiles appoint Dante one of a council of twelve, under Alessandro da Romena. He appears to have been much dissatisfied with his colleagues. "Paradise," xvii. 61.
Robert of Brunne translates into English verse the "Manuel de Peches," a treatise written in French by Robert Grosseteste, Bishop of Lincoln.

1304 Dante joins with the exiles in an unsuccessful attack on the city of Florence.
May. The bridge over the Arno breaks down during a representation of the infernal torments exhibited on that river. "Hell," xxvi. 9.
July 20. Petrarch, whose father had been banished two years before from Florence, is born at Arezzo.

A.D.

1305 Winceslaus II., King of Bohemia, dies. "Purgatory," vii. 99: "Paradise," xix. 123.

A conflagration happens at Florence. "Hell," xxvi. 9.

Sir William Wallace is executed at London.

1306 Dante visits Padua.

1307 He is in Lunigiana with the Marchese Marcello Malaspina. "Purgatory," viii. 133, xix. 140.

Dolcino, the fanatic, is burned. "Hell," xxviii. 53.

Edward II. of England comes to the throne.

1308 The Emperor Albert I. murdered. "Purgatory," vi. 98; "Paradise," xix. 114.

Corso Donati, Dante's political enemy, slain. "Purgatory," xxiv. 81.

He seeks an asylum at Verona, under the roof of the Signori della Scala. "Paradise," xvii. 69.

He wanders, about this time, over various parts of Italy. See his "Convito." He is at Paris a second time; and, according to one of the early commentators, visits Oxford.

Robert, the patron of Petrarch, is crowned King of Sicily. "Paradise," ix. 2.

Duns Scotus dies. He was born about the same time as Dante.

1309 Charles II., King of Naples, dies. "Paradise," xix. 125.

1310 The Order of the Templars abolished. "Purgatory," xx. 94.

Jean de Meun, the continuer of the Roman de la Rose, dies about this time.

Pier Crescenzi of Bologna writes his book on agriculture, in Latin.

1311 Fra Giordano da Rivalta, of Pisa, a Dominican, the author of sermons esteemed for the purity of the Tuscan language, dies.

1312 Robert, King of Sicily, opposes the coronation of the Emperor Henry VII. "Paradise," viii. 59.

1312 Ferdinand IV. of Castile dies, and is succeeded by Alonzo XI.

Dino Compagni, a distinguished Florentine, concludes his history of his own time, written in elegant Italian.

Gaddo Gaddi, the Florentine artist, dies.

1313 The Emperor Henry of Luxemburgh, by whom Dante had hoped to be restored to Florence, dies. "Paradise," xvii. 80, xxx. 135. Henry is succeeded by Lewis of Bavaria.

Dante takes refuge at Ravenna, with Guido Novello da Polenta.

Giovanni Boccaccio is born.

Pope Clement V. dies. "Hell," xix. 86; "Paradise," xxvii. 53, xxx. 141.

1314 Philip IV. of France dies. "Purgatory," vii. 108; "Paradise," xix. 117.

Louis X. succeeds.

Ferdinand IV. of Spain dies. "Paradise," xix. 122.

Giacopo da Carrara defeated by Can Grande, who makes himself master of Vicenza. "Paradise," ix. 45.

1315 Louis X. of France marries Clemenza, sister to our poet's friend, Charles Martel, King of Hungary. "Paradise," ix. 2.

1316 Louis X. of France dies, and is succeeded by Philip V.

John XXII. elected Pope. "Paradise," xxvii. 53.

Joinville, the French historian, dies about this time.

1320 About this time John Gower is born, eight years before his friend Chaucer.

1321 July. Dante dies at Ravenna, of a complaint brought on by disappointment at his failure in a negotiation which he had been conducting with the Venetians, for his patron Guido Novello da Polenta.

His obsequies are sumptuously performed at Ravenna, by Guido, who himself died in the ensuing year.

B

In the midway of this our mortal life
I found me in a gloomy wood, astray
                                    Cant. I.

THE VISION OF DANTE.

Ibell.

CANTO I.

ARGUMENT.

The writer, having lost his way in a gloomy forest, and being hindered by certain wild beasts from ascending a mountain, is met by Virgil, who promises to show him the punishments of Hell, and afterwards of Purgatory ; and that he shall then be conducted by Beatrice into Paradise. He follows the Roman poet.

IN the midway[1] of this our mortal life,
  I found me in a gloomy wood, astray
Gone from the path direct : and e'en to tell,
It were no easy task, how savage wild
That forest, how robust and rough its growth,
Which to remember[2] only, my dismay
Renews, in bitterness not far from death.
Yet, to discourse of what there good befell,
All else will I relate discover'd there.

    How first I enter'd it I scarce can say,
Such sleepy dulness in that instant weigh'd
My senses down, when the true path I left ;
But when a mountain's foot I reach'd, where closed
The valley that had pierced my heart with dread,
I look'd aloft, and saw his shoulders broad
Already vested with that planet's beam,[3]
Who leads all wanderers safe through every way.

[1] *In the midway.*—That the era of the Poem is intended by these words to be fixed to the thirty-fifth year of the poet's age, A.D. 1300, will appear more plainly in Canto xxi., where that date is explicitly marked. In his " Convito," human life is compared to an arch or bow, the highest point of which is, in those well framed by nature, at their thirty-fifth year " Opere di Dante," ediz. Ven. 8vo, 1793, tom. i., p. 105

[2] *Which to remember.*—" Even when I remember I am afraid, and trembling taketh hold on my flesh," Job xxi. 6.

[3] *That planet's beam.*—The sun.

Then was a little respite to the fear,
That in my heart's recesses[1] deep had lain
All of that night, so pitifully past:
And as a man, with difficult short breath,
Forespent with toiling, 'scaped from sea to shore,
Turns[2] to the perilous wide waste, and stands
At gaze; e'en so my spirit, that yet fail'd,
Struggling with terror, turn'd to view the straits
That none hath past and lived. My weary frame
After short pause re-comforted, again
I journey'd on over that lonely steep,
The hinder foot[3] still firmer. Scarce the ascent
Began, when, lo! a panther,[4] nimble, light,
And cover'd with a speckled skin, appear'd;
Nor, when it saw me, vanish'd; rather strove
To check my onward going; that ofttimes,
With purpose to retrace my steps, I turn'd.

 The hour was morning's prime, and on his way
Aloft the sun ascended with those stars[5]
That with him rose when Love divine first moved
Those its fair works: so that with joyous hope
All things conspired to fill me, the gay skin[6]
Of that swift animal, the matin dawn,
And the sweet season. Soon that joy was chased,
And by new dread succeeded, when in view
A lion[7] came, 'gainst me as it appear'd,

---

[1] *My heart's recesses.*—Nel lago del cuor. Lombardi cites an imitation of this by Redi in his "Ditirambo":

> "I buon vini son quegli, che acquetano
>   Le procelle si fosche e rubelle,
>   Che nel lago del cuor l'anime inquietano."

[2] *Turns.*—So in our poet's second psalm:

> "Come colui, che andando per lo bosco,
>   Da spino punto, a quel si volge e guarda."

"Even as one, in passing through a wood,
 Pierced by a thorn, at which he turns and looks."

[3] *The hinder foot.*—It is to be remembered that in ascending a hill the weight of the body rests on the hinder foot.

[4] *A panther.*—Pleasure or luxury.

[5] *With those stars.*—The sun was in Aries, in which sign he supposes it to have begun its course at the creation.

[6] *The gay skin.*—A late editor of the "Divina Commedia," Signor Zotti, has spoken of the present translation as the only one that has rendered this passage rightly; but Mr. Hayley had shown me the way, in his very skilful version of the first three Cantos of the "Inferno," inserted in the Notes to his "Essay on Epic Poetry":

"I now was raised to hope sublime
 By these bright omens of my fate benign,
 The beauteous beast and the sweet hour of prime."

All the commentators whom I have seen understand our poet to say that the season of the year and the hour of the day induced him to hope for the gay skin of the panther; and there is something in the sixteenth Canto, verse 107, which countenances their interpretation, although that which I have followed still appears to me the more probable.

[7] *A lion.*—Pride or ambition.

A lion came, 'gainst me as it appear'd,
With his head held aloft, and hunger-mad.
Canto I., lines 43, 44.

With his head held aloft and hunger-mad,
That e'en the air was fear-struck. A she-wolf[1]
Was at his heels, who in her leanness seem'd
Full of all wants, and many a land hath made
Disconsolate ere now. She with such fear
O'erwhelmed me, at the sight of her appall'd,
That of the height all hope I lost. As one
Who, with his gain elated, sees the time
When all unwares is gone, he inwardly
Mourns with heart-griping anguish; such was I,
Haunted by that fell beast, never at peace,
Who coming o'er against me, by degrees
Impell'd me where the sun in silence rests.[2]

While to the lower space with backward step
I fell, my ken discern'd the form of one
Whose voice seem'd faint through long disuse of speech.
When him in that great desert I espied,
"Have mercy on me," cried I out aloud,
"Spirit! or living man! whate'er thou be."

He answer'd: "Now not man, man once I was,
And born of Lombard parents, Mantuans both
By country, when the power of Julius[3] yet
Was scarcely firm. At Rome my life was past,
Beneath the mild Augustus, in the time

---

[1] *A she-wolf.*—Avarice. It cannot be doubted that the image of these three beasts coming against him is taken by our author from the prophet Jeremiah (v. 6): " Wherefore a lion out of the forest shall slay them, and a wolf of the evenings shall spoil them, a leopard shall watch over their cities." Rossetti, following Dionisi and other later commentators, interprets Dante's leopard to denote Florence, his lion the King of France, and his wolf the Court of Rome. It is far from improbable that our author might have had a second allegory of this sort in his view ; even as Spenser, in the introductory letter to his poem, tells us that " in the ' Faëry Queen ' he meant Glory in his general intention, but in his particular he conceived the most excellent and glorious person of his sovereign the Queen. And yet," he adds, " in some places else I do otherwise shadow her." Such involution of allegorical meanings may well be supposed to have been frequently present to the mind of Dante throughout the composition of this poem. Whether his acute and eloquent interpreter, Rossetti, may not have been carried much too far in the pursuit of a favourite hypothesis, is another question ; and I must avow my disbelief of the secret jargon imputed to our poet and the other writers of that time in the " Comment on the Divina Commedia," and in the " Spirito Antipapale," the latter of which works is familiarised to the English reader in Miss Ward's faithful translation

[2] *Where the sun in silence rests.*—

    " The sun to me is dark,
    And silent as the moon,
    When she deserts the night,
    Hid in her vacant interlunar cave."
            Milton, Samson Agonistes.

The same metaphor will recur, Canto v., verse 29 :

    " Into a place I came
    Where light was silent all."

[3] *When the power of Julius.*—

    " Nacqui sub Julio, ancorchè fosse tardi."

This is explained by the commentators : " Although it were rather late with respect to my birth, before Julius Cæsar assumed the supreme authority, and made himself perpetual dictator." Virgil indeed was born twenty-five years before that event.

Of fabled deities and false. A bard
Was I, and made Anchises' upright son
The subject of my song, who came from Troy,
When the flames preyed on Ilium's haughty towers.[1]
But thou, say wherefore to such perils past
Return'st thou ? wherefore not this pleasant mount
Ascendest, cause and source of all delight ?"
"And art thou then that Virgil, that well-spring,
From which such copious floods of eloquence
Have issued ?" I with front abash'd replied.
"Glory and light of all the tuneful train !
May it avail me, that I long with zeal
Have sought thy volume, and with love immense
Have conn'd it o'er. My master thou, and guide ![2]
Thou he from whom alone I have derived
That style, which for its beauty into fame
Exalts me. See the beast, from whom I fled.
Oh, save me from her, thou illustrious sage !
For every vein and pulse throughout my frame
She hath made tremble." He, soon as he saw
That I was weeping, answer'd, "Thou must needs
Another way pursue, if thou wouldst 'scape
From out that savage wilderness. This beast,
At whom thou criest, her way will suffer none
To pass, and no less hindrance makes than death :
So bad and so accursed in her kind,
That never sated is her ravenous will,
Still after food[3] more craving than before.
To many an animal in wedlock vile
She fastens, and shall yet to many more,
Until that greyhound[4] come, who shall destroy

---

[1] *Ilium's haughty towers.*—

　　　　"Ceciditque superbum
Ilium."　　　　　　*Virgil, Æneid,* iii. 3.

[2] *My master thou, and guide !*—

　　"Tu se' lo mio maestro, e' l mio autore,
　　Tu se' solo colui."

　　"Thou art my father, thou my author, thou."
　　　　　　Milton, Paradise Lost, ii. 804.

[3] *Still after food.*—So Frezzi :

　　" La voglia sempre ha fame, e mai non s'empie,
　　　Ed al più pasto più riman digiuna."
　　　　　　Il Quadriregio, lib. ii., cap. xi.
Venturi observes that the verse in the original is
borrowed by Berni.

[4] *That greyhound.*—This passage has been commonly understood as a eulogium on the liberal spirit
of his Veronese patron, Can Grande della Scala.

He, soon as he saw
That I was weeping, answer'd.

Canto I. lines 87, 88.

Her with sharp pain. He will not life support
By earth nor its base metals, but by love,
Wisdom, and virtue ; and his land shall be
The land 'twixt either Feltro.[1] In his might
Shall safety to Italia's plains[2] arise,
For whose fair realm, Camilla, virgin pure,
Nisus, Euryalus, and Turnus fell.
He, with incessant chase, through every town
Shall worry, until he to hell at length
Restore her, thence by envy first let loose.
I, for thy profit pondering, now devise
That thou mayst follow me ; and I, thy guide,
Will lead thee hence through an eternal space,
Where thou shalt hear despairing shrieks, and see
Spirits of old tormented, who invoke
A second death ;[3] and those next view, who dwell
Content in fire,[4] for that they hope to come,
Whene'er the time may be, among the blest,
Into whose regions if thou then desire
To ascend, a spirit worthier[5] than I
Must lead thee, in whose charge, when I depart,
Thou shalt be left : for that Almighty King,
Who reigns above, a rebel to his law
Adjudges me; and therefore hath decreed

---

[1] *'Twixt either Feltro.*—Verona, the country of Can della Scala, is situated between Feltro, a city in the Marca Trivigiana, and Monte Feltro, a city in the territory of Urbino. But Dante perhaps does not merely point out the place of Can Grande's nativity, for he may allude further to a prophecy, ascribed to Michael Scot, which imported that the " Dog of Verona would be lord of Padua and of all the Marca Trivigiana." It was fulfilled in the year 1329, a little before Can Grande's death. See G. Villani, " Hist." lib. x., cap. cv. and cxli., and some lively criticism by Gasparo Gozzi, entitled, " Giudizio degli Antichi Poeti," &c., printed at the end of the Zatta edition of " Dante," tom. iv., part ii., p. 15. The prophecy, it is likely, was a forgery ; for Michael died before 1300, when Can Grande was only nine years old. See " Hell," xx. 115, and " Paradise," xvii. 75. Troya has given a new interpretation to Dante's prediction, which he applies to Uguccione della Faggiuola, whose country also was situated between two Feltros. See the " Veltro Allegorico di Dante," p. 110. But after all the pains he has taken, this very able writer fails to make it clear that Uguccione, though he acted a prominent part as a Ghibelline leader, is intended here or in " Purgatory," c. xxxiii. 38. The main proofs rest on an ambiguous report mentioned by Boccaccio of the " Inferno " being dedicated to him, and on a suspicious letter attributed to a certain friar Ilario, in which the friar describes Dante addressing him as a stranger, and desiring him to convey that portion of the poem to Uguccione. There is no direct allusion to him throughout the " Divina Commedia," as there is to the other chief public protectors of our poet during his exile.

[2] *Italia's plains.*—" Umile Italia," from Virgil. " Æneid," lib. iii. 522 :

  " Humilemque videmus
  Italiam."

[3] *A second death.*—" And in those days shall men seek death, and shall not find it ; and shall desire to die, and death shall flee from them," Rev. ix. 6.

[4] *Content in fire.*—The spirits in Purgatory.

[5] *A spirit worthier.*—Beatrice, who conducts the poet through Paradise.

That, to his city, none through me should come.
He in all parts hath sway; there rules, there holds
His citadel and throne. Oh, happy those,
Whom there he chooses!" I to him in few:
"Bard! by that God, whom thou didst not adore,
I do beseech thee (that this ill and worse
I may escape) to lead me where thou saidst,
That I Saint Peter's gate[1] may view, and those
Who, as thou tell'st, are in such dismal plight."
  Onward he moved, I close his steps pursued.

[1] *Saint Peter's gate.*—The gate of Purgatory, which the poet feigns to be guarded by an angel placed on that station by St. Peter.

Onward he moved, I close his steps pursued.
Canto I. line 132.

Now was the day departing.

Canto II., line 1.

CANTO II.

ARGUMENT.

After the invocation, which poets are used to prefix to their works, he shows that, on a consideration of his own strength, he doubted whether it sufficed for the journey proposed to him, but that, being comforted by Virgil, he at last took courage, and followed him as his guide and master.

NOW was the day[1] departing, and the air,
　　Embrown'd with shadows, from their toils released
All animals on earth ; and I alone
Prepared myself the conflict to sustain,
Both of sad pity, and that perilous road,
Which my unerring memory shall retrace.

　　O Muses ! Oh, high genius ! now vouchsafe
Your aid. Oh, mind ![2] that all I saw hast kept
Safe in a written record, here thy worth
And eminent endowments come to proof.
I thus began : "Bard ! thou who art my guide,
Consider well, if virtue be in me
Sufficient, ere to this high enterprise
Thou trust me. Thou hast told that Silvius' sire,[3]
Yet clothed in corruptible flesh, among
The immortal tribes had entrance, and was there
Sensibly present. Yet if Heaven's great Lord,
Almighty foe to ill, such favour show'd
In contemplation of the high effect,
Both what and who from him should issue forth,

---

1 *Now was the day.*—A compendium of Virgil's description, " Æneid," lib. iv. 522. Compare Apollonius Rhodius, lib. iii. 744, and lib. iv. 1058.

> " The day gan failin : and the darke night,
> That revith bestis from their businesse,
> Berafte me my booke," &c.
> 　　*Chaucer, The Assemble of Foules.*

2 *Oh, mind.*—

> " Oh, thought ! that write all that I met,
> And in the tresorie it set
> Of my braine, now shall men see
> If any virtue in thee be."
> 　　*Chaucer, Temple of Fame,* b. ii , v. 18.

3 *Silvius' sire.*—Æneas.

It seems in reason's judgment well deserved ;
Sith he of Rome and of Rome's empire wide,
In heaven's empyreal height was chosen sire :
Both which, if truth be spoken, were ordain'd
And stablish'd for the holy place, where sits
Who to great Peter's sacred chair succeeds.
He from this journey, in thy song renown'd,
Learn'd things, that to his victory gave rise
And to the Papal robe. In after-times
The chosen vessel[1] also travell'd there,[2]
To bring us back assurance in that faith
Which is the entrance to salvation's way.
But I, why should I there presume ? or who
Permits it ? not Æneas I, nor Paul.
Myself I deem not worthy, and none else
Will deem me. I, if on this voyage then
I venture, fear it will in folly end.
Thou, who art wise, better my meaning know'st,
Than I can speak." As one, who unresolves
What he hath late resolved, and with new thoughts
Changes his purpose, from his first intent
Removed ; e'en such was I on that dun coast,
Wasting in thought my enterprise, at first
So eagerly embraced. " If right thy words
I scan," replied that shade magnanimous,
" Thy soul is by vile fear assail'd,[3] which oft
So overcasts a man, that he recoils
From noblest resolution, like a beast
At some false semblance in the twilight gloom.
That from this terror thou mayst free thyself,
I will instruct thee why I came, and what
I heard in that same instant, when for thee
Grief touch'd me first. I was among the tribe,

------- .   ---

[1] *The chosen vessel.*—St. Paul. Acts ix. 15 : " But the Lord said unto him, Go thy way : for he is a chosen vessel unto me."

[2] *There*—This refers to " the immortal tribes," v. 16 ; St. Paul having been caught up to heaven—2Cor. xii. 2.

[3] *Thy soul is by vile fear assail'd.*—

     " L'anima tua è da viltate offesa."

So in Berni, " Orl. Inn.," lib. iii., c. i., st. 53 : " Se l'alma avete offesa da viltate."

I, who now bid thee on this errand forth,
Am Beatrice.

Cant. II., lines 70, 71.

Who rest suspended,[1] when a dame, so blest
And lovely I besought her to command,
Call'd me ; her eyes were brighter than the star
Of day ; and she, with gentle voice and soft,
Angelically tuned, her speech address'd :
'Oh, courteous shade of Mantua ! thou whose fame
Yet lives, and shall live long as Nature lasts ![2]
A friend, not of my fortune but myself,[3]
On the wide desert in his road has met
Hindrance so great, that he through fear has turn'd.
Now much I dread lest he past help have stray'd,
And I be risen too late for his relief,
From what in heaven of him I heard. Speed now,
And by thy eloquent persuasive tongue,
And by all means for his deliverance meet,
Assist him. So to me will comfort spring.
I, who now bid thee on this errand forth,
Am Beatrice ;[4] from a place I come
Re-visited with joy. Love brought me thence,
Who prompts my speech. When in my Master's sight
I stand, thy praise to him I oft will tell.'
    "She then was silent, and I thus began :
'O Lady ! by whose influence alone
Mankind excels whatever is contain'd[5]
Within that heaven which hath the smallest orb,
So thy command delights me, that to obey,
If it were done already, would seem late.
No need hast thou further to speak thy will ;
Yet tell the reason, why thou art not loth

---

[1] *Who rest suspended.*—The spirits in Limbo, neither admitted to a state of glory nor doomed to punishment.

[2] *As Nature lasts.*—"Quanto 'l moto lontana." "Mondo," instead of "moto," which Lombardi claims as a reading peculiar to the Nidobeatina edition and some MSS., is also in Landino's edition of 1484. Of this Monti was not aware. See his "Proposta," under the word "Lontanare."

[3] *A friend, not of my fortune but myself.*—"Se non fortunæ sed hominibus solere esse amicum."— *Cornelii Nepotis Attici Vitæ,* c. ix.

"Cætera fortunæ, non mea turba, fuit."
        Ovid, Tristia, lib. i., el. 5, 34.

"My fortune and my seeming destiny
He made the bond, and broke it not with me."
    Coleridge's Death of Wallenstein, Act i., sc. 7.

[4] *Beatrice.*—The daughter of Folco Portinari, who is here invested with the character of celestial wisdom or theology. See the "Life of Dante" prefixed.

[5] *Whatever is contain'd.*—Every other thing comprised within the lunar heaven, which, being the lowest of all, has the smallest circle.

To leave that ample space, where to return
Thou burnest, for this centre here beneath.'

   "She then : 'Since thou so deeply wouldst inquire,
I will instruct thee briefly why no dread
Hinders my entrance here. Those things alone
Are to be fear'd whence evil may proceed ;
None else, for none are terrible beside.
I am so framed by God, thanks to his grace !
That any sufferance of your misery
Touches me not, nor flame of that fierce fire
Assails me. In high heaven a blessed dame[1]
Resides, who mourns with such effectual grief
That hindrance, which I send thee to remove,
That God's stern judgment to her will inclines.
To Lucia[2] calling, her she thus bespake :
"Now doth thy faithful servant need thy aid,
And I commend him to thee." At her word
Sped Lucia, of all cruelty the foe,
And coming to the place, where I abode
Seated with Rachel, her of ancient days,
She thus address'd me : "Thou true praise of God !
Beatrice ! why is not thy succour lent
To him, who so much loved thee, as to leave
For thy sake all the multitude admires ?
Dost thou not hear how pitiful his wail,
Nor mark the death, which in the torrent flood,
Swollen mightier than a sea, him struggling holds ?"
Ne'er among men did any with such speed
Haste to their profit, flee from their annoy,
As, when these words were spoken, I came here,
Down from my blessed seat, trusting the force
Of thy pure eloquence, which thee, and all
Who well have mark'd it, into honour brings.

   "When she had ended, her bright beaming eyes

---

[1] *A blessed dame.*—The Divine Mercy.

[2] *Lucia.*—The enlightening Grace of Heaven, as it is commonly explained. But Lombardi has well observed, that as our poet places her in the Paradise, c. xxxii., amongst the souls of the blessed, so it is probable that she, like Beatrice, had a real existence ; and he accordingly supposes her to have been St. Lucia the martyr, although she is here representative of an abstract idea.

Tearful she turn'd aside ; whereat I felt
Redoubled zeal to serve thee. As she will'd,
Thus am I come : I saved thee from the beast,
Who thy near way across the goodly mount
Prevented. What is this comes o'er thee then ?
Why, why dost thou hang back ? why in thy breast
Harbour vile fear ? why hast not courage there,
And noble daring ; since three maids,[1] so blest,
Thy safety plan, e'en in the court of heaven ;
And so much certain good my words forebode ? "

    As florets,[2] by the frosty air of night
Bent down and closed, when day has blanch'd their leaves,
Rise all unfolded on their spiry stems ;
So was my fainting vigour new restored,
And to my heart such kindly courage ran,
That I as one undaunted soon replied :
"Oh, full of pity she, who undertook
My succour ! and thou kind, who didst perform
So soon her true behest ! With such desire
Thou hast disposed me to renew my voyage,
That my first purpose fully is resumed.
Lead on : one only will is in us both.
Thou art my guide, my master thou, and lord."

    So spake I ; and when he had onward moved,
I enter'd on the deep and woody way.

---

[1] *Three maids.*—The Divine Mercy, Lucia, and Beatrice.

[2] *As florets.*—

> " Come fioretto dal notturno gelo
>   Chinato e chiuso, poi che il sol l'imbianca,
>   S'apre e si leva dritto sopra il stelo."
>
> *Boccaccio, Il Filostrato.* p. iii., st. 13.

> " But right as floures through the cold of night
>   Iclosed, stoppen in her stalkes lowe,
>   Redressen hem agen the sunne bright,
>   And spreden in her kinde course by rowe," &c.
>
> *Chaucer, Troilus and Creseide.* b. ii.

It is from Boccaccio rather than Dante that Chaucer has taken this simile, which he applies to Troilus on the same occasion as Boccaccio has done. He appears indeed to have imitated or rather paraphrased the " Filostrato " in his " Troilus and Creseide " ; for it is not yet known who that Lollius is, from whom he professes to take the poem, and who is again mentioned in the " House of Fame," b. iii. The simile in the text has been imitated by many others ; among whom see Berni, " Orl. Inn.," lib. i., c. xii., st. 80 ; Marino, " Adone," c. xvii., st. 63, and son. " Donna vestita di nero " ; and Spenser's " Faëry Queen," b. iv., c. xii., st. 34, and b. vi., c. ii., st. 35 ; and Boccaccio again in the " Teseide," lib. ix., st. 28.

CANTO III.

ARGUMENT.

Dante, following Virgil, comes to the gate of Hell; where, after having read the dreadful words that are written thereon, they both enter. Here, as he understands from Virgil, those were punished who had passed their time (for living it could not be called) in a state of apathy and indifference both to good and evil. Then pursuing their way, they arrive at the river Acheron; and there find the old ferryman, Charon, who takes the spirits over to the opposite shore; which as soon as Dante reaches, he is seized with terror, and falls into a trance.

"THROUGH me you pass into the city of woe:
   Through me you pass into eternal pain:
Through me among the people lost for aye.
Justice the founder of my fabric moved:
To rear me was the task of power divine,
Supremest wisdom, and primeval love.[1]
Before me things create were none, save things
Eternal, and eternal I endure.
All hope abandon,[2] ye who enter here."

   Such characters, in colour dim, I mark'd
Over a portal's lofty arch inscribed.
Whereat I thus: "Master, these words import
Hard meaning." He as one prepared replied:
"Here thou must all distrust behind thee leave;
Here be vile fear extinguish'd. We are come
Where I have told thee we shall see the souls
To misery doom'd, who intellectual good
Have lost." And when his hand[3] he had stretch'd forth
To mine, with pleasant looks, whence I was cheer'd,
Into that secret place he led me on.
   Here sighs,[4] with lamentations and loud moans,

---

[1] *Power divine, Supremest wisdom, and primeval love* — The three Persons of the Blessed Trinity

[2] *All hope abandon* —

   "Lasciate ogni speranza voi ch' entrate."

So Berni, "Orl. Inn." lib. i., c. viii., st. 53:

   "Lascia pur della vita ogni speranza."

[3] *And when his hand.—*

   "With that my hand in his he caught anone:
   On which I comfort caught, and went in fast."

     Chaucer, The Assemble of Foules.

[4] *Here sighs.—*"Post hæc omnia ad loca tartarea, et ad os infernalis baratri deductus sum, qui simile videbatur puteo, loca vero eadem horridis tenebris,

All hope abandon, ye who enter here.

Canto III. line 9.

Resounded through the air pierced by no star,
That e'en I wept at entering. Various tongues,
Horrible languages, outcries of woe,
Accents of anger, voices deep and hoarse,
With hands together smote that swell'd the sounds,
Made up a tumult, that for ever whirls
Round through that air with solid darkness stain'd,
Like to the sand[1] that in the whirlwind flies.
I then, with error[2] yet encompass'd, cried,
"Oh, master! what is this I hear? what race
Are these, who seem so overcome with woe?"

　　He thus to me : "This miserable fate
Suffer the wretched souls of those who lived
Without or praise or blame, with that ill band
Of angels mix'd, who nor rebellious proved,
Nor yet were true to God, but for themselves
Were only. From his bounds Heaven drove them forth,
Not to impair his lustre ; nor the depth
Of Hell receives them, lest the accursed tribe[3]
Should glory thence with exultation vain."

　　I then : "Master! what doth aggrieve them thus,
That they lament so loud?" He straight replied :
"That will I tell thee briefly. These of death
No hope may entertain ; and their blind life
So meanly passes, that all other lots
They envy. Fame[4] of them the world hath none,
Nor suffers ; mercy and justice scorn them both.
Speak not of them, but look, and pass them by."

---

f.etoribus exhalantibus, stridoribus quoque et nimiis plena erant ejulatibus, juxta quem infernum vermis erat infinitæ magnitudinis, liga:us maxima catena." *Alberici Visio*, § 9.

[1] *Like to the sand.*—" Unnumber'd as the sands
　　Of Barca or Cyrene's torrid soil,
　　Levied to side with warring winds, and poise
　　Their lighter wings."
　　　　　　Milton. Paradise Lost, b. ii., 903.

[2] *With error.*—Instead of "error," Vellutello's edition of 1544 has "orror," a reading remarked also by Landino, in his notes. So much mistaken is the collater of the Monte Casino MS. in calling it "lezione da niuno notata," "a reading which no one has observed."

[3] *Lest the accursed tribe.*—Lest the rebellious angels should exult at seeing those who were neutral, and therefore less guilty, condemned to the same punishment with themselves. Rossetti, in a long note on this passage, has ably exposed the plausible interpretation of Monti, who would have "alcuna gloria" mean "no glory," and thus make Virgil say "that the evil ones would derive no honour from the society of the neutral." A similar mistake in the same word is made elsewhere by Lombardi. See my note on c. xii., v. 9.

[4] *Fame.*—
　　" Cancell'd from heaven and sacred memory,
　　Nameless in dark oblivion let them dwell."
　　　　　　Milton, Paradise Lost, b. vi. 380.
　　" Therefore eternal silence be their doom."
　　　　　　Ibid., 385.

And I, who straightway look'd, beheld a flag,[1]
Which whirling ran around so rapidly,
That it no pause obtain'd : and following came
Such a long train of spirits, I should ne'er
Have thought that death so many had despoil'd.
      When some of these I recognised, I saw
And knew the shade of him, who to base fear
Yielding, abjured his high estate.[2] Forthwith
I understood, for certain, this the tribe
Of those ill spirits both to God displeasing
And to his foes. These wretches, who ne'er lived,
Went on in nakedness, and sorely stung
By wasps and hornets, which bedew'd their cheeks
With blood, that, mix'd with tears, dropp'd to their feet,
And by disgustful worms was gather'd there.
      Then looking further onwards, I beheld
A throng upon the shore of a great stream :
Whereat I thus : "Sir ! grant me now to know
Whom here we view, and whence impell'd they seem
So eager to pass o'er, as I discern
Through the blear light ?"[3] He thus to me in few :
"This shalt thou know, soon as our steps arrive
Beside the woful tide of Acheron."
      Then with eyes downward cast, and fill'd with shame,
Fearing my words offensive to his ear,
Till we had reach'd the river, I from speech
Abstain'd. And, lo ! toward us in a bark
Comes on an old man,[4] hoary white with eld,

---

[1] *A flag.*—   " All the grisly legions that troop
            Under the sooty flag of Acheron."
                              Milton, Comus.
                        Who to base fear
Yielding, abjured his high estate.—
This is commonly understood of Celestine V., who ab-
dicated the Papal power in 1294. Venturi mentions a
work written by Innocenzio Barcellini, of the Celestine
order, and printed at Milan in 1701, in which an attempt
is made to put a different interpretation on this passage.
Lombardi would apply it to some one of Dante's fellow-
citizens, who, refusing through avarice or want of spirit,
to support the party of the Bianchi at Florence, had been
the main occasion of the miseries that befell them. But
the testimony of Fazio degli Uberti, who lived so near the
time of our author, seems almost decisive on this point.
He expressly speaks of the Pope Celestine as being in hell.
See the " Dittamondo," l. iv., cap. xxi. The usual interpretation is further confirmed in a passage in canto xxvii. v.
101. Petrarch, while he passes a high encomium on Celestine for his abdication of the Papal power, gives us to
understand that there were others who thought it a dis-
graceful act. See the " De Vitâ Solit.," b. ii., sect. iii., c. 18.
[3] *Through the blear light.*—" Lo fioco lume." So
Filicaja, canz. vi., st. 12 : " Qual fioco lume."
[4] *An old man.*—
 " Portitor has horrendus aquas et flumina servat
  Terribili squalore Charon, cui plurima mento
  Canities inculta jacet ; stant lumina flammâ."
                        Virgil, Æneid, lib. vi. 298.

And, lo! toward us in a bark
Comes on an old man, hoary white with eld,
Crying, "Woe to you, wicked spirits!"
Canto III., lines 76—78.

Crying, "Woe to you, wicked spirits ! hope not
Ever to see the sky again. I come
To take you to the other shore across,
Into eternal darkness, there to dwell
In fierce heat and in ice.[1] And thou, who there
Standest, live spirit ! get thee hence, and leave
These who are dead." But soon as he beheld
I left them not, "By other way," said he,
"By other haven shalt thou come to shore,
Not by this passage ; thee a nimbler boat[2]
Must carry." Then to him thus spake my guide :
"Charon ! thyself torment not : so 'tis will'd,
Where will and power are one : ask thou no more."

    Straightway in silence fell the shaggy cheeks
Of him, the boatman o'er the livid lake,[3]
Around whose eyes glared wheeling flames. Meanwhile
Those spirits, faint and naked, colour changed,
And gnashed their teeth, soon as the cruel words
They heard. God and their parents they blasphemed,
The human kind, the place, the time, and seed,
That did engender them and give them birth.

    Then all together sorely wailing drew
To the curst strand, that every man must pass
Who fears not God. Charon, demoniac form,
With eyes of burning coal,[4] collects them all,
Beckoning, and each, that lingers, with his oar
Strikes. As fall off the light autumnal leaves,[5]

---

[1] *In fierce heat and in ice.*—
          "The bitter change
Of fierce extremes, extremes by change more fierce,
From beds of raging fire to starve in ice
Their soft ethereal warmth."
        Milton, Paradise Lost, b. ii. 601.
       "The delighted spirit
To bathe in fiery floods, or to reside
In thrilling regions of thick-ribbed ice."
Shakespeare, Measure for Measure, Act iii., sc. i.
See note to c. xxxii. 23.

[2] *A nimbler boat.*—He perhaps alludes to the bark
"swift and light," in which the Angel conducts the
spirits to Purgatory. See " Purgatory," c. ii. 40.

[3] *The livid lake.*—" Vada livida."
        Virgil, Æneid, lib. vi. 320.

"Totius ut lacûs putidæque paludis
Lividissima, maximeque est profunda vorago."
        Catullus, xviii. 10.

[4] *With eyes of burning coal.*—
"His looks were dreadful, and his fiery eyes,
Like two great beacons, glared bright and wide."
      Spenser, Faëry Queen, b. vi., c. vii., st. 42.

[5] *As fall off the light autumnal leaves.*—
"Quam multa in silvis autumni frigore primo
Lapsa cadunt folia."
        Virgil, Æneid, lib. vi. 300.
"Thick as autumnal leaves, that strew the brooks
In Vallombrosa, where the Etrurian shades
High over-arch'd embower."
      Milton, Paradise Lost, b. i. 304.
Compare Apollonius Rhodius, lib. iv. p. 214.

D

One still another following, till the bough
Strews all its honours on the earth beneath ;
E'en in like manner Adam's evil brood
Cast themselves, one by one, down from the shore,
Each at a beck, as falcon at his call.[1]
Thus go they over through the umber'd wave ;
And ever they on the opposing bank
Be landed, on this side another throng
Still gathers. "Son," thus spake the courteous guide,
"Those who die subject to the wrath of God
All here together come from every clime,
And to o'erpass the river are not loth :
For so Heaven's justice goads them on, that fear
Is turned into desire. Hence ne'er hath past
Good spirit. If of thee Charon complain,
Now mayst thou know the import of his words."
This said, the gloomy region trembling shook
So terribly, that yet with clammy dews
Fear chills my brow. The sad earth gave a blast,
That, lightning, shot forth a vermilion flame,
Which all my senses conquer'd quite, and I
Down dropp'd, as one with sudden slumber seized.

----

[1] *As falcon at his call.*—This is Vellutello's explanation, and seems preferable to that commonly given : "as a bird that is enticed to the cage by the call of another."

CANTO IV.

ARGUMENT.

The Poet, being roused by a clap of thunder, and following his guide onwards, descends into Limbo, which is the first circle of Hell, where he finds the souls of those who, although they have lived virtuously, and have not to suffer for great sins, nevertheless, through lack of baptism, merit not the bliss of Paradise. Hence he is led on by Virgil to descend into the second circle.

BROKE the deep slumber in my brain a crash
    Of heavy thunder, that I shook myself,
As one by main force roused. Risen upright,
My rested eyes I moved around, and search'd,
With fixèd ken, to know what place it was
Wherein I stood. For certain, on the brink
I found me of the lamentable vale,
The dread abyss, that joins a thundrous sound [1]
Of plaints innumerable. Dark and deep,
And thick with clouds o'erspread, mine eye in vain
Explored its bottom, nor could aught discern.

    "Now let us to the blind world there beneath
Descend," the bard began, all pale of look :
"I go the first, and thou shalt follow next."

    Then I, his alter'd hue perceiving, thus :
"How may I speed, if thou yieldest to dread,
Who still art wont to comfort me in doubt ? "

    He then : "The anguish of that race below
With pity stains my cheek, which thou for fear
Mistakest. Let us on. Our length of way
Urges to haste." Onward, this said, he moved ;
And entering, led me with him, on the bounds
Of the first circle that surrounds the abyss.

---

[1] *A thundrous sound.*—Imitated, as Mr. Thyer has remarked, by Milton, in "Paradise Lost," book viii. line 242 :

"But long, ere our approaching, heard within
Noise, other than the sound of dance or song,
Torment, and loud lament, and furious rage."

Here, as mine ear could note, no plaint was heard
Except of sighs, that made the eternal air
Tremble, not caused by tortures, but from grief
Felt by those multitudes, many and vast,
Of men, women, and infants. Then to me
The gentle guide : "Inquirest thou not what spirits
Are these which thou beholdest ? Ere thou pass
Farther, I would thou know, that these of sin
Were blameless ; and if aught they merited,
It profits not, since baptism was not theirs,
The portal[1] to thy faith. If they before
The Gospel lived, they served not God aright;
And among such am I. For these defects.
And for no other evil, we are lost ;
Only so far afflicted, that we live
Desiring without hope."[2] Sore grief assail'd
My heart at hearing this, for well I knew
Suspended in that Limbo many a soul
Of mighty worth. "Oh, tell me, sire revered !
Tell me, my master !" I began, through wish
Of full assurance in that holy faith
Which vanquishes all error ; "say, did e'er
Any, or through his own or other's merit,
Come forth from thence, who afterward was blest ?"

Piercing the secret purport[3] of my speech,
He answer'd : "I was new to that estate,
When I beheld a puissant one[4] arrive
Amongst us, with victorious trophy crown'd.
He forth[5] the shade of our first parent drew,

---

[1] *Portal.*—" Porta della fede." This was an alteration made in the text by the Academicians della
Crusca, on the authority, as it would appear, of only
two MSS. The other reading is " parte della fede "
" part of the faith."

[2] *Desiring without hope.*—

" And with desire to languish without hope."
Milton, Paradise Lost, b. x. 995.

[3] *Secret purport.*—Lombardi well observes that
Dante seems to have been restrained by awe and
reverence from uttering the name of Christ in this
place of torment; and that for the same cause,

probably, it does not occur once throughout the
whole of this first part of the poem.

[4] *A puissant one.*—Our Saviour.

[5] *He forth.*—The author of the " Quadriregio" has
introduced a sublime description into his imitation of
this passage :

" Pose le reni là dove si serra ;
Ma Cristo lui e 'l catarcion d'acciajo
E queste porte allora gettò a terra.
Quando in la grotta entrò 'l lucido rajo,
Adamo disse ; Questo è lo splendore
Che mi spirò in faccia da primajo.
Venuto se' aspettato Signore." L. ii., cap. 3.

Only so far afflicted, that we live
Desiring without hope.
                    Canto IV., lines 38, 39.

Abel his child, and Noah, righteous man,
Of Moses lawgiver for faith approved,
Of patriarch Abraham, and David king,
Israel with his sire and with his sons,
Nor without Rachel whom so hard he won,
And others many more, whom he to bliss
Exalted. Before these, be thou assured,
No spirit of human kind was ever saved."

We, while he spake, ceased not our onward road,
Still passing through the wood; for so I name
Those spirits thick beset. We were not far
On this side from the summit, when I kenn'd
A flame, that o'er the darken'd hemisphere
Prevailing shined. Yet we a little space
Were distant, not so far but I in part
Discover'd that a tribe in honour high
That place possess'd. "Oh thou, who every art
And science valuest! who are these, that boast
Such honour, separate from all the rest?"

He answer'd: "The renown of their great names,
That echoes through your world above, acquires
Favour in heaven, which holds them thus advanced."
Meantime a voice I heard: "Honour the bard
Sublime![1] his shade returns, that left us late!"
No sooner ceased the sound, than I beheld
Four mighty spirits toward us bend their steps,
Of semblance neither sorrowful nor glad.[2]

When thus my master kind began: "Mark him,
Who in his right hand bears that falchion keen,
The other three preceding, as their lord.
This is that Homer, of all bards supreme:
Flaccus the next, in satire's vein excelling;

"Satan hung writhing round the holt; but him,
The huge portcullis, and those gates of brass,
Christ threw to earth. As down the cavern stream'd
The radiance: ' Light,' said Adam, ' this, that breathed
First on me. Thou art come, expected Lord!' "
Much that follows is closely copied by Frezzi from
our poet.

[1] *Honour the bard sublime!*—" Onorate l' altissimo poeta." So Chiabrera, " Canz. Erioche," 32·
" Onorando l' altissimo poeta."

[2] *Of semblance neither sorrowful nor glad.*—
" She nas to sober ne to glad."
Chaucer's Dream.

The third is Naso; Lucan is the last.
Because they all that appellation own,
With which the voice singly accosted me,
Honouring they greet me thus, and well they judge."
So I beheld united the bright school
Of him the monarch of sublimest song,[1]
That o'er the others like an eagle soars.

When they together short discourse had held,
They turn'd to me, with salutation kind
Beckoning me; at the which my master smiled:
Nor was this all; but greater honour still
They gave me, for they made me of their tribe;
And I was sixth amid so learn'd a band.
Far as the luminous beacon on we pass'd,
Speaking of matters, then befitting well
To speak, now fitter left untold.[2] At foot
Of a magnificent castle we arrived,
Seven times with lofty walls begirt, and round
Defended by a pleasant stream. O'er this
As o'er dry land we pass'd. Next, through seven gates,
I with those sages enter'd, and we came
Into a mead with lively verdure fresh.

There dwelt a race, who slow their eyes around
Majestically moved, and in their port
Bore eminent authority: they spake
Seldom, but all their words were tuneful sweet.
We to one side retired, into a place

---

[1] *The monarch of sublimest song.*—Homer. It appears, from a passage in the "Convito," that there was no Latin translation of Homer in Dante's time. "Sappio ciascuno," &c., p. 20. "Every one should know that nothing, harmonised by musical enchainment, can be transmuted from one tongue into another without breaking all its sweetness and harmony. And this is the reason why Homer has never been turned from Greek into Latin, as the other writers we have of theirs." This sentence, I fear, may well be regarded as conclusive against the present undertaking. Yet would I willingly bespeak for it at least so much indulgence as Politian claimed for himself, when in the Latin translation which he afterwards made of Homer, but which has since unfortunately perished, he ventured on certain liberties, both of phraseology and metre, for which the nicer critics of his time thought fit to call him to an account: "Ego vero tametsi rudis in primis non adeo tamen obtusi sum pectoris in versibus maxime faciundis, ut spatia ista morasque non sentiam. Vero cum mihi de Græco pæne ad verbum forent antiquissima interpretanda carmina, fateor affectavi equidem ut in verbis obsoletam vetustatem, sic in mensurâ ipsâ et numero gratam quandam ut speravi novitatem." Ep. lib. i., Baptistæ Guarini.

[2] *Fitter left untold.*—
    "Che'l tacere è bello."
So our poet, in Canzone 14:
    "La vide in parte che'l tacere è bello."
Ruccellai, "Le Api," 780:
    "Ch' a dire è brutto ed a tacerlo è bello."
And Bembo:
    "Vie più bello è il tacerle, che il favellarne."
                    Gli Asol., lib. i.

So I beheld united the bright school
Of him the monarch of sublimest song,
That o'er the others like an eagle soars.

Canto IV, lines 89—91.

Open, and bright, and lofty, whence each one
Stood manifest to view. Incontinent,
There on the green enamel[1] of the plain
Were shown me the great spirits, by whose sight
I am exalted in my own esteem. `

Electra[2] there I saw accompanied
By many, among whom Hector I knew,
Anchises' pious son, and with hawk's eye
Cæsar all armed, and by Camilla there
Penthesilea. On the other side,
Old King Latinus seated by his child
Lavinia, and that Brutus I beheld
Who Tarquin chased, Lucretia, Cato's wife
Marcia, with Julia[3] and Cornelia there ;
And sole apart retired, the Soldan fierce.[4]

Then when a little more I raised my brow,
I spièd the master of the sapient throng,[5]

---

[1] *Green enamel.*—" Verde smalto." Dante here uses a metaphor that has since become very common in poetry.
" O'er the smooth enamell'd green."
　　　　　　　　　　Milton, Arcades.
" Enamelling, and perhaps pictures in enamel, were common in the Middle Ages," &c. *Warton, History of English Poetry,* v. i., c. xiii., p. 376. " This art flourished most at Limoges, in France. So early as the year 1197, we have *duas tabulas æneas superauratas de labore Limogiæ*. ` Chart. ann. 1197 apud Ughelin,' tom. vii., ` Ital. Sacr.,'p. 1274." *Warton.* Ibid. Additions to v. i. printed in vol. ii. Compare Walpole's " Anecdotes of Painting in England," vol. i., c. ii.

[2] *Electra.*—The daughter of Atlas, and mother of Dardanus, the founder of Troy. See Virgil, " Æneid," viii. 134, as referred to by Dante in the treatise " De Monarchiâ," lib. ii. " Electra, scilicet, nata magni nominis regis Atlantis, ut de ambobus testimonium reddit poeta noster in octavo, ubi Æneas ad Evandrum sic ait. ` Dardanus Iliacæ,' " &c.

[3] *Julia.*—The daughter of Julius Cæsar, and wife of Pompey.

[4] *The Soldan fierce.*—Saladin, or Salaheddin, the rival of Richard Cœur de Lion. See D'Herbelot, " Bibl. Orient. "; the " Life of Saladin," by Bohao'edin Ebn Shedad, published by Albert Schultens, with a Latin translation ; and Knolle's " History of the Turks," pp. 57 to 73. " About this time (1193) died the great Sultan Saladin, the greatest terror of the Christians, who, mindful of man's fragility, and the vanity of worldly honours, commanded, at the time of his death, no solemnity to be used at his burial ; but only his shirt, in manner of an ensign, made fast unto the point of a lance, to be carried before his dead body as an ensign, a plain priest going before, and crying aloud unto the people in this sort : ` Saladin, Conqueror of the East, of all the greatness and riches he had in his life, carrieth not with him anything more than his shirt.' A sight worthy so great a king, as wanted nothing to his eternal commendation more than the true knowledge of his salvation in Christ Jesus. He reigned about sixteen years with great honour." He is introduced by Petrarch in the " Triumph of Fame," c. ii. ; and by Boccaccio in the " Decameron," G. x., N. 9.

[5] *The master of the sapient throng.*—" Maestro di color che sanno. *Aristotle.* Petrarch assigns the first place to Plato. See " Triumph of Fame," c. iii.
" Volsimi da man manca, e vidi Plato
　　Che 'n quella schiera andò piu presso al segno
　　A qual aggiunge, a chi dal cielo è dato.
　Aristotile poi pien d'alto ingegno."
Pulci, in his " Morgante Maggiore," c. xviii., says :
" Tu se' il maestro di color che sanno."
The reverence in which the Stagirite was held by our author cannot be better shown than by a passage in his " Convito," p. 142 : " Che Aristotile sia degnissimo," &c. " That Aristotle is most worthy of trust and obedience, may be thus proved. Amongst the workmen or artificers of different arts and operations, which are in order to some final art or operation, he who is the artist or operator in that ought chiefly to be obeyed and trusted by the rest, as being the one who alone considers the ultimate end of all the other ends. Thus, he who exercises the occupation of a knight ought to be obeyed by the sword-cutler, the bridle-maker, the armourer, and by all those trades which are in order to the occupation of a knight. And because all human operations respect a certain end.

Seated amid the philosophic train.
Him all admire, all pay him reverence due.
There Socrates and Plato both I mark'd
Nearest to him in rank, Democritus,
Who sets the world at chance,[1] Diogenes,
With Heraclitus, and Empedocles,
And Anaxagoras, and Thales sage,
Zeno, and Dioscorides well read
In Nature's secret lore. Orpheus I mark'd
And Linus, Tully and moral Seneca,
Euclid and Ptolemy, Hippocrates,
Galenus, Avicen,[2] and him who made
That commentary vast, Averroes.[3]

    Of all to speak at full were vain attempt;
For my wide theme so urges, that ofttimes
My words fall short of what bechanced. In two
The six associates part. Another way
My sage guide leads me, from that air serene,
Into a climate ever vexed with storms :
And to a part I come, where no light shines.

---

which is that of human life, to which man, inasmuch as
he is man, is ordained, the master or artist, who considers
of and teaches us that, ought chiefly to be obeyed and
trusted. Now this is no other than Aristotle ; and he
is therefore the most deserving of trust and obedience."

[1] *Democritus, who sets the world at chance.*—
Democritus, who maintained the world to have been
formed by the fortuitous concourse of atoms.

[2] *Avicen.*—See D'Herbelot, " Bibl. Orient.," article
" Sina." He died in 1050. Pulci here again imitates
our poet :

    " Avicenna quel che il sentimento
    Intese di Aristotile e i segreti,
    Averrois che fece il gran comento."
        Morgante Maggiore, c. xxv.

Chaucer, in the Prologue to the " Canterbury Tales,"
makes the Doctour of Phisike familiar with

        " Avicen,
    Averrois."

  " Sguarda Avicenna mio con tre corone,
    Ch' egli fù Prence, e di scienza pieno,
    E util tanto all' umane persone."
      Frezzi, Il Quadriregio, l. iv., cap. 9.

" Fuit Avicenna vir summi ingeni, magnus Philosophus, excellens medicus, et summus apud suos Theologus." Sebastian Scheffer, Introd. in " Artem
Medicam," p. 63, as quoted in the " Historical Observations on the Quadriregio." Ediz. 1725.

[3] *Him who made that commentary vast, Averroes.*—

" Il gran Platone, e l' altro che sta attento,
Mirando il cielo, e sta a lui a lato
Averrois, che fece il gran comento."
    Frezzi, Il Quadriregio, l. iv., cap. 9.

Averroes, called by the Arabs Ibn Roschd, translated
and commented the works of Aristotle. According to
Tiraboschi (" Storia della Lett. Ital.," t. v., l. ii., c. ii.,
§ 4) he was the source of modern philosophical impiety.
The critic quotes some passages from Petrarch
(" Senil.," l. v., ep. iii., et " Oper.," v. ii., p. 1143) to
show how strongly such sentiments prevailed in the
time of that poet, by whom they were held in horror
and detestation. He adds that this fanatic admirer of
Aristotle translated his writings with that felicity
which might be expected from one who did not know
a syllable of Greek, and who was therefore compelled
to avail himself of the unfaithful Arabic versions.
D'Herbelot, on the other hand, informs us that
" Averroes was the first who translated Aristotle from
Greek into Arabic, before the Jews had made their translation ; and that we had for a long time no other text of
Aristotle except that of the Latin translation, which was
made from this Arabic version of this great philosopher
(Averroes), who afterwards added to it a very ample
commentary, of which Thomas Aquinas, and the other
scholastic writers, availed themselves, before the Greek
originals of Aristotle and his commentators were known
to us in Europe." According to D'Herbelot, he died
in 1198; but Tiraboschi places that event about 1206.

CANTO V.

Coming into the second circle of Hell, Dante at the entrance beholds Minos the infernal Judge, by whom he is admonished to beware how he enters those regions. Here he witnesses the punishment of carnal sinners, who are lost about ceaselessly in the dark air by the most furious winds. Amongst these, he meets with Francesca of Rimini, through pity at whose sad tale he falls fainting to the ground.

FROM the first circle[1] I descended thus
    Down to the second, which, a lesser space
Embracing, so much more of grief contains,
Provoking bitter moans. There Minos stands,
Grinning with ghastly feature;[2] he, of all
Who enter, strict examining the crimes,
Gives sentence, and dismisses them beneath,
According as he foldeth him around :
For when before him comes the ill-fated soul,
It all confesses ; and that judge severe
Of sins, considering what place in hell
Suits the transgression, with his tail so oft
Himself encircles, as degrees beneath
He dooms it to descend. Before him stand
Alway a numerous throng ; and in his turn
Each one to judgment passing, speaks, and hears
His fate, thence downward to his dwelling hurl'd.
    " Oh thou ! who to this residence of woe
Approachest !" when he saw me coming, cried
Minos, relinquishing his dread employ,
"Look how thou enter here ; beware in whom
Thou place thy trust ; let not the entrance broad

---

1 *From the first circle.*—Chiabrera's twenty-first sonnet is on a painting, by Cesare Corte, from this canto. Mr. Fuseli, a much greater name, has lately employed his wonder-working pencil on the same subject.

2 *Grinning with ghastly feature.*—Hence Milton :

    " Death
Grinn'd horrible a ghastly smile."
       Paradise Lost, b. ii. 845.

E.

Deceive thee to thy harm." To him my guide :
"Wherefore exclaimest ? Hinder not his way
By destiny appointed ; so 'tis will'd,
Where will and power are one. Ask thou no more."
    Now 'gin the rueful wailings to be heard.
Now am I come where many a plaining voice
Smites on mine ear. Into a place I came
Where light was silent all. Bellowing there groan'd
A noise, as of a sea in tempest torn
By warring winds. The stormy blast of hell
With restless fury drives the spirits on,
Whirl'd round and dashed amain with sore annoy.
When they arrive before the ruinous sweep,
There shrieks are heard, there lamentations, moans,
And blasphemies 'gainst the good Power in heaven.
    I understood, that to this torment sad
The carnal sinners are condemn'd, in whom
Reason by lust is sway'd. As in large troops
And multitudinous, when winter reigns,
The starlings on their wings are borne abroad ;
So bears the tyrannous gust those evil souls.
On this side and on that, above, below,
It drives them : hope of rest to solace them
Is none nor e'en of milder pang. As cranes,
Chanting their dolorous notes,[1] traverse the sky,
Stretch'd out in long array ; so I beheld
Spirits, who came loud wailing, hurried on
By their dire doom. Then I : "Instructor ! who
Are these, by the black air so scourged ?"—"The first
'Mong those, of whom thou question'st," he replied,
"O'er many tongues was empress. She in vice
Of luxury was so shameless, that she made

---

[1] *As cranes, chanting their dolorous notes.*—
This simile is imitated by Lorenzo de' Medici,
in his "Ambra," a poem, first published by
Mr. Roscoe, in the Appendix to his "Life of
Lorenzo":

"Marking the tracts of air, the clamorous cranes
Wheel their due flight in varied ranks descried ;
And each with outstretch'd neck his rank maintains,
In marshall'd order through the ethereal void."

         Roscoe, v. i., c. v., p. 257, 4to edit.

Compare Homer, "Iliad," iii. 3 ; Virgil, "Æneid," l.
x. 264 ; Oppian, "Halieut." lib. i. 620 ; Ruccellai,
"Le Api," 942 ; and Dante's "Purgatory," xxiv.
63.

Bard! willingly
I would address these two together coming,
Which seem so light before the wind.
Canto V., lines 72—74.

Liking[1] be lawful by promulged decree,
To clear the blame she had herself incurr'd.
This is Semiramis, of whom 'tis writ,
That she succeeded Ninus her espoused;[2]
And held the land, which now the Soldan rules.
The next in amorous fury slew herself,
And to Sicheus' ashes broke her faith :
Then follows Cleopatra, lustful queen."

There mark'd I Helen, for ·whose sake so long
The time was fraught with evil ; there the great
Achilles, who with love fought to the end.
Paris I saw, and Tristan ; and beside,
A thousand more he show'd me, and by name
Pointed them out, whom love bereaved of life.

When I had heard my sage instructor name
These dames and knights of antique days, o'erpower'd
By pity, well nigh in a maze my mind
Was lost ; and I began : "Bard ! willingly
I would address those two together coming,
Which seem so light before the wind." He thus :
"Note thou, when nearer they to us approach.
Then by that love which carries them along,
Entreat ; and they will come." Soon as the wind
Sway'd them toward us, I thus framed my speech :
"Oh, wearied spirits ! come, and hold discourse
With us, if by none else restrain'd." As doves
By fond desire invited, on wide wings
And firm, to their sweet nest returning home,
Cleave the air, wafted by their will along ;
Thus issued, from that troop where Dido ranks,

[1] *Liking.*—"His lustes were as law in his degree."
  Chaucer. Monke's Tale. Nero.

[2] *That she succeeded Ninus her espoused.*—

  " Che succedette a Nino e fu sua sposa."

M. Artaud, in his " Histoire de Dante," p. 580,
mentions a manuscript work called " Attacanti's
Quadragesimale de reditu peccatoris ad Deum," in
which the line is thus cited :

  " Che sugger dette a Nino e fu sua sposa."
  " Who suckled Ninus, and was his wife."

This remarkable reading had been before noticed by

Federici : " Intorno ad alcune varianti nel testo della
' Divina Commedia.' Edit. Milan, 1830." See the
" Biblioteca Italiana," tom. 82, p. 282. It appears
from the treatise " De Monarchiâ " (l. ii.) that Dante
derived his knowledge of Assyrian history from his
favourite author Orosius (l. i., c. iv.), who relates that
Semiramis both succeeded Ninus through the artifice
of personating her son, and that she committed incest
with her son ; but as the name of her husband Ninus
only is there recorded, and as other historians called
the son Ninias, it is probable that the common reading
is right.

They, through the ill air speeding : with such force
My cry prevail'd, by strong affection urged.

 "Oh, gracious creature and benign ! who go'st
Visiting, through this element obscure,[1]
Us, who the world with bloody stain imbrued ;
If, for a friend, the King of all, we own'd,
Our prayer to him should for thy peace arise,
Since thou hast pity on our evil plight.
Of whatsoe'er to hear or to discourse
It pleases thee, that will we hear, of that
Freely with thee discourse, while e'er the wind,
As now, is mute. The land[2] that gave me birth
Is situate on the coast, where Po descends
To rest in ocean with his sequent streams.

 "Love, that in gentle heart is quickly learnt,[3]
Entangled him by that fair form, from me
Ta'en in such cruel sort, as grieves me still :
Love, that denial takes from none beloved,[4]
Caught me with pleasing him so passing well,
That, as thou seest, he yet deserts me not.
Love brought us to one death : Caïna[5] waits
The soul who spilt our life." Such were their words ;
At hearing which, downward I bent my looks,
And held them there so long, that the bard cried :
"What art thou pondering ?" I in answer thus :

 Element obscure.—"L'aer perso." Much is said by the commentators concerning the exact sense of the word "perso." It cannot be explained in clearer terms than those used by Dante himself in his "Convito" : "Il perso è un colore misto di purpureo e nero, ma vince il nero." p. 185. "It is a colour mixed of purple and black, but the black prevails." The word recurs several times in this poem. Chaucer also uses it, in the Prologue to the "Canterbury Tales," Doctour of Phisike :

 "In sanguin and in perse he clad was alle."

[2] *The land.*—Ravenna.

[3] *Love, that in gentle heart is quickly learnt.*—

 "Amor, ch'al cor gentil ratto s'apprende."

A line taken by Marino, "Adone," c. cxli., st. 251. That the reader of the original may not be misled as to the exact sense of the word "s'apprende," which I have rendered "is learnt," it may be right to apprise him that it signifies "is caught," and that it is a metaphor from a thing taking fire. Thus it is used by Guido Guinicelli, whom indeed our poet seems here to have had in view :

 "Fuoco d'Amore in gentil cor s'apprende,
  Come vertute in pietra preziosa."

Sonetti, &c., di diversi Antichi Toscani. Ediz Giunti. 1527, l. ix., p. 107.

 "The fire of love in gentle heart is caught,
  As virtue in the precious stone."

[4] *Love, that denial takes from none beloved.*—

 "Amor ch' a null' amato amar perdona."

So Boccaccio, in his "Filocopo," l. 1 :

 "Amore, mai non perdonò l'amore a nullo amato."

And Pulci, in the "Morgante Maggiore," c. iv. :

 "E perchè amor mai volontier perdona,
  Che non sia al fin sempre amato chi ama."

Indeed, many of the Italian poets have repeated this verse.

[5] *Caïna.*—The place to which murderers are doomed.

" Alas ! by what sweet thoughts, what fond desire
Must they at length to that ill pass have reach'd ! "
        Then turning, I to them my speech address'd,
And thus began : " Francesca ![1] your sad fate
Even to tears my grief and pity moves.
But tell me ; in the time of your sweet sighs,
By what, and how Love granted, that ye knew
Your yet uncertain wishes ? "   She replied :
" No greater grief than to remember days
Of joy, when misery is at hand.[2]   That kens
Thy learn'd instructor.   Yet so eagerly
If thou art bent to know the primal root,
From whence our love gat being, I will do
As one who weeps and tells his tale.   One day,
For our delight we read of Lancelot,[3]
How him love thrall'd.   Alone we were, and no
Suspicion near us.   Oft-times by that reading
Our eyes were drawn together, and the hue
Fled from our alter'd cheek.   But at one point [4]
Alone we fell.   When of that smile we read,
The wished smile so rapturously kiss'd

---

[1] *Francesca.*—Francesca, daughter of Guido da Polenta, lord of Ravenna, was given by her father in marriage to Lanciotto, son of Malatesta, lord of Rimini, a man of extraordinary courage, but deformed in his person. His brother Paolo, who unhappily poss ssed those graces which the husband of Francesca wanted, engaged her affections ; and being taken in adultery, they were both put to death by the enraged Lanciotto. See Notes to canto xxvii., vs. 38 and 43. Troya relates that they were buried together ; and that three centuries after the bodies were found at Rimini, whither they had been removed from Pesaro, with the silken garments yet fresh.—" Veltro Allegorico di Dante," Ediz. 1826. p. 33. The whole of this passage is alluded to by Petrarch, in his " Triumph of Love." c. iii. :

> " Ecco quei che le carte empion di sogni
> Lancilotto Tristano e gli altri erranti :
> Onde convien che 'l vulgo errante agogni ;
> Vedi Ginevra, Isotta e l'altre amanti ;
> E la coppia d'Arimino che 'nsieme
> Vanno facendo dolorosi pianti."

Mr. Leigh Hunt has expanded the present episode into a beautiful poem, in his " Story of Rimini."

[2] *No greater grief than to remember days of joy. when misery is at hand.*—Imitated by Chaucer :

> " For of Fortunis sharp adversite
> The worste kind of infortune is this,
> A man to have been in prosperite.
> And it remembir when it passid is."
>
> *Troilus and Creseide.* b iii.

By Marino :

> " Che non ha doglia il misero maggiore,
> Che ricordar la gioia entro il dolore."
>
> *Adone.* c. xiv., st. 100

And by Fortiguerra :

> " Rimembrare il ben perduto
> Fa più meschino lo presente stato."
>
> *Ricciardetto,* c. xi., st. 83.

The original, perhaps, was in Boëtius, " De Consolatione Philosophiæ " ; " In omni adversitate fortunæ infelicissimum genus est infortunii fuisse felicem et non esse." l. 2, pr. 4. Boëtius, and Cicero, " De Amicitiâ," were the two first books that engaged the attention of Dante, as he himself tells us in the " Convito," p. 68.

[3] *Lancelot.*—One of the Knights of the Round Table, and the lover of Ginevra, or Guinever, celebrated in romance. The incident alluded to seems to have made a strong impression on the imagination of Dante, who introduces it again in the " Paradise." canto xvi.

[4] *At one point.*—" Questo quel punto fû, che sol mi vinse." *Tasso, Il Torrismondo.* a. i., s. 3.

By one so deep in love, then he, who ne'er
From me shall separate, at once my lips
All trembling kiss'd. The book and writer both
Were love's purveyors. In its leaves that day
We read no more."[1] While thus one spirit spake,
The other wail'd so sorely, that heart-struck
I, through compassion fainting, seem'd not far
From death, and like a corse fell to the ground.[2]

---

[1] *In its leaves that day we read no more.*—Nothing can exceed the delicacy with which Francesca in these words intimates her guilt.

[2] *And like a corse fell to the ground.*—

"E caddi, come corpo morto cade."

So Pulci :

"E cadde, come morto in terra cade."
Morgante Maggiore, c. xxii.

And Ariosto :

"E cada, come corpo morto cade."
Orlando Furioso, c. ii., st. 55.

"And when I saw him, I fell at his feet as dead."—Rev. i. 17.

In its leaves that day
We read no more.

Canto V., lines 134, 135.

CANTO VI.

On his recovery, the poet finds himself in the third circle, where the gluttonous are punished. Their torment is, to lie in the mire, under a continual and heavy storm of hail, snow, and discoloured water ; Cerberus meanwhile barking over them with his threefold throat, and rending them piecemeal. One of these, who on earth was named Ciacco, foretells the divisions with which Florence is about to be distracted. Dante proposes a question to his guide, who solves it ; and they proceed towards the fourth circle.

M Y sense reviving,[1] that erewhile had droop'd
　　With pity for the kindred shades, whence grief
O'ercame me wholly, straight around I see
New torments, new tormented souls, which way
Soe'er I move, or turn, or bend my sight.
In the third circle I arrive, of showers
Ceaseless, accursed, heavy and cold, unchanged
For ever, both in kind and in degree.
Large hail, discolour'd water, sleety flaw
Through the dun midnight air streamed down amain :
Stank all the land whereon that tempest fell.
　　Cerberus, cruel monster, fierce and strange,
Through his wide threefold throat, barks as a dog
Over the multitude immersed beneath.
His eyes glare crimson, black his unctuous beard,
His belly large, and claw'd the hands, with which
He tears the spirits, flays them, and their limbs
Piecemeal disparts. Howling there spread, as curs,
Under the rainy deluge, with one side
The other screening, oft they roll them round,
A wretched, godless crew. When that great worm[2]

---

[1] *My sense reviving.*—

　"Al tornar della mente, che si chiuse,
　　Dinanzi alla pietà de' duo cognati."

Berni has made a sportive application of these lines, in his "Orl. Inn.," lib. iii., c. viii., st. 1.

[2] *That great worm.*—"Juxta—infernum vermis erat infinitæ magnitudinis ligatus maximâ catenâ."—*Alberici Visio*, § 9. In canto xxxiv. Lucifer is called

"The abhorred worm, that boreth through the world." This is imitated by Ariosto, "Orlando Furioso," c. xlvi., st. 76. Shakespeare, Milton, and Cowper, who well understood that the most common words are often the most impressive, have used the synonymous

F

Descried us, savage Cerberus, he oped
His jaws, and the fangs show'd us; not a limb
Of him but trembled. Then my guide, his palms
Expanding on the ground, thence fill'd with earth
Raised them, and cast it in his ravenous maw.
E'en as a dog, that yelling bays for food
His keeper, when the morsel comes, lets fall
His fury, bent alone with eager haste
To swallow it; so dropp'd the loathsome cheeks
Of demon Cerberus, who thundering stuns
The spirits, that they for deafness wish in vain.

We, o'er the shade thrown prostrate by the brunt
Of the heavy tempest passing, set our feet
Upon their emptiness, that substance seem'd.

They all along the earth extended lay,
Save one, that sudden raised himself to sit,
Soon as that way he saw us pass. "Oh, thou!"
He cried, "who through the infernal shades art led,
Own, if again thou know'st me. Thou wast framed
Or ere my frame was broken." I replied:
"The anguish thou endurest perchance so takes
Thy form from my remembrance, that it seems
As if I saw thee never. But inform
Me who thou art, that in a place so sad
Art set, and in such torment, that although
Other be greater, none disgusteth more."
He thus in answer to my words rejoin'd:
"Thy city, heap'd with envy to the brim,
Aye, that the measure overflows its bounds,
Held me in brighter days. Ye citizens
Were wont to name me Ciacco.[1] For the sin
Of gluttony, damned vice, beneath this rain,
E'en as thou seest, I with fatigue am worn:

---

term in our language with good effect; as Pindar
has done in Greek:

  "Ἀπὸ Ταυγέτου μὲν Λάκαιναν
    ἐπὶ θηρσὶ κύνα τρέχειν πυκαιώτατον ἑρπετόν."

Heyne's Pindar, Fragm. Epinic. ii. 2, in Hieron.

[1] *Ye citizens were wont to name me Ciacco.*—So called from his inordinate appetite; *ciacco*, in Italian, signifying a pig. The real name of this glutton has not been transmitted to us. He is introduced in Boccaccio's "Decameron," Giorn. ix. Nov. 8.

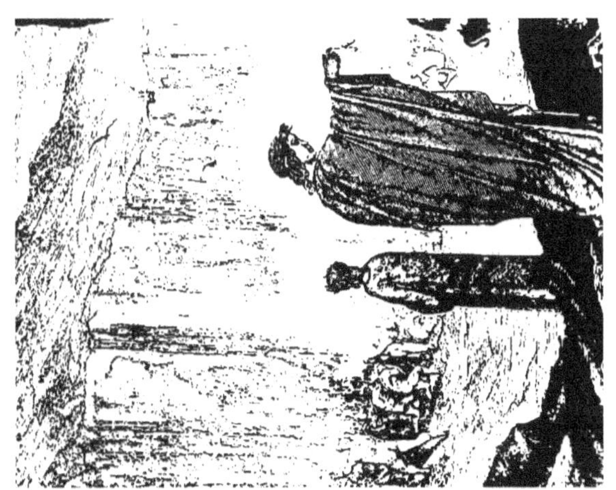

Nor I sole spirit in this woe : all these
Have by like crime incurr'd like punishment."

No more he said, and I my speech resumed :
"Ciacco ! thy dire affliction grieves me much,
Even to tears. But tell me, if thou know'st
What shall at length befall the citizens
Of the divided city ;[1] whether any
Just one inhabit there : and tell the cause
Whence jarring Discord hath assail'd it thus."

He then : "After long striving they will come
To blood ; and the wild party from the woods[2]
Will chase the other[3] with much injury forth.
Then it behoves that this must fall,[4] within
Three solar circles ;[5] and the other rise
By borrow'd force of one, who under shore
Now rests.[6] It shall a long space hold aloof
Its forehead, keeping under heavy weight
The other opprest, indignant at the load,
And grieving sore. The just are two in number,[7]
But they neglected. Avarice, envy, pride,[8]
Three fatal sparks, have set the hearts of all
On fire." Here ceased the lamentable sound ;
And I continued thus : "Still would I learn
More from thee, further parley still entreat.
Of Farinata and Tegghiaio[9] say,

[1] *The divided city.*—The city of Florence, divided into the Bianchi and Neri factions.

[2] *The wild party from the woods.*—So called because it was headed by Veri de' Cerchi, whose family had lately come into the city from Acone, and the woody country of the Val di Nievole.

[3] *The other.*—The opposite party of the Neri, at the head of which was Corso Donati.

[4] *This must fall.*—The Bianchi.

[5] *Three solar circles.*—Three years.

[6] *Of one, who under shore now rests.*—Charles of Valois, by whose means the Neri were replaced.

[7] *The just are two in number.*—Who these two were the commentators are not agreed. Some understand them to be Dante himself and his friend Guido Cavalcanti. But this would argue a presumption, which our poet himself elsewhere contradicts ; for, in the "Purgatory," he owns his consciousness of not being exempted from one at least of "the three fatal sparks, which had set the hearts of all on fire" (see canto xiii, 126). Others refer the encomium to Barduccio and Giovanni Vespignano, adducing the following passage from Villani in support of their opinion : "In the year 1331 died in Florence two just and good men, of holy life and conversation, and bountiful in almsgiving, although laymen. The one was named Barduccio, and was buried in S. Spirito, in the place of the Frati Romitani ; the other, named Giovanni da Vespignano, was buried in S. Pietro Maggiore. And by each God showed open miracles, in healing the sick and lunatic after divers manners ; and for each there was ordained a solemn funeral, and many images of wax set up in discharge of vows that had been made."—*G. Villani*, lib. x., cap. clxxix.

[8] *Avarice, envy, pride.*—

" Invidia, superbia ed avarizia
Veden moltiplicar tra miei figliuoli."

Fazio degli Uberti, Dittamondo, lib. i., cap. xxix.

[9] *Of Farinata and Tegghiaio.*—See canto x. and Notes, and canto xvi. and Notes.

They who so well deserved; of Giacopo,[1]
Arrigo, Mosca,[2] and the rest, who bent
Their minds on working good. Oh! tell me where
They bide, and to their knowledge let me come.
For I am prest with keen desire to hear
If heaven's sweet cup, or poisonous drug of hell,
Be to their lip assigned." He answer'd straight:
"These are yet blacker spirits. Various crimes
Have sunk them deeper in the dark abyss.
If thou so far descendest, thou mayst see them.
But to the pleasant world, when thou return'st,
Of me make mention, I entreat thee, there.
No more I tell thee, answer thee no more."

  This said, his fixed eyes he turn'd askance,
A little eyed me, then bent down his head,
And 'midst his blind companions with it fell.

  When thus my guide: "No more his bed he leaves,
Ere the last angel-trumpet blow. The Power
Adverse to these shall then in glory come,
Each one forthwith to his sad tomb repair,
Resume[3] his fleshly vesture and his form,
And hear the eternal doom re-echoing rend
The vault." So pass'd we through that mixture foul
Of spirits and rain, with tardy steps; meanwhile
Touching,[4] though slightly, on the life to come.
For thus I question'd: "Shall these tortures, sir,
When the great sentence passes, be increased,
Or mitigated, or as now severe?"

  He then: "Consult thy knowledge;[5] that decides,
That, as each thing to more perfection grows,
It feels more sensibly both good and pain.

---

[1] *Giacopo.*—Giacopo Rusticucci. See canto xvi.

[2] *Arrigo, Mosca.*—Of Arrigo no mention afterwards occurs. Mosca degli Uberti is introduced in canto xxviii.

[3] *Resume.*—Imitated by Frezzi:

" Allor ripiglieran la carne e l'ossa :
  Li rei oscuri, e i buon con splendori
  Per la virtù della divina possa."
    Il Quadriregio, lib. iv., cap. xv.

[4] *Touching.*—Conversing, though in a slight and superficial manner, on the life to come.

[5] *Consult thy knowledge.*—We are referred to the following passage in St. Augustine: "Cum fiet resurrectio carnis, et bonorum gaudia et malorum tormenta majora erunt." "At the resurrection of the flesh, both the happiness of the good and the torments of the wicked will be increased."

Though ne'er to true perfection may arrive
This race accurst, yet nearer then, than now,
They shall approach it."   Compassing that path,
Circuitous we journey'd ; and discourse,
Much more than I relate, between us pass'd :
Till at the point, whence the steps led below,
Arrived, there Plutus, the great foe, we found.

CANTO VII.

In the present canto Dante describes his descent into the fourth circle, at the beginning of which he sees Plutus stationed. Here one like doom awaits the prodigal and the avaricious; which is, to meet in direful conflict, rolling great weights against each other with mutual upbraidings. From hence Virgil takes occasion to show how vain the goods that are committed into the charge of Fortune; and this moves our author to inquire what being that Fortune is, of whom he speaks: which question being resolved, they go down into the fifth circle, where they find the wrathful and gloomy tormented in the Stygian lake. Having made a compass round great part of this lake, they come at last to the base of a lofty tower.

"AH me! O Satan! Satan!"[1] loud exclaim'd
　　Plutus, in accent hoarse of wild alarm:
And the kind sage, whom no event surprised,
To comfort me thus spake: "Let not thy fear
Harm thee, for power in him, be sure, is none
To hinder down this rock thy safe descent."
Then to that swoln lip turning, "Peace!" he cried,
"Curst wolf! thy fury inward on thyself
Prey, and consume thee! Through the dark profound,
Not without cause, he passes. So 'tis will'd
On high, there where the great Archangel pour'd
Heaven's vengeance on the first adulterer proud."[2]

　　As sails, full spread and bellying with the wind,
Drop suddenly collapsed, if the mast split;
So to the ground down dropp'd the cruel fiend.

---

[1] *Ah me! O Satan! Satan!*—"Pape Satan, Pape Satan, aleppe." *Pape* is said by the commentators to be the same as the Latin word *papæ*, "strange!" Of *aleppe* they do not give a more satisfactory account. See the "Life of Benvenuto Cellini," translated by Dr. Nugent, v. ii., b. iii., c. vii., p. 113, where he mentions "having heard the words *Paix, paix, Satan! allez, paix!* in the courts of justice at Paris. I recollected what Dante said, when he with his master Virgil entered the gates of hell: for Dante, and Giotto the painter, were together in France, and visited Paris with particular attention, where the court of justice may be considered as hell. Hence it is that Dante, who was likewise perfect master of the French, made use of that expression; and I have often been surprised that it was never understood in that sense."

[2] *The first adulterer proud.*—Satan. The word "fornication," or "adultery," "strupo," is here used for a revolt of the affections from God, according to the sense in which it is often applied in Scripture. But Monti, following Grassi's "Essay on Synonymes," supposes "strupo" to mean "troop"; the word *strup* being still used in the Piedmontese dialect for "a flock of sheep," and answering to *troupeau* in French. In that case, "superbo strupo" would signify "the troop of rebel angels who sinned through pride."

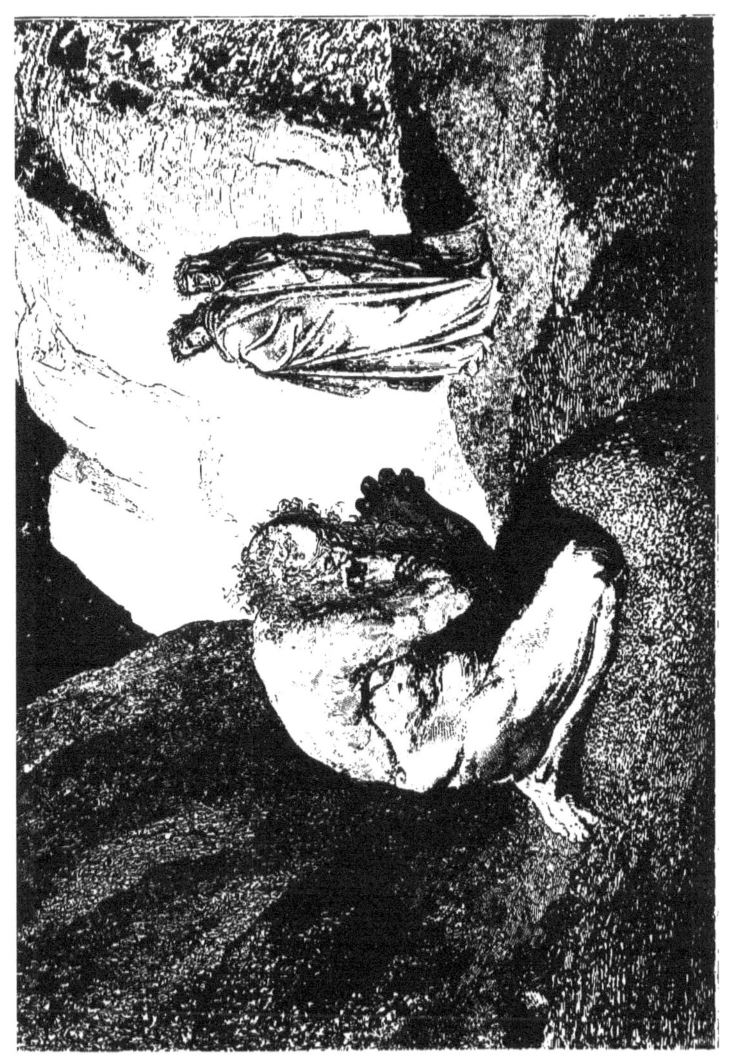

Thus we, descending to the fourth steep ledge,
Gain'd on the dismal shore, that all the woe
Hems in of all the universe. Ah me !
Almighty Justice ! in what store thou heap'st
New pains, new troubles,[1] as I here beheld.
Wherefore doth fault of ours bring us to this ?
　　E'en as a billow,[2] on Charybdis rising,
Against encounter'd billow dashing breaks ;
Such is the dance this wretched race must lead,
Whom more than elsewhere numerous here I found
From one side and the other, with loud voice,
Both roll'd on weights, by main force of their breasts,
Then smote together, and each one forthwith
Roll'd them back voluble, turning again ;
Exclaiming these, "Why holdest thou so fast ? "
Those answering, "And why castest thou away ? "
So, still repeating their despiteful song,
They to the opposite point, on either hand,
Traversed the horrid circle ; then arrived,
Both turn'd them round, and through the middle space
Conflicting met again. At sight whereof
I, stung with grief, thus spake : "Oh, say, my guide !
What race is this. Were these, whose heads are shorn,
On our left hand, all separate to the Church ? "
　　He straight replied : "In their first life, these all
In mind were so distorted, that they made,
According to due measure, of their wealth
No use. This clearly from their words collect,
Which they howl forth, at each extremity
Arriving of the circle, where their crime
Contrary in kind disparts them. To the Church
Were separate those, that with no hairy cowls

[1] *In what store thou heap'st*
New pains, new troubles.—
Some understand "chi stipa" to mean either " who
can imagine," or "who can describe the torments,"
&c. I have followed Landino, whose words, though
very plain, seem to have been mistaken by Lombardi :
"Chi stipa, chi accumula, ed insieme raccoglie :
quasi dica, tu giustizia aduni tanti supplicii."

[2] *E'en as a billow.—*
" As when two billows in the Irish sowndes,
　Forcibly driven with contrarie tides,
　Do meet together, each aback rebounds
　With roaring rage, and dashing on all sides,
　That filleth all the sea with foam, divides
　The doubtful current into divers wayes."
　　　　Spenser, Faëry Queen, b. iv., c. i., st. 42.

Are crown'd, both popes and cardinals,[1] o'er whom
Avarice dominion absolute maintains."
　　I then: "'Mid such as these some needs must be,
Whom I shall recognise, that with the blot
Of these foul sins were stain'd." He answering thus:
"Vain thought conceivest thou. That ignoble life,
Which made them vile before, now makes them dark,
And to all knowledge indiscernible.
For ever they shall meet in this rude shock:
These from the tomb with clenched grasp shall rise,
Those with close-shaven locks. That ill they gave,
And ill they kept, hath of the beauteous world
Deprived, and set them at this strife, which needs
No labour'd phrase of mine to set it off.
Now mayst thou see, my son, how brief, how vain,
The goods committed into Fortune's hands,
For which the human race keep such a coil!
Not all the gold[2] that is beneath the moon,
Or ever hath been, of these toil-worn souls
Might purchase rest for one." I thus rejoin'd:
"My guide! of thee this also would I learn;
This Fortune, that thou speak'st of, what it is,
Whose talons grasp the blessings of the world."
　　He thus: "Oh, beings blind! what ignorance
Besets you! Now my judgment hear and mark.
He, whose transcendent wisdom[3] passes all,
The heavens creating, gave them ruling powers
To guide them; so that each part shines[4] to each,
Their light in equal distribution pour'd.
By similar appointment he ordain'd,
Over the world's bright images to rule,

---

[1] *Popes and cardinals.*—Ariosto having personified
Avarice as a strange and hideous monster, says of
her—

　　"Peggio facea nella Romana corte,
　　Che v'avea uccisi cardinali e papi."
　　　　Orlando Furioso, c. xxvi., st. 32.
"Worse did she in the court of Rome, for there
　She had slain popes and cardinals."

[2] *Not all the gold.*—
　　"Tutto l'oro ch' è sotta la luna."

"For all the golde under the colde mone."
　　　　Chaucer, Legende of Hypermnestra.

[3] *He, whose transcendent wisdom.*—Compare
Frezzi:
　　"Dio è primo prince in ogni parte
　　Sempre e di tutto," &c.
　　　　Il Quadriregio, lib. ii., cap. ii.

[4] *Each part shines.*—Each hemisphere of the
heavens shines upon that hemisphere of the earth
which is placed under it.

Superintendence of a guiding hand
And general minister,[1] which, at due time,
May change the empty vantages of life
From race to race, from one to other's blood.
Beyond prevention of man's wisest care :
Wherefore one nation rises into sway,
Another languishes, e'en as her will
Decrees, from us conceal'd, as in the grass,
The serpent train. Against her nought avails
Your utmost wisdom. She with foresight plans,
Judges, and carries on her reign, as theirs
The other powers divine. Her changes know
None intermission, by necessity[2]
She is made swift, so frequent come who claim
Succession in her favours. This is she
So execrated e'en by those whose debt
To her is rather praise : they wrongfully
With blame requite her, and with evil word ;
But she is blessed, and for that recks not :
Amidst the other primal beings glad,
Rolls on her sphere, and in her bliss exults.
Now on our way pass we, to heavier woe
Descending : for each star[3] is falling now,
That mounted at our entrance, and forbids
Too long our tarrying." We the circle cross'd
To the next steep, arriving at a well,
That boiling pours itself down to a fosse
Sluiced from its source. Far murkier was the wave
Than sablest grain : and we in company
Of the inky waters, journeying by their side,

---

[1] *General minister.*—Lombardi cites an apposite passage from Augustine, "De Civitate Dei," lib. v. : —" Nos eas causas, quæ dicuntur fortuitæ (unde etiam fortuna nomen accepit) non dicimus nullas, sed latentes, easque tribuimus, vel veri Dei, vel quorum libet spirituum voluntati."

[2] *By necessity.*—This sentiment called forth the reprehension of Francesco Stabili, commonly called Cecco d'Ascoli, in his " Acerba," lib. i., c. i. :

  " In ciò peccasti, O Fiorentin poeta,
   Ponendo che li ben della fortuna
   Necessitati sieno con lor meta.
  Non è fortuna, cui ragion non vinca.
  Or pensa Dante, se prova nessuna
  Si può più fare che questa convinca."
" Herein, oh bard of Florence, didst thou err,
 Laying it down that fortune's largesses
 Are fated to their goal. Fortune is none,
 That reason cannot conquer. Mark thou, Dante,
 If any argument may gainsay this."

[3] *Each star.*—So Boccaccio : "Giù ogni stella a cader cominciò, che salia."—*Decameron*, Giorn. 3, at the end.

Enter'd, though by a different track,[1] beneath.
Into a lake, the Stygian named, expands
The dismal stream, when it hath reach'd the foot
Of the grey wither'd cliffs. Intent I stood
To gaze, and in the marish sunk descried
A miry tribe, all naked, and with looks
Betokening rage. They with their hands alone
Struck not, but with the head, the breast, the feet,
Cutting each other piecemeal with their fangs.

 The good instructor spake : " Now seest thou, son,
The souls of those whom anger overcame.
This too for certain know, that underneath
The water dwells a multitude, whose sighs
Into these bubbles make the surface heave,
As thine eye tells thee wheresoe'er it turn.
Fix'd in the slime, they say, 'Sad once were we,
In the sweet air made gladsome by the sun.
Carrying a foul and lazy mist within :
Now in these murky settlings are we sad.'
Such dolorous strain they gurgle in their throats,
But word distinct can utter none." Our route
Thus compass'd we, a segment widely stretch'd
Between the dry embankment, and the core
Of the loath'd pool, turning meanwhile our eyes
Downward on those who gulp'd its muddy lees ;
Nor stopp'd, till to a tower's low base we came.

---

[1] A different track.—"Una via diversa." Some understand this "a strange path"; as the word is used in the preceding canto—" fiera crudele e diversa," "monster fierce and strange"; and in the " Vita Nuova "—" visi diversi ed orribili a vedere," " visages strange and horrible to see."

CANTO VIII.

ARGUMENT

A signal having been made from the tower, Phlegyas, the ferryman of the lake, speedily crosses it, and conveys Virgil and Dante to the other side. On their passage they meet with Filippo Argenti, whose fury and torment are described. They then arrive at the city of Dis, the entrance whereto is denied, and the portals closed against them by many demons.

MY theme pursuing[1] I relate, that ere
   We reach'd the lofty turret's base, our eyes
Its height ascended, where we mark'd uphung
Two cressets, and another saw from far
Return the signal, so remote, that scarce
The eye could catch its beam. I, turning round
To the deep source of knowledge, thus inquired :
"Say what this means ; and what, that other light
In answer set : what agency doth this ?"

   "There on the filthy waters," he replied,
"E'en now what next awaits us mayst thou see,
If the marsh-gendered fog conceal it not."

   Never was arrow from the cord dismiss'd
That ran its way so nimbly through the air,
As a small barque, that through the waves I spied
Toward us coming, under the sole sway
Of one that ferried it, who cried aloud,
"Art thou arrived, fell spirit ?"—"Phlegyas, Phlegyas,

---

[1] *My theme pursuing.*—It is related by some of the early commentators, that the seven preceding cantos were found at Florence after our poet's banishment, by some one who was searching over his papers, which were left in that city ; that by this person they were taken to Dino Frescobaldi ; and that he, being much delighted with them, forwarded them to the Marchese Morello Malaspina, at whose entreaty the poem was resumed. This account, though very circumstantially related, is rendered improbable by the prophecy of Ciacco in the sixth canto, which must have been written after the events to which it alludes. The manner in which the present canto opens furnishes no proof of the truth of the report ; for, as Maffei remarks in his " Osservazioni Letterarie," tom. ii., p. 240, referred to by Lombardi, it might as well be affirmed that Ariosto was interrupted in his " Orlando Furioso," because he begins c. xvi.—

   " Dico la bella storia ripigliando,"

and c. xxii.—

   " Ma tornando al lavor, che vario ordisco."

[2] *Phlegyas.*—Phlegyas, who was so incensed against Apollo, for having violated his daughter Coronis, that he set fire to the temple of that deity, by whose vengeance he was cast into Tartarus. See Virgil, " Æneid." l. vi. 618.

This time thou criest in vain," my lord replied ;
" No longer shalt thou have us, but while o'er
The slimy pool we pass." As one who hears
Of some great wrong he hath sustain'd, whereat
Inly he pines, so Phlegyas inly pined
In his fierce ire. My guide, descending, stepp'd
Into the skiff, and bade me enter next,
Close at his side ; nor, till my entrance, seem'd
The vessel freighted. Soon as both embark'd,
Cutting the waves, goes on the ancient prow,
More deeply than with others is its wont.

While we our course o'er the dead channel held,
One drench'd in mire before me came, and said,
" Who art thou, that thus comest ere thine hour ? "

I answer'd, " Though I come, I tarry not :
But who art thou, that art become so foul ? "

" One, as thou seest, who mourn," he straight replied.

To which I thus : " In mourning and in woe,
Curst spirit ! tarry thou. I know thee well,
E'en thus in filth disguised." Then stretch'd he forth
Hands to the barque ; whereof my teacher sage
Aware, thrusting him back : " Away ! down there
To the other dogs !" then, with his arms my neck
Encircling, kiss'd my cheek, and spake : " Oh soul,
Justly disdainful ! blest was she in whom
Thou wast conceived.[2] He in the world was one
For arrogance noted : to his memory
No virtue lends its lustre ; even so
Here is his shadow furious. There above,
How many now hold themselves mighty kings,
Who here like swine shall wallow in the mire,
Leaving behind them horrible dispraise."

I then : " Master ! him fain would I behold
Whelm'd in these dregs, before we quit the lake."

---

[1] *While we our course.*—" Solcando noi per quella
morta gora."—*Frezzi, Il Quadriregio*, lib. ii., cap. 7.
[2] *In whom thou wast conceived.*—" Che 'n te
s'incinse." Several of the commentators have stumbled
at this word, which is the same as *enceinte* in French,
and *incieus* in Latin. For many instances in which
it is thus used, see the notes on Boccaccio's " Decameron," p. 101, in the Giunti edition, 1573.

My teacher sage
Aware, thrusting him back: "Away! down there
To the other dogs!"

Cant. VIII., lines 39—41

He thus : " Or ever to thy view the shore
Be offer'd, satisfied shall be that wish,
Which well deserves completion." Scarce his words
Were ended, when I saw the miry tribes
Set on him with such violence, that yet
For that render I thanks to God, and praise.
"To Filippo Argenti !" [1] cried they all :
And on himself the moody Florentine
Turn'd his avenging fangs. Him here we left,
Nor speak I of him more. But on mine ear
Sudden a sound of lamentation smote,
Whereat mine eye unbarr'd I sent abroad.

And thus the good instructor : " Now, my son,
Draws near the city, that of Dis is named,[2]
With its grave denizens, a mighty throng."

I thus : " The minarets already, sir !
There, certes, in the valley I descry,
Gleaming vermilion, as if they from fire
Had issued." He replied : " Eternal fire,
That inward burns, shows them with ruddy flame
Illumed ; as in this nether hell thou seest."

We came within the fosses deep, that moat
This region comfortless. The walls appear'd
As they were framed of iron. We had made
Wide circuit, ere a place we reach'd, where loud
The mariner cried vehement, " Go forth :
The entrance is here." Upon the gates I spied
More than a thousand, who of old from heaven
Were shower'd.[3] With ireful gestures, " Who is this,"
They cried, "that, without death first felt, goes through
The regions of the dead ? " My sapient guide
Made sign that he for secret parley wish'd ;

---

1 *Filippo Argenti.*—Boccaccio tells us, " He was a
man remarkable for the large proportions and extraordinary vigour of his bodily frame, and the extreme
waywardness and irascibility of his temper."—*Decameron*, Giorn. ix., Nov. 8.

2 *The city, that of Dis is named.*—So Ariosto.
"Orlando Furioso," c. xl., st. 32 :

" Fatto era un stagno più sicuro e brutto,
  Di quel che cinge la città di Dite."

3 *From heaven were shower'd.*—" Da ciel piovuti."
Thus Frezzi : " Li maladetti piovuti da cielo."—*Il
Quadriregio*, lib. iv. cap. 4. And Pulci, in the
passage cited in the note to canto xxi. 117.

Whereat their angry scorn abating, thus
They spake: "Come thou alone; and let him go,
Who hath so hardily enter'd this realm.
Alone return he by his witless way;
If well he know it, let him prove. For thee
Here shalt thou tarry, who through clime so dark
Hast been his escort." Now bethink thee, reader!
What cheer was mine at sound of those curst words.
I did believe I never should return.

"Oh, my loved guide! who more than seven times
Security hast render'd me, and drawn
From peril deep, whereto I stood exposed,
Desert me not," I cried, "in this extreme.
And, if our onward going be denied,
Together trace we back our steps with speed."

My liege, who thither had conducted me,
Replied, "Fear not: for of our passage none
Hath power to disappoint us, by such high
Authority permitted. But do thou
Expect me here; meanwhile, thy wearied spirit
Comfort, and feed with kindly hope, assured
I will not leave thee in this lower world."

This said, departs the sire benevolent,
And quits me. Hesitating I remain
At war, 'twixt will and will not,[2] in my thoughts.

I could not hear what terms he offer'd them,
But they conferr'd not long, for all at once
Pellmell[3] rush'd back within. Closed were the gates,
By those our adversaries, on the breast
Of my liege lord: excluded, he return'd

---

[1] *Seven times.*—"The commentators," says Venturi, "perplex themselves with the inquiry what seven perils these were from which Dante had been delivered by Virgil. Reckoning the beasts in the first canto as one of them, and adding Charon, Minos, Cerberus, Plutus, Phlegyas, and Filippo Argenti, as so many others, we shall have the number; and if this be not satisfactory, we may suppose a determinate to have been put for an indeterminate number."

[2] *At war, 'twixt will and will not.*—"Che sì, e nò nel capo mi tenzona." Thus our poet in his eighth canzone:

  "Ch' il sì, e'l nò tututto in vostra mano
  Ha posto amore."

And Boccaccio, "Ninf. Fiesol," st. 233: Il sì e il nò nel capo gli contende." The words I have adopted are Shakespeare's," Measure for Measure,"Act. ii., sc. 1.

[3] *Pellmell.*—"A pruova." "Certatim." "A l'envi." I had before translated "To trial," and have to thank Mr. Carlyle for detecting the error.

I could not hear what terms he offer'd them,
But they conferr'd not long.

Canto VIII., lines 110, 111.

To me with tardy steps. Upon the ground
His eyes were bent, and from his brow erased
All confidence, while thus in sighs he spake :
" Who hath denied me these abodes of woe ? "
Then thus to me : " That I am anger'd, think
No ground of terror : in this trial I
Shall vanquish, use what arts they may within
For hindrance. This their insolence, not new,[1]
Erewhile at gate less secret they display'd,
Which still is without bolt ; upon its arch
Thou saw'st the deadly scroll : and even now,
On this side of its entrance, down the steep,
Passing the circles, unescorted, comes
One whose strong might can open us this land.'

---

[1] *This their insolence, not new.*—Virgil assures our poet that these evil spirits had formerly shown the ame insolence when our Saviour descended into hell. They attempted to prevent him from entering at the gate, over which Dante had read the fatal inscription—" that gate which,' says the Roman poet, " an angel had just passed, by whose aid we shall overcome this opposition, and gain admittance into the city "

CANTO IX.

ARGUMENT.

After some hindrances, and having seen the hellish furies and other monsters, the poet, by the help of an angel, enters the city of Dis, wherein he discovers that the heretics are punished in tombs burning with intense fire: and he, together with Virgil, passes onwards between the sepulchres and the walls of the city.

THE hue,[1] which coward dread on my pale cheeks
  Imprinted when I saw my guide turn back,
Chased that from his which newly they had worn,
And inwardly restrain'd it. He, as one
Who listens, stood attentive : for his eye
Not far could lead him through the sable air,
And the thick-gathering cloud. "It yet behoves
We win this fight ;" thus he began : "if not,
Such aid to us is offer'd.—Oh ! how long
Me seems it, ere the promised help arrive."

  I noted, how the sequel of his words
Cloked their beginning ; for the last he spake
Agreed not with the first. But not the less
My fear was at his saying ; sith I drew
To import worse, perchance, than that he held,
His mutilated speech. "Doth ever any
Into this rueful concave's extreme depth
Descend, out of the first degree, whose pain
Is deprivation merely of sweet hope ?"

  Thus I inquiring. "Rarely," he replied,
"It chances, that among us any makes
This journey, which I wend. Erewhile, 'tis true,
Once came I here beneath, conjured by fell
Erictho,[2] sorceress, who compell'd the shades

---

[1] *The hue.*—Virgil, perceiving that Dante was pale with fear, restrained those outward tokens of displeasure which his own countenance had betrayed.

[2] *Erictho.*—Erictho, a Thessalian sorceress, according to Lucan, " Pharsalia," l. vi., was employed by Sextus, son of Pompey the Great, to conjure up a spirit, who should inform him of the issue of the civil wars between his father and Cæsar.

Back to their bodies. No long space my flesh
Was naked of me,[1] when within these walls
She made me enter, to draw forth a spirit
From out of Judas' circle. Lowest place
Is that of all, obscurest, and removed
Furthest from heaven's all-circling orb. The road
Full well I know: thou therefore rest secure.
That lake, the noisome stench exhaling, round
The city of grief encompasses, which now
We may not enter without rage." Yet more
He added: but I hold it not in mind,
For that mine eye toward the lofty tower
Had drawn me wholly, to its burning top;
Where, in an instant, I beheld uprisen
At once three hellish furies, stain'd with blood:
In limb and motion feminine they seem'd;
Around them greenest hydras twisting roll'd
Their volumes; adders and cerastes[2] crept
Instead of hair, and their fierce temples bound.

He, knowing well the miserable hags
Who tend the queen of endless woe, thus spake:
"Mark thou each dire Erynnis. To the left,
This is Megæra; on the right hand, she
Who wails, Alecto; and Tisiphone
I' th' midst." This said, in silence he remain'd.
Their breast they each one clawing tore; themselves
Smote with their palms, and such shrill clamour raised
That to the bard I clung, suspicion-bound.
"Hasten Medusa: so to adamant
Him shall we change;" all looking down exclaim'd:

---

[1]   *No long space my flesh
was naked of me.*

"Quæ corpus complexa animæ tam fortis inane."—
Ovid, Metamorphoses, l. xiii., fab. 2. Dante appears
to have fallen into an anachronism. Virgil's death
did not happen till long after this period. But
Lombardi shows, in opposition to the other commentators, that the anachronism is only apparent.
Erictho might well have survived the battle of
Pharsalia long enough to be employed in her
magical practices at the time of Virgil's decease.

[2] *Adders and cerastes.*

   "Vipereum crinem vittis innexa cruentis."
         Virgil, Æneid, l. vi. 281.
   "Spinâque vagi torquente cerastæ
  *   *   * et torrida dipsas
Et gravis in geminum vergens caput amphisbæna."
        Lucan, Pharsalia, l. ix. 719.
So Milton:
   "Scorpion and asp, and amphisbæna dire,
    Cerastes horn'd, hydrus and elops drear,
    And dipsas."   *Paradise Lost,* b. x. 524.

"E'en when by Theseus' might assail'd, we took
No ill revenge." Turn thyself round, and keep
Thy countenance hid; for if the Gorgon dire
Be shown, and thou shouldst view it, thy return
Upwards would be for ever lost. This said,
Himself, my gentle master, turn'd me round;
Nor trusted he my hands, but with his own
He also hid me. Ye of intellect
Sound and entire, mark well the lore[1] conceal'd
Under close texture of the mystic strain.

And now there came o'er the perturbed waves
Loud-crashing, terrible, a sound that made
Either shore tremble, as if of a wind[2]
Impetuous, from conflicting vapours sprung,
That 'gainst some forest driving all his might,
Plucks off the branches, beats them down, and hurls
Afar;[3] then, onward passing, proudly sweeps
His whirlwind rage, while beasts and shepherds fly.

Mine eyes he loosed, and spake: "And now direct
Thy visual nerve along that ancient foam,
There, thickest where the smoke ascends." As frogs
Before their' foe the serpent, through the wave
Ply swiftly all, till at the ground each one
Lies on a heap; more than a thousand spirits
Destroy'd, so saw I fleeing before one
Who pass'd with unwet feet the Stygian sound.
He, from his face removing the gross air,
Oft his left hand forth stretch'd, and seem'd alone
By that annoyance wearied. I perceived

---

[1] *The lore.*—The poet probably intends to call the reader's attention to the allegorical and mystic sense of the present canto, and not, as Venturi supposes, to that of the whole work. Landino supposes this hidden meaning to be, that in the case of those vices which proceed from incontinence and intemperance, reason, which is figured under the person of Virgil, with the ordinary grace of God, may be a sufficient safeguard; but that in the instance of more heinous crimes, such as those we shall hereafter see punished, a special grace, represented by the angel, is requisite for our defence.

[2] *A wind.*—Imitated by Berni:

"Com' un gruppo di vento in la marina
L' onde, e le navi sottosopra caccia,
Ed in terra con furia repentina
Gli arbori abbatte, sveglie, sfronda e straccia.
Smarriti fuggon i lavoratori
E per le selve le fiere e' pastori."
   Orlando Innamorato, lib. i., c. ii., st. 6.

[3] *Afar.*—"Porta i fiori," "carries away the blossoms," is the common reading. "Porta fuori," which is the right reading, adopted by Lombardi in his edition from the Nidobeatina, for which he claims it exclusively, I had also seen in Landino's edition of 1484, and adopted from thence, long before it was my chance to meet with Lombardi.

That he was sent from heaven ; and to my guide
Turn'd me, who signal made, that I should stand
Quiet, and bend to him. Ah me ! how full
Of noble anger seem'd he. To the gate
He came, and with his wand[1] touch'd it, whereat
Open without impediment it flew.
    " Outcasts of heaven ! Oh, abject race, and scorn'd ! "
Began he, on the horrid grunsel standing,
" Whence doth this wild excess of insolence
Lodge in you ? wherefore kick you 'gainst that will
Ne'er frustrate of its end, and which so oft
Hath laid on you enforcement of your pangs ?
What profits, at the fates to butt the horn ?
Your Cerberus,[2] if ye remember, hence
Bears still, peel'd of their hair, his throat and maw."
    This said, he turn'd back o'er the filthy way,
And syllable to us spake none ; but wore
The semblance of a man by other care
Beset, and keenly prest, than thought of him
Who in his presence stands. Then we our steps
Toward that territory moved, secure
After the hallow'd words. We, unopposed,
There enter'd ; and, my mind eager to learn
What state a fortress like to that might hold,
I, soon as enter'd, throw mine eye around,
And see, on every part, wide-stretching space,
Replete with bitter pain and torment ill.
    As where Rhone stagnates on the plains of Arles,[3]

---

[1] *With his wand.*—

  "She with her rod did softly smite the raile.
   Which straight flew ope,"
      Spenser, Faëry Queen, b. iv., c. iii., st. 46.

[2] *Your Cerberus.*—Cerberus is feigned to have been dragged by Hercules, bound with a threefold chain, of which, says the angel, he still bears the marks. Lombardi blames the other interpreters for having supposed that the angel attributes this exploit to Hercules, a fabulous hero, rather than to our Saviour. It would seem as if the good father had forgotten that Cerberus is himself no less a creature of the imagination than the hero who encountered him.

[3] *The plains of Arles.*—In Provence. See Ariosto, " Orlando Furioso," c. xxxix., st. 72 :

  " Fu da ogni parte in quest' ultima guerra
    (Benche la cosa non fu ugual divisa,
    Ch' assai più andar dei Saracin sotterra
    Per man di Bradamante e di Marfisa)
    Se ne vede ancor segno in quella terra,
    Che presso ad Arli, ove il Rodano stagna,
    Piena de sepolture è la campagna."

These sepulchres are mentioned in the " Life of Charlemagne," which goes under the name of Archbishop Turpin, cap. 28 and 30, and by Fazio degli Uberti, " Dittamondo," l. iv. cap. xxi.

Or as at Pola,[1] near Quarnaro's gulf,
That closes Italy and laves her bounds,
The place is all thick spread with sepulchres;
So was it here, save what in horror here
Excell'd : for 'midst the graves were scatter'd flames,
Wherewith intensely all throughout they burn'd,[2]
That iron for no craft there hotter needs.

    Their lids all hung suspended ; and beneath,
From them forth issued lamentable moans,
Such as the sad and tortured well might raise.

    I thus : "Master ! say who are these, interr'd
Within these vaults, of whom distinct we hear
The dolorous sighs." He answer thus return'd :
"The arch-heretics are here, accompanied
By every sect their followers ; and much more,
Than thou believest, the tombs are freighted : like
With like is buried ; and the monuments
Are different in degrees of heat." This said,
He to the right hand turning, on we pass'd
Betwixt the afflicted and the ramparts high.

---

[1] *At Pola.*—A city of Istria, situated near the Gulf of Quarnaro, in the Adriatic Sea.

[2] *They burn'd.*—Mr. Darley observes, that in the Incantation of Hervor (v. "Northern Antiquities," vol. ii.) the spirit of Angantyr lies in a tomb "all on fire."

He answer thus return'd:
"The arch-heretics are here, accompanied
By every sect their followers."
                              Can. IX., lines 124—126.

CANTO X.

Dante, having obtained permission from his guide, holds discourse with Farinata degli Uberti and Cavalcante Cavalcanti, who lie in their fiery tombs that are yet open, and not to be closed up till after the last judgment. Farinata predicts the poet's exile from Florence; and shows him that the condemned have knowledge of future things, but are ignorant of what is at present passing, unless it be revealed by some new comer from earth.

NOW by a secret pathway we proceed,
  Between the walls, that hem the region round,
And the tormented souls : my master first,
I close behind his steps. "Virtue supreme !"
I thus began : " who through these ample orbs
In circuit lead'st me, even as thou will'st ;
Speak thou, and satisfy my wish. May those,
Who lie within these sepulchres, be seen ?
Already all the lids are raised, and none
O'er them keeps watch." He thus in answer spake :
" They shall be closed all, what time they here
From Josaphat[1] return'd shall come, and bring
Their bodies, which above they now have left
The cemetery on this part obtain,
With Epicurus, all his followers,
Who with the body make the spirit die.
Here therefore satisfaction shall be soon,
Both to the question asked, and to the wish[2]
Which thou conceal'st in silence." I replied :
" I keep not, guide beloved ! from thee my heart
Secreted, but to shun vain length of words ;
A lesson erewhile taught me by thyself."

[1] *Josaphat.*—It seems to have been a common opinion among the Jews, as well as among many Christians, that the general judgment will be held in the valley of Josaphat, or Jehoshaphat : " I will also gather all nations, and will bring them down into the valley of Jehoshaphat, and will plead with them there for my people and for my heritage Israel, whom they have scattered among the nations, and parted my land." Joel iii. 2.

[2] *The wish.*—The wish, that Dante had not expressed, was to see and converse with the followers of Epicurus ; among whom, we shall see, were Farinata degli Uberti and Cavalcante Cavalcanti.

"O Tuscan ! thou, who through the city of fire
Alive art passing, so discreet of speech :
Here, please thee, stay awhile. Thy utterance
Declares the place of thy nativity
To be that noble land, with which perchance
I too severely dealt." Sudden that sound
Forth issued from a vault, whereat, in fear,
I somewhat closer to my leader's side
Approaching, he thus spake : "What dost thou ? Turn :
Lo ! Farinata [1] there, who hath himself
Uplifted : from his girdle upwards, all
Exposed, behold him." On his face was mine
Already fix'd : his breast and forehead there
Erecting, seem'd as in high scorn he held
E'en hell. Between the sepulchres, to him
My guide thrust me, with fearless hands and prompt ;
This warning added : "See thy words be clear."

He, soon as there I stood at the tomb's foot,
Eyed me a space ; then in disdainful mood
Address'd me : "Say what ancestors were thine."

I, willing to obey him, straight reveal'd
The whole, nor kept back aught : when he, his brow
Somewhat uplifting, cried : " Fiercely were they
Adverse to me, my party, and the blood
From whence I sprang : twice,[2] therefore, I abroad
Scatter'd them." "Though driven out, yet they each time
From all parts," answer'd I, "return'd ; an art
Which yours have shown they are not skill'd to learn.'

Then, peering forth from the unclosed jaw,
Rose from his side a shade,[3] high as the chin,
Leaning, methought, upon its knees upraised.

---

[1] *Farinata.*—Farinata degli Uberti, a noble Florentine, was the leader of the Ghibelline faction, when
they obtained a signal victory over the Guelfi at
Montaperto, near the river Arbia. Macchiavelli calls
him "a man of exalted soul, and great military
talents," "History of Florence," b. ii. His grandson,
Bonifacio, or, as he is commonly called, Fazio degli
Uberti, wrote a poem, entitled the " Dittamondo," in
imitation of Dante. I shall have frequent occasion to
refer to it throughout these Notes. At the conclusion
of cap. 27, l. ii, he makes mention of his ancestor
Farinata. See Note 4 to Life of Dante.

[2] *Twice.*—The first time in 1248, when they were
driven out by Frederick II.—see G. Villani, lib. vi., c.
xxxiv. : and the second time in 1260. See Note to v. 83.

[3] *Rose from his side a shade.*—The spirit of Cavalcante Cavalcanti, a noble Florentine, of the Guelph
party.

He, soon as there I stood at the tomb's foot,
Eyed me a space; then in disdainful mood
Address'd me: "Say what ancestors were thine."
Canto X., lines 40—42.

It look'd around, as eager to explore
If there were other with me ; but perceiving
That fond imagination quench'd, with tears
Thus spake : " If thou through this blind prison go'st,
Led by thy lofty genius and profound,
Where is my son ?[1] and wherefore not with thee ?"

     I straight replied : " Not of myself I come
By him, who there expects me, through this clime
Conducted, whom perchance Guido thy son
Had in contempt."[2]   Already had his words
And mode of punishment read me his name,
Whence I so fully answer'd.   He at once
Exclaim'd, up starting, " How ! saidst thou, he *had*?[3]
No longer lives he ?   Strikes not on his eye
The blessed daylight ?"   Then, of some delay
I made ere my reply, aware, down fell
Supine, nor after forth appear'd he more.

     Meanwhile the other, great of soul, near whom
I yet was station'd, changed not countenance stern,

---

[1] *My son.*—Guido, the son of Cavalcante Cavalcanti ; " he whom I call the first of my friends," says Dante in his " Vita Nuova," where the commencement of their friendship is related. From the character given of him by contemporary writers, his temper was well formed to assimilate with that of our poet. " He was," according to G. Villani, lib. viii., c. xli., " of a philosophical and elegant mind, if he had not been too delicate and fastidious." And Dino Compagni terms him " a young and noble knight, brave and courteous, but of a lofty, scornful spirit, much addicted to solitude and study." Muratori, *Rerum Italicarum Scriptores*, t. 9. lib. i., p. 481. He died, either in exile at Serrazana, or soon after his return to Florence, December, 1300, during the spring of which year the action of this poem is supposed to be passing.

[2] *Guido thy son had in contempt.*—Guido Cavalcanti, being more given to philosophy than poetry, was perhaps no great admirer of Virgil. Some poetical compositions by Guido are, however, still extant ; and his reputation for skill in the art was such as to eclipse that of his predecessor and namesake, Guido Guinicelli. His " Canzone sopra il Terreno Amore" was thought worthy of being illustrated by numerous and ample commentaries : Crescimbeni, " Istoria della Volgar Poesia," lib. v. Our author addressed him in a playful sonnet, of which the following spirited translation is found in the notes to Hayley's " Essay on Epic Poetry," ep. iii. :—

" Henry ! I wish that you, and Charles, and I,
By some sweet spell within a barque were placed,
   A gallant barque with magic virtue graced,
   Swift at our will with every wind to fly ;
So that no changes of the shifting sky,
   No stormy terrors of the watery waste,
   Might bar our course, but heighten still our taste
Of sprightly joy, and of our social tie :
Then that my Lucy, Lucy fair and free,
   With those soft nymphs, on whom your souls are bent,
   The kind magician might to us convey,
To talk of love throughout the livelong day :
   And that each fair might be as well content,
   As I in truth believe our hearts would be."
The two friends, here called Henry and Charles, are, in the original, Guido and Lapo, concerning the latter of whom see the Life of Dante prefixed : and Lucy is Monna Bice. A more literal version of the sonnet may be found in the " Canzoniere of Dante, translated by Charles Lyell, Esq.," 8vo, London, 1835, p. 407.

[3] *Saidst thou, he had.*—In Æschylus the shade of Darius is represented as inquiring with similar anxiety after the fate of his son Xerxes :—

"*Atossa*. Μονάδα δὲ Ξέρξην ἔρημον φασὶν οὐ πολλῶν μέτα -
Darius. Πῶς δε δὴ καὶ ποῖ τελευτᾷν ; ἔστι τις σωτηρία : "
           ΠΕΡΣΑΙ, 741, *Blomfield's edit.*

" *Atossa*.—Xerxes astonish'd, desolate, alone—
   Ghost of Dar. How will this end ? Nay, pause not.
   Is he safe ? "—*The Persians. Potter's Trans.*

Nor moved the neck, nor bent his ribbed side.
"And if," continuing the first discourse,
"They in this art," he cried, "small skill have shown ;
That doth torment me more e'en than this bed.
But not yet fifty times[1] shall be relumed
Her aspect, who reigns here queen of this realm,[2]
Ere thou shalt know the full weight of that art.
So to the pleasant world mayst thou return,[3]
As thou shalt tell me why, in all their laws,
Against my kin this people is so fell."

 "The slaughter[4] and great havoc," I replied,
"That colour'd Arbia's flood with crimson stain—
To these impute, that in our hallow'd dome
Such orisons[5] ascend." Sighing he shook
The head, then thus resumed : " In that affray
I stood not singly, nor, without just cause,
Assuredly, should with the rest have stirr'd ;
But singly there I stood,[6] when, by consent
Of all, Florence had to the ground been razed,
The one who openly forbade the deed."

---

[1] *Not yet fifty times.*—" Not fifty months shall be passed, before thou shalt learn, by woful experience, the difficulty of returning from banishment to thy native city."

[2] *Queen of this realm.*—The moon, one of whose titles in heathen mythology was Proserpine, queen of the shades below.

[3] *So to the pleasant world mayst thou return.*—
 " E se tu mai nel dolce mondo reggi."
Lombardi would construe this : " And if thou ever remain in the pleasant world." His chief reasons for thus departing from the common interpretation are, first that " se " in the sense of " so " cannot be followed by " mai," any more than in Latin *sic* can be followed by *unquam ;* and next that " reggi is too unlike *riedi* to be put for it. A more intimate acquaintance with the early Florentine writers would have taught him that " mai " is used in other senses than those which *unquam* appears to have had, particularly in that of *pur,* " yet ; " as may be seen in the notes to the " Decameron," p. 43, ed. Giunti, 1573 ; and that the old writers both of prose and verse changed *riedo* into *reggio,* as of *fiedo* they made *feggio,* " Inf." c. xv., v. 30, and c. xvii., v. 75. See page 98 of the same notes to the " Decameron," where a poet before Dante's time is said to have translated " Redeunt flores " " Reggiono i fiori."

[4] *The slaughter.*—" By means of Farinata degli Uberti, the Guelfi were conquered by the army of King Manfredi, near the river Arbia, with so great a slaughter, that those who escaped from that defeat took refuge, not in Florence, which city they considered as lost to them, but in Lucca." *Macchiavelli, History of Florence,* b. ii., and G. Villani, lib. vi., c. lxxx. and lxxxi.

[5] *Such orisons.*—This appears to allude to certain prayers which were offered up in the churches of Florence, for deliverance from the hostile attempts of the Uberti : or, it may be, that the public councils being held in churches, the speeches delivered in them against the Uberti are termed " orisons," or prayers.

[6] *Singly there I stood.*—Guido Novello assembled a council of the Ghibellini at Empoli ; where it was agreed by all, that, in order to maintain the ascendancy of the Ghibelline party in Tuscany, it was necessary to destroy Florence, which could serve only (the people of that city being Guelfi) to enable the party attached to the Church to recover its strength. This cruel sentence, passed upon so noble a city, met with no opposition from any of its citizens or friends, except Farinata degli Uberti, who openly and without reserve forbade the measure : affirming, that he had endured so many hardships, and encountered so many dangers, with no other view than that of being able to pass his days in his own country.—*Macchiavelli, History of Florence,* b. ii.

"So may thy lineage[1] find at last repose,"
I thus adjured him, "as thou solve this knot,
Which now involves my mind. If right I hear,
Ye seem to view beforehand that which time
Leads with him, of the present uninform'd."

"We view,[2] as one who hath an evil sight,"
He answer'd, "plainly, objects far remote ;
So much of his large splendour yet imparts
The Almighty Ruler : but when they approach,
Or actually exist, our intellect
Then wholly fails ; nor of your human state,
Except what others bring us, know we aught.
Hence therefore mayst thou understand, that all
Our knowledge in that instant shall expire,
When on futurity the portals close."

Then conscious of my fault,[3] and by remorse
Smitten, I added thus : "Now shalt thou say
To him there fallen, that his offspring still
Is to the living join'd ; and bid him know,
That if from answer, silent, I abstain'd,
'Twas that my thought was occupied, intent
Upon that error, which thy help hath solved."

But now my master summoning me back
I heard, and with more eager haste besought
The spirit to inform me, who with him
Partook his lot. He answer thus return'd :
"More than a thousand with me here are laid.
Within is Frederick,[4] second of that name,

---

[1] *So may thy lineage.*—"Deh se riposi mai vostra semenza." Here Lombardi is again mistaken, as at v. 80 above. Let me take this occasion to apprise the reader of Italian poetry, that one not well versed in it is very apt to misapprehend the word " se," as I think Cowper has done in translating Milton's Italian verses. A good instance of the different meanings in which it is used is afforded in the following lines by Bernardo Capello :—

> " E tu, che dolcemente i fiori e l' erba
> Con lieve corso mormorando bagni,
> Tranquillo fiume di vaghezza pieno ;
> Se 'l cielo al mar si chiaro t' accompagni ;
> Se punto di pietade in te si serba :
> Le mie lagrime accogli entro al tuo seno."

Here the first " se " signifies " so," and the second " if."

[2] *We view.*—"The departed spirits know things past and to come ; yet are ignorant of things present. Agamemnon foretells what should happen unto Ulysses, yet ignorantly inquires what is become of his own son."—*Browne on Urn Burial,* ch. iv.

[3] *My fault.*—Dante felt remorse for not having returned an immediate answer to the inquiry of Cavalcante, from which delay he was led to believe that his son Guido was no longer living.

[4] *Frederick.*—The Emperor Frederick II., who died in 1250. See Notes to canto xiii.

I

And the Lord Cardinal;[1] and of the rest
I speak not." He, this said, from sight withdrew.
But I my steps toward the ancient bard
Reverting, ruminated on the words
Betokening me such ill. Onward he moved,
And thus, in going, question'd : " Whence the amaze
That holds thy senses wrapt ? " I satisfied
The inquiry, and the sage enjoin'd me straight :
" Let thy safe memory store what thou hast heard
To thee importing harm ; and note thou this,"
With his raised finger bidding me take heed,
" When thou shalt stand before her gracious beam,[2]
Whose bright eye all surveys, she of thy life
The future tenour will to thee unfold."

Forthwith he to the left hand turn'd his feet :
We left the wall, and towards the middle space
Went by a path that to a valley strikes,
Which e'en thus high exhaled its noisome steam.

---

[1] *The Lord Cardinal.*—Ottaviano Ubaldini, a Florentine, made cardinal in 1245, and deceased about 1273. On account of his great influence, he was generally known by the appellation of " the Cardinal." It is reported of him that he declared, if there were any such thing as a human soul, he had lost his for the Ghibellini. " I know not," says Tiraboschi, " whether it is on sufficient grounds that Crescimbeni numbers among the poets of this age the Cardinal Uttaviano, or Ottaviano degli Ubaldini, a Florentine, archdeacon and procurator of the church of Bologna, afterwards made cardinal by Innocent IV. in 1245, and employed in the most important public affairs, wherein, however, he showed himself, more than became his character, a favourer of the Ghibellines. He died, not in the year 1272, as Ciaconio and other writers have reported, but at soonest after the July of 1273, at which time he was in Mugello with Pope Gregory X."— *Tiraboschi Della Poes. It., Mr. Mathias' edit.,* t. i., p. 140.

[2] *Her gracious beam.*—Beatrice

From the profound abyss, behind the lid
Of a great monument we stood retired.
Canto XI., lines 6, 7.

CANTO XI.

—

ARGUMENT.

Dante arrives at the verge of a rocky precipice which encloses the seventh circle, where he sees the sepulchre of Anastasius the heretic ; behind the lid of which pausing a little, to make himself capable by degrees of enduring the fetid smell that steamed upward from the abyss, he is instructed by Virgil concerning the manner in which the three following circles are disposed, and what description of sinners is punished in each. He then inquires the reason why the carnal, the gluttonous, the avaricious and prodigal, the wrathful and gloomy, suffer not their punishments within the city of Dis. He next asks how the crime of usury is an offence against God ; and at length the two poets go towards the place from whence a passage leads down to the seventh circle.

UPON the utmost verge of a high bank,
   By craggy rocks environ'd round, we came,
Where woes beneath, more cruel yet, were stow'd :
And here, to shun the horrible excess
Of fetid exhalation upward cast
From the profound abyss, behind the lid
Of a great monument we stood retired,
Whereon this scroll I mark'd : "I have in charge
Pope Anastasius,[1] whom Photinus drew
From the right path."—"Ere our descent, behoves
We make delay, that somewhat first the sense,
To the dire breath accustom'd, afterward
Regard it not." My master thus ; to whom
Answering I spake : "Some compensation find,
That the time pass not wholly lost." He then :
"Lo ! how my thoughts e'en to thy wishes tend.
My son,[2] within these rocks," he thus began,
"Are three close circles in gradation placed,
As these which now thou leavest. Each one is full

---

[1] *Pope Anastasius.*—The commentators are not agreed concerning the person who is here mentioned as a follower of the heretical Photinus. By some he is supposed to have been Anastasius II.; by others, the fourth of that name ; while a third set contend that our poet has confounded him with Anastasius I., Emperor of the East. Fazio degli Uberti, like our author, makes him a pope :

"Anastasio papa in quel tempo era,
  Di Fotin vago a mal grado de sui."

Dittamondo, l. ii., cap. xiv.

[2] *My son.*—The remainder of the present canto may be considered as a syllabus of the whole of this part of the poem.

Of spirits accurst ; but that the sight alone
Hereafter may suffice thee, listen how
And for what cause in durance they abide.
    "Of all malicious act abhorr'd in heaven,
The end is injury ; and all such end
Either by force or fraud[1] works other's woe.
But fraud, because of man peculiar evil,
To God is more displeasing ; and beneath,
The fraudulent are therefore doom'd to endure
Severer pang. The violent occupy
All the first circle ; and because, to force,
Three persons are obnoxious, in three rounds,
Each within other separate, is it framed.
To God, his neighbour, and himself, by man
Force may be offer'd ; to himself I say,
And his possessions, as thou soon shalt hear
At full. Death, violent death, and painful wounds
Upon his neighbour he inflicts ; and wastes,
By devastation, pillage, and the flames,
His substance. Slayers, and each one that smites
In malice, plunderers, and all robbers, hence
The torment undergo of the first round,
In different herds. Man can do violence
To himself and his own blessings : and for this,
He in the second round must aye deplore
With unavailing penitence his crime.
Whoe'er deprives himself of life and light,
In reckless lavishment his talent wastes,
And sorrows[2] there where he should dwell in joy.
To God may force be offer'd, in the heart
Denying and blaspheming his high power,
And Nature with her kindly law contemning.
And thence the inmost round marks with its seal

---

[1] *Either by force or fraud.*—" Cum autem duobus modiis, id est, aut vi, aut fraude, fiat injuria . . . utrumque homini alienissimum ; sed fraus odio digna majore."—*Cic. de Off.*, lib. i., c. xiii.

[2] *And sorrows.*—This fine moral, that not to enjoy our being is to be ungrateful to the Author of it, is well expressed in Spenser, "Faëry Queen," b. iv., c. viii., st. 15 :—

" For he whose daies in wilful woe are worne,
    The grace of his Creator doth despise,
    That will not use his gifts for thankless
        nigardise."

Sodom, and Cahors,[1] and all such as speak
Contemptuously of the Godhead in their hearts.
        "Fraud, that in every conscience leaves a sting,
May be by man employ'd on one, whose trust
He wins, or on another who withholds
Strict confidence. Seems as the latter way
Broke but the bond of love which Nature makes.
Whence in the second circle have their nest,
Dissimulation, witchcraft, flatteries,
Theft, falsehood, simony, all who seduce
To lust, or set their honesty at pawn,
With such vile scum as these. The other way
Forgets both Nature's general love, and that
Which thereto added afterward gives birth
To special faith. Whence in the lesser circle,
Point of the universe, dread seat of Dis,
The traitor is eternally consumed."
        I thus : "Instructor, clearly thy discourse
Proceeds, distinguishing the hideous chasm
And its inhabitants with skill exact.
But tell me this : they of the dull, fat pool,
Whom the rain beats, or whom the tempest drives,
Or who with tongues so fierce conflicting meet,
Wherefore within the city fire-illumed
Are not these punish'd, if God's wrath be on them ?
And if it be not, wherefore in such guise
Are they condemn'd ?" He answer thus return'd :
"Wherefore in dotage wanders thus thy mind,
Not so accustom'd ? or what other thoughts
Possess it ? Dwell not in thy memory
The words, wherein thy ethic page[2] describes
Three dispositions adverse to Heaven's will,
Incontinence, malice, and mad brutishness,

---

[1] *Cahors.*—A city of Guienne, much frequented by usurers.

[2] *Thy ethic page.*—He refers to Aristotle's Ethics : "Μετὰ δὲ ταῦτα λεκτέον, ἄλλην ποιησαμένους ἀρχὴν, ὅτι τῶν περὶ τὰ ἤθη φευκτῶν τρία ἐστὶν εἴδη, κακία, ἀκρασία, θηριότης."—*Ethic Nicomach*, lib vii., c. i. "In the next place, entering on another division of the subject, let it be defined, that respecting morals there are three sorts of things to be avoided—malice, incontinence, and brutishness."

And how incontinence the least offends
God, and least guilt incurs ? If well thou note
This judgment, and remember who they are,
Without these walls to vain repentance doom'd,
Thou shalt discern why they apart are placed
From these fell spirits, and less wreakful pours
Justice divine on them its vengeance down."

    "Oh, sun ! who healest all imperfect sight,
Thou so content'st me, when thou solvest my doubt,
That ignorance not less than knowledge charms.
Yet somewhat turn thee back," I in these words
Continued, " where thou saidst, that usury
Offends celestial Goodness ; and this knot
Perplex'd unravel." He thus made reply :
" Philosophy, to an attentive ear,
Clearly points out, not in one part alone,
How imitative Nature takes her course
From the celestial mind, and from its art :
And where her laws[1] the Stagirite unfolds,
Not many leaves scann'd o'er, observing well
Thou shalt discover, that your art on her
Obsequious follows, as the learner treads
In his instructor's step ; so that your art
Deserves the name of second in descent[2]
From God. These two, if thou recall to mind
Creation's holy book,[3] from the beginning
Were the right source of life and excellence
To human kind. But in another path
The usurer walks ; and Nature in herself
And in her follower thus he sets at nought,

---

[1] *Her laws.* — Aristotle's Physics. "Ἡ τέχνη μιμεῖται τὴν φύσιν."—*Aristotle,* ΦΥΣ. ΑΚΡ., lib. ii., c. 2. "Art imitates Nature." See the " Coltivazione " of Alamanni, lib. i.

         " L'arte umana
Altro non è da dir ch' un dolce sprone,
Un correger soave, un pio sostegno,
Uno esperto imitar, comporre accorto
Un sollecito attar con studio e'ngegno
La cagion natural, l' effetto, e l' opra."

[2] *Second in descent.* —
    " Sì che vostr' arte a Dio quasi è nipote."
So Frezzi :
    " Giustizia fu da cielo, e di Dio è figlia,
     E ogni bona legge a Dio è nipote."
        Il Quadriregio, lib. iv., cap. 2.

[3] *Creation's holy book.*—Gen. ii. 15 : " And the Lord God took the man, and put him into the garden of Eden to dress it and to keep it." And Gen. iii. 19: " In the sweat of thy face shalt thou eat bread."

Placing elsewhere his hope.[1]   But follow now
My steps on forward journey bent ; for now
The Pisces play with undulating glance
Along the horizon, and the Wain[2] lies all
O'er the north-west ; and onward there a space
Is our steep passage down the rocky height."

---

[1] *Placing elsewhere his hope.*—The usurer, trusting in the produce of his wealth, lent out on usury, despises Nature directly, because he does not avail himself of her means for maintaining or enriching himself; and indirectly, because he does not avail himself of the means which Art, the follower and imitator of Nature, would afford him for the same purposes.

[2] *Wain.*—The constellation Boötes, or Charles's Wain.

CANTO XII.

ARGUMENT.

Descending by a very rugged way into the seventh circle, where the violent are punished, Dante and his leader find it guarded by the Minotaur; whose fury being pacified by Virgil, they step downwards from crag to crag; till, drawing near the bottom, they descry a river of blood, wherein are tormented such as have committed violence against their neighbour. At these, when they strive to emerge from the blood, a troop of Centaurs, running along the side of the river, aim their arrows; and three of their band opposing our travellers at the foot of the steep, Virgil prevails so far, that one consents to carry them both across the stream; and on their passage Dante is informed by him of the course of the river, and of those that are punished therein.

THE place, where to descend the precipice
   We came, was rough as Alp; and on its verge
Such object lay, as every eye would shun.
   As is that ruin, which Adice's stream[1]
On this side Trento struck, shouldering the wave,
Or loosed by earthquake or for lack of prop;
For from the mountain's summit, whence it moved
To the low level, so the headlong rock
Is shiver'd, that some passage[2] it might give
To him who from above would pass; e'en such
Into the chasm was that descent: and there
At point of the disparted ridge lay stretch'd
The infamy of Crete,[3] detested brood
Of the feign'd heifer:[4] and at sight of us
It gnaw'd itself, as one with rage distract.
To him my guide exclaim'd: "Perchance thou deem'st
The King of Athens[5] here, who, in the world

---

[1] *Adice's stream.*—After a great deal having been said on the subject, it still appears very uncertain at what part of the river this fall of the mountain happened.

[2] *Some passage.*—Lombardi erroneously, I think, understands by "alcuna via" "no passage:" in which sense "alcuno" is certainly sometimes used by some old writers. Moni, as usual, agrees with Lombardi. See Note to c. iii., v. 40.

[3] *The infamy of Crete.*—The Minotaur.

[4] *The feign'd heifer.*—Pasiphaë.

[5] *The King of Athens.*—Theseus, who was enabled by the instruction of Ariadne, the sister of the Minotaur, to destroy that monster. "Duca d'Atene." So Chaucer calls Theseus:

> "Whilom, as olde stories tellen us,
> There was a duk, that highte Theseus."
> *The Knighte's Tale.*

And Shakespeare

And there
At point of the disparted ridge lay stretch'd
The infamy of Crete, detested broad
Of the feign'd heifer.

Canto XII., lines 11—14.

Above, thy death contrived. Monster ! avaunt !
He comes not tutor'd by thy sister's art,[1]
But to behold your torments is he come."

Like to a bull,[2] that with impetuous spring
Darts, at the moment when the fatal blow
Hath struck him, but unable to proceed
Plunges on either side ; so saw I plunge
The Minotaur ; whereat the sage exclaim'd :
" Run to the passage ! while he storms, 'tis well
That thou descend." Thus down our read we tool:
Through those dilapidated crags, that oft
Moved underneath my feet, to weight[3] like theirs
Unused. I pondering went, and thus he spake :
" Perhaps thy thoughts are of this ruin'd steep,
Guarded by the brute violence, which I
Have vanquish'd now. Know then, that when I erst
Hither descended to the nether hell,
This rock was not yet fallen. But past doubt
(If well I mark), not long ere He arrived,[4]
Who carried off from Dis the mighty spoil
Of the highest circle, then through all its bounds
Such trembling seized the deep concave and foul,
I thought the universe was thrill'd with love,
Whereby, there are who deem, the world hath oft
Been into chaos turn'd :[5] and in that point,
Here, and elsewhere, that old rock toppled down.
But fix thine eyes beneath : the river of blood[6]

" Happy be Theseus, our renowned Duke."
  Midsummer Night's Dream, Act i., sc. i.
" This is in reality," observes Mr. Douce, " no mis-
application of a modern title, as Mr. Steevens con-
ceived, but a legitimate use of the word in its primitive
Latin sense of leader, and so it is often used in the
Bible. Shakespeare might have found Duke Theseus
in the Book of Troy, or in Turberville's Ovid's
Epistles. See the argument to that of Phædra and
Hippolytus."—*Douce's Illustrations of Shakespeare*,
8vo, 1807, vol. i., p. 179.

[1] *Thy sister's art.*—Ariadne.

[2] *Like to a bull.*—

" Ὡς δ' ὅταν ὀξὺν ἔχων πέλεκυν αἰζήϊος ἀνὴρ,
Κόψας ἐξόπιθεν κεράων βοὸς ἀγραύλοιο,
Ἵνα τάμῃ διὰ πᾶσαν, ὁ δὲ προθορὼν ἐρίπῃσιν."
  Homer, Iliad, l. xvii. 522.

" As when some vigorous youth with sharpen'd axe
A pastured bullock smites behind the horns,
And hews the muscle through : he at the stroke
Springs forth and falls." *Cowper's Translation*.

[3] *To weight.*—

" Incumbent on the dusky air
That felt unusual weight."
  Milton, Paradise Lost, b. i. 227.

[4] *He arrived.*—Our Saviour, who, according to
Dante, when he ascended from hell, carried with him
the souls of the patriarchs, and of other just men, out
of the first circle. See canto iv.

[5] *Been into chaos turn'd.*—This opinion is attributed to Empedocles.

[6] *The river of blood.*—" Deinde vidi locum (? lacum)

Approaches, in the which all those are steep'd,
Who have by violence injured." Oh, blind lust!
Oh, foolish wrath! who so dost goad us on
In the brief life, and in the eternal then
Thus miserably o'erwhelm us. I beheld
An ample fosse, that in a bow was bent,
As circling all the plain; for so my guide
Had told. Between it and the rampart's base,
On trail ran Centaurs, with keen arrows arm'd,
As to the chase they on the earth were wont.

At seeing us descend they each one stood;
And issuing from the troop, three sped with bows
And missile weapons chosen first; of whom
One cried from far: "Say, to what pain ye come
Condemn'd, who down this steep have journey'd. Speak
From whence ye stand, or else the bow I draw."

To whom my guide: "Our answer shall be made
To Chiron, there, when nearer him we come.
Ill was thy mind, thus ever quick and rash."
Then me he touch'd, and spake: "Nessus is this,
Who for the fair Deïanira died,
And wrought himself revenge[1] for his own fate.
He in the midst, that on his breast looks down,
Is the great Chiron who Achilles nursed;
That other, Pholus, prone to wrath." Around
The fosse these go by thousands, aiming shafts
At whatsoever spirit dares emerge[2]
From out the blood, more than his guilt allows.

We to those beasts, that rapid strode along,
Drew near; when Chiron took an arrow forth,
And with the notch push'd back his shaggy beard

---

magnum totum, ut mihi videbatur, plenum sanguine.
Sed dixit mihi Apostolus, sed non sanguis, sed ignis
est ad concremandos homicidas, et odiosos deputatus.
Hanc tamen similitudinem propter sanguinis effu-
sionem retinet."—*Alberici Visio*, § 7.

[1] *And wrought himself revenge.*—Nessus, when
dying by the hand of Hercules, charged Deïanira to
preserve the gore from his wound; for that if the
affections of Hercules should at any time be estranged
from her, it would act as a charm and recall them.

Deïanira had occasion to try the experiment; and the
venom acting, as Nessus had intended, caused
Hercules to expire in torments. See the "Trachiniæ" of Sophocles.

[2] *Emerge.*—"Multos in eis vidi usque ad talos
demergi, alios usque ad genua, vel femora, alios
usque ad pectus juxta peccati vidi modum: alios vero
qui majoris criminis noxa tenebantur in ipsis sum-
mitatibus supersedere conspexi."—*Alberici Visio*,
§ 3.

We to those beasts, that rapid strode along,
Drew near.

Canto XII, lines 73, 74.

To the cheek-bone, then, his great mouth to view
Exposing, to his fellows thus exclaim'd :
"Are ye aware, that he who comes behind
Moves what he touches ? The feet of the dead
Are not so wont." My trusty guide, who now
Stood near his breast, where the two natures join,
Thus made reply : " He is indeed alive,
And solitary so must needs by me
Be shown the gloomy vale, thereto induced
By strict necessity, not by delight.
She left her joyful harpings in the sky,
Who this new office to my care consign'd.
He is no robber, no dark spirit I.
But by that virtue, which empowers my step
To tread so wild a path, grant us, I pray,
One of thy band, whom we may trust secure,
Who to the ford may lead us, and convey
Across, him mounted on his back ; for he
Is not a spirit that may walk the air."

Then on his right breast turning, Chiron thus
To Nessus[1] spake : " Return, and be their guide.
And if you chance to cross another troop,
Command them keep aloof." Onward we moved,
The faithful escort by our side, along
The border of the crimson-seething flood,
Whence, from those steep'd within, loud shrieks arose.

Some there I mark'd, as high as to their brow
Immersed, of whom the mighty Centaur thus :
" These are the souls of tyrants, who were given
To blood and rapine. Here they wail aloud
Their merciless wrongs. Here Alexander dwells,
And Dionysius fell, who many a year
Of woe wrought for fair Sicily. That brow,

---

1 *Nessus.*—Our poet was probably induced, by the
following line in Ovid, to assign to Nessus the task of
conducting them over the ford :
" Nessus adit membrisque valens scitusque vadorum."
Metamorphoses. l. ix.
And Ovid's authority was Sophocles, who says of this
centaur—

" Ὃς τὸν βαθύρρουν ποταμὸν Εὔηνον βροτοὺς
Μισθοῦ πόρευε χερσὶν οὔτε πομπίμοις
Κώπαις ἐρέσσων, οὔτε λαίφεσιν νεώς."
Trachiniæ. 570.

" He in his arms, across Evenus' stream
Deep-flowing, bore the passenger for hire,
Without or sail or billow-cleaving oar."

Whereon the hair so jetty clustering hangs,
Is Azzolino;[1] that with flaxen locks
Obizzo of Este,[2] in the world destroy'd
By his foul step-son." To the bard revered
I turn'd me round, and thus he spake : "Let him
Be to thee now first leader, me but next
To him in rank." Then further on a space
The Centaur passed, near some, who at the throat
Were extant from the wave ; and, showing us
A spirit by itself apart retired,
Exclaim'd : " He[3] in God's bosom smote the heart,
Which yet is honour'd on the bank of Thames."

   A race I next espied who held the head,
And even all the bust, above the stream.
'Midst these I many a face remember'd well.
Thus shallow more and more the blood became,
So that at last it but imbrued the feet ;
And there our passage lay athwart the fosse.

   "As ever on this side the boiling wave
Thou seest diminishing," the Centaur said,
" So on the other, be thou well assured,
It lower still and lower sinks its bed,
Till in that part it re-uniting join,
Where 'tis the lot of tyranny to mourn.

[1] *Azzolino.*—Azzolino, or Ezzolino di Romano, a most cruel tyrant in the Marca Trivigiana, Lord of Padua, Vicenza, Verona, and Brescia, who died in 1260. His atrocities form the subject of a Latin tragedy, called " Eccerinis," by Albertino Mussato, of Padua, the contemporary of Dante, and the most elegant writer of Latin verse of that age. See also the " Paradise," canto ix. ; Berni, " Orlando Innamorato," lib. ii., c. xxv., st. 50 ; Ariosto, " Orlando Furioso," c. iii., st. 33 ; and Tassoni, " Secchia Rapita," c. viii., st. 11.

[2] *Obizzo of Este*, Marquis of Ferrara and of the Marca d'Ancona, was murdered by his own son (whom, for that most unnatural act, Dante calls his step-son) for the sake of the treasures which his rapacity had amassed. See Ariosto, " Orlando Furioso," c. iii., st. 32. He died in 1293, according to Gibbon, " Ant. of the House of Brunswick," Posthumous Works, v. ii., 4to.

[3] *He.*—" Henrie, the brother of this Edmund, and son to the aforesaid King of Almaine (Richard, brother of Henry III. of England), as he returned from Affrike, where he had been with Prince Edward, was slain at Viterbo in Italy (whither he was come about business which he had to do with the Pope), by the hand of Guy de Montfort, the son of Simon de Montfort, Earl of Leicester, in revenge of the same Simon's death. The murther was committed afore the high altar, as the same Henrie kneeled there to hear divine service."—A.D. 1272. *Holinshed's Chronicles*, p. 275. See also G. Villani, " Hist.," lib. vii., c. xl., where it is said " that the heart of Henry was put into a golden cup, and placed on a pillar at London Bridge over the river Thames, for a memorial to the English of the said outrage." Lombardi suggests that " ancor si cola " in the text may mean, not that " the heart was still honoured," but that it was put into a perforated cup in order that the blood dripping from it might excite the spectators to revenge. This is surely too improbable.

    " Un poco prima dove più si stava
      Sicuro Enrico, il conte di Monforte
      L'alma del corpo col coltel gli cava."
Fazio degli Uberti, Dittamondo, l. ii., cap. xxix.

There Heaven's stern justice lays chastising hand
On Attila, who was the scourge of earth,
On Sextus and on Pyrrhus,[1] and extracts
Tears ever by the seething flood unlock'd
From the Rinieri, of Corneto this,
Pazzo the other named,[2] who fill'd the ways
With violence and war." This said, he turn'd,
And quitting us, alone re-pass'd the ford.

----

[1] *On Sextus and on Pyrrhus.*—Sextus, either the son of Tarquin the Proud, or of Pompey the Great: and Pyrrhus, King of Epirus.

[2] *The Rinieri, of Corneto this, Pazzo the other named.*—Two noted marauders. The latter was of the noble family of Pazzi in Florence.

CANTO XIII.

———

ARGUMENT

Still in the seventh circle, Dante enters its second compartment, which contains both those who have done violence on their own persons and those who have violently consumed their goods; the first changed into rough and knotted trees whereon the harpies build their nests, the latter chased and torn by black female mastiffs. Among the former, Piero delle Vigne is one, who tells him the cause of his having committed suicide, and moreover in what manner the souls are transformed into those trunks. Of the latter crew he recognises Lano, a Siennese, and Giacomo, a Paduan ; and lastly, a Florentine, who had hung himself from his own roof, speaks to him of the calamities of his countrymen.

ERE Nessus yet had reach'd the other bank,
We enter'd on a forest,[1] where no track
Of steps had worn a way. Not verdant there
The foliage, but of dusky hue ; not light
The boughs and tapering, but with knares deform'd
And matted thick : fruits there were none, but thorns
Instead, with venom fill'd. Less sharp than these,
Less intricate the brakes, wherein abide
Those animals, that hate the cultured fields,
Betwixt Corneto and Cecina's stream.[2]

Here the brute Harpies make their nest, the same
Who from the Strophades[3] the Trojan band
Drove with dire boding of their future woe.
Broad are their pennons,[4] of the human form
Their neck and countenance, arm'd with talons keen
The feet, and the huge belly fledge with wings.
These sit and wail on the drear mystic wood.

The kind instructor in these words began :
" Ere further thou proceed, know thou art now

———

[1] *A forest.*—" Inde in aliam vallem nimis terribiliorem deveni plenam subtilissimis arboribus in modum hastarum sexaginta brachiorum longitudinem habentibus, quarum omnium capita, ac si sudes acutissima erant, et spinosa."—*Alberici Visio,* § 4.

[2] *Betwixt Corneto and Cecina's stream.*—A wild and woody tract of country, abounding in deer, goats, and wild boars. Cecina is a river not far to the south of Leghorn ; Corneto, a small city on the same coast, in the patrimony of the Church.

[3] *The Strophades.*—See Virgil," Æneid," lib. iii. 210.

[4] *Broad are their pennons.*—

" Virginei volucrum vultus, fœdissima ventris
Proluvies, uncæque manus, et pallida semper
Ora fame."

Virgil, Æneid, lib. iii. 216.

Here the brute Harpies make their nest.

Canto XIII. Line 13.

I' th' second round, and shalt be, till thou come
Upon the horrid sand : look therefore well
Around thee, and such things thou shalt behold,
As would my speech discredit." On all sides
I heard sad plainings breathe, and none could see
From whom they might have issued. In amaze
Fast bound I stood. He, as it seem'd, believed
That I had thought so many voices came
From some amid those thickets close conceal'd,
And thus his speech resumed : "If thou lop off
A single twig from one of those ill plants,
The thought thou hast conceived shall vanish quite."

Thereat a little stretching forth my hand,
From a great wilding gather'd I[1] a branch,
And straight the trunk exclaim'd, "Why pluck'st thou me ?"
Then, as the dark blood trickled down its side,
These words it added : "Wherefore tear'st me thus ?
Is there no touch of mercy in thy breast ?
Men once were we, that now are rooted here.
Thy hand might well have spared us, had we been
The souls of serpents." As a brand yet green,
That burning at one end from the other sends
A groaning sound, and hisses with the wind
That forces out its way, so burst at once
Forth from the broken splinter words and blood.

I, letting fall the bough, remain'd as one
Assail'd by terror ; and the sage replied :
"If he, oh, injured spirit ! could have believed
What he hath seen but in my verse described,[2]
He never against thee had stretch'd his hand.
But I, because the thing surpass'd belief,
Prompted him to this deed, which even now

Gather'd I.—So Frezzi :

   " A quelle frasche stesi su la mano,
     E d'una vetta un ramuscel ne colsi ;
     Allora ella gridò : oimè, fa piano,
    E sangue vivo usci, ond' io lo tolsi."

       Il Quadriregio, lib. i., cap. 4.

[2] *In my verse described.*—The commentators explain this, " If he could have believed, in consequence of my assurance alone, that of which he hath now had ocular proof, he would not have stretched forth his hand against thee." But I am of opinion that Dante makes Virgil allude to his own story of Polydorus, in the third book of the " Æneid."

Myself I rue. But tell me who thou wast;
That, for this wrong to do thee some amends,
In the upper world (for thither to return
Is granted him) thy fame he may revive."
"That pleasant word of thine,"[1] the trunk replied,
"Hath so inveigled me, that I from speech
Cannot refrain, wherein if I indulge
A little longer, in the snare detain'd,
Count it not grievous. I it was,[2] who held
Both keys to Frederick's heart, and turn'd the wards,
Opening and shutting, with a skill so sweet,
That besides me, into his inmost breast
Scarce any other could admittance find.
The faith I bore to my high charge was such,
It cost me the life-blood that warm'd my veins.
The harlot,[3] who ne'er turn'd her gloating eyes
From Cæsar's household, common vice and pest
Of courts, 'gainst me inflamed the minds of all;
And to Augustus they so spread the flame,
That my glad honours changed to bitter woes.
My soul, disdainful and disgusted, sought
Refuge in death from scorn, and I became,
Just as I was, unjust toward myself.
By the new roots, which fix this stem, I swear,
That never faith I broke to my liege lord,
Who merited such honour; and of you,
If any to the world indeed return,

---

[1] *That pleasant word of thine.*—"Since you have inveigled me to speak by holding forth so gratifying an expectation, let it not displease you if I am as it were detained in the snare you have spread for me, so as to be somewhat prolix in my answer."

[2] *I it was.*—Piero delle Vigne, a native of Capua, who from a low condition raised himself, by his eloquence and legal knowledge, to the office of Chancellor to the Emperor Frederick II.; whose confidence in him was such, that his influence in the empire became unbounded. The courtiers, envious of his exalted situation, contrived, by means of forged letters, to make Frederick believe that he held a secret and traitorous intercourse with the Pope, who was then at enmity with the Emperor. In consequence of this supposed crime, he was cruelly condemned, by h[is] too credulous sovereign, to lose his eyes; and bein[g] driven to despair by his unmerited calamity and di[s]grace, he put an end to his life by dashing out h[is] brains against the walls of a church, in the year 124[9]. Both Frederick and Piero delle Vigne compose[d] verses in the Sicilian dialect, which are now extan[t]. A canzone by each of them may be seen in the nint[h] book of the "Sonetti" and "Canzoni di diversi Auto[ri] Toscani," published by the Giunti in 1527.

[3] *The harlot.*—Envy. Chaucer alludes to this, i[n] the Prologue to the "Legende of Good Women":

    "Envie is lavender to the court alway,
      For she ne parteth neither night ne day
      Out of the house of Cesar: thus saith Dant."

Clear he from wrong my memory, that lies
Yet prostrate under envy's cruel blow."
   First somewhat pausing, till the mournful words
Were ended, then to me the bard began :
"Lose not the time ; but speak, and of him ask,
If more thou wish to learn." Whence I replied :
"Question thou him again of whatsoe'er
Will, as thou think'st, content me ; for no power
Have I to ask, such pity is at my heart."
   He thus resumed : "So may he do for thee
Freely what thou entreatest, as thou yet
Be pleased, imprison'd spirit ! to declare,
How in these gnarled joints the soul is tied ;
And whether any ever from such frame
Be loosen'd, if thou canst, that also tell."
   Thereat the trunk breathed hard, and the wind soon
Changed into sounds articulate like these :
"Briefly ye shall be answer'd. When departs
The fierce soul from the body, by itself
Thence torn asunder, to the seventh gulf
By Minos doom'd, into the wood it falls,
No place assign'd, but wheresoever chance
Hurls it ; there sprouting, as a grain of spelt,
It rises to a sapling, growing thence
A savage plant. The Harpies, on its leaves
Then feeding, cause both pain, and for the pain
A vent to grief. We, as the rest, shall come
For our own spoils, yet not so that with them
We may again be clad ; for what a man
Takes from himself it is not just he have.
Here we perforce shall drag them ; and throughout
The dismal glade our bodies shall be hung,
Each on the wild thorn of his wretched shade."
   Attentive yet to listen to the trunk
We stood, expecting further speech, when us
A noise surprised ; as when a man perceives
The wild boar and the hunt approach his place
Of station'd watch, who of the beasts and boughs

Loud rustling round him hears. And, lo! there came
Two naked, torn with briers, in headlong flight,
That they before them broke each fan o' th' wood.[1]
"Haste now," the foremost cried, "now haste thee, death!"
The other, as seem'd, impatient of delay,
Exclaiming, "Lano![2] not so bent for speed
Thy sinews, in the lists of Toppo's field."
And then, for that perchance no longer breath
Sufficed him, of himself and of a bush
One group he made. Behind them was the wood
Full of black female mastiffs, gaunt and fleet,
As greyhounds that have newly slipt the leash.
On him, who squatted down, they stuck their fangs,
And having rent him piecemeal bore away
The tortured limbs. My guide then seized my hand,
And led me to the thicket, which in vain
Mourn'd through its bleeding wounds: "O Giacomo
Of Sant' Andrea![3] what avails it thee,"
It cried, "that of me thou hast made thy screen?
For thy ill life, what blame on me recoils?"

When o'er it he had paused, my master spake:
"Say who wast thou, that at so many points
Breathest out with blood thy lamentable speech?"

He answer'd: "Oh, ye spirits! arrived in time
To spy the shameful havoc that from me
My leaves have sever'd thus, gather them up,
And at the foot of their sad parent-tree
Carefully lay them. In that city[4] I dwelt,

---

[1] *Each fan o' th' wood.*—Hence perhaps Milton:
   "Leaves and fuming rills, Aurora's fan,"
                 Paradise Lost, b. v. 6.
Some have translated "rosta" "impediment," instead of "fan."

[2] *Lano!*—Lano, a Siennese, who being reduced by prodigality to a state of extreme want, found his existence no longer supportable; and having been sent by his countrymen on a military expedition to assist the Florentines against the Aretini, took that opportunity of exposing himself to certain death, in the engagement which took place at Toppo, near Arezzo. See G. Villani, "Hist.," lib. vii., c. cxix.

[3] *O Giacomo of Sant' Andrea!*—Jacopo da S. Andrea, a Paduan, who, having wasted his prope in the most wanton acts of profusion, killed himself despair.

[4] *In that city.*—"I was an inhabitant of F ence, that city which changed her first patron M for St. John the Baptist; for which reason vengeance of the deity thus slighted will never appeased; and if some remains of his statue w not still visible on the bridge over the Arno, would have been already levelled to the ground; thus the citizens, who raised her again from the as to which Attila had reduced her, would have labou

"Haste now," the foremost cried, "now haste thee, death!"
Canto XIII., line 120.

Who for the Baptist her first patron changed,
Whence he for this shall cease not with his art
To work her woe : and if there still remain'd not
On Arno's passage some faint glimpse of him,
Those citizens, who rear'd once more her walls
Upon the ashes left by Attila,
Had labour'd without profit of their toil.
I slung the fatal noose[1] from my own roof."

---

in vain."　See " Paradise," canto xvi. 44.　The relic of antiquity, to which the superstition of Florence attached so high an importance, was carried away by a flood, that destroyed the bridge on which it stood, in the year 1337, but without the ill effects that were apprehended from the loss of their fancied Palladium.

[1] *I slung the fatal noose.*—We are not informed who this suicide was ; some calling him Rocco de' Mozzi, and others Lotto degli Angli.

CANTO XIV.

ARGUMENT.

They arrive at the beginning of the third of those compartments into which this seventh circle is divided. It is a plain of dry and hot sand, where three kinds of violence are punished; namely, against God, against Nature, and against Art; and those who have thus sinned are tormented by flakes of fire, which are eternally showering down upon them. Among the violent against God is found Capaneus, whose blasphemies they hear. Next, turning to the left along the forest of self-slayers, and having journeyed a little onwards, they meet with a streamlet of blood that issues from the forest and traverses the sandy plain. Here Virgil speaks to our poet of a huge ancient statue that stands within Mount Ida in Crete, from a fissure in which statue there is a dripping of tears, from which the said streamlet, together with the three other infernal rivers, are formed.

SOON as the charity of native land
 Wrought in my bosom, I the scatter'd leaves
Collected, and to him restored, who now
Was hoarse with utterance. To the limit thence
We came, which from the third the second round
Divides, and where of justice is display'd
Contrivance horrible. Things then first seen
Clearlier to manifest, I tell how next
A plain we reach'd, that from its sterile bed
Each plant repell'd. The mournful wood waves round
Its garland on all sides, as round the wood
Spreads the sad fosse. There, on the very edge,
Our steps we stay'd. It was an area wide
Of arid sand and thick, resembling most
The soil that erst by Cato's foot[1] was trod.

 Vengeance of heaven! Oh! how shouldst thou be fear'd
By all, who read what here mine eyes beheld.

 Of naked spirits many a flock I saw,
All weeping piteously, to different laws
Subjected; for on the earth some lay supine,
Some crouching close were seated, others paced

---

[1] *By Cato's foot.*—See Lucan, " Pharsalia," lib. ix.

Incessantly around ; the latter tribe
More numerous, those fewer who beneath
The torment lay, but louder in their grief.
　　　O'er all the sand fell slowly wafting down
Dilated flakes of fire,[1] as flakes of snow
On Alpine summit, when the wind is hush'd,
As, in the torrid Indian clime,[2] the son
Of Ammon saw, upon his warrior band
Descending, solid flames, that to the ground
Came down ; whence he bethought him with his troop
To trample on the soil ; for easier thus
The vapour was extinguish'd, while alone :
So fell the eternal fiery flood, wherewith
The marle glow'd underneath, as under stove[3]
The viands, doubly to augment the pain.
Unceasing was the play of wretched hands,
Now this, now that way glancing, to shake off
The heat, still falling fresh.　I thus began :
"Instructor ! thou who all things overcomest,
Except the hardy demons that rush'd forth
To stop our entrance at the gate, say who
Is yon huge spirit, that, as seems, heeds not
The burning, but lies writhen in proud scorn,
As by the sultry tempest immatured ?"
　　　Straight he himself, who was aware I ask'd
My guide of him, exclaim'd : "Such as I was
When living, dead such now I am.　If Jove
Weary his workman out, from whom in ire
He snatch'd the lightnings, that at my last day
Transfix'd me ; if the rest he weary out,
At their black smithy labouring by turns,
In Mongibello,[4] while he cries aloud,

---

[1] *Dilated flakes of fire.*—Compare Tasso, "Gieru-
salemme Liberata," c. x., st. 61 :
　　" Al fin giungemmo al loco, ove già scese
　　Fiamma del cielo in dilatate falde,
　　E di natura vendicò l' offese
　　Sovra la gente in mal oprar si salde."
[2] *As, in the torrid Indian clime.*—Landino refers
to Albertus Magnus for the circumstance here alluded to.

[3] *As under stove.*—So Frezzi :
　　" Si come l' esca al foco del focile."
　　　　　　　　　　　Lib. i., cap. 17.
[4] *In Mongibello.*—
　　" More hot than Ætn' or flaming Mongibell."
　　　　Spenser, *Faëry Queen*, b. ii., c. ix., st. 29.
　　" Siccome alla fucina in Mongibello
　　Fabrica tuono il demonio Vulcano,

'Help, help, good Mulciber!' as erst he cried
In the Phlegræan warfare; and the bolts
Launch he, full aim'd at me, with all his might;
He never should enjoy a sweet revenge."

Then thus my guide, in accent higher raised
Than I before had heard him: "Capaneus!
Thou art more punish'd, in that this thy pride
Lives yet unquench'd: no torment, save thy rage,
Were to thy fury pain proportion'd full."

Next turning round to me, with milder lip
He spake: "This of the seven kings was one,[1]
Who girt the Theban walls with siege, and held,
As still he seems to hold, God in disdain,
And sets his high omnipotence at nought.
But, as I told him, his despiteful mood
Is ornament well suits the breast that wears it.
Follow me now; and look thou set not yet
Thy foot in the hot sand, but to the wood
Keep ever close." Silently on we pass'd
To where there gushes from the forest's bound
A little brook, whose crimson'd wave yet lifts
My hair with horror. As the rill, that runs
From Bulicame,[2] to be portion'd out
Among the sinful women; so ran this
Down through the sand; its bottom and each bank
Stone-built, and either margin at its side,
Whereon I straight perceived our passage lay.

"Of all that I have shown thee, since that gate
We enter'd first, whose threshold is to none
Denied, nought else so worthy of regard,
As is this river, has thine eye discern'd,
O'er which the flaming volley all is quench'd."

Batte folgori e foco col martello,
E con esso i suoi fabri in ogni mano."
Berni, Orlando Innamorato, lib. i., c. xvi., st. 21.

See Virgil, "Æneid," lib. viii. 416. It would be endless to refer to parallel passages in the Greek writers.

[1] *This of the seven kings was one.*—Compare Æschylus, "Seven Chiefs," 425; Euripides, "Phœnissæ," 1170; and Statius, "Thebais," lib. x. 821.

[2] *Bulicame.*—A warm medicinal spring near Viterbo; the waters of which, as Landino and Vellutelli affirm, passed by a place of ill fame. Venturi conjectures that Dante would imply that it was the scene of much licentious merriment among those who frequented its baths.

So spake my guide ; and I him thence besought,
That having given me appetite to know,
The food he too would give, that hunger craved.
  "In midst of ocean," forthwith he began,
"A desolate country lies, which Crete is named ;
Under whose monarch,[1] in old times, the world
Lived pure and chaste. A mountain rises there,
Call'd Ida, joyous once with leaves and streams,
Deserted now like a forbidden thing.
It was the spot which Rhea, Saturn's spouse,
Chose for the secret cradle of her son ;
And better to conceal him, drown'd in shouts
His infant cries. Within the mount, upright
An ancient form there stands, and huge, that turns
His shoulders towards Damiata ; and at Rome,
As in his mirror, looks. Of finest gold
His head[2] is shaped, pure silver are the breast
And arms, thence to the middle is of brass,
And downward all beneath well-temper'd steel,
Save the right foot of potter's clay, on which
Than on the other more erect he stands.
Each part, except the gold, is rent throughout ;
And from the fissure tears distil, which join'd
Penetrate to that cave. They in their course
Thus far precipitated down the rock,
Form Acheron, and Styx, and Phlegethon ;
Then by this straiten'd channel passing hence
Beneath, e'en to the lowest depth of all,
Form there Cocytus, of whose lake (thyself
Shalt see it) I here give thee no account."
  Then I to him : "If from our world this sluice
Be thus derived ; wherefore to us but now

---

[1] *Under whose monarch.—*

  "Credo pudicitiam Saturno rege moratam
    In terris."   *Juvenal, Satires,* vi.

  "In Saturn's reign, at Nature's early birth,
    There was a thing call'd chastity on earth."
                              Dryden.

[2] *His head.—*This is imitated by Frezzi, in the
"Quadriregio," lib. iv., cap. 14 :
  "La statua grande vidi in un gran piano," &c.
" This image's head was of fine gold, his breast and
his arms of silver, his belly and his thighs of brass,
his legs of iron, his feet part of iron and part of clay."
—*Dan.* ii. 32, 33.

Appears it at this edge ? " He straight replied :
" The place, thou know'st, is round : and though great part
Thou have already past, still to the left
Descending to the nethermost, not yet
Hast thou the circuit made of the whole orb.
Wherefore, if aught of new to us appear,
It needs not bring up wonder in thy looks."
 Then I again inquired : " Where flow the streams
Of Phlegethon and Lethe ? for of one
Thou tell'st not ; and the other, of that shower,
Thou say'st, is form'd." He answer thus return'd :
" Doubtless thy questions all well pleased I hear.
Yet the red seething wave [1] might have resolved
One thou proposest. Lethe thou shalt see,
But not within this hollow, in the place
Whither,[2] to lave themselves, the spirits go,
Whose blame hath been by penitence removed."
He added : " Time is now we quit the wood.
Look thou my steps pursue : the margins give
Safe passage, unimpeded by the flames ;
For over them all vapour is extinct."

---

[1] *The red seething wave.*—This he might have known was Phlegethon.

[2] *In the place whither.*—On the other side of Purgatory.

CANTO XV.

ARGUMENT.

Taking their way upon one of the mounds by which the streamlet, spoken of in the last canto, was embanked, and having gone so far as they could no longer have discerned the forest if they had turned round to look for it, they meet a troop of spirits that come along the sand by the side of the pier. These are they who have done violence to Nature; and amongst them Dante distinguishes Brunetto Latini, who had been formerly his master; with whom, turning a little backward, he holds a discourse which occupies the remainder of this canto.

ONE of the solid margins bears us now
    Envelop'd in the mist, that, from the stream
Arising, hovers o'er, and saves from fire
Both piers and water. As the Flemings rear
Their mound, 'twixt Ghent and Bruges, to chase back
The ocean, fearing his tumultuous tide
That drives toward them; or the Paduans theirs
Along the Brenta, to defend their towns
And castles, ere the genial warmth be felt
On Chiarentana's[1] top; such were the mounds,
So framed, though not in height or bulk to these
Made equal, by the master, whosoe'er
He was, that raised them here. We from the wood
Were now so far removed, that turning round
I might not have discern'd it, when we met
A troop of spirits, who came beside the pier.

    They each one eyed us, as at eventide
One eyes another under a new moon;
And toward us sharpen'd their sight, as keen
As an old tailor at his needle's eye.[2]

    Thus narrowly explored by all the tribe,
I was agnised of one, who by the skirt
Caught me, and cried, " What wonder have we here ? "

    And I, when he to me outstretch'd his arm,

---

[1] *Ere the genial warmth be felt on Chiarentana's top.*—A part of the Alps where the Brenta rises: which river is much swollen as soon as the snow begins to dissolve on the mountains.

[2] *As an old tailor at his needle's eye.*—In Fazio degli Uberti's " Dittamondo." l. iv., cap. 4. the tailor is introduced in a simile scarcely less picturesque :

  " Perchè tanto mi stringe a questo punto
    La lunga tema, ch' io fo come il sarto
    Che quando affretta spesso passa il punto."

Intently fix'd my ken on his parch'd looks,
That, although smirch'd with fire, they hinder'd not
But I remember'd him ; and towards his face
My hand inclining, answer'd : "Ser Brunetto !"[1]

---

[1] *Brunetto.*—"Ser Brunetto, a Florentine, the secretary or chancellor of the city, and Dante's preceptor, hath left us a work so little read, that both the subject of it and the language of it have been mistaken. It is in the French spoken in the reign of St. Louis, under the title of 'Tresor'; and contains a species of philosophical course of lectures divided into theory and practice, or, as he expresses it, '*un enchaussement des choses divines et humaines,*'" &c. —*Sir R. Clayton's Translation of Tenhove's " Memoirs of the Medici,"* vol. i., ch. ii., p. 104. The " Tresor " has never been printed in the original language. There is a fine manuscript of it in the British Museum, with an illuminated portrait of Brunetto in his study, prefixed. Mus. Brit. MSS. 17, E. 1, Tesor. It is divided into four books · the first, on Cosmogony and Theology ; the second, a translation of Aristotle's Ethics ; the third, on Virtues and Vices ; the fourth, on Rhetoric. For an interesting memoir relating to this work, see " Hist. de l'Acad. des Inscriptions," tom. vii. 296. His " Tesoretto," one of the earliest productions of Italian poetry, is a curious work, not unlike the writings of Chaucer in style and numbers ; though Bembo remarks that his pupil, however largely he had stolen from it, could not have much enriched himself. As it is perhaps but little known, I will here add a slight sketch of it. Brunetto describes himself as returning from an embassy to the King of Spain, on which he had been sent by the Guelph party from Florence. On the plain of Roncesvalles he meets a scholar on a bay mule—

> " Un scolaio
> Sur un muletto baio "—
> There a scholar I espied
> On a bay mule that did ride "—

who tells him that the Guelfi are driven out of the city with great loss. Struck with grief at these mournful tidings, and musing with his head bent downwards, he loses his road, and wanders into a wood. Here Nature, whose figure is described with sublimity, appears, and discloses to him the secrets of her operations. After this, he wanders into a desert—

> " Deh che paese fiero
> Trovai in quella parte
> Che s'io sapessi d'arte
> Quivi mi bisognava.
> Che quanto più mirava
> Più mi parea selvaggio,
> Quivi non a viaggio.
> Quivi non a persone.
> Quivi non a magione.
> Non bestia non uccello,
> Non fiume non ruscello.

> Non formica non mosca,
> Non cosa ch'io conosca
> Ed io pensando forte
> Dottai ben della morte,
> E non è maraviglia,
> Che ben trecento miglia,
> Durava d'ogni lato,
> Quel paese smagato "—

> " Well-away ! what fearful ground
> In that savage part I found.
> If of art I aught could ken
> Well behoved me use it then.
> More I look'd, the more I deem'd
> That it wild and desert seem'd
> Not a road was there in sight,
> Not a house, and not a wight ·
> Not a bird, and not a brute,
> Not a rill, and not a root :
> Not an emmet, not a fly,
> Not a thing I mote descry.
> Sore I doubted therewithal
> Whether death would me befall ;
> Nor was wonder, for around
> Full three hundred miles of ground
> Right across on every side
> Lay the desert bare and wide "—

and proceeds on his way, under the protection of a banner with which Nature had furnished him, till on the third day he finds himself in a pleasant champaign, where are assembled many emperors, kings, and sages :

> " Un gran piano giocondo
> Lo più gajo del mondo
> E lo più degnitoso "
> " Wide and far the champaign lay,
> None in all the earth so gay."

It is the habitation of Virtue and her daughters, the four Cardinal Virtues. Here Brunetto sees also Courtesy, Bounty, Loyalty, and Prowess, and hears the instructions they give to a knight, which occupy about a fourth part of the poem. Leaving this territory, he passes over valleys, mountains, woods, forests, and bridges, till he arrives in a beautiful valley covered with flowers on all sides, and the richest in the world ; but which was continually shifting its appearance from a round figure to a square, from obscurity to light, and from populousness to solitude. This is the region of Pleasure, or Cupid, who is accompanied by four ladies—Love, Hope, Fear, and Desire. In one part of it he meets with Ovid, and is instructed by him how to conquer the passion of love, and to escape from that place. After his escape, he makes his confession to a friar, and then returns to the forest of visions ; and, ascending a mountain, meets

And are ye here?"   He thus to me: "My son!
Oh, let it not displease thee, if Brunetto
Latini but a little space with thee
Turn back, and leave his fellows to proceed."

        I thus to him replied: "Much as I can,
I thereto pray thee; and if thou be willing
That I here seat me with thee, I consent;
His leave, with whom I journey, first obtain'd."

        "Oh, son!" said he, "whoever of this throng
One instant stops, lies then a hundred years,
No fan to ventilate him, when the fire
Smites sorest. Pass thou therefore on. I close
Will at thy garments walk, and then rejoin
My troop, who go mourning their endless doom."

        I dared not from the path descend to tread
On equal ground with him, but held my head
Bent down, as one who walks in reverent guise.

        "What chance or destiny," thus he began,
"Ere the last day, conducts thee here below?
And who is this that shows to thee the way?"

        "There up aloft," I answer'd, "in the life
Serene, I wander'd in a valley lost,
Before mine age[1] had to its fulness reach'd.
But yester-morn I left it: then once more
Into that vale returning, him I met;
And by this path homeward he leads me back."

---

with Ptolemy, a venerable old man. Here the narrative breaks off. The poem ends, as it began, with an address to Rustico di Filippo, on whom he lavishes every sort of praise. It has been observed that Dante derived the idea of opening his poem, by describing himself as lost in a wood, from the "Tesoretto" of his master. I know not whether it has been remarked that the crime of usury is branded by both these poets as offensive to God and Nature:

> "Un altro, che non cura
>   Di Dio ne di Natura,
> Si diventa usuriere "—
> " One, that holdeth not in mind
>   Law of God or Nature's kind,
> Taketh him to usury "—

or that the sin for which Brunetto is condemned by his pupil is mentioned in his "Tesoretto" with great horror. But see what is said on this subject by Perticari, "Degli Scrittori del Trecento," l. i., c. iv. Dante's twenty-fifth sonnet is a jocose one, addressed to Brunetto, of which a translation is inserted in the Life of Dante, prefixed. He died in 1294. G. Villani sums up his account of him by saying that he was himself a worldly man; but that he was the first to refine the Florentines from their grossness, and to instruct them in speaking properly, and in conducting the affairs of the republic on principles of policy.

[1] *Before mine age.*—On the whole, Vellutello's explanation of this is, I think, most satisfactory. He supposes it to mean, "before the appointed end of his life was arrived—before his days were accomplished." Lombardi, concluding that the fulness of age must be the same as "the midway of this our mortal life" (see canto i., v. 1), understands that he had lost himself in the wood before that time, and that he then only discovered his having gone astray.

"If thou," he answer'd, "follow but thy star,
Thou canst not miss at last a glorious haven;
Unless in fairer days my judgment err'd.
And if my fate so early had not chanced,
Seeing the heavens thus bounteous to thee, I
Had gladly given thee comfort in thy work.
But that ungrateful and malignant race,
Who in old times came down from Fesole,[1]
Ay, and still smack of their rough mountain-flint,
Will for thy good deeds show thee enmity.
Nor wonder; for amongst ill-savour'd crabs
It suits not the sweet fig-tree lay her fruit.
Old fame reports them in the world for blind,[2]
Covetous, envious, proud. Look to it well:
Take heed thou cleanse thee of their ways. For thee,
Thy fortune hath such honour in reserve,
That thou by either party shalt be craved
With hunger keen: but be the fresh herb far
From the goat's tooth. The herd of Fesole
May of themselves make litter, not touch the plant,
If any such yet spring on their rank bed,
In which the holy seed revives, transmitted
From those true Romans, who still there remain'd,
When it was made the nest of so much ill."

"Were all my wish fulfill'd," I straight replied,
"Thou from the confines of man's nature yet
Hadst not been driven forth; for in my mind
Is fix'd, and now strikes full upon my heart,
The dear, benign, paternal image, such
As thine was, when so lately thou didst teach me
The way for man to win eternity:
And how I prized the lesson, it behoves,
That, long as life endures, my tongue should speak.
What of my fate thou tell'st, that write I down;
And, with another text[3] to comment on,

---

[1] *Fesole.*—See G. Villani, "Hist.," lib. iv., cap. v., and Macchiavelli, "History of Florence," b. ii.

[2] *Blind.*—It is said that the Florentines were thus called, in consequence of their having been deceived by a shallow artifice practised on them by the Pisans in the year 1117. See G. Villani, lib. iv., cap. xxx.

[3] *With another text.*—He refers to the prediction of Farinata, in canto x.

For her I keep it, the celestial dame,
Who will know all, if I to her arrive.
This only would I have thee clearly note :
That, so my conscience have no plea against me,
Do Fortune as she list, I stand prepared.
Not new or strange such earnest to mine ear.
Speed Fortune then her wheel, as likes her best ;
The clown his mattock ; all things have their course."

  Thereat my sapient guide upon his right
Turn'd himself back, then looked at me, and spake :
" He listens to good purpose who takes note."

  I not the less still on my way proceed,
Discoursing with Brunetto, and inquire
Who are most known and chief among his tribe.

  " To know of some is well ;" he thus replied,
" But of the rest silence may best beseem.
Time would not serve us for report so long.
In brief I tell thee, that all these were clerks,
Men of great learning and no less renown,
By one same sin polluted in the world.
With them is Priscian ;[1] and Accorso's son,
Francesco,[2] herds among that wretched throng :
And, if the wish of so impure a blotch
Possess'd thee, him[3] thou also mightst have seen,
Who by the servants' servant[4] was transferr'd
From Arno's seat to Bacchiglione, where
His ill-strain'd nerves he left. I more would add,
But must from further speech and onward way

---

[1] *Priscian.*—There is no reason to believe, as the commentators observe, that the grammarian of this name was stained with the vice imputed to him ; and we must therefore suppose that Dante puts the individual for the species, and implies the frequency of the crime among those who abused the opportunities which the education of youth afforded them, to so abominable a purpose.

[2] *Francesco.*—Accorso, a Florentine, interpreted the Roman law at Bologna, and died in 1229, at the age of seventy-eight. His authority was so great as to exceed that of all the other interpreters, so that Cino da Pistoia termed him the " Idol of Advocates." His sepulchre, and that of his son Francesco, here spoken of, is at Bologna, with this short epitaph : " Sepulcrum Accursii Glossatoris et Francisci ejus Filii." See Guido Panziroli, " De Claris Legum Interpretibus," lib. ii., cap. xxix., Lips., 4to, 1721.

[3] *Him.*—Andrea de' Mozzi, who, that his scandalous life might be less exposed to observation, was translated either by Nicholas III. or Boniface VIII. from the see of Florence to that of Vicenza, through which passes the river Bacchiglione. At the latter of these places he died.

[4] *The servants' servant.*—Servo de' servi. So Ariosto, Sat. iii. :

    " Degli servi
    Io sia il gran servo."

Alike desist ; for yonder I behold
A mist new-risen on the sandy plain.
A company, with whom I may not sort,
Approaches. I commend my Treasure to thee,[1]
Wherein I yet survive ; my sole request."

    This said, he turn'd, and seemed as one of those
Who o'er Verona's champaign try their speed
For the green mantle ; and of them he seem'd,
Not he who loses but who gains the prize.

---

[1] *I commend my Treasure to thee.*—Brunetto's great work, the " Trésor."

    " Sieti raccomandato il mio Tesoro."

So Giusto de' Conti, in his Bella Mano, Son. " Occhi : "

    " Siavi raccomandato il mio Tesoro."

CANTO XVI.

NOW came I where the water's din was heard,
    As down it fell into the other round,
Resounding like the hum of swarming bees :
When forth together issued from a troop,
That pass'd beneath the fierce tormenting storm,
Three spirits, running swift. They towards us came,
And each one cried aloud, "Oh ! do thou stay,
Whom, by the fashion of thy garb, we deem
To be some inmate of our evil land."

    Ah me ! what wounds I mark'd upon their limbs,
Recent and old, inflicted by the flames.
E'en the remembrance of them grieves me yet.

    Attentive to their cry, my teacher paused,
And turn'd to me his visage, and then spake :
"Wait now : our courtesy these merit well ;
And were 't not for the nature of the place,
Whence glide the fiery darts, I should have said,
That haste had better suited thee than them."

    They, when we stopp'd, resumed their ancient wail,
And, soon as they had reach'd us, all the three
Whirl'd round together in one restless wheel.
As naked champions, smear'd with slippery oil,
Are wont, intent, to watch their place of hold
And vantage, ere in closer strife they meet ;
Thus each one, as he wheel'd, his countenance
At me directed, so that opposite

L.

The neck moved ever to the twinkling feet.
   "If woe of this unsound and dreary waste,"
Thus one began, "added to our sad cheer
Thus peel'd with flame, do call forth scorn on us
And our entreaties, let our great renown
Incline thee to inform us who thou art,
That dost imprint, with living feet unharm'd,
The soil of Hell. He, in whose track thou seest
My steps pursuing, naked though he be
And reft of all, was of more high estate
Than thou believest; grandchild of the chaste
Gualdrada,[1] him they Guidoguerra call'd,
Who in his lifetime many a noble act[2]
Achieved, both by his wisdom and his sword.
The other, next to me that beats the sand,
Is Aldobrandi,[3] name deserving well,
In the upper world, of honour; and myself,
Who in this torment do partake with them,

---

[1] *Gualdrada.*—Gualdrada was the daughter of Bellincione Berti, of whom mention is made in the "Paradise," canto xv. and xvi. He was of the family of Ravignani, a branch of the Adimari. The Emperor Otho IV., being at a festival in Florence where Gualdrada was present, was struck with her beauty; and inquiring who she was, was answered by Bellincione that she was the daughter of one who, if it was His Majesty's pleasure, would make her admit the honour of his salute. On overhearing this she arose from her seat, and blushing, in an animated tone of voice desired her father that he would not be so liberal in his offers, for that no man should ever be allowed that freedom except him who should be her lawful husband. The emperor was not less delighted by her resolute modesty than he had before been by the loveliness of her person; and calling to him Guido, one of his barons, gave her to him in marriage, at the same time raising him to the rank of a count, and bestowing on her the whole of Casentino, and a part of the territory of Romagna, as her portion. Two sons were the offspring of this union, Guglielmo and Ruggieri: the latter of whom was father of Guidoguerra, a man of great military skill and prowess, who, at the head of four hundred Florentines of the Guelph party, was signally instrumental to the victory obtained at Benevento by Charles of Anjou, over Manfredi, King of Naples, in 1265. One of the consequences of this victory was the expulsion of the Ghibellini, and the re-establishment of the Guelfi at Florence. Borghini ("Disc. dell' Orig. di Firenze," ediz. 1755, p. 6), as cited by Lombardi, endeavours by a comparison o[f] dates to throw discredit on the above relation o[f] Gualdrada's answer to her father, which is found in G[iov.] Villani, lib. v., c. xxxvii.: and Lombardi adds, that i[f] it had been true, Bellincione would have been worth[y] of a place in the eighteenth canto of "Hell," rathe[r] than of being mentioned with praise in the "Para[-] dise": to which it may be answered, that the proposa[l] of the father, however irreconcilable it may be to ou[r] notions of modern refinement, might possibly in thos[e] times have been considered rather as a sportive sall[y] than as a serious exposure of his daughter's innocence[.] The incident is related, in a manner very unfavour[-] able to Berti, by Francesco Sansovino, in one of hi[s] "Novelle," inserted by Mr. Thomas Roscoe in hi[s] entertaining selection from the Italian novelists, v[ol.] iii., p. 137.

[2] *Many a noble act.*—

   "Molto egli oprò col senno e con la mano."
      Tasso, Gierusalemme Liberata, c. i., st. 1.

[3] *Aldobrandi.*—Tegghiaio Aldobrandi was of th[e] noble family of Adimari, and much esteemed for hi[s] military talents. He endeavoured to dissuade th[e] Florentines from the attack which they meditate[d] against the Siennese; and the rejection of his couns[el] occasioned the memorable defeat which the form[er] sustained at Montaperto, and the consequent banish[-] ment of the Guelfi from Florence.

Am Rusticucci,[1] whom, past doubt, my wife,
Of savage temper, more than aught beside
Hath to this evil brought." If from the fire
I had been shelter'd, down amidst them straight
I then had cast me ; nor my guide, I deem,
Would have restrain'd my going : but that fear
Of the dire burning vanquish'd the desire,
Which made me eager of their wish'd embrace.

  I then began : "Not scorn, but grief much more,
Such as long time alone can cure, your doom
Fix'd deep within me, soon as this my lord
Spake words, whose tenor taught me to expect
That such a race, as ye are, was at hand.
I am a countryman of yours, who still
Affectionate have utter'd, and have heard
Your deeds and names renown'd. Leaving the gall,
For the sweet fruit I go, that a sure guide
Hath promised to me. But behoves, that far
As to the centre first I downward tend."

  "So may long space thy spirit guide thy limbs,"
He answer straight return'd ; "and so thy fame
Shine bright when thou art gone, as thou shalt tell,
If courtesy and valour, as they wont,
Dwell in our city, or have vanish'd clean :
For one amidst us late condemn'd to wail,
Borsiere,[2] yonder walking with his peers,
Grieves us no little by the news he brings."

  "An upstart multitude and sudden gains,
Pride and excess, O Florence ! have in thee
Engender'd, so that now in tears thou mourn'st !"

  Thus cried I, with my face upraised, and they
All three, who for an answer took my words,
Look'd at each other, as men look when truth
Comes to their ear. "If at so little cost."[3]

---

[1] *Rusticucci.*—Giacopo Rusticucci, a Florentine, markable for his opulence and the generosity of his irit.

[2] *Borsiere.*—Guglielmo Borsiere, another Floren-ie, whom Boccaccio, in a story which he relates of m, terms " a man of courteous and elegant manners, and of great readiness in conversation."—*Decameron,* Giorn. i., Nov. 8.

[3] *At so little cost.*—They intimate to our poet (as Lombardi well observes) the inconveniences to which his freedom of speech was about to expose him in the future course of his life.

They all at once rejoin'd, "thou satisfy
Others who question thee, oh happy thou!
Gifted with words so apt to speak thy thought,
Wherefore, if thou escape this darksome clime,
Returning to behold the radiant stars,
When thou with pleasure shalt retrace the past,[1]
See that of us thou speak among mankind."
    This said, they broke the circle, and so swift
Fled, that as pinions seem'd their nimble feet.
    Not in so short a time might one have said
"Amen," as they had vanish'd. Straight my guide
Pursued his track. I followed: and small space
Had we past onward, when the water's sound
Was now so near at hand, that we had scarce
Heard one another's speech for the loud din.
    E'en as the river,[2] that first holds its course
Unmingled, from the Mount of Vesulo,
On the left side of Apennine, toward
The east, which Acquacheta higher up
They call, ere it descend into the vale,
At Forli,[3] by that name no longer known,
Rebellows o'er Saint Benedict, roll'd on
From the Alpine summit down a precipice,
Where space[4] enough to lodge a thousand spreads;
Thus downward from a craggy steep we found
That this dark wave resounded, roaring loud,
So that the ear its clamour soon had stunn'd.
    I had a cord[5] that braced my girdle round,
Wherewith I erst had thought fast bound to take

---

[1] *When thou with pleasure shalt retrace the past.*—
    " Quando ti giovera dicere io fui."
So Tasso, " Gierusalemme Liberata," c. xv., st. 38 :
    " Quando mi giovera narrar altrui
      Le novita vedute, e dire ; io fui."

[2] *E'en as the river.*—He compares the fall of Phlegethon to that of the Montone (a river in Romagna) from the Apennine above the Abbey of St. Benedict. All the other streams that rise between the sources of the Po and the Montone, and fall from the left side of the Apennine, join the Po, and accompany it to the sea.

[3] *At Forli.*—Because there it loses the name of Acquacheta, and takes that of Montone.

[4] *Where space.*—Either because the abbey was capable of containing more than those who occupied it, or because (says Landino) the lords of that territory, as Boccaccio related on the authority of the abbot, had intended to build a castle near the waterfall, and to collect within its walls the population of the neighbouring villages.

[5] *A cord.*—This passage, as it is confessed by Landino, involves a fiction sufficiently obscure. His own attempt to unravel it does not much lessen the difficulty. That which Lombardi has made is something better. It is believed that our poet, in the earlier part of is life, had entered into the order of St. Francis. By observing the rules of that profession,

The painted leopard. This when I had all
Unloosen'd from me (so my master bade)
I gather'd up, and stretch'd it forth to him.
Then to the right he turn'd, and from the brink
Standing few paces distant, cast it down
Into the deep abyss. "And somewhat strange,"
Thus to myself I spake, "signal so strange
Betokens, which my guide with earnest eye
Thus follows." Ah! what caution must men use
With those who look not at the deed alone,
But spy into the thoughts with subtle skill.[1]

　　"Quickly shall come," he said, "what I expect:
Thine eye discover quickly that, whereof
Thy thought is dreaming." Ever to that truth,[2]
Which but the semblance of a falsehood wears,
A man, if possible, should bar his lip;
Since, although blameless, he incurs reproach.
But silence here were vain; and by these notes,[3]
Which now I sing, reader, I swear to thee,
So may they favour find to latest times!
That through the gross and murky air I spied
A shape come swimming up, that might have quell'd
The stoutest heart with wonder; in such guise
As one returns, who hath been down to loose
An anchor grappled fast against some rock,
Or to aught else that in the salt wave lies,
Who, upward springing, close draws in his feet.

---

he had designed to mortify his carnal appetites, or, as he expresses it, "to take the painted leopard" (that animal, which, as we have seen in a note to the first canto, represented Pleasure) "with this cord." This part of the habit he is now desired by Virgil to take off; and it is thrown down the gulf, to allure Geryon to them with the expectation of carrying down one who had cloaked his iniquities under the garb of penitence and self-mortification; and thus (to apply to Dante on this occasion the words of Milton)—

"He, as Franciscan, thought to pass disguised."

[1] *But spy into the thoughts with subtle skill.*—
"Sorrise Uranio, che per entro vede
　　Gli altrui pensier col senno."
　　Menzini, Sonetto. Mentre io dormia.

[2] *Ever to that truth.*—This memorable apophthegm is repeated by Luigi Pulci and Trissino:

"Sempre a quel ver, ch' ha faccia di menzogna,
　E più senno tacer la lingua cheta,
　Che spesso senza colpa fa vergogna."
　　　　Morgante Maggiore, c. xxiv.
"La verità che par mensogna,
　Si dovrebbe tacer dall' uom ch' è saggio."
　　　　Italia Lib., c. xvi

[3] *By these notes.*—So Frezzi:
"Per queste rime mie, lettor, ti giuro."
　　　　Il Quadriregio, lib. iii., cap. 16.
In like manner, Pindar confirms his veracity by an oath:
"Ναὶ μὰ γὰρ Ὅρκον, ἐμὰν δόξαν."
　　　　Nem., xi. 30;
which is imitated, as usual, by Chiabrera:
"Ed io lungo il Permesso
　Sacro alle Muse obligherò mia fede."
　　　　Canz. Eroiche, xliii. 75.

CANTO XVII.

—

ARGUMENT

The monster Geryon is described ; to whom while Virgil is speaking in order that he may carry them both down to the next circle, Dante, by permission, goes a little further along the edge of the void, to descry the third species of sinners contained in this compartment, namely, those who have done violence to Art ; and then returning to his master, they both descend, seated on the back of Geryon.

"LO ! the fell monster[1] with the deadly sting,
    Who passes mountains, breaks through fenced walls,
And firm embattled spears, and with his filth
Taints all the world." Thus me my guide address'd,
And beckon'd him, that he should come to shore,
Near to the stony causeway's utmost edge.
    Forthwith that image vile of Fraud appear'd,
His head and upper part exposed on land,
But laid not on the shore his bestial train.
His face the semblance of a just man's wore,
So kind and gracious was its outward cheer ;
The rest was serpent all : two shaggy claws
Reach'd to the arm-pits ; and the back and breast,
And either side, were painted o'er with nodes
And orbits. Colours variegated more
Nor Turks nor Tartars e'er on cloth of state
With interchangeable embroidery wove,
Nor spread Arachne o'er her curious loom.
As oft-times a light skiff, moor'd to the shore,
Stands part in water, part upon the land ;
Or, as where dwells the greedy German boor,
The beaver settles, watching for his prey ;
So on the rim, that fenced the sand with rock,
Sat perch'd the fiend of evil. In the void

[1] *The fell monster.*—Fraud.

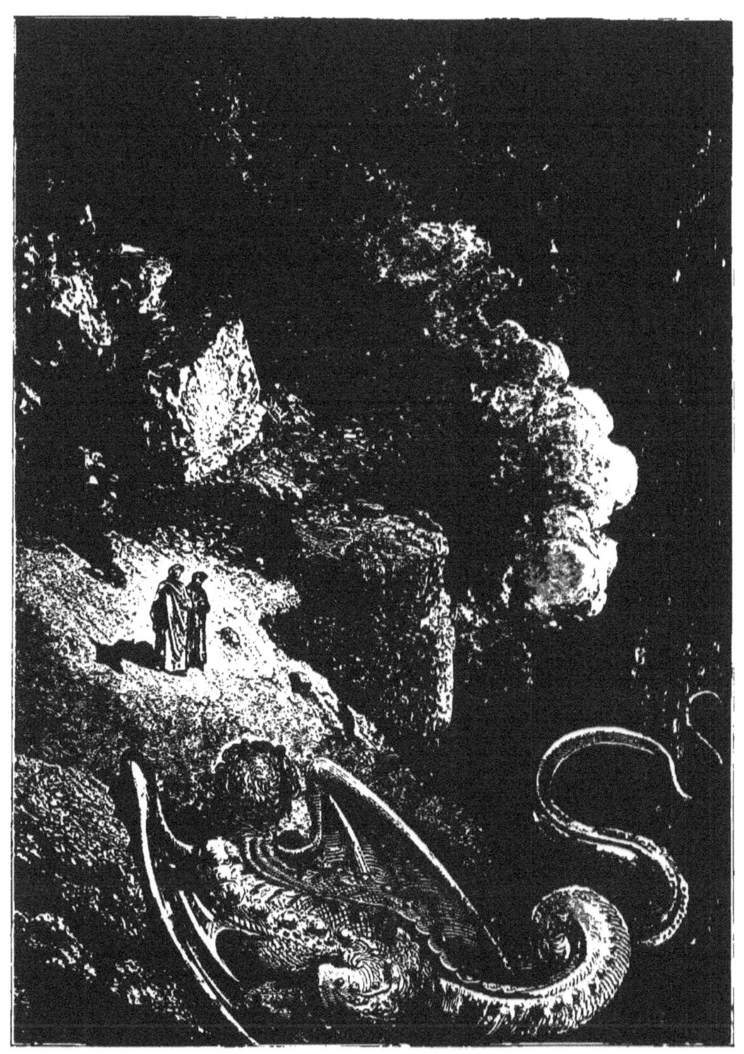

Forthwith that image vile of Fraud appear'd.

Canto *XVII.*, line 7.

Glancing, his tail upturned its venomous fork,
With sting like scorpion's arm'd. Then thus my guide :
" Now need our way must turn few steps apart,
Far as to that ill beast, who couches there."
　　Thereat, toward the right our downward course
We shaped, and, better to escape the flame
And burning marle, ten paces on the verge
Proceeded. Soon as we to him arrive,
A little further on mine eye beholds
A tribe of spirits, seated on the sand
Near to the void. Forthwith my master spake :
" That to the full thy knowledge may extend
Of all this round contains, go now, and mark
The mien these wear : but hold not long discourse.
Till thou returnest, I with him meantime
Will parley, that to us he may vouchsafe
The aid of his strong shoulders." Thus alone,
Yet forward on the extremity I paced
Of that seventh circle, where the mournful tribe
Were seated. At the eyes forth gush'd their pangs.
Against the vapours and the torrid soil
Alternately their shifting hands they plied.
Thus use the dogs in summer still to ply
Their jaws and feet by turns, when bitten sore
By gnats, or flies, or gadflies swarming round.
　　Noting the visages of some, who lay
Beneath the pelting of that dolorous fire,
One of them all I knew not ; but perceived,
That pendent from his neck each bore a pouch[1]
With colours and with emblems various mark'd,
On which it seem'd as if their eye did feed.
　　And when, amongst them, looking round I came,
A yellow purse[2] I saw with azure wrought,
That wore a lion's countenance and port.

---

[1] *A pouch.*—A purse, whereon the armorial bearings of each were emblazoned. According to Landino, our poet implies that the usurer can pretend to no other honour than such as he derives from his purse and his family. The description of persons by their heraldic insignia is remarkable on several occasions in this poem.

[2] *A yellow purse.*—The arms of the Gianfigliazzi of Florence.

Then, still my sight pursuing its career,
Another[1] I beheld, than blood more red,
A goose display of whiter wing than curd.
And one who bore a fat and azure swine[2]
Pictured on his white scrip, address'd me thus :
"What dost thou in this deep ? Go now and know,
Since yet thou livest, that my neighbour here
Vitaliano[3] on my left shall sit.
A Paduan with these Florentines am I.
Oft-times they thunder in mine ears, exclaiming,
'Oh ! haste that noble knight,[4] he who the pouch
With the three goats[5] will bring.'" This said, he writhed
The mouth, and loll'd the tongue out, like an ox
That licks his nostrils. I, lest longer stay
He ill might brook, who bade me stay not long,
Backward my steps from those sad spirits turn'd.

My guide already seated on the haunch
Of the fierce animal I found ; and thus
He me encouraged. "Be thou stout : be bold.
Down such a steep flight must we now descend.
Mount thou before : for, that no power the tail
May have to harm thee, I will be i' th' midst."

As one,[6] who hath an ague fit so near,
His nails already are turn'd blue, and he
Quivers all o'er, if he but eye the shade ;
Such was my cheer at hearing of his words.
But shame[7] soon interposed her threat, who makes
The servant bold in presence of his lord.

---

[1] *Another.*—Those of the Ubbriachi, another Florentine family of high distinction.

[2] *A fat and azure swine.*—The arms of the Scrovigni, a noble family of Padua.

[3] *Vitaliano.*—Vitaliano del Dente, a Paduan.

[4] *That noble knight.*—Giovanni Bujamonti, a Florentine usurer, the most infamous of his time.

[5] *Goats.*—Monti, in his "Proposta," had introduced a facetious dialogue, on the supposed mistake made in the interpretation of this word "becchi" by the compilers of the Della Crusca Dictionary, who translated it "goats," instead of "beaks." He afterwards saw his own error, and had the ingenuousness to confess it in the Appendix, p. 274. Having in the former editions of this work been betrayed into the same misunderstanding of my author, I cannot do less than follow so good an example, by acknowledging and correcting it.

[6] *As one.*—Dante trembled with fear, like a man who, expecting the return of a quartan ague, shakes even at the sight of a place made cool by the shade.

[7] *But shame.*—I have followed the reading in Vellutello's edition :

 "Ma vergogna mi fe le sue minacce ";
which appears preferable to the common one,

 "Ma vergogna mi fer," &c.
It is necessary that I should observe this, because it has been imputed to me as a mistake.

New terror I conceived at the steep plunge.
Canto XVII., line 117.

I settled me upon those shoulders huge,
And would have said, but that the words to aid
My purpose came not, "Look thou clasp me firm.'
      But he whose succour then not first I proved,
Soon as I mounted, in his arms aloft,
Embracing, held me up ; and thus he spake :
"Geryon ! now move thee : be thy wheeling gyres
Of ample circuit, easy thy descent.
Think on the unusual burden thou sustain'st."
      As a small vessel, backening out from land,
Her station quits ; so thence the monster loosed,
And, when he felt himself at large, turn'd round
There, where the breast had been, his forked tail.
Thus, like an eel, outstretch'd at length he steer'd,
Gathering the air up with retractile claws.
      Not greater was the dread, when Phaëton
The reins let drop at random, whence high heaven,
Whereof signs yet appear, was wrapt in flames ;
Nor when ill-fated Icarus perceived,
By liquefaction of the scalded wax,
The trusted pennons loosen'd from his loins,
His sire exclaiming loud, "Ill way thou keep'st,"
Than was my dread, when round me on each part
The air I view'd, and other object none
Save the fell beast. He, slowly sailing, wheels
His downward motion, unobserved of me,
But that the wind, arising to my face,
Breathes on me from below. Now on our right
I heard the cataract beneath us leap
With hideous crash ; whence bending down to explore,
New terror I conceived at the steep plunge ;
For flames I saw, and wailings smote mine ear :
So that, all trembling, close I crouch'd my limbs,
And then distinguish'd, unperceived before,
By the dread torments that on every side
Drew nearer, how our downward course we wound.
      As falcon, that hath long been on the wing,
But lure nor bird hath seen, while in despair

The falconer cries, "Ah me ! thou stoop'st to earth,"
Wearied descends, whence nimbly he arose
In many an airy wheel, and 'lighting sits
At distance from his lord in angry mood ;
So Geryon 'lighting places us on foot
Low down at base of the deep-furrow'd rock,
And, of his burden there discharged, forthwith
Sprang forward, like an arrow from the string.

CANTO XVIII.

ARGUMENT.

The poet describes the situation and form of the eighth circle, divided into ten gulfs, which contain as many different descriptions of fraudulent sinners; but in the present canto he treats only of two sorts: the first is of those who, either for their own pleasure or for that of another, have seduced any woman from her duty; and these are scourged of demons in the first gulf: the other sort is of flatterers, who in the second gulf are condemned to remain immersed in filth.

THERE is a place within the depths of hell
   Call'd Malebolge, all of rock dark-stain'd
With hue ferruginous, e'en as the steep
That round it circling winds. Right in the midst
Of that abominable region yawns
A spacious gulf profound, whereof the frame
Due time shall tell. The circle, that remains,
Throughout its round, between the gulf and base
Of the high craggy banks, successive forms
Ten bastions, in its hollow bottom raised.

   As where, to guard the walls, full many a fosse
Begirds some stately castle, sure defence [1]
Affording to the space within; so here
Were modell'd these: and as like fortresses,
E'en from their threshold to the brink without,
Are flank'd with bridges; from the rock's low base
Thus flinty paths advanced, that 'cross the moles
And dikes struck onward far as to the gulf,

---

1 *Sure defence.*—

   "La parte dov' e' son rendon sicura."

This is the common reading; besides which there are two others:

   "La parte dove il sol rende figura;

and

   "La parte dov' ei son rende figura:"

the former of which two, Lombardi says, is found in Daniello's edition, printed at Venice, 1568; in that printed in the same city with the commentaries of Landino and Vellutello, 1572; and also in some MSS. The latter, which has very much the appearance of being genuine, was adopted by Lombardi himself, on the authority of a text supposed to be in the handwriting of Filippo Villani, but so defaced by the alterations made in it by some less skilful hand, that the traces of the old ink were with difficulty recovered; and it has, since the publication of Lombardi's edition, been met with also in the Monte Casino MS. Monti is decided in favour of Lombardi's reading, and Biagioli opposed to it.

That in one bound collected cuts them off.
Such was the place, wherein we found ourselves
From Geryon's back dislodged. The bard to left
Held on his way, and I behind him moved.

On our right hand new misery I saw,
New pains, new executioners of wrath,
That swarming peopled the first chasm. Below
Were naked sinners. Hitherward they came
Meeting our faces, from the middle point:
With us beyond,[1] but with a larger stride.
E'en thus the Romans,[2] when the year returns
Of Jubilee, with better speed to rid
The thronging multitudes, their means devise
For such as pass the bridge; that on one side
All front toward the castle, and approach
Saint Peter's fane, on the other towards the mount.

Each diverse way, along the grisly rock,
Horn'd demons I beheld, with lashes huge,
That on their back unmercifully smote.
Ah! how they made them bound at the first stripe!
None for the second waited, nor the third.

Meantime, as on I pass'd, one met my sight,
Whom soon as view'd, "Of him," cried I, "not yet
Mine eye hath had his fill." I therefore stay'd[3]
My feet to scan him, and the teacher kind
Paused with me, and consented I should walk
Backward a space; and the tormented spirit,
Who thought to hide him, bent his visage down.
But it avail'd him nought; for I exclaim'd:
"Thou who dost cast thine eye upon the ground,
Unless thy features do belie thee much,

---

[1] *Beyond.*—Beyond the middle point they tended the same way with us, but their pace was quicker than ours.

[2] *E'en thus the Romans.*—In the year 1300, Pope Boniface VIII., to remedy the inconvenience occasioned by the press of people who were passing over the bridge of St. Angelo during the time of the Jubilee, caused it to be divided lengthwise by a partition; and ordered that all those who were going to St. Peter's should keep one side, and those returning the other.

G. Villani, who was present, describes the order that was preserved, lib. viii., c. xxxvi. It was at this time, and on this occasion, as the honest historian tells us, that he first conceived the design of "compiling his book."

[3] *I therefore stay'd.*—"I piedi affissi" is the reading of the Nidobeatina edition; but Lombardi is under an error when he tells us that the other editions have "gli occhi affissi:" for Vellutello's at least, printed in 1544, agrees with the Nidobeatina.

M

Venedico[1] art thou. But what brings thee
Into this bitter seasoning ?"[2] He replied :
" Unwillingly I answer to thy words.
But thy clear speech, that to my mind recalls
The world I once inhabited, constrains me.
Know then 'twas I who led fair Ghisola
To do the Marquis' will, however fame
The shameful tale have bruited. Nor alone
Bologna hither sendeth me to mourn.
Rather with us the place is so o'erthrong'd,
That not so many tongues this day are taught,
Betwixt the Reno and Savena's stream,
To answer Sipa[3] in their country's phrase.
And if of that securer proof thou need,
Remember but our craving thirst for gold."

Him speaking thus, a demon with his thong
Struck, and exclaim'd, " Away, corrupter ! here
Women are none for sale." Forthwith I join'd
My escort, and few paces thence we came
To where a rock forth issued from the bank.
That easily ascended, to the right
Upon its splinter turning, we depart
From those eternal barriers. When arrived
Where, underneath, the gaping arch lets pass
The scourged souls : " Pause here," the teacher said,
" And let these others miserable now
Strike on thy ken ; faces not yet beheld,
For that together they with us have walk'd."

From the old bridge we eyed the pack, who came
From the other side toward us, like the rest,
Excoriate from the lash. My gentle guide,
By me unquestion'd, thus his speech resumed :
" Behold that lofty shade, who this way tends,
And seems too woe-begone to drop a tear.

---

[1] *Venedico.*—Venedico Caccianimico, a Bolognese, who prevailed on his sister Ghisola to prostitute herself to Obizzo da Este, Marquis of Ferrara.

[2] *Seasoning.*—Salse. Monti, in his " Proposta," takes this to be the name of a place.

[3] *To answer Sipa.*—He denotes Bologna by its situation between the rivers Savena to the east, and Reno to the west of that city : and by a peculiarity of dialect, the use of the affirmative *sipa* instead either of *si*, or, as Monti will have it, of *sia*.

How yet the regal aspect he retains !
Jason is he, whose skill and prowess won
The ram from Colchos. To the Lemnian isle
His passage thither led him, when those bold
And pitiless women had slain all their males.
There he with tokens and fair witching words
Hypsipyle[1] beguiled, a virgin young,
Who first had all the rest herself beguiled.
Impregnated, he left her there forlorn.
Such is the guilt condemns him to this pain.
Here too Medea's injuries are avenged.
All bear him company, who like deceit
To his have practised. And thus much to know
Of the first vale suffice thee, and of those
Whom its keen torments urge." Now had we come
Where, crossing the next pier, the straiten'd path
Bestrides its shoulders to another arch.

 Hence, in the second chasm we heard the ghosts,
Who gibber in low melancholy sounds,
With wide-stretch'd nostrils snort, and on themselves
Smite with their palms. Upon the banks a scurf,
From the foul steam condensed, encrusting hung,
That held sharp combat with the sight and smell.

 So hollow is the depth, that from no part,
Save on the summit of the rocky span,
Could I distinguish aught. Thus far we came ;
And thence I saw, within the fosse below,
A crowd immersed in ordure, that appear'd
Draff of the human body. There beneath
Searching with eye inquisitive, I mark'd
One with his head so grimed, 'twere hard to deem
If he were clerk or layman. Loud he cried :
" Why greedily thus bendest more on me,
Than on these other filthy ones, thy ken ?"

 " Because, if true my memory," I replied,
" I heretofore have seen thee with dry locks ;

---

[1] *Hypsipyle.*—See Apollonius Rhodius, l. i., and Valerius Flaccus, l. ii. Hypsipyle deceived the other women, by concealing her father Thoas, when they had agreed to put all their males to death.

"Why greedily thus bendest more on me,
Than on these other filthy ones thy look?"

Canto XVIII., lines 116, 117.

Thaïs is this, the harlot, whose false lip
Answer'd her doting paramour that ask'd,
"Thankest me much?"

Canto XVIII., lines 130—132.

And thou Alessio[1] art, of Lucca sprung.
Therefore than all the rest I scan thee more."
    Then beating on his brain, these words he spake:
"Me thus low down my flatteries have sunk,
Wherewith I ne'er enough could glut my tongue."
    My leader thus: "A little further stretch
Thy face, that thou the visage well mayst note
Of that besotted, sluttish courtesan,
Who there doth rend her with defiled nails,
Now crouching down, now risen on her feet.
Thaïs[2] is this, the harlot, whose false lip
Answer'd her doting paramour that ask'd,
'Thankest me much?'—'Say rather, wondrously,'
And, seeing this, here satiate be our view."

---

[1] *Alessio.*—Alessio, of an ancient and considerable family in Lucca, called the Interminei.

[2] *Thaïs.*—He alludes to that passage in the "Eunuchus" of Terence, where Thraso asks if Thaïs was obliged to him for the present he had sent her; and Gnatho replies, that she had expressed her obligation in the most forcible terms—

" *Thaïs.* Magnas vero agere gratias Thaïs mihi ?
 Gnatho. Ingentes."

Eunuchus. Act iii., sc. i.

CANTO XIX.

ARGUMENT.

They come to the third gulf, wherein are punished those who have been guilty of simony. These are fixed with the head downwards in certain apertures, so that no more of them than the legs appears without, and on the soles of their feet are seen burning flames. Dante is taken down by his guide into the bottom of the gulf: and there finds Pope Nicholas V., whose evil deeds, together with those of other pontiffs, are bitterly reprehended. Virgil then carries him up again to the arch, which affords them a passage over the following gulf.

WOE to thee, Simon Magus ! woe to you,
   His wretched followers ! who the things of God,
Which should be wedded unto goodness, them,
Rapacious as ye are, do prostitute
For gold and silver in adultery.
Now must the trumpet sound for you, since yours
Is the third chasm. Upon the following vault
We now had mounted, where the rock impends
Directly o'er the centre of the fosse.

   Wisdom Supreme ! how wonderful the art,
Which thou dost manifest in heaven, in earth,
And in the evil world, how just a meed
Allotting by thy virtue unto all.

   I saw the livid stone, throughout the sides
And in its bottom full of apertures,
All equal in their width, and circular each.
Nor ample less nor larger they appear'd
Than in Saint John's fair dome[1] of me beloved,
Those framed to hold the pure baptismal streams,
One of the which I brake, some few years past,
To save a whelming infant : and be this
A seal to undeceive whoever doubts

---

[1] *Saint John's fair dome.*—The apertures in the rock were of the same dimensions as the fonts of St. John the Baptist at Florence ; one of which, Dante says, he had broken, to rescue a child that was playing near and fell in. He intimates that the motive of his breaking the font had been maliciously represented by his enemies.

There stood I like the friar, that doth shrive
A wretch for murder doom'd.

Canto XIX., lines 10, 11.

The motive of my deed. From out the mouth
Of every one emerged a sinner's feet,
And of the legs high upward as the calf.
The rest beneath was hid. On either foot
The soles were burning; whence the flexile joints
Glanced with such violent motion, as had snapt
Asunder cords or twisted withs. As flame,
Feeding on unctuous matter, glides along
The surface, scarcely touching where it moves;
So here, from heel to point, glided the flames.

　　"Master! say who is he, than all the rest
Glancing in fiercer agony, on whom
A ruddier flame doth prey?" I thus inquired.

　　"If thou be willing," he replied, "that I
Carry thee down, where least the slope bank falls,
He of himself shall tell thee, and his wrongs."

　　I then: "As pleases thee, to me is best.
Thou art my lord; and know'st that ne'er I quit
Thy will: what silence hides, that knowest thou."

　　Thereat on the fourth pier we came, we turn'd,
And on our left descended to the depth,
A narrow strait, and perforated close.
Nor from his side my leader set me down,
Till to his orifice he brought, whose limb
Quivering express'd his pang. "Whoe'er thou art,
Sad spirit! thus reversed, and as a stake
Driven in the soil," I in these words began;
"If thou be able, utter forth thy voice."

　　There stood I like the friar, that doth shrive
A wretch for murder doom'd, who, e'en when fix'd,[1]
Calleth him back, whence death awhile delays.

　　He shouted: "Ha! already standest there?
Already standest there, O Boniface![2]

---

[1] *When fix'd.*—The commentators on Boccaccio's "Decameron," p. 72, ediz. Giunti, 1573, cite the words of the statute by which murderers were sentenced thus to suffer at Florence: "Assassinus trahatur ad caudam muli seu asini usque ad locum justitiæ; et ibidem plantetur capite deorsum, ita quod moriatur." "Let the assassin be dragged at the tail of a mule or ass to the place of justice; and there let him be set in the ground with his face downward, so that he die."

[2] *O Boniface!*—The spirit mistakes Dante for Boniface VIII., who was then alive; and who he did not expect would have arrived so soon, in consequence, as

By many a year the writing play'd me false.
So early dost thou surfeit with the wealth,
For which thou fearedst not in guile[1] to take
The lovely lady, and then mangle her?"
    I felt as those who, piercing not the drift
Of answer made them, stand as if exposed
In mockery, nor know what to reply;
When Virgil thus admonish'd: "Tell him quick,
'I am not he, not he whom thou believest.'"
    And I, as was enjoin'd me, straight replied.
    That heard, the spirit all did wrench his feet,
And, sighing, next in woful accent spake:
"What then of me requirest? If to know
So much imports thee, who I am, that thou
Hast therefore down the bank descended, learn
That in the mighty mantle I was robed,[2]
And of a she-bear was indeed the son,
So eager to advance my whelps, that there
My having in my purse above I stow'd,
And here myself. Under my head are dragg'd
The rest, my predecessors in the guilt
Of simony. Stretch'd at their length, they lie
Along an opening in the rock. 'Midst them
I also low shall fall, soon as he comes,
For whom I took thee, when so hastily
I question'd. But already longer time
Hath past, since my soles kindled, and I thus
Upturn'd have stood, than is his doom to stand
Planted with fiery feet. For after him
One yet of deeds more ugly shall arrive,
From forth the west, a shepherd without law,[3]
Fated to cover both his form and mine.

---

it should seem, of a prophecy, which predicted the death of that pope at a later period. Boniface died in 1303.

[1] *In guile.*—"Thou didst presume to arrive by fraudulent means at the Papal power, and afterwards to abuse it."

[2] *In the mighty mantle I was robed.*—Nicholas III. of the Orsini family, whom the poet therefore calls "figliuol dell' orsa," "son of the she-bear." He died in 1281.

[3] *From forth the west, a shepherd without law.*—Bertrand de Got, Archbishop of Bordeaux, who succeeded to the pontificate in 1305, and assumed the title of Clement V. He transferred the holy see to Avignon in 1308 (where it remained till 1376), and died in 1314.

He a new Jason[1] shall be call'd, of whom
In Maccabees we read; and favour such
As to that priest his king indulgent show'd,
Shall be of France's monarch[2] shown to him."

I know not if I here too far presumed,
But in this strain I answer'd: "Tell me now
What treasures from Saint Peter at the first
Our Lord demanded, when he put the keys
Into his charge? Surely he asked no more
But 'Follow me!' Nor Peter,[3] nor the rest,
Or gold or silver of Matthias took,
When lots were cast upon the forfeit place
Of the condemned soul.[4] Abide thou then;
Thy punishment of right is merited:
And look thou well to that ill-gotten coin,
Which against Charles[5] thy hardihood inspired.
If reverence of the keys restrain'd me not,
Which thou in happier time didst hold, I yet
Severer speech might use. Your avarice
O'ercasts the world with mourning, under foot[6]
Treading the good, and raising bad men up,
Of shepherds like to you, the Evangelist[7]

---

[1] *A new Jason.*—"But after the death of Seleucus, when Antiochus, called Epiphanes, took the kingdom, Jason, the brother of Onias, laboured underhand to be high priest, promising unto the king, by intercession, three hundred and threescore talents of silver, and of another revenue eighty talents."—2 *Macc.* iv. 7, 8.

[2] *Of France's monarch.*—Philip IV. of France. See G. Villani, lib. viii., c. lxxx.

[3] *Nor Peter.*—Acts i. 26.

[4] *The condemned soul.*—Judas.

[5] *Against Charles.*—Nicholas III. was enraged against Charles I., King of Sicily, because he rejected with scorn a proposition made by that pope for an alliance between their families. See G. Villani, "Hist.," lib. vii., c. liv.

[6] *Under foot.*—
   "So shall the world go on,
To good malignant, to bad men benign."
       Milton, Paradise Lost, b. xii., 538.

[7] *The Evangelist.*—Rev. xvii. 1, 2, 3. Petrarch, in one of his Epistles, had his eye on these lines : " *Gaude* (*inquam*) *et ad aliquid utilis inventa gloriare bonorum hostis et malorum hospes, atque asylum pessima rerum Babylon feris, Rhodani ripis im- posita, famosa dicam an infamis meretrix, fornicata cum regibus terræ. Illa equidem ipsa es quam in spiritu sacer vidit Evangelista. Illa eadem, inquam, es, non alia, sedens super aquas multas, sive ad littora tribus cincta fluminibus sive rerum atque divitiarum turba mortalium quibus lasciviens ac secura insides opum immemor æternarum sive ut idem qui vidit, exposuit. Populi et gentes et linguæ aquæ sunt, super quas meretrix sedes, recognosce habitum," &c.—*Petrarchæ Opera, ed. fol. Basil*, 1554, *Epist. sine titulo Liber*, ep. xvi., p. 720. The text is here probably corrupted. The construction certainly may be rendered easier by omitting the *ad* before *littora*, and substituting a comma for a full stop after *exposuit*. With all the respect that is due to a venerable prelate and truly learned critic I cannot but point out a mistake he has fallen into, relating to this passage, when he observes that "numberless passages in the writings of Petrarch speak of Rome under the name of Babylon. But an equal stress is not to be laid on all these. It should be remembered that the popes, in Petrarch's time, resided at Avignon, greatly to the disparagement of themselves, as he thought, and especially of Rome; of which this singular man was

Was ware, when her, who sits upon the waves,
With kings in filthy whoredom he beheld;
She who with seven heads tower'd at her birth,
And from ten horns her proof of glory drew,
Long as her spouse in virtue took delight.
Of gold and silver ye have made your god,
Differing wherein from the idolater,
But that he worships one, a hundred ye?
Ah, Constantine![1] to how much ill gave birth,
Not thy conversion, but that plenteous dower,
Which the first wealthy Father gain'd from thee."

  Meanwhile, as thus I sung, he, whether wrath
Or conscience smote him, violent upsprang
Spinning on either sole. I do believe
My teacher well was pleased, with so composed
A lip he listen'd ever to the sound

---

little less than idolatrous. The situation of the place, surrounded by waters, and his splenetic concern for the *exiled* church (for under this idea he painted to himself the Pope's migration to the banks of Avignon), brought to his mind the condition of the Jewish Church in the Babylonian captivity; and this parallel was all, perhaps, that he meant to insinuate in most of those passages. But when he applies the prophecies to Rome, as to the *Apocalyptic* Babylon (as he clearly does in the epistle under consideration), his meaning is not equivocal, and we do him but justice to give him an honourable place among the TESTES VERITATIS."—*An Introduction to the Study of the Prophecies, &c., by Richard Hurd, D.D.*, serm. vii., p. 239, note Y, ed. 1772. Now, a reference to the words printed in italics, which the Bishop of Worcester has omitted in his quotation, will make it sufficiently evident that *Avignon*, and not *Rome*, is here alluded to by Petrarch. The application that is made of these prophecies by two men so eminent for their learning and sagacity as Dante and Petrarch is, however, very remarkable, and must be satisfactory to those who have renounced the errors and corruptions of the Papacy. Such applications were indeed frequent in the middle ages, as may be seen in the "Sermons" above referred to. Balbo observes that it is not Rome, as most erroneously interpreted, but Avignon and the court there, that is termed Babylon by Dante and Petrarch. "Vita di Dante," v. ii., p. 102.

[1] *Ah, Constantine!*—He alludes to the pretended gift of the Lateran by Constantine to Sylvester, of which Dante himself seems to imply a doubt, in his treatise "De Monarchiâ": "Ergo scindere Imperium, Imperatori non licet. Si ergo aliquæ dignitates per Constantinum essent alienatæ (ut dicunt) ab Imperio," &c. Lib. iii. "Therefore, to make a rent in the empire exceeds the lawful power of the emperor himself. If, then, some dignities were by Constantine alienated (as they report) from the empire," &c. In another part of the same treatise he speaks of the alienation with less doubt indeed, but not with less disapprobation: "O felicem populum! O Ausoniam te gloriosam! si vel numquam infirmator imperii tui extitisset; vel numquam sua pia intentio ipsum fefellisset." "Oh, happy people! Oh, glorious Italy! if either he who thus weakened thine empire had never been born, or had never suffered his pious intentions to mislead him." Lib. ii., *ad finem*. The gift is by Ariosto very humorously placed in the moon, among the things lost or abused on earth:

  " Di varj fiori ad un gran monte passa,
   Ch' ebber già buono odore, or puzzan forte,
   Questo era il dono (se però dir lece)
   Che Costantino al buon Silvestro fece."
      Orlando Furioso, c. xxxiv., st. 80.

Milton has translated both this passage and that in the text. Prose Works, vol. i., p. 11, ed. 1753:

  " Ah, Constantine! of how much ill was cause
   Not thy conversion, but those rich domains
   That the first wealthy pope received of thee."

  " Then passed he to a flowery mountain green,
   Which once smelt sweet, now stinks as odiously;
   This was that gift, if you the truth will have,
   That Constantine to good Silvester gave."

Of the true words I utter'd.   In both arms
He caught, and, to his bosom lifting me,
Upward retraced the way of his descent.

    Nor weary of his weight, he press'd me close
Till to the summit of the rock we came,
Our passage from the fourth to the fifth pier
His cherish'd burden there gently he placed
Upon the rugged rock and steep, a path
Not easy for the clambering goat to mount.

    Thence to my view another vale appear'd.

CANTO XX.

ARGUMENT.

The poet relates the punishment of such as presumed, while living, to predict future events. It is to have their faces reversed and set the contrary way on their limbs, so that, being deprived of the power to see before them, they are constrained ever to walk backwards. Among these Virgil points out to him Amphiaraûs, Tiresias, Aruns, and Manto (from the mention of whom he takes occasion to speak of the origin of Mantua), together with several others, who had practised the arts of divination and astrology.

AND now the verse proceeds to torments new,
  Fit argument of this the twentieth strain
Of the first song, whose awful theme records
The spirits whelm'd in woe. Earnest I look'd
Into the depth, that open'd to my view,
Moisten'd with tears of anguish, and beheld
A tribe, that came along the hollow vale,
In silence weeping : such their step as walk
Quires, chanting solemn litanies, on earth.

  As on them more direct mine eye descends,
Each wondrously seem'd to be reversed[1]
At the neck-bone, so that the countenance
Was from the reins averted ; and because
None might before him look, they were compell'd
To advance with backward gait. Thus one perhaps
Hath been by force of palsy clean transposed,
But I ne'er saw it nor believe it so.

  Now, reader ! think within thyself, so God
Fruit of thy reading give thee ! how I long
Could keep my visage dry,[2] when I beheld

---

[1] *Reversed.—*
" But very uncouth sight was to behold
How he did fashion his untoward pace ;
For as he forward moved his footing old,
So backward still was turn'd his wrinkled face ;
Unlike to men, who, ever as they trace,
Both feet and face one way are wont to lead."
    Spenser, Faëry Queen, b. i., c. viii., st. 31.
[2] *How I long could keep my visage dry.—*
" Sight so deform what heart of man could long
Dry-eyed behold ? Adam could not, but wept."
    Milton, Paradise Lost, b. xi., 495.

Near me our form distorted in such guise,
That on the hinder parts fallen from the face
The tears down-streaming roll'd. Against a rock
I leant and wept, so that my guide exclaim'd,
"What! and art thou, too, witless as the rest?
Here pity most doth show herself alive,
When she is dead. What guilt exceedeth his,
Who with Heaven's judgment in his passion strives?
Raise up thy head, raise up, and see the man
Before whose eyes[1] earth gaped in Thebes, when all
Cried out 'Amphiaraüs, whither rushest?
Why leavest thou the war?' He not the less
Fell ruining[2] far as to Minos down,
Whose grapple none eludes. Lo! how he makes
The breast his shoulders; and who once too far
Before him wish'd to see, now backward looks,
And treads reverse his path. Tiresias[3] note,
Who semblance changed, when woman he became
Of male, through every limb transform'd; and then
Once more behoved him with his rod to strike
The two entwining serpents, ere the plumes,
That mark'd the better sex, might shoot again.
　　"Aruns,[4] with rere his belly facing, comes.
On Luni's mountains 'midst the marbles white,

---

[1] *Before whose eyes.*—Amphiaraüs, one of the seven kings who besieged Thebes. He is said to have been swallowed up by an opening of the earth. See Lidgate's "Storie of Thebes," part iii., where it is told how the "Bishop Amphiaraüs" fell down to hell:

　　"And thus the devill, for his outrages.
　　Like his desert payed him his wages."

A different reason for his being doomed thus to perish is assigned by Pindar:

　　"ὁ δ' 'Αμφιάρηϊ," &c. *Nem.* ix.

　　"For thee, Amphiaraüs, earth,
　　By Jove's all-riving thunder cleft.
　　Her mighty bosom open'd wide,
　　Thee and thy plunging steeds to hide,
　　Or ever on thy back the spear
　　Of Periclymenus impress'd
　　A wound to shame thy warlike breast.
　　For struck with panic fear
　　The gods' own children flee."

[2] *Ruining.*—"Ruinare." Hence, perhaps, Milton, "Paradise Lost," b. vi., 868:

　　　　"Heaven ruining from heaven."

[3] *Tiresias.*—

"Duo magnorum viridi coëuntia sylvâ
Corpora serpentum baculi violaverat ictu.
Deque viro factus (mirabile) fœmina, septem
Egerat autumnos. Octavo rursus eosdem
Vidit. Et, est vestræ si tanta potentia plagæ,
Nunc quoque vos feriam. Percussis anguibus isdem
Forma prior rediit, genitivaque venit imago."
　　　　Ovid. Metamorphoses, lib. iii.

[4] *Aruns.*—Aruns is said to have dwelt in the mountains of Luni (from whence that territory is still called Lunigiana), above Carrara, celebrated for its marble. Lucan, "Pharsalia," lib. i. 575. So Boccaccio, in the "Fiammetta," lib. iii.: "Quale Arunte," &c. "Like Aruns, who, amidst the white marbles of Luni, contemplated the celestial bodies and their motions." Compare Fazio degli Uberti," "Dittamondo," l. iii., cap. vi.

Where delves Carrara's hind, who wons beneath,
A cavern was his dwelling, whence the stars
And main sea wide in boundless view he held.
    "The next, whose loosen'd tresses overspread
Her bosom, which thou seest not (for each hair
On that side grows) was Manto,[1] she who search'd
Through many regions, and at length her seat
Fix'd in my native land: whence a short space
My words detain thy audience. When her sire
From life departed, and in servitude
The city dedicate to Bacchus mourn'd,
Long time she went a wanderer through the world.
Aloft in Italy's delightful land
A lake there lies, at foot of that proud Alp
That o'er the Tyrol locks Germania in,
Its name Benacus, from whose ample breast
A thousand springs, methinks, and more, between
Camonica[2] and Garda, issuing forth,
Water the Apennine. There is a spot[3]
At midway of that lake, where he who bears
Of Trento's flock the pastoral staff, with him
Of Brescia, and the Veronese, might each
Passing that way his benediction give.
A garrison of goodly site and strong[4]
Peschiera[5] stands, to awe with front opposed
The Bergamese and Brescian, whence the shore
More slope each way descends. There, whatsoe'er

---

[1] *Manto.*—The daughter of Tiresias of Thebes, a city dedicated to Bacchus. From Manto, Mantua, the country of Virgil, derives its name. The poet proceeds to describe the situation of that place.

[2] *Camonica.*—Lombardi, instead of

    " Fra Garda, e val Camonica e Apennino,
reads,

    " Fra Garda e val Camonica Pennino,"
from the Nidobeatina edition (to which he might have added that of Vellutello in 1544), and two MSS., all of which omit the second conjunction, the only part of the alteration that affects the sense. I have re-translated the passage, which in the former editions stood thus:

            " Which a thousand rills
Methinks, and more, water between the vale
Camonica and Garda, and the height
Of Apennine remote."

It should be added that Vellutello reads " Valdimonica " for " Val Camonica ; " but which of these is right remains to be determined by a collation of editions and MSS., and still more perhaps by a view of the country in the neighbourhood of the lake (now called the Lago di Garda), with a reference to this passage.

[3] *There is a spot.*—Prato di Fame, where the dioceses of Trento, Verona, and Brescia meet.

[4] *A garrison of goodly site and strong.*—

        " Gaza, bello e forte arnese
Da fronteggiar i regni di Soria."
            Tasso, Gierusalemme Liberata, c. i., st. 67.

[5] *Peschiera.*—A garrison situated to the south of the lake, where it empties itself and forms the Mincius.

Benacus' bosom holds not, tumbling o'er
Down falls, and winds a river flood beneath
Through the green pastures. Soon as in his course
The stream makes head, Benacus then no more
They call the name, but Mincius, till at last
Reaching Governo, into Po he falls.
Not far his course hath run, when a wide flat
It finds, which overstretching as a marsh
It covers, pestilent in summer oft.
Hence journeying, the savage maiden saw
Midst of the fen a territory waste
And naked of inhabitants. To shun
All human converse, here she with her slaves,
Plying her arts, remain'd, and lived, and left
Her body tenantless. Thenceforth the tribes,
Who round were scatter'd, gathering to that place,
Assembled ; for its strength was great, enclosed
On all parts by the fen. On those dead bones
They rear'd themselves a city, for her sake
Calling it Mantua, who first chose the spot,
Nor ask'd another omen for the name ;
Wherein more numerous the people dwelt,
Ere Casalodi's madness[1] by deceit
Was wrong'd of Pinamonte. If thou hear
Henceforth another origin[2] assign'd
Of that my country, I forewarn thee now,
That falsehood none beguile thee of the truth."

  I answer'd, "Teacher, I conclude thy words
So certain, that all else shall be to me
As embers lacking life. But now of these,
Who here proceed, instruct me, if thou see
Any that merit more especial note,
For thereon is my mind alone intent."

---

[1] *Casalodi's madness.*—Alberto da Casalodi, who had got possession of Mantua, was persuaded, by Pinamonte Buonacorsi, that he might ingratiate himself with the people by banishing to their own castles the nobles, who were obnoxious to them. No sooner was this done, than Pinamonte put himself at the head of the populace, drove out Casalodi and his adherents, and obtained the sovereignty for himself.

[2] *Another origin.*—Lombardi refers to Servius on the Tenth Book of the " Æneid : " " Alii a Tarchone Tyrrheni fratre conditam dicunt Mantuam autem ideo nominatam quia Etrusca lingua Mantum ditem patrem appellant."

He straight replied : "That spirit, from whose cheek
The beard sweeps o'er his shoulders brown, what time
Græcia was emptied of her males, that scarce
The cradles were supplied, the seer was he
In Aulis, who with Calchas gave the sign
When first to cut the cable. Him they named
Eurypilus : so sings my tragic strain,[1]
In which majestic measure well thou know'st,
Who know'st it all. That other, round the loins
So slender of his shape, was Michael Scot,[2]
Practised in every slight of magic wile.
"Guido Bonatti[3] see : Asdente[4] mark,

---

[1] *So sings my tragic strain.*—
"Suspensi Eurypilum scitatum oracula Phœbi
Mittimus." *Virgil, Æneid,* ii. 114.

[2] *Michael Scot.*—"Egli non ha ancora guari, che in questa città fu un gran maestro in negromanzia, il quale ebbe nome Michele Scotto, perciò che di Scozia era."—*Boccaccio, Decameron,* Giorn. viii., Nov. 9. " It is not long since there was in this city (Florence) a great master in necromancy, who was called Michele Scotto, because he was from Scotland." See also G. Villani, " Hist.," lib. x., cap. cv. and cxli., and lib. xii., cap. xviii. ; and Fazio degli Uberti, " Dittamondo," l. ii., cap. xxvii. I make no apology for adding the following curious particulars extracted from the notes to Mr. Scott's " Lay of the Last Minstrel," a poem in which a happy use is made of the superstitions relating to the subject of this note :—" Sir Michael Scott, of Balwearie, flourished during the thirteenth century, and was one of the ambassadors sent to bring the Maid of Norway to Scotland upon the death of Alexander III. He was a man of much learning, chiefly acquired in foreign countries. He wrote a commentary upon Aristotle, printed at Venice in 1496, and several treatises upon natural philosophy, from which he appears to have been addicted to the abstruse studies of judicial astrology, alchemy, physiognomy, and chiromancy. Hence he passed among his contemporaries for a skilful magician. Dempster informs us that he remembers to have heard in his youth, that the magic books of Michael Scott were still in existence, but could not be opened without danger, on account of the fiends who were thereby invoked. Dempsteri, ' Historia Ecclesiastica,' 1627, lib. xii., p. 495. Leslie characterises Michael Scott as ' Singulari philosophiæ astronomiæ ac medicinæ laude præstans, dicebatur penitissimos magiæ recessus indagasse.' A personage thus spoken of by biographers and historians loses little of his mystical fame in vulgar tradition. Accordingly, the memory of Sir Michael Scott survives in many a legend ; and in the south of Scotland any work of great labour and antiquity is ascribed either to the agency of Auld Michael, of Sir William Wallace, or of the devil. Tradition varies concerning the place of his burial : some contend for Holme Coltrame, in Cumberland, others for Melrose Abbey ; but all agree that his books of magic were interred in his grave, or preserved in the convent where he died."—*The Lay of the Last Minstrel, by Walter Scott, Esq.,* Lond., 4to, 1805, p. 234, Notes. Mr. Warton, speaking of the new translations of Aristotle, from the original Greek into Latin, about the twelfth century, observes : " I believe the translators understood very little Greek. Our countryman, Michael Scotus, was one of the first of them ; who was assisted by Andrew, a Jew. Michael was astrologer to Frederic II., Emperor of Germany, and appears to have executed his translations at Toledo, in Spain, about the year 1220. These new versions were perhaps little more than corrections from those of the early Arabians, made under the inspection of the learned Spanish Saracens," *History of English Poetry,* vol. i., dissert. ii., and sect. ix., p. 292. Among the Canonici MSS. in the Bodleian, I have seen (No. 520) the astrological works of Michael Scot, on vellum, with an illuminated portrait of him at the beginning.

[3] *Guido Bonatti.*—An astrologer of Forli, on whose skill Guido da Montefeltro, lord of that place, so much relied, that he is reported never to have gone into battle except in the hour recommended to him as fortunate by Bonatti. Landino and Vellutello speak of a book which he composed on the subject of his art. Macchiavelli mentions him in the " History of Florence," l. i., p. 24, ed. 1550. " He flourished about 1230 and '1260. Though a learned astronomer, he was seduced by astrology, through which he was greatly in favour with many princes of that time. His many works are miserably spoiled by it."—*Bettinelli, Risorgimento d'Italia,* t. i., p. 118, 8vo, 1786. He is referred to in Brown's " Vulgar Errors," b. iv., c. xii.

[4] *Asdente.*—A shoemaker at Parma, who deserted

Who now were willing he had tended still
The thread and cordwain, and too late repents.
    " See next the wretches, who the needle left,
The shuttle and the spindle, and became
Diviners : baneful witcheries they wrought
With images and herbs. But onward now :
For now doth Cain with fork of thorns[1] confine
On either hemisphere, touching the wave
Beneath the towers of Seville. Yesternight
The moon was round. Thou mayst remember well :
For she good service did thee in the gloom
Of the deep wood." This said, both onward moved.

his business to practise the arts of divination. How much this man had attracted the public notice appears from a passage in our author's " Convito," where it is said, in speaking of the derivation of the word " noble," that " if those who were best known were accounted the most noble, Asdente, the shoemaker of Parma, would be more noble than any one in that city."

[1] *Cain with fork of thorns.*—By Cain and the thorns, or what is still vulgarly called the Man in the Moon, the poet denotes that luminary. The same superstition is alluded to in the " Paradise," canto ii. 52. The curious reader may consult Brand on " Popular Antiquities," 4to, 1813, vol. ii. p. 476, and Douce's " Illustrations of Shakespeare," 8vo, 1807, v. i., p. 10.

CANTO XXI.

ARGUMENT.

Still in the eighth circle, which bears the name of Malebolge, they look down from the bridge that passes over its fifth gulf, upon the barterers or public peculators. These are plunged in a lake of boiling pitch, and guarded by demons, to whom Virgil, leaving Dante apart, presents himself; and licence being obtained to pass onward both pursue their way.

THUS we from bridge to bridge, with other talk,
The which my drama cares not to rehearse,
Pass'd on; and to the summit reaching, stood
To view another gap, within the round
Of Malebolge, other bootless pangs.
Marvellous darkness shadow'd o'er the place.
In the Venetians' arsenal[1] as boils
Through wintry months tenacious pitch, to smear
Their unsound vessels; for the inclement time
Sea-faring men restrains, and in that while
His barque one builds anew, another stops
The ribs of his that hath made many a voyage,
One hammers at the prow, one at the poop,
This shapeth oars, that other cables twirls,
The mizen one repairs, and main-sail rent;
So, not by force of fire but art divine,
Boil'd[2] here a glutinous thick mass, that round
Limed all the shore beneath. I that beheld,
But therein nought distinguish'd, save the bubbles
Raised by the boiling, and one mighty swell
Heave,[3] and by turns subsiding fall. While there

---

[1] *In the Venetians' arsenal.*—
  "Come dentr' ai Navai della gran terra,
  Tra le lacune del mar d'Adria posta,
  Serban la pece la togata gente,
  Ad uso di lor navi e di lor triremi;
  Per solcar poi sicuri il mare ondoso," &c.
        Ruccellai, Le Api, v. 165.

Dryden seems to have had the passage in the text before him in his "Annus Mirabilis, st. 146 &c.

[2] *Boil'd.*—"Vidi flumen magno de Inferno precedere ardens, atque piceum."—*Alberici Visio*, § xvii.

[3] *One mighty swell heave.*—"Vidi etiam os putei magnum flammas emittentem, et nunc sursum nunc deorsum descendentem."—*Alberici Visio*, § xi.

This said,
They grappled him with more than hundred hooks,
Canto XXI. lines 50, 51.

I fix'd my ken below, "Mark! mark!" my guide
Exclaiming, drew me towards him from the place
Wherein I stood. I turn'd myself, as one
Impatient to behold that which beheld
He needs must shun, whom sudden fear unmans,
That he his flight delays not for the view.
Behind me I discern'd a devil black,
That running up advanced along the rock.
Ah! what fierce cruelty his look bespake.
In act how bitter did he seem, with wings
Buoyant outstretch'd and feet of nimblest tread.
His shoulder, proudly eminent and sharp,
Was with a sinner charged; by either haunch
He held him, the foot's sinew griping fast.

    "Ye of our bridge!" he cried, "keen-talon'd fiends!
Lo! one of Santa Zita's elders.[1]   Him
Whelm ye beneath, while I return for more.
That land hath store of such. All men are there,
Except Bonturo, barterers:[2] of 'no'
For lucre there an 'ay' is quickly made."

    Him dashing down, o'er the rough rock he turn'd;
Nor ever after thief a mastiff loosed
Sped with like eager haste. That other sank,
And forthwith writhing to the surface rose.
But those dark demons, shrouded by the bridge,
Cried, " Here the hallow'd visage[3] saves not : here
Is other swimming than in Serchio's wave,[4]
Wherefore, if thou desire we rend thee not,
Take heed thou mount not o'er the pitch." This said,
They grappled him with more than hundred hooks,
And shouted, " Cover'd thou must sport thee here ;
So, if thou canst, in secret mayst thou filch."

One of Santa Zita's elders.—The elders or chief
magistrates of Lucca, where Santa Zita was held in
especial veneration. The name of this sinner is supposed to have been Martino Botaio.

[2] Except Bonturo, barterers.—This is said ironically of Bonturo de' Dati. By barterers are meant
peculators of every description ; all who traffic the
interests of the public for their own private advantage.

[3] The hallow'd visage.—A representation of the
head of our Saviour worshipped at Lucca.

[4] Is other swimming than in Serchio's wave.—

    " Qui si nuota altrimenti che nel Serchio."

Serchio is the river that flows by Lucca. So Pulci,
" Morgante Maggiore," c. xxiv. :

    " Qui si nuota nel sangue, e non nel Serchio."

E'en thus the cook bestirs him, with his grooms,
To thrust the flesh[1] into the caldron down
With flesh-hooks, that it float not on the top.

Me then my guide bespake : "Lest they descry
That thou art here, behind a craggy rock
Bend low and screen thee : and whate'er of force
Be offer'd me, or insult, fear thou not ;
For I am well advised, who have been erst
In the like fray." Beyond the bridge's head
Therewith he pass'd ; and reaching the sixth pier,
Behoved him then a forehead terror-proof.

With storm and fury, as when dogs rush forth
Upon the poor man's back, who suddenly
From whence he standeth makes his suit ; so rush'd
Those from beneath the arch, and against him
Their weapons all they pointed. He, aloud :
"Be none of you outrageous : ere your tine
Dare seize me, come forth from amongst you one,
Who having heard my words, decide he then
If he shall tear these limbs." They shouted loud
"Go, Malacoda !" Whereat one advanced,
The others standing firm, and as he came,
"What may this turn avail him ?" he exclaim'd.

"Believest thou, Malacoda ! I had come
Thus far from all your skirmishing secure,"
My teacher answer'd, "without will divine
And destiny propitious ? Pass we then ;
For so Heaven's pleasure is, that I should lead
Another through this savage wilderness."

Forthwith so fell his pride, that he let drop
The instrument of torture at his feet,
And to the rest exclaim'd, "We have no power
To strike him." Then to me my guide : "Oh, thou !
Who on the bridge among the crags dost sit
Low crouching, safely now to me return."

I rose and towards him moved with speed ; the fiends

---

[1] *The flesh.*—"In eundem flumen corruunt : rur- | ibidem cruciantur, donec in morem carnium excocti,"
sumque assurgentes, ac denuo recidentes, tamdiu | &c.—*Alberici Visio,* § xvii.

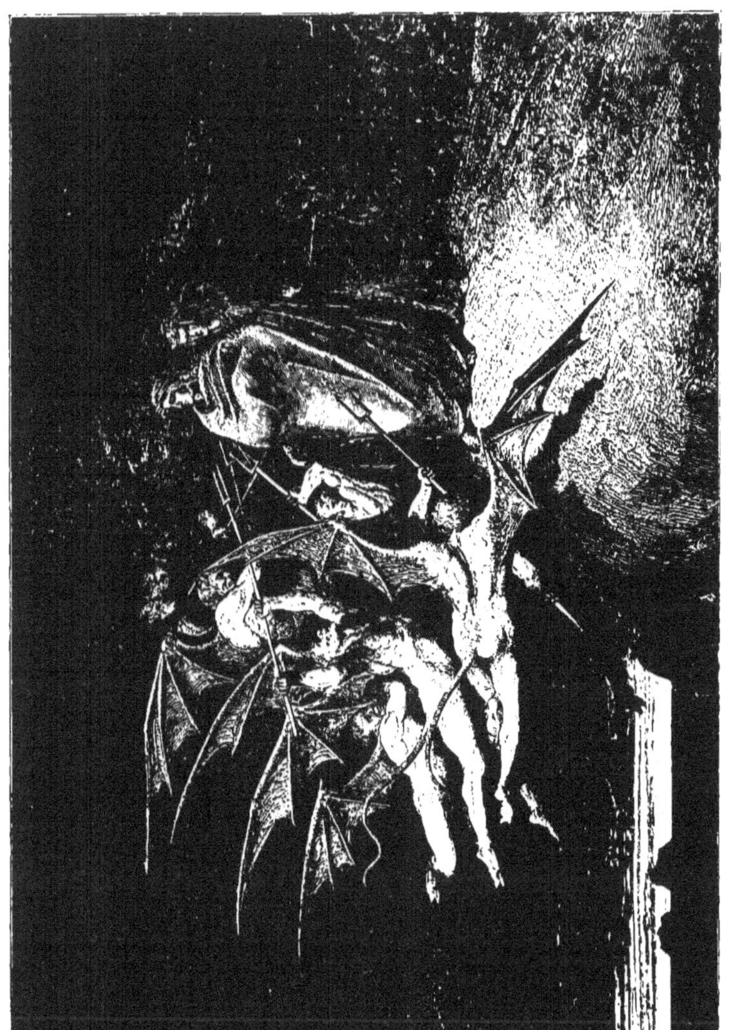

"Be none of you outrageous."
Canto XVI., line 72

Meantime all forward drew : me terror seized,
Lest they should break the compact they had made.
Thus issuing from Caprona,[1] once I saw
The infantry, dreading lest his covenant
The foe should break ; so close he hemm'd them round.

   I to my leader's side adhered, mine eyes
With fixed and motionless observance bent
On their unkindly visage. They their hooks
Protruding, one the other thus bespake :
"Wilt thou I touch him on the hip ?" To whom
Was answer'd, "Even so ; nor miss thy aim."

   But he, who was in conference with my guide,
Turn'd rapid round ; and thus the demon spake :
"Stay, stay thee, Scarmiglione ! " Then to us
He added : "Further footing to your step
This rock affords not, shiver'd to the base
Of the sixth arch. But would ye still proceed,
Up by this cavern go : not distant far,
Another rock will yield you passage safe.
Yesterday,[2] later by five hours than now,
Twelve hundred threescore years and six had fill'd
The circuit of their course, since here the way
Was broken. Thitherward I straight despatch
Certain of these my scouts, who shall espy
If any on the surface bask. With them
Go ye : for ye shall find them nothing fell.
Come Alichino, forth," with that he cried,
"And Calcabrina, and Cagnazzo[3] thou !
The troop of ten let Barbariccia lead.

---

1 *From Caprona.*—The surrender of the castle of Caprona to the combined forces of Florence and Lucca, on condition that the garrison should march out in safety, to which event Dante was a witness, took place in 1290. See G. Villani, " Hist.," lib. vii., c. cxxxvi.

2 *Yesterday.*—This passage fixes the era of Dante's descent at Good Friday, in the year 1300 (thirty-four years from our blessed Lord's incarnation being added to 1266), and at the thirty-fifth year of our poet's age. See canto i., v. 1. The awful event alluded to, the Evangelists inform us, happened "at the ninth hour," that is, our sixth, when "the rocks were rent," and the convulsion, according to Dante, was felt even in the depths of hell. See canto xii., v. 38.

3 *Cagnazzo.*—Pulci introduces some of these demons in a very pleasant adventure, related near the beginning of the second canto of his " Morgante Maggiore : "

  " Non senti tu, Orlando, in quella tomba
   Quelle parole, che colui rimbomba ?
   Io voglio andar a scoprir quello avello,
   Là dove e' par che quella voce s'oda,
   Ed escane Cagnazzo, e Farfarello,
   O Libicocco, col suo Malacoda :
   E finalmente s'accostava a quello,

With Libicocco, Draghinazzo haste,
Fang'd Ciriatto, Graffiacane fierce,
And Farfarello, and mad Rubicant.
Search ye around the bubbling tar.   For these,
In safety lead them, where the other crag
Uninterrupted traverses the dens."

    I then : " Oh, master !¹ what a sight is there.
Ah ! without escort, journey we alone,
Which, if thou know the way, I covet not.
Unless thy prudence fail thee, dost not mark
How they do gnarl upon us, and their scowl
Threatens us present tortures ? "   He replied :
" I charge thee, fear not : let them, as they will,
Gnarl on : 'tis but in token of their spite
Against the souls who mourn in torment steep'd."

    To leftward o'er the pier they turn'd ; but each
Had first between his teeth prest close the tongue,
Toward their leader for a signal looking,
Which he with sound obscene² triumphant gave.

Però che Orlando questa impresa loda,
E disse ; scuopri, se vi fussi dentro
Quanti ne piovon mai dal ciel nel centro."
                      Stanze xxx. 1.
" ' Perceivest the words, Orlando, which this fellow
Doth in our ears out of that tomb rebellow ?
I'll go, and straight the sepulchre uncase,
From whence, as seems to me, that voice was heard ;
Be Farfarel and Cagnazzo to my face,
Or Libicoc with Malacoda, stirr'd : '
And finally he drew near to the place ;

The emprize Orlando praising with this word :
' Uncase it, though within as many dwell,
As ever were from heaven rain'd down to hell.' "

¹ *Oh, master !*—Lombardi tells us that every
edition, except his favourite Nidobeatina, has " O me "
printed separately, instead of " Omè." This is not
the case at least with Landino's of 1484. But there
is no end of these inaccuracies.

² *With sound obscene.*—Compare the original with
Aristophanes, " Nubes." 165 :

        " σάλπιγξ ὁ πρωκτός ἐστίν."

CANTO XXII.

ARGUMENT.

Virgil and Dante proceed, accompanied by the demons, and see other sinners of the same description in the same gulf. The device of Ciampolo, one of these, to escape from the demons, who had laid hold on him.

IT hath been heretofore my chance to see
  Horsemen with martial order shifting camp,
To onset sallying, or in muster ranged,
Or in retreat sometimes outstretch'd for flight :
Light-armed squadrons and fleet foragers
Scouring thy plains, Arezzo! have I seen
And clashing tournaments, and tilting jousts,
Now with the sound of trumpets, now of bells,
Tabors,[1] or signals made from castled heights,
And with inventions multiform, our own,
Or introduced from foreign land; but ne'er
To such a strange recorder I beheld,
In evolution moving, horse nor foot,
Nor ship, that tack'd by sign from land or star.

  With the ten demons on our way we went;
Ah, fearful company! but in the church[2]
With saints, with gluttons at the tavern's mess.

  Still earnest on the pitch I gazed, to mark
All things whate'er the chasm contain'd,[3] and those
Who burn'd within. As dolphins[4] that, in sign

---

[1] *Tabors.*—"Tabour, a drum, a common accompaniment of war, is mentioned as one of the instruments of martial music in this battle (in Richard Cœur-de-Lion) with characteristical propriety. It was imported into the European armies from the Saracens in the holy war. Joinville describes a superb barque or galley belonging to a Saracen chief which, he says, was filled with cymbals, tabours, and Saracen horns. 'Hist. de S. Loys,' p. 30."—*Warton's History of English Poetry*, v. i., § iv., p. 167.

[2] *In the church.*—This proverb is repeated by Pulci, "Morgante Maggiore," c. xvii.

[3] *Whate'er the chasm contain'd.*—Monti, in his "Proposta," interprets "contegno" to mean, not "contents," but "state," "condition."

[4] *As dolphins.*—

"Li lieti delfini
Givan saltando sopra l'onde chiare,
Che sogliou di fortuna esser divini."
  Frezzi, Il Quadriregio. lib. i., cap. xv.

O

To mariners, heave high their arched backs,
That thence forewarn'd they may advise to save
Their threaten'd vessel ; so, at intervals,
To ease the pain, his back some sinner show'd,
Then hid more nimbly than the lightning-glance.

      E'en as the frogs, that of a watery moat
Stand at the brink, with the jaws only out,
Their feet and of the trunk all else conceal'd,
Thus on each part the sinners stood ; but soon
As Barbariccia was at hand, so they
Drew back under the wave. I saw, and yet
My heart doth stagger, one, that waited thus,
As it befalls that oft one frog remains,
While the next springs away : and Graffiacan,[1]
Who of the fiends was nearest, grappling seized
His clotted locks, and dragg'd him sprawling up,
That he appear'd to me an otter. Each
Already by their names I knew, so well
When they were chosen I observed, and mark'd
How one the other call'd. "O Rubicant
See that his hide thou with thy talons flay,"
Shouted together all the cursed crew.

      Then I : "Inform thee, master ! if thou may,
What wretched soul is this, on whom their hands
His foes have laid." My leader to his side
Approach'd, and whence he came inquired ; to whom
Was answer'd thus : "Born in Navarre's domain,[2]
My mother placed me in a lord's retinue ;
For she had borne me to a losel vile,
A spendthrift of his substance and himself.
The good king Thibault[3] after that I served :

----

[1] *Graffiacan.*—Fuseli, in a note to his third
Lecture, observes, that "the Minos of Dante, in
Messer Biagio da Cesena, and his Charon, have been
recognised by all ; but less the shivering wretch held
over the barge by a hook, and evidently taken from
this passage." He is speaking of Michael Angelo's
" Last Judgment."

[2] *Born in Navarre's domain.*—The name of this
peculator is said to have been Ciampolo.

[3] *The good king Thibault.*—" Thibault I., King of
Navarre, died on the 8th of June, 1233, as much to be
commended for the desire he showed of aiding the
war in the Holy Land, as reprehensible and faulty for
his design of oppressing the rights and privileges of
the Church ; on which account it is said that the
whole kingdom was under an interdict for the space
of three entire years. Thibault undoubtedly merits
praise, as for his other endowments, so especially for his cultivation of the liberal arts, his
exercise and knowledge of music and poetry, in

To peculating here my thoughts were turn'd,
Whereof I give account in this dire heat."

Straight Ciriatto, from whose mouth a tusk
Issued on either side, as from a boar,
Ripp'd him with one of these. 'Twixt evil claws
The mouse had fallen : but Barbariccia cried,
Seizing him with both arms : " Stand thou apart,
While I do fix him on my prong transpierced."
Then added, turning to my guide his face,
" Inquire of him, if more thou wish to learn
Ere he again be rent." My leader thus :
" Then tell us of the partners in thy guilt ;
Knowest thou any sprung of Latian land
Under the tar ? " " I parted," he replied,
" But now from one, who sojourn'd not far thence ;
So were I under shelter now with him,
Nor hook nor talon then should scare me more."

" Too long we suffer," Libicocco cried ;
Then, darting forth a prong, seized on his arm,
And mangled bore away the sinewy part.
Him Draghinazzo by his thighs beneath
Would next have caught ; whence angrily their chief,
Turning on all sides round, with threatening brow
Restrain'd them. When their strife a little ceased,
Of him, who yet was gazing on his wound,
My teacher thus without delay inquired :
" Who was the spirit, from whom by evil hap
Parting, as thou hast told, thou camest to shore ? "

" It was the friar Gomita,"[1] he rejoin'd,
" He of Gallura, vessel of all guile,

---

which he so much excelled, that he was accustomed to
compose verses and sing them to the viol, and to
exhibit his poetical compositions publicly in his palace,
that they might be criticised by all."—*Mariana,
History of Spain*, b. xiii., c. ix. An account of
Thibault, and two of his songs, with what were
probably the original melodies, may be seen in Dr.
Burney's " History of Music," v. ii., c. iv. His poems,
which are in the French language, were edited by M.
l'Evêque de la Ravallière ; Paris, 1742, 2 vols. 12mo.
Dante twice quotes one of his verses in the " Treatise
de Vulgari Eloquentia," lib. i., c. ix., and lib. ii., c. v.,
and refers to him again, lib. ii., c. vi. From " the
good king Thibault " are descended the good, but
more unfortunate monarch, Louis XVI. of France,
and consequently the present legitimate sovereign of
that realm. See Henault, " Abrégé Chron.," 1252, 3, 4.

1 *The friar Gomita.*—He was entrusted by Nino
de' Visconti with the government of Gallura, one of
the four jurisdictions into which Sardinia was divided.
Having his master's enemies in his power, he took a
bribe from them, and allowed them to escape.
Mention of Nino will recur in the Notes to canto
xxxiii.

Who had his master's enemies in hand,
And used them so that they commend him well.
Money he took, and them at large dismiss'd ;
So he reports ; and in each other charge
Committed to his keeping play'd the part
Of barterer to the height. With him doth herd
The chief of Logodoro, Michel Zanche.[1]
Sardinia is a theme whereof their tongue
Is never weary. Out ! alas ! behold
That other, how he grins. More would I say,
But tremble lest he mean to maul me sore."

    Their captain then to Farfarello turning,
Who roll'd his moony eyes in act to strike,
Rebuked him thus : " Off, cursed bird ! avaunt !"

    " If ye desire to see or hear," he thus
Quaking with dread resumed, " or Tuscan spirits
Or Lombard, I will cause them to appear.
Meantime let these ill talons bate their fury,
So that no vengeance they may fear from them,
And I, remaining in this self-same place,
Will, for myself but one, make seven appear,
When my shrill whistle shall be heard : for so
Our custom is to call each other up."

    Cagnazzo at that word deriding grinn'd,
Then wagg'd the head and spake : " Hear his device,
Mischievous as he is, to plunge him down."

    Whereto he thus, who fail'd not in rich store
Of nice-wove toils : " Mischief, forsooth, extreme !
Meant only to procure myself more woe."

    No longer Alichino then refrain'd,
But thus, the rest gainsaying, him bespake :
" If thou do cast thee down, I not on foot
Will chase thee, but above the pitch will beat
My plumes. Quit we the vantage ground, and let
The bank be as a shield ; that we may see,
If singly thou prevail against us all."

---

[1] *Michel Zanche.*—The president of Logodoro, another of the four Sardinian jurisdictions. See canto xxxiii. 136, Note.

In pursuit
He therefore sped, exclaiming, " Thou art caught."
Canto XXII., lines 125, 126

But the other proved
A goshawk able to rend well his foe;
And in the boiling lake both fell.
Canto XXII, lines 137—139.

Now, reader, of new sport expect to hear.
They each one turn'd his eyes to the other shore,
He first, who was the hardest to persuade.
The spirit of Navarre chose well his time,
Planted his feet on land, and at one leap
Escaping, disappointed their resolve.
Them quick resentment stung, but him the most
Who was the cause of failure : in pursuit
He therefore sped, exclaiming, "Thou art caught."
But little it avail'd ; terror outstripp'd
His following flight ; the other plunged beneath,
And he with upward pinion raised his breast :
E'en thus the water-fowl, when she perceives
The falcon near, dives instant down, while he
Enraged and spent retires. That mockery
In Calcabrina fury stirr'd, who flew
After him, with desire of strife inflamed ;
And, for the barterer had 'scaped, so turn'd
His talons on his comrade. O'er the dyke
In grapple close they join'd ; but the other proved
A goshawk able to rend well his foe ;
And in the boiling lake both fell. The heat
Was umpire[1] soon between them ; but in vain
To lift themselves they strove, so fast were glued
Their pennons. Barbariccia, as the rest,
That chance lamenting, four in flight despatch'd
From the other coast, with all their weapons arm'd.
They, to their post on each side speedily
Descending, stretch'd their hooks toward the fiends,
Who flounder'd, inly burning from their scars :
And we departing left them to that broil.

---

[1] *Umpire.*—Schermidor. The reader, if he thinks it worth while, may consult the " Preposta " of Monti on this word, which, with Lombardi, he would alter to *sghermitor.*

CANTO XXIII.

ARGUMENT.

The enraged demons pursue Dante, but he is preserved from them by Virgil. On reaching the sixth gulf, he beholds the punishment of the hypocrites; which is, to pace continually round the gulf under the pressure of caps and hoods that are gilt on the outside, but leaden within. He is addressed by two of these, Catalano and Loderingo, knights of Saint Mary, otherwise called Joyous Friars of Bologna. Caïaphas is seen fixed to a cross on the ground, and lies so stretched along the way, that all tread on him in passing.

IN silence and in solitude we went,
    One first, the other following his steps,
As minor friars journeying on their road.

    The present fray had turn'd my thoughts to muse
Upon old Æsop's fable,[1] where he told
What fate unto the mouse and frog befell;
For language hath not sounds more like in sense,
Than are these chances, if the origin
And end of each be heedfully compared.
And as one thought bursts from another forth,
So afterward from that another sprang,
Which added doubly to my former fear.
For thus I reason'd: "These through us have been
So foil'd, with loss and mockery so complete,
As needs must sting them sore. If anger then
Be to their evil will conjoin'd, more fell
They shall pursue us, than the savage hound
Snatches the leveret panting 'twixt his jaws."

    Already I perceived my hair stand all
On end with terror, and look'd eager back.

    "Teacher," I thus began, "it speedily
Thyself and me thou hide not, much I dread
Those evil talons. Even now behind

---

[1] *Æsop's fable.*—The frog, who offered to carry the mouse across a ditch, with the intention of drowning him, when both were carried off by a kite. It is not among those Greek fables which go under the name of Æsop.

Scarcely had his feet
Reach'd to the lowest of the bed beneath,
When over us the steep they reach'd.
Canto XXIII., lines 52—54.

They urge us : quick imagination works
So forcibly, that I already feel them."

He answer'd : " Were I form'd of leaded glass,
I should not sooner draw unto myself
Thy outward image, than I now imprint
That from within. This moment came thy thoughts
Presented before mine, with similar act
And countenance similar, so that from both
I one design have framed. If the right coast
Incline so much, that we may thence descend
Into the other chasm, we shall escape
Secure from this imagined pursuit."

He had not spoke[1] his purpose to the end,
When I from far beheld them with spread wings
Approach to take us. Suddenly my guide
Caught me, even as a mother that from sleep
Is by the noise aroused, and near her sees
The climbing fires, who snatches up her babe
And flies ne'er pausing, careful more of him
Than of herself, that but a single vest
Clings round her limbs. Down from the jutting beach
Supine he cast him to that pendent rock,
Which closes on one part the other chasm.

Never ran water with such hurrying pace
Adown the tube to turn a land-mill's wheel,
When nearest it approaches to the spokes,
As then along that edge my master ran,
Carrying me in his bosom, as a child,
Not a companion. Scarcely had his feet
Reach'd to the lowest of the bed beneath,
When over us the steep they reach'd : but fear
In him was none ; for that high Providence,
Which placed them ministers of the fifth fosse,
Power of departing thence took from them all.

---

[1] *He had not spoke.*—" Cumque ego cum angelis relictus starem pavidus, unus ex illis tartareis ministris horridis (? horridus) hispidis (? hispidus) aspectuque procerus festinus adveniens me impellere et quomodocumque nocere conabatur : cum ecce apostolus velocius accurrens, meque subito arripiens in quendam locum gloriose projecit visionis."—*Alberici Visio,* § xv.

There in the depth we saw a painted tribe,
Who paced with tardy steps around, and wept,
Faint in appearance and o'ercome with toil.
Caps had they on, with hoods, that fell low down
Before their eyes, in fashion like to those
Worn by the monks in Cologne.[1] Their outside
Was overlaid with gold, dazzling to view,
But leaden all within, and of such weight,
That Frederick's[2] compared to these were straw.
Oh, everlasting wearisome attire !

We yet once more with them together turn'd
To leftward, on their dismal moan intent.
But by the weight opprest, so slowly came
The fainting people, that our company
Was changed, at every movement of the step.

Whence I my guide address'd : "See that thou find
Some spirit, whose name may by his deeds be known,
And to that end look round thee as thou go'st."

Then one, who understood the Tuscan voice,
Cried after us aloud : "Hold in your feet,
Ye who so swiftly speed through the dusk air.
Perchance from me thou shalt obtain thy wish."

Whereat my leader, turning, me bespake :
"Pause, and then onward at their pace proceed."

I stayed, and saw two spirits in whose look
Impatient eagerness of mind was mark'd
To overtake me ; but the load they bare
And narrow path retarded their approach.

Soon as arrived, they with an eye askance
Perused me, but spake not : then turning, each
To other thus conferring said : "This one
Seems, by the action of his throat, alive ;
And, be they dead, what privilege allows
They walk unmantled by the cumbrous stole ?
Then thus to me : "Tuscan, who visitest

---

[1] *Monks in Cologne.* — They wore large cowls.

[2] *Frederick's.*—The Emperor Frederick II. is said to have punished those who were guilty of high treason by wrapping them in lead, and casting them into a furnace.

"That pierced spirit, whom intent
Thou view'st, was he who gave the Pharisees
Counsel, that it were fitting for one man
To suffer for the people."

Canto XXIII., lines 117—120.

P

The college of the mourning hypocrites,
Disdain not to instruct us who thou art."

"By Arno's pleasant stream," I thus replied,
"In the great city I was bred and grew,
And wear the body I have ever worn.
But who are ye, from whom such mighty grief,
As now I witness, courseth down your cheeks ?
What torment breaks forth in this bitter woe ? "

"Our bonnets gleaming bright with orange hue," [1]
One of them answer'd, " are so leaden gross,
That with their weight they make the balances
To crack beneath them. Joyous friars [2] we were,
Bologna's natives ; Catalano I,
He Loderingo named ; and by thy land
Together taken, as men used to take
A single and indifferent arbiter,
To reconcile their strifes. How there we sped,
Gardingo's vicinage [3] can best declare."

"Oh, friars !" I began, "your miseries——"
But there brake off, for one had caught mine eye,
Fix'd to a cross with three stakes on the ground :
He, when he saw me, writhed himself, throughout
Distorted, ruffling with deep sighs his beard.
And Catalano, who thereof was 'ware,

---

[1] *Gleaming bright with orange hue.*—It is observed by Venturi, that the word " rance " does not here signify " rancid or disgustful," as it is explained by the old commentators, but " orange-coloured," in which sense it occurs in the " Purgatory," canto ii. 9. By the erroneous interpretation Milton appears to have been misled : " Ever since the day peepe, till now the sun was grown somewhat *ranke.*"—*Prose Works*, v. i., p. 160, ed. 1753.

[2] *Joyous friars.*—" Those who ruled the city of Florence on the part of the Ghibellines, perceiving this discontent and murmuring, which they were fearful might produce a rebellion against themselves, in order to satisfy the people, made choice of two knights, Frati Godenti (joyous friars) of Bologna, on whom they conferred the chief power in Florence ; one named M. Catalano de' Malavolti, the other M. Loderingo di Liandolo ; one an adherent of the Guelph, the other of the Ghibelline party. It is to be remarked, that the Joyous Friars were called Knights of St. Mary, and became knights on taking that habit. Their robes were white, the mantle sable, and the arms a white field and red cross with two stars. Their office was to defend widows and orphans ; they were to act as mediators. They had internal regulations, like other religious bodies. The above-mentioned M. Loderingo was the founder of that order. But it was not long before they too well deserved the appellation given them, and were found to be more bent on enjoying themselves than on any other object. These two friars were called in by the Florentines, and had a residence assigned them in the palace belonging to the people, over against the Abbey. Such was the dependence placed on the character of their order, that it was expected they would be impartial, and would save the commonwealth any unnecessary expense ; instead of which, though inclined to opposite parties, they secretly and hypocritically concurred in promoting their own advantage rather than the public good."—*G. Villani*, b. vii., c. xiii. This happened in 1266.

[3] *Gardingo's vicinage.*—The name of that part of the city which was inhabited by the powerful Ghibelline family of the Uberti, and destroyed under the partial and iniquitous administration of Catalano and Loderingo.

Thus spake : "That pierced spirit,[1] whom intent
Thou view'st, was he who gave the Pharisees
Counsel, that it were fitting for one man
To suffer for the people. He doth lie
Transverse ; nor any passes, but him first
Behoves make feeling trial how each weighs.
In straits like this along the fosse are placed
The father of his consort,[2] and the rest
Partakers in that council, seed of ill
And sorrow to the Jews."   I noted then,
How Virgil gazed with wonder upon him,
Thus abjectly extended on the cross
In banishment eternal.   To the friar
He next his words addressed : "We pray ye tell,
If so be lawful, whether on our right
Lies any opening in the rock, whereby
We both may issue hence, without constraint
On the dark angels, that compell'd they come
To lead us from this depth."   He thus replied :
"Nearer than thou dost hope, there is a rock
From the great[3] circle moving, which o'ersteps
Each vale of horror, save that here his cope
Is shatter'd.   By the ruin ye may mount :
For on the side it slants, and most the height
Rises below."   With head bent down awhile
My leader stood ; then spake : "He warn'd us ill,[4]
Who yonder hangs the sinners on his hook.

　　To whom the friar : "At Bologna erst
I many vices of the devil heard ;
Among the rest was said, 'He is a liar,[5]
And the father of lies !'"   When he had spoke,
My leader with large strides proceeded on,
Somewhat disturb'd with anger in his look.

　　I therefore left the spirits heavy laden,
And, following, his beloved footsteps mark'd.

---

[1] *That pierced spirit.*—Caīaphas.

[2] *The father of his consort.*—Annas, father-in-law
to Caīaphas.

[3] *Great.*—In the former editions it was printed
' next." The error was observed by Mr. Carlyle.

[4] *He warn'd us ill.*—He refers to the falsehoc
told him by the demon, canto xxi. 108.

[5] *He is a liar.*—*John* viii. 44.   Dante ha
perhaps heard this text from one of the pulpits i
Bologna.

CANTO XXIV.

———

ARGUMENT.

Under the escort of his faithful master, Dante, not without difficulty, makes his way out of the sixth gulf, and in the seventh sees the robbers tormented by venomous and pestilent serpents. The soul of Vanni Fucci, who had pillaged the sacristy of Saint James in Pistoia, predicts some calamities that impended over that city, and over the Florentines.

IN the year's early nonage,[1] when the sun
  Tempers his tresses in Aquarius' urn,
And now towards equal day the nights recede;
Whenas the rime upon the earth puts on
Her dazzling sister's image,[2] but not long
Her milder sway endures; then riseth up
The village hind, whom fails his wintry store,[3]
And looking out beholds the plain around
All whiten'd; whence impatiently he smites
His thighs, and to his hut returning in,
There paces to and fro, wailing his lot,
As a discomfited and helpless man;
Then comes he forth again, and feels new hope
Spring in his bosom, finding e'en thus soon
The world hath changed its countenance, grasps his crook,
And forth to pasture drives his little flock:
So me my guide dishearten'd, when I saw
His troubled forehead; and so speedily
That ill was cured; for at the fallen bridge
Arriving, towards me with a look as sweet,

---

[1] *In the year's early nonage.*—"At the latter part of January, when the sun enters into Aquarius, and the equinox is drawing near, when the hoar-frosts in the morning often wear the appearance of snow, but are melted by the rising sun."

[2] *Her dazzling sister's image.*—

"λιγνὺν μέλαιναν, αἰόλην πυρὸς κάσιν."
Æschylus, *Septen contra Thebas*, v. 490; *Blomfield's edit.*

"κάσις
πηλοῦ ξύνουρος, διψία κόνις."
Æschylus, *Agamemnon*, v. 478, *Blomfield.*

[3] *Whom fails his wintry store.*—

"A cui la roba manca."

So in the "Purgatorio," c. xiii. 61:

"Così gli ciechi a cui la roba manca."

He turn'd him back, as that I first beheld
At the steep mountain's foot. Regarding well
The ruin, and some counsel first maintain'd
With his own thought, he open'd wide his arm
And took me up. As one, who, while he works,
Computes his labour's issue, that he seems
Still to foresee the effect ; so lifting me
Up to the summit of one peak, he fix'd
His eye upon another. "Grapple that,"
Said he, "but first make proof, if it be such
As will sustain thee." For one capt with lead
This were no journey. Scarcely he, though light,
And I, though onward push'd from crag to crag,
Could mount. And if the precinct of this coast
Were not less ample than the last, for him
I know not, but my strength had surely fail'd.
But Malebolge all toward the mouth
Inclining of the nethermost abyss,
The site of every valley hence requires,
That one side upward slope, the other fall.

      At length the point from whence[1] the utmost stone
Juts down, we reach'd ; soon as to that arrived,
So was the breath exhausted from my lungs
I could no further, but did seat me there.

      "Now needs thy best of man ;" so spake my guide :
"For not on downy plumes,[2] nor under shade
Of canopy reposing, fame is won ;
Without which whosoe'er consumes his days,
Leaveth such vestige of himself on earth,
As smoke in air, or foam upon the wave.
Thou therefore rise : vanquish thy weariness[3]

---

[1] *From whence.*—Mr.Carlyle notes the mistake in my
former translation, and I have corrected it accordingly.
[2] *Not on downy plumes.*—

    " Lettor, tu dei pensar che, senza ardire,
     Senza affanno soffrir, l'uomo non puote
     Fama acquistar, ne gran cose fornire."
   Fazio degli Uberti, Dittamondo, lib. iv., cap. iv.
  " Nessun mai per fuggir, o per riposo,
    Venne in altezza fama over in gloria."
     Frezzi, Il Quadriregio, lib. ii., cap. ii.

  " Signor, non sotto l'ombra in piaggia molle
    Tra fonti e fior, tra Ninfe e tra Sirene,
    Ma in cima all' erto e faticoso colle
    Della virtù riposto è il nostro bene."
   Tasso, Gierusalemme Liberata, c. xvii., st. 61.
[3] *Vanquish thy weariness.*—
      " Quin corpus onustum
  Hesternis vitiis animum quoque prægravat unâ,
  Atque affigit humi divinæ particulam auræ."
     Horace, Sat. ii., lib. ii. 78.

By the mind's effort, in each struggle form'd
To vanquish, if she suffer not the weight
Of her corporeal frame to crush her down.
A longer ladder yet remains to scale.
From these to have escaped sufficeth not,
If well thou note me, profit by my words."

I straightway rose, and show'd myself less spent
Than I in truth did feel me. "On," I cried,
"For I am stout and fearless." Up the rock
Our way we held, more rugged than before,
Narrower, and steeper far to climb. From talk
I ceased not, as we journey'd, so to seem
Least faint; whereat a voice from the other fosse
Did issue forth, for utterance suited ill.
Though on the arch that crosses there I stood,
What were the words I knew not, but who spake
Seem'd moved in anger. Down I stoop'd to look;
But my quick eye might reach not to the depth
For shrouding darkness; wherefore thus I spake:
"To the next circle, teacher, bend thy steps,
And from the wall dismount we; for as hence
I hear and understand not, so I see
Beneath, and nought discern." "I answer not,"
Said he, "but by the deed. To fair request
Silent performance maketh best return."

We from the bridge's head descended, where
To the eighth mound it joins; and then, the chasm
Opening to view, I saw a crowd within
Of serpents terrible,[1] so strange of shape
And hideous, that remembrance in my veins
Yet shrinks the vital current. Of her sands[2]
Let Libya vaunt no more: if Jaculus,
Pareas and Chelyder be her brood,
Cenchris and Amphisbæna, plagues so dire

---

[1] *I saw a crowd within*
Of serpents terrible.—
"Vidi locum horridum tenebrosum fœtoribus exhalantibus flammis crepitantibus serpentibus, draconibus
. . . repletum."—*Alberici Visio.* § 12.

[2] *Sands.*—Compare Lucan, "Pharsalia." lib. ix. 703.

Or in such numbers swarming ne'er she show'd,
Not with all Ethiopia, and whate'er
Above the Erythræan sea is spawn'd.

  Amid this dread exuberance of woe
Ran naked spirits wing'd with horrid fear,
Nor hope had they of crevice where to hide,
Or heliotrope[1] to charm them out of view.
With serpents were their hands behind them bound,
Which through their reins infix'd the tail and head,
Twisted in folds before. And, lo! on one
Near to our side, darted an adder up,
And, where the neck is on the shoulders tied,
Transpierced him. Far more quickly than e'er pen
Wrote O or I, he kindled, burn'd, and changed
To ashes all, pour'd out upon the earth.
When there dissolved he lay, the dust again
Uproll'd spontaneous, and the self-same form
Instant resumed. So mighty sages tell,
The Arabian Phœnix,[2] when five hundred years
Have well nigh circled, dies, and springs forthwith
Renascent : blade nor herb throughout his life
He tastes, but tears of frankincense[3] alone
And odorous amomum : swaths of nard

---

[1] *Heliotrope.*—" Viridi colore est (gemma helio-
tropion) non ita acuto sed nubilo magis et represso,
stellis puniceis superspersa. Causa nominis de effectu
lapidis est et potestate. Dejecta in labris æneis radios
solis mutat sanguineo repercussu, utraque aquâ splen-
dorem aëris abjicit et avertit. Etiam illud posse dicitur,
ut herbâ ejusdem nominis mixta et præcantationibus
legitimis consecrata, eum, a quocunque gestabitur,
subtrahat visibus obviorum."—*Solinus,* c. xl. " A
stone," says Boccaccio, in his humorous tale of
" Calandrino," "which we lapidaries call heliotrope,
of such extraordinary virtue, that the bearer of it is
effectually concealed from the sight of all present."—
Decameron, Giorn. viii., Nov. 3. In Chiabrera's
" Ruggiero," Scaltrimento begs of Sofia, who is send-
ing him on a perilous errand, to lend him the heliotrope :

       " In mia man fida
    L'elitropia, per cui possa involarmi
    Secondo il mio talento agli occhi altrui," c. vi.
  " Trust to my hand the heliotrope, by which
    I may at will from others' eyes conceal me."
Compare Ariosto, " Il Negromante," Act iii., sc. 3 ;

Pulci, " Morgante Maggiore," c. xxv. ; and Fortiguerra,
" Ricciardetto," c. x., st. 17. Gower, in his " Con-
fessio Amantis," lib. vii., enumerates it among the
jewels in the diadem of the sun :

       "Jaspis and helitropius."

  [2] *The Arabian Phœnix.*—This is translated from
Ovid, " Metamorphoses," lib. xv. :

" Una est quæ reparat, seque ipsa reseminat ales ;
  Assyrii Phœnica vocant. Nec fruge neque herbis,
  Sed thuris lacrymis, et succo vivit amomi.
  Hæc ubi quinqu · suæ complevit secula vitæ,
  Ilicis in ramis, tremulæve cacumine palmæ,
  Unguibus et pando nidum sibi construit ore.
  Qua simul ut casias, et nardi lenis aristas,
  Quassaque cum fulvâ substravit cinnama myrrhâ.
  Se super imponit, finitque in odoribus ævum."
See also Petrarch, Canzone " Qual piu," &c.

  [3] *Tears of frankincense.*—

    " Incenso e mirra è quello onde si pasce."
Fazio degli Uberti, " Dittamondo," in a gorgeous description of the phœnix, lib. ii., cap. v

And myrrh his funeral shroud. As one that falls,
He knows not how, by force demoniac dragg'd
To earth, or through obstruction fettering up
In chains invisible the powers of man,
Who, risen from his trance, gazeth around,[1]
Bewilder'd with the monstrous agony
He hath indured, and wildly staring sighs ;
So stood aghast the sinner when he rose.

Oh ! how severe God's judgment, that deals out
Such blows in stormy vengeance. Who he was
My teacher next inquired ; and thus in few
He answer'd : " Vanni Fucci[2] am I call'd,
Not long since rained down from Tuscany
To this dire gullet. Me the bestial life
And not the human pleased, mule that I was,
Who in Pistoia found my worthy den."

I then to Virgil : " Bid him stir not hence ;
And ask him what crime did thrust him hither : once
A man I knew him, choleric and bloody."

The sinner heard and feigned not, but towards me
His mind directing and his face, wherein
Was dismal shame depictured, thus he spake :
"It grieves me more to have been caught by thee
In this sad plight, which thou beholdest, than
When I was taken from the other life.
I have no power permitted to deny
What thou inquirest. I am doom'd thus low
To dwell, for that the sacristy by me
Was rifled of its goodly ornaments,
And with the guilt another falsely charged.
But that thou mayst not joy to see me thus,
So as thou e'er shalt 'scape this darksome realm,
Open thine ears and hear what I forebode.

---

[1] *Gazeth around.*—

   " Su mi levai senza far più parole,
     Cogli occhi intorno stupido mirando,
     Si come l'Epilentico far suole."

    Frezzi, Il Quadriregio, lib. ii., cap. iii.

[2] *Vanni Fucci.*—He is said to have been an illegitimate offspring of the family of Lazari, in Pistoia, and, having robbed the sacristy of the church of St. James in that city, to have charged Vanni della Nona with the sacrilege ; in consequence of which accusation the latter suffered death.

Reft of the Neri first Pistoia[1] pines ;
Then Florence[2] changeth citizens and laws ;
From Valdimagra,[3] drawn by wrathful Mars,
A vapour rises, wrapt in turbid mists,
And sharp and eager driveth on the storm
With arrowy hurtling o'er Piceno's field,
Whence suddenly the cloud shall burst, and strike
Each helpless Bianco prostrate to the ground.
This have I told, that grief may rend thy heart."

[1] *Pistoia.*—" In May, 1301, the Bianchi party of Pistoia, with the assistance and favour of the Bianchi, who ruled Florence, drove out the party of the Neri from the former place, destroying their houses, palaces, and farms."—*G. Villani, Hist.*, lib. viii., c. xliv.

[2] *Then Florence.*—" Soon after the Bianchi will be expelled from Florence, the Neri will prevail, and the laws and people will be changed."

[3] *From Valdimagra.*—The commentators explain this prophetical threat to allude to the victory obtained by the Marquis Morello Malaspina of Valdimagra (a tract of country now called the Lunigiana), who put himself at the head of the Neri, and defeated their opponents, the Bianchi, in the Campo Piceno near Pistoia, soon after the occurrence related in the preceding note on line 142. Of this engagement I find no mention in Villani. Balbo (" Vita di Dante," v. ii., p. 143) refers to Gerini, " Memorie Storiche di Lunigiana," tom. ii., p. 123, for the whole history of this Morello or Moroello. Currado Malaspina is introduced in the eighth canto of the " Purgatory," where it appears, that although on the present occasion they espoused contrary sides, most important favours were nevertheless conferred by that family on our poet, at a subsequent period of his exile, in 1307.

CANTO XXV.

ARGUMENT.

The sacrilegious Fucci vents his fury in blasphemy, is seized by serpents, and flying is pursued by Cacus in the form of a centaur, who is described with a swarm of serpents on his haunch, and a dragon on his shoulders breathing forth fire. Our poet then meets with the spirits of three of his countrymen, two of whom undergo a marvellous transformation in his presence.

WHEN he had spoke, the sinner raised his hands[1]
Pointed in mockery, and cried: "Take them, God!
I level them at thee." From that day forth
The serpents were my friends; for round his neck
One of them rolling twisted, as it said,
"Be silent, tongue!" Another, to his arms
Upgliding, tied them, riveting itself
So close, it took from them the power to move.
Pistoia! ah, Pistoia! why dost doubt
To turn thee into ashes, cumbering earth
No longer, since in evil act so far
Thou hast undone thy seed?[2] I did not mark,
Through all the gloomy circles of the abyss,
Spirit, that swell'd so proudly 'gainst his God;
Not him,[3] who headlong fell from Thebes. He fled,
Nor utter'd more; and after him there came
A centaur full of fury, shouting, "Where,
Where is the caitiff?" On Maremma's marsh[4]

---

[1] *His hands.*—
  "Le mani alzò, con ambeduo le fiche."
So Frezzi:
  "E fe le fiche a Dio 'l superbo vermo."
      Il Quadriregio, lib. ii., cap. xix.
  "Io vidi l'ira poi con crudel faccia;
    E fe le fiche a Dio il mostro rio,
    Stringendo i denti ed alzando le braccia."
      Ibid., lib. iii., c. x.
And Trissino:
  "Poi facea con le man le fiche al cielo
    Dicendo: Togli, Iddio; che puoi più farmi?"
      L'Ital. Liberata, c. xii.

"The practice of thrusting out the thumb between the first and second fingers, to express the feelings of insult and contempt, has prevailed very generally among the nations of Europe, and for many ages had been denominated 'making the fig,' or described at least by some equivalent expression."—*Douce's Illustrations of Shakespeare*, vol. i., p. 402, ed. 1807. The passage in the original text has not escaped this diligent commentator.

[2] *Thy seed.*—Thy ancestry.

[3] *Not him.*—Capaneus, canto xiv.

[4] *On Maremma's Marsh.*—An extensive tract near the sea-shore of Tuscany.

Swarm not the serpent tribe, as on his haunch
They swarm'd, to where the human face begins.
Behind his head, upon the shoulders, lay
With open wings a dragon, breathing fire
On whomsoe'er he met. To me my guide :
"Cacus[1] is this, who underneath the rock
Of Aventine spread oft a lake of blood.
He, from his brethren parted, here must tread
A different journey, for his fraudful theft
Of the great herd that near him stall'd ; whence found
His felon deeds their end, beneath the mace
Of stout Alcides, that perchance laid on
A hundred blows,[2] and not the tenth was felt."

While yet he spake, the centaur sped away :
And under us three spirits came, of whom
Nor I nor he was ware, till they exclaim'd,
"Say who are ye !" We then brake off discourse,
Intent on these alone. I knew them not :
But, as it chanceth oft, befell, that one
Had need to name another. "Where," said he,
"Doth Cianfa[3] lurk ?" I, for a sign my guide
Should stand attentive, placed against my lips
The finger lifted. If, oh, reader ! now
Thou be not apt to credit what I tell,
No marvel ; for myself do scarce allow
The witness of mine eyes. But as I look'd
Toward them, lo ! a serpent with six feet
Springs forth on one, and fastens full upon him :
His midmost grasp'd the belly, a forefoot
Seized on each arm (while deep in either cheek[4]
He flesh'd his fangs) ; the hinder on the thighs
Were spread, 'twixt which the tail inserted curl'd

---

[1] *Cacus.*—Virgil, " Æneid," lib. viii. 193.

[2] *A hundred blows.*—Less than ten blows, out of
the hundred Hercules gave him, had deprived him of
feeling.

[3] *Cianfa.*—He is said to have been of the family of
Donati at Florence.

[4] *In either cheek.*—" Ostendit mihi post hoc
apostolus lacum magnum tetrum, et aquæ sulphureæ
plenum, in quo animarum multitudo demersa est,
plenum serpentibus ac scorpionibus ; stabant vero ibi
et dæmones serpentes tenentes et ora vultus et capita
hominum cum eisdem serpentibus percutientes."—
Alberici Visio, § xxiii.

The other two
Look'd on, exclaiming, " Ah! how dost thou change,
Agnello!"   Canto XXV., lines 56—61.

Upon the reins behind. Ivy ne'er clasp'd[1]
A dodder'd oak, as round the other's limbs
The hideous monster intertwined his own.
Then, as they both had been of burning wax,
Each melted into other, mingling hues,
That which was either now was seen no more.
Thus up the shrinking paper,[2] ere it burns,
A brown tint glides, not turning yet to black,
And the clean white expires. The other two
Look'd on, exclaiming, "Ah ! how dost thou change,
Agnello ![3] See ! thou art nor double now,
Nor only one." The two heads now became
One, and two figures blended in one form
Appear'd, where both were lost. Of the four lengths
Two arms were made : the belly and the chest,
The thighs and legs, into such members changed
As never eye hath seen. Of former shape
All trace was vanish'd. Two, yet neither, seem'd
That image miscreate, and so pass'd on
With tardy steps. As underneath the scourge
Of the fierce dog-star that lays bare the fields,
Shifting from brake to brake the lizard seems
A flash of lightning, if he thwart the road ;
So toward the entrails of the other two
Approaching seem'd an adder all on fire,
As the dark pepper-grain livid and swart.
In that part,[4] whence our life is nourish'd first,
One he transpierced ; then down before him fell
Stretch'd out. The pierced spirit look'd on him,

---

[1] *Ivy ne'er clasp'd.*—
    "'Οποία κισσὸς δρυὸς ὅπως τῆσδ' ἕξομαι."
                Euripides, Hecuba, v. 102.
" Like ivy to an oak, how will I cling to her !"

[2] *Thus up the shrinking paper.*—Many of the commentators suppose that by "papiro" is here meant the wick of a lamp or candle, and Lombardi adduces an extract from Pier Crescenzio (" Agricolt.," lib. vi., cap ix.) to show that this use was then made of the plant. But Tiraboschi has proved that paper made of linen came into use towards the latter half of the fourteenth century, and that the inventor of it was Pier da Fabiano, who carried on his manufactory in the city of Trevigi ; whereas paper of cotton, with, perhaps, some linen mixed, was used during the twelfth century. —*Storia della Lett. Ital.,* tom. v., lib. i., c. iv., § iv.

    " All my bowels crumble up to dust.
    I am a scribbled form, drawn with a pen
    Upon a parchment ; and against this fire
    Do I shrink up."
            Shakespeare, King John, Act v., sc. 7.

[3] *Agnello !*—Agnello Brunelleschi.
[4] *In that part.*—The navel.

But spake not ; yea, stood motionless and yawn'd,
As if by sleep or feverous fit assail'd.[1]
He eyed the serpent, and the serpent him.
One from the wound, the other from the mouth
Breathed a thick smoke, whose vapoury columns join'd.
　　　Lucan[2] in mute attention now may hear,
Nor thy disastrous fate, Sabellus, tell,
Nor thine, Nasidius. Ovid[3] now be mute.
What if in warbling fiction he record
Cadmus and Arethusa, to a snake
Him changed, and her into a fountain clear,
I envy not ; for never face to face
Two natures thus transmuted did he sing,
Wherein both shapes were ready to assume
The other's substance. They in mutual guise
So answer'd, that the serpent split his train
Divided to a fork, and the pierced spirit
Drew close his steps together, legs and thighs
Compacted, that no sign of juncture soon
Was visible : the tail, disparted, took
The figure which the spirit lost; its skin
Softening, his indurated to a rind.
The shoulders next I mark'd, that entering join'd
The monster's arm-pits, whose two shorter feet
So lengthen'd, as the others dwindling shrunk.
The feet behind then twisting up became
That part that man conceals, which in the wretch
Was cleft in twain. While both the shadowy smoke
With a new colour veils, and generates
The excrescent pile on one, peeling it off
From the other body, lo ! upon his feet
One upright rose, and prone the other fell.
Nor yet their glaring and malignant lamps

---

[1] *As if by sleep or feverous fit assail'd.*—
　　　　"O Rome ! thy head
　Is drown'd in sleep, and all thy body fev'ry."
　　　　　　Ben Jonson's Catiline.
[2] *Lucan.*—"Pharsalia," lib. ix., 766 and 793 :

" Lucan di alcun di questi poetando
　Conta si come Sabello e Nasidio
　Fù punti e trasformati ivi passando."
　　Fazio degli Uberti, Dittamondo," l. v., cap. xvii.
[3] *Ovid.*—" Metamorphoses," lib. iv. and v.

Were shifted, though each feature changed beneath.
Of him who stood erect, the mounting face
Retreated towards the temples, and what there
Superfluous matter came, shot out in ears
From the smooth cheeks; the rest, not backward dragg'd,
Of its excess did shape the nose; and swell'd
Into due size protuberant the lips.
He, on the earth who lay, meanwhile extends
His sharpen'd visage,[1] and draws down the ears
Into the head, as doth the slug his horns.
His tongue, continuous before and apt
For utterance, severs; and the other's fork
Closing unites. That done, the smoke was laid.
The soul, transform'd into the brute, glides off,
Hissing along the vale, and after him
The other talking sputters; but soon turn'd
His new-grown shoulders on him, and in few
Thus to another spake : "Along this path
Crawling, as I have done, speed Buoso[2] now !"

So saw I fluctuate in successive change
The unsteady ballast of the seventh hold :
And here if aught my pen[3] have swerved, events
So strange may be its warrant. O'er mine eyes
Confusion hung, and on my thoughts amaze.

Yet scaped they not so covertly, but well
I mark'd Sciancato :[4] he alone it was
Of the three first that came, who changed not : thou
The other's fate, Gaville ![5] still dost rue.

---

[1] *His sharpen'd visage.*—Compare Milton, "Para-
se Lost," b. x. 511, &c.

[2] *Buoso.*—He is also said by some to have been of
e Donati family, but by others of the Abbati.

[3] *My pen.*—Lombardi justly prefers "la penna" to
la lingua;" but, when he tells us that the former is
the Nidobeatina, and the latter in the other editions,
 ought to have excepted at least Landino's of 1484,
 d Vellutello's of 1544, and, perhaps, many besides
 ese.

[4] *Sciancato.*—Puccio Sciancato, a noted robber,
whose family, Venturi says, he has not been able to
discover. The Latin annotator on the Monte Casino
MS. informs us that he was one of the Galigai of
Florence, the decline of which house is mentioned in
the "Paradise," canto xvi. 96.

[5] *Gaville !*—Francesco Guercio Cavalcante was
killed at Gaville, near Florence; and in revenge of
his death several inhabitants of that district were put
to death.

CANTO XXVI.

—

ARGUMENT.

Remounting by the steps, down which they had descended to the seventh gulf, they go forward to the arch that stretches over the eighth, and from thence behold numberless flames wherein are punished the evil counsellors, each flame containing a sinner, save one, in which were Diomede and Ulysses, the latter of whom relates the manner of his death.

FLORENCE, exult! for thou so mightily
    Hast thriven, that o'er land and sea[1] thy wings
Thou beatest, and thy name spreads over hell.
Among the plunderers, such the three I found
Thy citizens; whence shame to me thy son,
And no proud honour to thyself redounds.

    But if our minds,[2] when dreaming near the dawn,
Are of the truth presageful, thou ere long
Shalt feel what Prato[3] (not to say the rest)
Would fain might come upon thee; and that chance
Were in good time, if it befell thee now.
Would so it were, since it must needs befall!
For as time[4] wears me, I shall grieve the more.

    We from the depth departed; and my guide
Remounting scaled the flinty steps,[5] which late
We downward traced, and drew me up the steep.
Pursuing thus our solitary way

---

[1] *O'er land and sea.—*
"For he can spread thy name o'er lands and seas."
               Milton, Sonnet viii.

[2] *But if our minds.—*
"Namque sub Auroram, jam dormitante lucernâ,
  Somnia quo cerni tempore vera solent."
             Ovid. Epist. xix.
The same poetical superstition is alluded to in the "Purgatory." canto ix. and xxvii.

[3] *Shalt feel what Prato.—*The poet prognosticates the calamities which were soon to befall his native city, and which, he says, even her nearest neighbour, Prato, would wish her. The calamities more particularly pointed at are said to be the fall of a wooden bridge over the Arno, in May, 1304, where a large multitude were assembled to witness a representation of hell and the infernal torments, in consequence of which accident many lives were lost; and a conflagration, that in the following month destroyed more than 1,700 houses, many of them sumptuous buildings. See G. Villani, "Hist.," lib. viii., c. lxx. and lxxi.

[4] *As time.—*"I shall feel all calamities more sensibly as I am further advanced in life."

[5] *The flinty steps.—*Venturi. after Daniello and Volpi, explains the word in the original, "borni," to mean the stones that project from a wall. for other buildings to be joined to, which the workmen call "toothings."

The guide, who mark'd
How I did gaze attentive, thus began:
" Within these ardours are the spirits, each
Swathed in confining fire."

Canto XXVI. lines 46—49.

Among the crags and splinters of the rock,
Sped not our feet without the help of hands.

Then sorrow seized me, which e'en now revives,
As my thought turns again to what I saw,
And, more than I am wont,[1] I rein and curb
The powers of nature in me, lest they run
Where Virtue guides not ; that, if aught of good
My gentle star or something better gave me,
I envy not myself the precious boon.

As in that season, when the sun least veils
His face that lightens all, what time the fly
Gives way to the shrill gnat, the peasant then,
Upon some cliff reclined, beneath him sees
Fire-flies innumerous spangling o'er the vale,
Vineyard or tilth, where his day-labour lies ;
With flames so numberless throughout its space
Shone the eighth chasm, apparent, when the depth
Was to my view exposed. As he, whose wrongs[2]
The bears avenged, at its departure saw
Elijah's chariot, when the steeds erect
Raised their steep flight for heaven ; his eyes, meanwhile,
Straining pursued them, till the flame alone
Upsoaring, like a misty speck, he kenn'd :
E'en thus along the gulf moves every flame,
A sinner so enfolded close in each,
That none exhibits token of the theft.

Upon the bridge I forward bent to look,
And grasp'd a flinty mass, or else had fallen,
Though push'd not from the height. The guide, who mark'd
How I did gaze attentive, thus began :
"Within these ardours are the spirits, each
Swathed in confining fire." "Master ! thy word,"
I answer'd, "hath assured me ; yet I deem'd

---

1 *More than I am wont.*—" When I reflect on the
punishment allotted to those who do not give sincere
and upright advice to others, I am more anxious than
ever not to abuse to so bad a purpose those talents,
whatever they may be, which Nature, or rather Providence, has conferred on me." It is probable that
this declaration was the result of real feeling in the
mind of Dante, whose political character would have
given great weight to any opinion or party he
had espoused, and to whom indigence and exile
might have offered temptations to deviate from that
line of conduct which a strict sense of duty pre-
scribed.

2 *As he, whose wrongs.*—2 Kings ii.

Already of the truth, already wish'd
To ask thee who is in yon fire, that comes
So parted at the summit, as it seem'd
Ascending from that funeral pile[1] where lay
The Theban brothers." He replied : " Within,
Ulysses there and Diomede endure
Their penal tortures, thus to vengeance now
Together hasting, as erewhile to wrath.
These in the flame with ceaseless groans deplore
The ambush of the horse,[2] that open'd wide
A portal for that goodly seed to pass,
Which sow'd imperial Rome ; nor less the guile
Lament they, whence, of her Achilles 'reft,
Deïdamia yet in death complains.
And there is rued the stratagem that Troy
Of her Palladium spoil'd." " If they have power
Of utterance from within these sparks," said I,
" Oh, master ! think my prayer a thousand-fold
In repetition urged, that thou vouchsafe
To pause till here the horned flame arrive.
See how toward it with desire I bend."

He thus : " Thy prayer is worthy of much praise,
And I accept it therefore : but do thou
Thy tongue refrain : to question them be mine ;
For I divine thy wish ; and they perchance,
For they were Greeks,[3] might shun discourse with thee."

When there the flame had come, where time and place
Seem'd fitting to my guide, he thus began :
" Oh, ye, who dwell two spirits in one fire !
If, living, I of you did merit aught,
Whate'er the measure were of that desert,
When in the world my lofty strain I pour'd,

---

[1] *Ascending from that funeral pile.*—The flame is said to have divided on the funeral pile which consumed the bodies of Eteocles and Polynices.

" Ecce iterum fratris primos ut contigit artus
Ignis edax, tremuere rogi, et novus advena busto
Pellitur, exundant diviso vertice flammæ,
Alternosque apices abruptâ luce coruscant."
                    Statius, Thebais, lib. xii.

[2] *The ambush of the horse.*—" The ambush of the wooden horse, that caused Æneas to quit the city of Troy and seek his fortune in Italy, where his descendants founded the Roman Empire."

[3] *For they were Greeks.*—By this it is, perhaps, implied that they were haughty and arrogant. So, in our poet's twenty-fourth Sonnet, he says :

        " Ed ella mi rispose, come un Greco."

Move ye not on, till one of you unfold
In what clime death o'ertook him self-destroy'd."
    Of the old flame forthwith the greater horn
Began to roll, murmuring, as a fire
That labours with the wind, then to and fro
Wagging the top, as a tongue uttering sounds,
Threw out its voice, and spake : " When I escaped
From Circe, who beyond a circling year
Had held me near Caieta[1] by her charms,
Ere thus Æneas yet had named the shore ;
Nor fondness for my son,[2] nor reverence
Of my old father, nor return of love,
That should have crown'd Penelope with joy,
Could overcome in me the zeal I had
To explore the world, and search the ways of life,.
Man's evil and his virtue. Forth I sail'd
Into the deep illimitable main,
With but one barque, and the small faithful band
' That yet cleaved to me. As Iberia far,
Far as Marocco, either shore I saw,
And the Sardinian and each isle beside
Which round that ocean bathes. Tardy with age
Were I and my companions, when we came
To the strait pass,[3] where Hercules ordain'd
The boundaries not to be o'erstepp'd by man.
The walls of Seville to my right I left,
On the other hand already Ceuta past.
'Oh, brothers !' I began, ' who to the west
Through perils without number now have reach'd ;
To this the short remaining watch, that yet
Our senses have to wake, refuse not proof
Of the unpeopled world, following the track
Of Phœbus. Call to mind from whence ye sprang :

---

[1] *Caieta.*—Virgil, " Æneid," lib. vii. 1.
[2] *Nor fondness for my son.*—Imitated by Tasso,
" Gierusalemme Liberata," c. viii., st. 7 :
    " Ne timor di fatica ò di periglio,
    Ne vaghezza del regno, ne pietade
    Del vecchio genitor, si degno affetto
    Intiepidir nel generoso petto."

This imagined voyage of Ulysses into the Atlantic is alluded to by Pulci :
    " E sopratutto commendava Ulisse,
    Che per veder nell' altro mondo gisse."
        Morgante Maggiore, c. xxv.
And by Tasso, " Gierusalemme Liberata," c. xv. 25.
[3] *The strait pass.*—The straits of Gibraltar.

Ye were not form'd to live the life of brutes,
But virtue to pursue, and knowledge high.'
With these few words I sharpen'd for the voyage
The mind of my associates, that I then
Could scarcely have withheld them. To the dawn
Our poop we turn'd, and for the witless flight
Made our oars wings,[1] still gaining on the left.
Each star of the other pole night now beheld,[2]
And ours so low, that from the ocean floor
It rose not. Five times re-illumed, as oft
Vanish'd the light from underneath the moon,
Since the deep way we enter'd, when from far
Appeared a mountain dim,[3] loftiest methought
Of all I e'er beheld. Joy seized us straight ;
But soon to mourning changed. From the new land
A whirlwind sprung, and at her foremost side
Did strike the vessel. Thrice[4] it whirl'd her round
With all the waves ; the fourth time lifted up
The poop, and sank the prow : so fate decreed :
And over us the booming billow closed."[5]

---

[1] *Made our oars wings.*—
"Οὐδ' εὑῆρε' ἐρετμά, τά τε πτερὰ νηῦσι πέλονται."
So Chiabrera, " Canz. Eroiche," xiii. :
"Farò de' remi un volo."
And Tasso, *Ibid.*, 26.

[2] *Night now beheld.*—Petrarch is here cited by Lombardi :
"Ne lassu sopra il cerchio della luna
Vide mai tante stelle alcuna notte."
Canz., xxxvii. 1.
" Nor there above the circle of the moon
Did ever night behold so many stars."

[3] *A mountain dim.*—The mountain of Purgatory. Amongst the various opinions of theologians respecting the situation of the terrestrial paradise, Pietro Lombardo relates that " it was separated by a long space, either of sea or land, from the regions inhabited by men and placed in the ocean, reaching as far as to the lunar circle, so that the waters of the deluge did not reach it."—*Sent.*, lib. ii., dist. 17. Thus Lombardi.

[4] *Thrice.*—
" Ast illum ter fluctus ibidem
Torquet agens circum, et rapidus vorat æquore vortex."
Virgil, Æneid, lib. i. 116.

[5] *Closed.*—Venturi refers to Pliny and Solinus for the opinion that Ulysses was the founder of Lisbon, from whence he thinks it was easy for the fancy of a poet to send him on yet further enterprises. Perhaps the story (which it is not unlikely that our author will be found to have borrowed from some legend of the Middle Ages) may have taken its rise partly from the obscure oracle returned by the ghost of Tiresias to Ulysses (see the eleventh book of the " Odyssey "), and partly from the fate which there was reason to suppose had befallen some adventurous explorers of the Atlantic Ocean.

CANTO XXVII.

ARGUMENT.

The poet, treating of the same punishment as in the last canto, relates that he turned towards a flame in which
was the Count Guido da Montefeltro, whose inquiries respecting the state of Romagna he answers ; and
Guido is thereby induced to declare who he is, and why condemned to that torment.

NOW upward rose the flame, and still'd its light
    To speak no more, and now pass'd on with leave
From the mild poet gain'd ; when following came
Another, from whose top a sound confused,
Forth issuing, drew our eyes that way to look.
    As the Sicilian bull,[1] that rightfully
His cries first echoed who had shaped its mould,
Did so rebellow, with the voice of him
Tormented, that the brazen monster seem'd
Pierced through with pain ; thus, while no way they found,
Nor avenue immediate through the flame,
Into its language turn'd the dismal words :
But soon as they had won their passage forth,
Up from the point, which vibrating obey'd
Their motion at the tongue, these sounds were heard :
"Oh, thou ! to whom I now direct my voice,
That lately didst exclaim in Lombard phrase,
' Depart thou ; I solicit thee no more ; '
Though somewhat tardy I perchance arrive,
Let it not irk thee here to pause awhile,
And with me parley : lo ! it irks not me,
And yet I burn. If but e'en now thou fall
Into this blind world, from that pleasant land
Of Latium, whence I draw my sum of guilt,
Tell me if those who in Romagna dwell

---

1 *The Sicilian bull.*—The engine of torture invented by Perillus, for the tyrant Phalaris.

Have peace or war. For of the mountains there[1]
Was I, betwixt Urbino and the height
Whence Tiber first unlocks his mighty flood."

Leaning I listen'd yet with heedful ear,
When, as he touch'd my side, the leader thus:
"Speak thou: he is a Latian." My reply
Was ready, and I spake without delay:
"Oh, spirit! who art hidden here below
Never was thy Romagna without war
In her proud tyrants' bosoms, nor is now:
But open war there left I none. The state,
Ravenna hath maintain'd this many a year,
Is steadfast. There Polenta's eagle[2] broods;
And in his broad circumference of plume
O'ershadows Cervia. The green talons grasp
The land,[3] that stood erewhile the proof so long
And piled in bloody heap the host of France.

"The old mastiff of Verruchio and the young,[4]

---

[1] *Of the mountains there.*—Montefeltro.

[2] *Polenta's eagle.*—Guido Novello da Polenta, who bore an eagle for his coat of arms The name of Polenta was derived from a castle so called, in the neighbourhood of Brettinoro. Cervia is a small maritime city, about fifteen miles to the south of Ravenna. Guido was the son of Ostasio da Polenta, and made himself master of Ravenna in 1265. In 1322 he was deprived of his sovereignty, and died at Bologna in the year following. This last and most munificent patron of Dante is himself enumerated, by the historian of Italian literature, among the poets of his time. Tiraboschi, "Storia della Lett. Ital.," tom. v., lib. iii., c. ii., § xiii. The passage in the text might have removed the uncertainty which Tiraboschi expressed, respecting the duration of Guido's absence from Ravenna, when he was driven from that city in 1295, by the arms of Pietro, Archbishop of Monreale. It must evidently have been very short, since his government is here represented (in 1300) as not having suffered any material disturbance for many years. In the Proëmium to the Annotations on the "Decameron" of Boccaccio, written by those who were deputed to that work, ediz. Giunti, 1573, it is said of Guido Novello, "Del quale si leggono ancora alcune composizioni, per poche che elle sieno, secondo quella età, belle e leggiadre;" and in the collection edited by Allacci at Naples, 1661, p. 382, is a sonnet of his, which breathes a high and pure spirit of Platonism. Among the MSS. of the "Iliad" in the Ambrosian Library at Milan, described by Mai, there is one that was in the possession of Guido. *Iliadis Fragmenta, &c.,* fol., *Mediol.* 1819. Proëmium, p. xlviii. It was, perhaps, seen by Dante. To this account I must now subjoin that which has since been given, but without any reference to authorities, by Troya: "In the course of eight years, from 1310 to 1318, Guido III. of Polenta, father of Francesca, together with his sons Bernardino and Ostasio, had died. A third son, named Bannino, was father of Guido IV. Of these two it is not known whether they held the lordship of Ravenna. But it came to the sons of Ostasio, Guido V., called Novello, and Rinaldo, the archbishop: on the sons of Bernardino devolved the sovereignty of the neighbouring city of Cervia."—*Veltro Allegorico di Dante,* ed. 1826, p. 176.

[3] *The land.*—The territory of Forli, the inhabitants of which, in 1282, were enabled, by the stratagem of Guido da Montefeltro, who then governed it, to defeat with great slaughter the French army by which it had been besieged. See G. Villani, lib. vii., c. lxxxi. The poet informs Guido, its former ruler, that it is now in the possession of Sinibaldo degli Ordelaffi, whom he designates by his coat of arms, a lion vert.

[4] *The old mastiff of Verruchio and the young.*—Malatesta and Malatestino his son, lords of Rimini, called, from their ferocity, the mastiffs of Verruchio, which was the name of their castle. Malatestino was, perhaps, the husband of Francesca, daughter of Guido da Polenta. See notes to canto v. 113.

That tore Montagna[1] in their wrath, still make,
Where they are wont, an auger of their fangs.
　　"Lamone's city, and Santerno's,[2] range
Under the lion of the snowy lair,[3]
Inconstant partisan, that changeth sides,
Or ever summer yields to winter's frost.
And she whose flank is wash'd of Savio's wave,[4]
As 'twixt the level and the steep she lies,
Lives so 'twixt tyrant power and liberty.
　　"Now tell us, I entreat thee, who art thou:
Be not more hard than others. In the world,
So may thy name still rear its forehead high."
　　Then roar'd awhile the fire, its sharpen'd point
On either side waved, and thus breathed at last:
"If I did think my answer were to one
Who ever could return unto the world,
This flame should rest unshaken. But since ne'er,
If true be told me, any from this depth
Has found his upward way, I answer thee,
Nor fear less infamy record the words.
　　"A man of arms[5] at first, I clothed me then
In good Saint Francis' girdle, hoping so
To have made amends. And certainly my hope
Had fail'd not, but that he, whom curses light on,
The high priest,[6] again seduced me into sin.
And how, and wherefore, listen while I tell.
Long as this spirit moved the bones and pulp
My mother gave me, less my deeds bespake
The nature of the lion than the fox.[7]
All ways of winding subtlety I knew,

---

[1] *Montagna.*—Montagna de' Parcitati, a noble knight, and leader of the Ghibelline party at Rimini, murdered by Malatestino.

[2] *Lamone's city, and Santerno's.*—Lamone is the river at Faenza, and Santerno at Imola.

[3] *The lion of the snowy lair.*—Maghinardo Pagano, whose arms were a lion azure on a field argent; mentioned again in the "Purgatory," canto xiv. 122. See G. Villani *passim*, where he is called Maghinardo da Susinana.

[4] *Whose flank is wash'd of Savio's wave.*—Cesena, situated at the foot of a mountain, and washed by the river Savio, that often descends with a swollen and rapid stream from the Apennine.

[5] *A man of arms.*—Guido da Montefeltro.

[6] *The high priest.*—Boniface VIII.

[7] *The nature of the lion than the fox.*—

　　　　" Non furon leonine ma di volpe."

So Pulci. " Morgante Maggiore," c. xix. :

　　　　" E furon le sue opre e le sue colpe
　　　　Non creder leonine ma di volpe."

　　" Fraus quasi vulpeculæ, vis leonis videtur."

　　　　　　Cicero de Officiis, lib. i., c 13.

And with such art conducted, that the sound
Reach'd the world's limit. Soon as to that part
Of life I found me come, when each behoves
To lower sails[1] and gather in the lines ;
That, which before had pleased me, then I rued,
And to repentance and confession turn'd,
Wretch that I was ; and well it had bested me.
The chief of the new Pharisees[2] meantime,
Waging his warfare near the Lateran,
Not with the Saracens or Jews (his foes
All Christians were, nor against Acre one
Had fought,[3] nor traffick'd in the Soldan's land),
He, his great charge nor sacred ministry,
In himself reverenced, nor in me that cord
Which used to mark with leanness whom it girded.

---

[1] *To lower sails.*—Our poet had the same train of thought as when he wrote that most beautiful passage in his "Convito," beginning "E qui è da sapere, che siccome dice Tullio in quello di Senettute, la naturale morte," &c., p. 209. ✱ " As it hath been said by Cicero, in his treatise on old age, natural death is like a port and haven to us after a long voyage ; and even as the good mariner, when he draws near the port, lowers his sails, and enters it softly with a weak and inoffensive motion, so ought we to lower the sails of our worldly operations, and to return to God with all our understanding and heart, to the end that we may reach this haven with all quietness and with all peace. And herein we are mightily instructed by Nature in a lesson of mildness ; for in such a death itself there is neither pain nor bitterness : but, as ripe fruit is lightly and without violence loosened from its branch, so our soul without grieving departs from the body in which it hath been."✱

" So mayst thou live, till like ripe fruit thou drop
  Into thy mother's lap, or be with ease
Gather'd, not harshly pluck'd, for death mature."
Milton, Paradise Lost, b. xi. 537.

[2] *The chief of the new Pharisees.*—Boniface VIII., whose enmity to the family of Colonna prompted him to destroy their houses near the Lateran. Wishing to obtain possession of their other seat, Penestrino, he consulted with Guido da Montefeltro how he might accomplish his purpose, offering him at the same time absolution for his past sins, as well as for that which he was then tempting him to commit. Guido's advice was, that kind words and fair promises would put his enemies into his power ; and they accordingly soon afterwards fell into the snare laid for them, A.D. 1298. See G. Villani, lib. viii., c. xxiii. There is a relation similar to this in the history of Ferreto Vincentino,

lib. ii., anno 1294 ; and the writer adds that our poet had justly condemned Guido to the torments he has allotted him. See Muratori, "Script. Ital.," tom. ix., p. 970, where the editor observes : " Probrosi hujus facinoris narrationi fidem adjungere nemo probus velit, quod facile confinxerint Bonifacii æmuli," &c. And indeed it would seem as if Dante himself had either not heard or had not believed the report of Guido's having sold himself thus foolishly to the Pope, when he wrote the passage in the "Convito," cited in the Note to line 77 ; for he soon after speaks of him as one of those noble spirits " who when they approached the last haven, lowered the sails of their worldly operations, and gave themselves up to religion in their old age, laying aside every worldly delight and wish."

[3] *Nor against Acre one had fought.*—He alludes to the renegade Christians, by whom the Saracens, in April, 1291, were assisted to recover St. John d'Acre, the last possession of the Christians in the Holy Land. The regret expressed by the Florentine annalist, G. Villani, for the loss of this valuable fortress, is well worthy of observation, lib. vii., c. cxliv.: " From this event Christendom suffered the greatest detriment : for by the loss of Acre there no longer remained in the Holy Land any footing for the Christians ; and all our good maritime places of trade never afterwards derived half the advantage from their merchandise and manufactures ; so favourable was the situation of the city of Acre, in the very front of our sea, in the middle of Syria, and as it were in the middle of the inhabited world, seventy miles from Jerusalem, both source and receptacle of every kind of merchandise, as well from the east as from the west ; the resort of all people from all countries, and of the eastern nations of every different tongue ; so that it might be considered as the aliment of the world."

As in Soracte, Constantine besought,[1]
To cure his leprosy, Sylvester's aid ;
So me, to cure the fever of his pride,
This man besought : my counsel to that end
He ask'd ; and I was silent ; for his words
Seem'd drunken : but forthwith he thus resumed :
'From thy heart banish fear : of all offence
I hitherto absolve thee. In return,
Teach me my purpose so to execute,
That Penestrino cumber earth no more.
Heaven, as thou knowest, I have no power to shut
And open : and the keys are therefore twain,
The which my predecessor[2] meanly prized.'
    "Then yielding to the forceful arguments,
Of silence as more perilous I deem'd,
And answer'd : 'Father ! since thou washest me
Clear of that guilt wherein I now must fall,
Large promise with performance scant, be sure,
Shall make thee triumph in thy lofty seat.'
    "When I was number'd with the dead, then came
Saint Francis for me ; but a cherub dark
He met, who cried, 'Wrong me not ; he is mine,
And must below to join the wretched crew,
For the deceitful counsel which he gave.
E'er since I watch'd him, hovering at his hair.
No power can the impenitent absolve ;
Nor to repent, and will, at once consist,
By contradiction absolute forbid.'
Oh, misery ! how I shook myself, when he
Seized me, and cried, 'Thou haply thought'st me not
A disputant in logic so exact !'
To Minos down he bore me ; and the judge
Twined eight times round his callous back the tail,
Which biting with excess of rage, he spake :
'This is a guilty soul, that in the fire

[1] *As in Soracte, Constantine besought.*—So in Dante's treatise, "De Monarchiâ :" "Dicunt quidam adhuc, quod Constantinus Imperator, mundatus a leprâ intercessione Sylvestri, tunc summi pontificis, imperii sedem, scilicet Romam, donavit ecclesiæ, cum multis aliis imperii dignitatibus," lib. iii. Compare Fazio degli Uberti, "Dittamondo," lib. ii., cap. xii.

[2] *My predecessor.*—Celestine V. See notes to canto iii.

Must vanish.' Hence, perdition-doom'd, I rove
A prey to rankling sorrow, in this garb."
       When he had thus fulfill'd his words, the flame
In dolour parted, beating to and fro
And writhing its sharp horn. We onward went,
I and my leader, up along the rock,
Far as another arch, that overhangs
The fosse, wherein the penalty is paid
Of those who load them with committed sin.

CANTO XXVIII.

ARGUMENT.

They arrive in the ninth gulf, where the sowers of scandal, schismatics, and heretics are seen with their limbs miserably maimed or divided in different ways. Among these the poet finds Mahomet, Piero da Medicina, Curio, Mosca, and Bertrand de Born.

WHO, e'en in words unfetter'd, might at full
    Tell of the wounds and blood that now I saw,
Though he repeated oft the tale ? No tongue
So vast a theme could equal, speech and thought
Both impotent alike. If in one band
Collected, stood the people all, who e'er
Pour'd on Apulia's happy soil[1] their blood,
Slain by the Trojans,[2] and in that long war,[3]
When of the rings[4] the measured booty made
A pile so high, as Rome's historian writes
Who errs not ; with the multitude, that felt
The griding force of Guiscard's Norman steel,[5]
And those the rest,[6] whose bones are gather'd yet

---

[1] *Happy soil.*—There is a strange discordance here among the expounders. "'Fortunata terra,' because of the vicissitudes of fortune which it experienced," Landino. "Fortunate, with respect to those who conquered in it," Vellutello. "Or on account of its natural fertility," Venturi. "The context requires that we should understand by 'fortunata,' 'calamitous,' 'disgraziata,' to which sense the word is extended in the 'Vocabulary' of La Crusca," Lombardi. Volpi is silent. On this note the late Archdeacon Fisher favoured me with the following remark : "Volpi is, indeed, silent at the passage ; but in the article 'Puglia,' in his second Index, he writes, 'Dante la chiama fortunata, cioè pingue e feconda.' This is your own translation, and is the same word in meaning with εὐδαίμων and *felix*, in Xenophon's 'Anabasis' and Horace *passim*."

[2] *The Trojans.*—Some MSS. have "Romani," and Lombardi has admitted it into the text. Venturi had, indeed, before met with the same reading in some edition, but he has not told us in which.

[3] *In that long war.*—The war of Hannibal in

Italy. "When Mago brought news of his victories to Carthage, in order to make his successes more easily credited, he commanded the golden rings to be poured out in the senate-house, which made so large a heap, that, as some relate, they filled three *modii* and a half. A more probable account represents them not to have exceeded one *modius.*"—*Livy, Hist.*, lib. xxiii. 12.

[4] *The rings.*—So Frezzi :

> "Non quella, che riempiè i moggi d'anella."
> *Il Quadriregio*, lib. ii., cap. 9.

[5] *Guiscard's Norman steel.*—Robert Guiscard, who conquered the kingdom of Naples, and died in 1110. G. Villani, lib. iv., cap. xviii. He is introduced in the " Paradise," canto xviii.

[6] *And those the rest.*—The army of Manfredi, which, through the treachery of the Apulian troops, was overcome by Charles of Anjou in 1265, and fell in such numbers, that the bones of the slain were still gathered near Ceperano. G. Villani, lib. vii., cap. ix. See the " Purgatory," canto iii.

R

At Ceperano, there where treachery
Branded the Apulian name, or where beyond
Thy walls, O Tagliacozzo,[1] without arms
The old Alardo conquer'd; and his limbs
One were to show transpierced, another his
Clean lopt away; a spectacle like this
Were but a thing of nought, to the hideous sight
Of the ninth chasm. A rundlet, that hath lost
Its middle or side stave, gapes not so wide
As one I mark'd, torn from the chin throughout
Down to the hinder passage: 'twixt the legs
Dangling his entrails hung, the midriff lay
Open to view, and wretched ventricle,
That turns the englutted aliment to dross.

Whilst eagerly I fix on him my gaze,
He eyed me, with his hands laid his breast bare,
And cried, "Now mark how I do rip me: lo!
How is Mahomet mangled: before me
Walks Ali[2] weeping, from the chin his face
Cleft to the forelock; and the others all,
Whom here thou seest, while they lived, did sow
Scandal and schism, and therefore thus are rent.
A fiend is here behind, who with his sword
Hacks us thus cruelly, slivering again
Each of this realm, when we have compast round
The dismal way; for first our gashes close
Ere we re-pass before him. But, say who
Art thou, that standest musing on the rock,
Haply so lingering to delay the pain
Sentenced upon thy crimes." "Him death not yet,"
My guide rejoin'd, "hath overta'en, nor sin
Conducts to torment; but, that he may make
Full trial of your state, I who am dead
Must through the depths of hell, from orb to orb,
Conduct him. Trust my words; for they are true."

---

[1]   *Or where beyond*
Thy walls, O Tagliacozzo.—
He alludes to the victory which Charles gained over Conradino, by the sage advice of the Sieur de Valeri. in 1268. G. Villani, lib. vii., c. xxvii.

[2] *Ali.*—The disciple of Mahomet.

"Now mark how I do rip me: lo!
How is Mahomet mangled."
Canto XXVIII., lines 30, 31.

More than a hundred spirits, when that they heard,
Stood in the fosse to mark me, through amaze
Forgetful of their pangs. "Thou, who perchance
Shalt shortly view the sun, this warning thou
Bear to Dolcino:[1] bid him, if he wish not
Here soon to follow me, that with good store
Of food he arm him, lest imprisoning snows
Yield him a victim to Novara's power;
No easy conquest else:" with foot upraised
For stepping, spake Mahomet, on the ground
Then fix'd it to depart. Another shade,
Pierced in the throat, his nostrils mutilate
E'en from beneath the eyebrows, and one ear
Lopt off, who, with the rest, through wonder stood
Gazing, before the rest advanced, and bared
His windpipe, that without was all o'ersmear'd
With crimson stain. "Oh, thou!" said he, "whom sin
Condemns not, and whom erst (unless too near
Resemblance do deceive me) I aloft
Have seen on Latian ground, call thou to mind
Piero of Medicina,[2] if again
Returning, thou behold'st the pleasant land[3]
That from Vercelli slopes to Mercabò;
And there instruct the twain,[4] whom Fano boasts

---

[1] *Dolcino.*—"In 1305 a friar, called Dolcino, who belonged to no regular order, contrived to raise in Novara, in Lombardy, a large company of the meaner sort of people, declaring himself to be a true apostle of Christ, and promulgating a community of property and of wives, with many other such heretical doctrines. He blamed the Pope, cardinals, and other prelates of the holy Church, for not observing their duty, nor leading the angelic life, and affirmed that he ought to be pope. He was followed by more than 3,000 men and women, who lived promiscuously on the mountains together, like beasts, and, when they wanted provisions, supplied themselves by depredation and rapine. This lasted for two years, till many being struck with compunction at the dissolute life they led, his sect was much diminished; and, through failure of food and the severity of the snows, he was taken by the people of Novara, and burnt, with Margarita, his companion, and many other men and women whom his errors had seduced."—G. *Villani*, lib. viii., c. lxxxiv. Landino observes that he was possessed of singular eloquence, and that both he and Margarita endured their fate with a firmness worthy of a better cause. For a further account of him, see Muratori, "Rerum Italicarum Scriptores," tom. ix., p. 427. Fazio degli Uberti, speaking of the polygamy allowed by Mahomet, adds:

" E qui con fra Dolcin par che s'intenda."

Dittamondo, lib. v., cap. xii.

[2] *Medicina.*—A place in the territory of Bologna. Piero fomented dissensions among the inhabitants of that city, and among the leaders of the neighbouring states.

[3] *The pleasant land.*—Lombardy.

[4] *The twain.*—Guido del Cassero and Angiolello da Cagnano, two of the worthiest and most distinguished citizens of Fano, were invited by Malatestino da Rimini to an entertainment, on pretence that he had some important business to transact with them; and, according to instructions given by him, they were drowned in their passage near Cattolica, between Rimini and Fano.

Her worthiest sons, Guido and Angelo,
That if 'tis given us here to scan aright
The future, they out of life's tenement[1]
Shall be cast forth, and whelm'd under the waves
Near to Cattolica, through perfidy
Of a fell tyrant. 'Twixt the Cyprian isle
And Balearic, ne'er hath Neptune seen
An injury so foul, by pirates done,
Or Argive crew of old. That one-eyed traitor
(Whose realm, there is a spirit here were fain
His eye had still lack'd sight of) them shall bring
To conference with him, then so shape his end,
That they shall need not 'gainst Focara's wind[2]
Offer up vow nor prayer." I answering thus :
" Declare, as thou dost wish that I above
May carry tidings of thee, who is he,
In whom that sight doth wake such sad remembrance."
    Forthwith he laid his hand on the cheek-bone
Of one, his fellow-spirit, and his jaws
Expanding, cried : " Lo ! this is he I wot of :
He speaks not for himself : the outcast this,
Who overwhelm'd the doubt in Cæsar's mind,[3]
Affirming that delay to men prepared
Was ever harmful." Oh ! how terrified
Methought was Curio, from whose throat was cut
The tongue, which spake that hardy word. Then one,
Maim'd of each hand, uplifted in the gloom
The bleeding stumps, that they with gory spots
Sullied his face, and cried : " Remember thee
Of Mosca[4] too ; I who, alas ! exclaim'd,

---

[1] *Out of life's tenement.*—" Fuor di lor vasello " is construed, by the old Latin annotator on the Monte Casino MS. and by Lombardi, " out of the ship." Volpi understands " vasello " to mean " their city or country." Others take the word in the sense according to which, though not without some doubt, it is rendered in this translation.

[2] *Focara's wind.*—Focara is a mountain, from which a wind blows that is peculiarly dangerous to the navigators of that coast.

[3] *The doubt in Cæsar's mind.*—Curio, whose speech (according to Lucan) determined Julius Cæsar to proceed when he had arrived at Rimini (the ancient Ariminum) and doubted whether he should prosecute the civil war :

" Tolle moras : semper nocuit differre paratis."
                Pharsalia, l. i. 281.

" Haste, then, thy towering eagles on their way;
  When fair occasion calls, 'tis fatal to delay."
                —*Rowe.*

[4] *Mosca*—Buondelmonte was engaged to marry a lady of the Amidei family, but broke his promise, and united himself to one of the Donati. This was so much resented by the former, that a meeting of

By the hair
I: bore the sever'd member, lantern-wise
Pendent in hand, which look'd at us, and said,
" Woe's me!"   *Canto XXVIII., lines 116—119.*

'The deed once done, there is an end,' that proved,
A seed of sorrow to the Tuscan race."
　　　　I added : " Ay, and death to thine own tribe."
　　　　Whence, heaping woe on woe, he hurried off,
As one grief-stung to madness. But I there
Still linger'd to behold the troop, and saw
Thing, such as I may fear without more proof
To tell of, but that conscience makes me firm,
The boon companion,[1] who her strong breastplate
Buckles on him, that feels no guilt within,
And bids him on and fear not. Without doubt
I saw, and yet it seems to pass before me,
A headless trunk that even as the rest
Of the sad flock paced onward. By the hair
It bore the sever'd member, lantern-wise
Pendent in hand, which look'd at us, and said,
" Woe's me ! " The spirit lighted thus himself ;
And two there were in one, and one in two.
How that may be, he knows who ordereth so.
　　　　When at the bridge's foot direct he stood,
His arm aloft he rear'd, thrusting the head
Full in our view, that nearer we might hear
The words, which thus it utter'd : " Now behold
This grievous torment, thou, who breathing go'st
To spy the dead : behold, if any else
Be terrible as this. And, that on earth
Thou mayst bear tidings of me, know that I
Am Bertrand,[2] he of Born, who gave King John

---

themselves and their kinsmen was held, to consider of
the best means of revenging the insult. Mosca degli
Uberti, or de' Lamberti, persuaded them to resolve
on the assassination of Buondelmonte, exclaiming to
them, " The thing once done, there is an end." The
counsel and its effects were the source of many
terrible calamities to the state of Florence : " This
murder," says G. Villani, lib. v., cap. xxxviii., " was
the cause and beginning of the accursed Guelph and
Ghibelline parties in Florence." It happened in 1215.
See the " Paradise," canto xvi. 139.

   [1] *The boon companion.*—
" What stronger breastplate than a heart untainted ? "
　　　　Shakespeare, 2 Henry VI., Act iii., sc. 2.
   [2] *Bertrand.* — Bertrand de Born, Vicomte de

Hautefort, near Perigueux in Guienne, who incited
John to rebel against his father, Henry II. of England.
Bertrand holds a distinguished place among the Provençal poets. He is quoted in Dante, " De Vulgari
Eloquentia," lib. ii., cap. ii., where it is said " that he
treated of war, which no Italian poet had yet done."
" Arma vero nullum Italum adhuc poetasse invenio."
The triple division of subjects for poetry, made in this
chapter of the " De Vulgari Eloquentia," is very remarkable. For the translation of some extracts from
Bertrand de Born's poems, see Millot, " Hist. Littér-
aire des Troubadours," tom. i., p. 210; but the historical parts of that work are, I believe, not to be relied
on. Bertrand had a son of the same name, who wrote
a poem against John, King of England. It is that

The counsel mischievous.   Father and son
I set at mutual war.   For Absalom
And David more did not Ahithophel,
Spurring them on maliciously to strife.
For parting those so closely knit, my brain
Parted, alas ! I carry from its source,
That in this trunk inhabits.   Thus the law
Of retribution fiercely works in me."

species of composition called " the serventese," and is in the Vatican, a MS. in Cod. 3.204. See Bastero, " La Crusca Provenzale, Roma," 1724, p. 80. For many particulars respecting both Bertrands. consult Raynouard's " Poésies des Troubadours," in which excellent work. and in his " Lexique Roman," Paris, 1838, several of their poems, in the Provençal language, may be seen.

But Virgil roused me: "What yet gazest on?
Wherefore doth fasten yet thy sight below
Among the maim'd and miserable shades?"
Canto XXIX., lines 4—6.

CANTO XXIX.

ARGUMENT.

Dante, at the desire of Virgil, proceeds onward to the bridge that crosses the tenth gulf, from whence he hears the cries of the alchemists and forgers, who are tormented therein ; but not being able to discern anything on account of the darkness, they descend the rock, that bounds this the last of the compartments in which the eighth circle is divided, and then behold the spirits who are afflicted by divers plagues and diseases. Two of them, namely, Grifolino of Arezzo, and Capocchio of Sienna, are introduced speaking.

SO were mine eyes inebriate with the view
  Of the vast multitude, whom various wounds
Disfigured, that they long'd to stay and weep.

    But Virgil roused me : " What yet gazest on ?
Wherefore doth fasten yet thy sight below
Among the maim'd and miserable shades ?
Thou hast not shown in any chasm beside
This weakness. Know, if thou wouldst number them,
That two and twenty miles the valley winds
Its circuit, and already is the moon
Beneath our feet : the time permitted now
Is short ; and more, not seen, remains to see."

    " If thou," I straight replied, " hadst weighed the cause,
For which I look'd, thou hadst perchance excused
The tarrying still." My leader part pursued
His way, the while I follow'd, answering him,
And adding thus : " Within that cave I deem,
Whereon so fixedly I held my ken,
There is a spirit dwells, one of my blood,
Wailing the crime that costs him now so dear."

    Then spake my master : " Let thy soul no more
Afflict itself for him. Direct elsewhere
Its thought, and leave him. At the bridge's foot
I mark'd how he did point with menacing look
At thee, and heard him by the others named

Geri of Bello.[1] Thou so wholly then
Wert busied with his spirit, who once ruled
The towers of Hautefort, that thou lookedst not
That way, ere he was gone." "Oh, guide beloved!
His violent death yet unavenged," said I,
" By any, who are partners in his shame,
Made him contemptuous; therefore, as I think,
He pass'd me speechless by; and, doing so,
Hath made me more compassionate his fate."

So we discoursed to where the rock first show'd
The other valley, had more light been there,
E'en to the lowest depth. Soon as we came
O'er the last cloister in the dismal rounds
Of Malebolge, and the brotherhood
Were to our view exposed, then many a dart
Of sore lament assail'd me, headed all
With points of thrilling pity, that I closed
Both ears against the volley with mine hands.

As were the torment,[2] if each lazar-house
Of Valdichiana,[3] in the sultry time
'Twixt July and September, with the isle
Sardinia and Maremma's pestilent fen,[4]
Had heap'd their maladies all in one fosse
Together; such was here the torment: dire
The stench, as issuing steams from fester'd limbs.

---

[1] *Geri of Bello.*—A kinsman of the poet's, who was murdered by one of the Sacchetti family. His being placed here may be considered as a proof that Dante was more impartial in the allotment of his punishments than has generally been supposed. He was the son of Bello, who was brother to Bellincione, our poet's grandfather. Pelli, " Mem. per la Vita di Dante," " Opere di Dante." Zatta, ediz., tom. iv., part ii., p. 23.

[2] *As were the torment.*—It is very probable that these lines gave Milton the idea of his celebrated description :

" Immediately a place
Before their eyes appear'd, sad, noisome, dark.
A lazar-house it seem'd, wherein were laid
Numbers of all diseased, all maladies," &c.
Paradise Lost, b. xi. 477.

Yet the enumeration of diseases which follows appears to have been taken by Milton from the " Quadriregio:"

" Quivi eran zoppi, monchi, sordi, e orbi,
Quivi era il mal podagrico e di fianco,
Quivi la frenesia cogli occhi torbi.
Quivi il dolor gridante, e non mai stanco,
Quivi il catarro con la gran cianfarda,
L'asma, la polmonia quivi eran' anco.
L'idropisia quivi era grave e tarda,
Di tutte febbri quel piano era pieno,
Quivi quel mal, che par che la carne arda."
Lib. ii., cap. 8.

[3] *Of Valdichiana.*—The valley through which passes the river Chiana, bounded by Arezzo, Cortona, Montepulciano, and Chiusi. In the heat of autumn it was formerly rendered unwholesome by the stagnation of the water, but has since been drained by the Emperor Leopold II. The Chiana is mentioned as a remarkably sluggish stream, in the " Paradise," canto xiii. 21.

[4] *Maremma's pestilent fen.*—See note to canto xxv. 18.

Then my sight
Was livelier to explore the depth, wherein
The minister of the most mighty Lord,
All-searching Justice, dooms to punishment
The forgers noted on her dread record.

Canto *XXIX.*, *lines* *52—56.*

We on the utmost shore of the long rock
Descended still to leftward. Then my sight
Was livelier to explore the depth, wherein
The minister of the most mighty Lord,
All-searching Justice, dooms to punishment
The forgers noted on her dread record.

More rueful was it not methinks to see
The nation in Ægina[1] droop, what time
Each living thing, e'en to the little worm,
All fell, so full of malice was the air
(And afterwards, as bards of yore have told,
The ancient people were restored anew
From seed of emmets), than was here to see
The spirits, that languish'd through the murky vale,
Up-piled on many a stack. Confused they lay,
One o'er the belly, o'er the shoulders one
Roll'd of another ; sideling crawl'd a third
Along the dismal pathway. Step by step
We journey'd on, in silence looking round,
And listening those diseased, who strove in vain
To lift their forms. Then two I mark'd, that sat
Propt 'gainst each other, as two brazen pans
Set to retain the heat. From head to foot,
A tetter bark'd them round. Nor saw I e'er
Groom currying so fast, for whom his lord
Impatient waited, or himself perchance
Tired with long watching, as of these each one
Plied quickly his keen nails, through furiousness
Of ne'er abated pruriency. The crust
Came drawn from underneath in flakes, like scales
Scraped from the bream, or fish of broader mail.

"Oh, thou ! who with thy fingers rendest off
Thy coat of proof," thus spake my guide to one,
"And sometimes makest tearing pincers of them,
Tell me if any born of Latian land
Be among these within ; so may thy nails

---

[1] *In Ægina.*—He alludes to the fable of the ants changed into myrmidons, Ovid, " Metamorphoses,"
b. vii.

Serve thee for everlasting to this toil."
    "Both are of Latium," weeping he replied,
"Whom tortured thus thou seest: but who art thou
That hast inquired of us?" To whom my guide:
"One that descend with this man, who yet lives,
From rock to rock, and show him hell's abyss.

    Then started they asunder, and each turn'd
Trembling toward us, with the rest, whose ear
Those words redounding struck. To me my liege
Address'd him: "Speak to them whate'er thou list.

    And I therewith began: "So may no time
Filch your remembrance from the thoughts of men
In the upper world, but after many suns
Survive it, as ye tell me, who ye are,
And of what race ye come. Your punishment,
Unseemly and disgustful in its kind,
Deter you not from opening thus much to me."

    "Arezzo was my dwelling,"[1] answer'd one,
"And me Albero of Sienna brought
To die by fire: but that, for which I died,
Leads me not here. True is, in sport I told him,
That I had learn'd to wing my flight in air;
And he, admiring much, as he was void
Of wisdom, will'd me to declare to him
The secret of mine art: and only hence,
Because I made him not a Dædalus,
Prevail'd on one supposed his sire to burn me,
But Minos to this chasm, last of the ten,
For that I practised alchemy on earth,
Has doom'd me. Him no subterfuge eludes."

    Then to the bard I spake: "Was ever race
Light as Sienna's?[2] Sure not France herself
Can show a tribe so frivolous and vain."
    The other leprous spirit heard my words,

---

[1] *Arezzo was my dwelling.*—Grifolino of Arezzo,
who promised Albero, son of the Bishop of Sienna,
that he would teach him the art of flying: and, because
he did not keep his promise, Albero prevailed on his
father to have him burnt for a necromancer.

[2]   *Was ever race
    Light as Sienna's?*—

The same imputation is again cast on the Siennese.
"Purgatory," canto xiii. 141.

And thus return'd : "Be Stricca[1] from this charge
Exempted, he who knew so temperately
To lay out fortune's gifts ; and Niccolo,
Who first the spice's costly luxury
Discover'd in that garden,[2] where such seed
Roots deepest in the soil : and be that troop
Exempted, with whom Caccia of Asciano
Lavish'd his vineyards and wide-spreading woods,
And his rare wisdom Abbagliato[3] show'd
A spectacle for all. That thou mayst know
Who seconds thee against the Siennese
Thus gladly, bend this way thy sharpen'd sight,
That well my face may answer to thy ken ;
So shalt thou see I am Capocchio's ghost,[4]
Who forged transmuted metals by the power
Of alchemy ; and if I scan thee right,
Thou needs must well remember how I aped
Creative nature by my subtle art."

---

[1] *Stricca.*—This is said ironically. Stricca, Niccolo Salimbeni, Caccia of Asciano, and Abbagliato or Meo de' Folcacchieri, belonged to a company of prodigal and luxurious young men in Sienna, called the "*brigata godereccia.*" Niccolo was the inventor of a new manner of using cloves in cookery, not very well understood by the commentators, and which was termed the "*costuma ricca.*" Pagliarini, in his Historical Observations on the "Quadriregio," lib. iii., cap. 13, adduces a passage from a MS. history of Sienna, in which it is told that these spendthrifts, out of a sum raised from the sale of their estates, built a palace, which they inhabited in common, and made the receptacle of their apparatus for luxurious enjoyment ; and that, amongst their other extravagances, they had their horses shod with silver, and forbade their servants to pick up the precious shoes if they dropped off. The end was, as might be expected, extreme poverty and wretchedness. Landino says they spent 200,000 florins in twenty months. Horses shod with silver are mentioned by Fazio degli Uberti :

"Ancora in questo tempo si fù visto
Quel Roberto Guiscardo, che d'argento
I cavagli ferrò per far l'acquisto."

Dittamondo, l. ii., c. 24, as corrected by Perticari.

[2] *In that garden.*—Sienna.

[3] *Abbagliato.* — Lombardi understands "Abbagliato" not to be the name of a man, but to be the epithet to "senno," and construes "E l'abbagliato suo senno proferse," "and manifested to the world the blindness of their understanding." So little doubt, however, is made of there being such a person, that Allacci speaks of his grandfather Folcacchiero de' Folcacchieri of Sienna as one who may dispute with the Sicilians the praise of being the first inventor of Italian poetry. Tiraboschi, indeed, observes that this genealogy is not authenticated by Allacci ; yet it is difficult to suppose that he should have mentioned it at all, if Meo de' Folcacchieri, or Abbagliato, as he was called, had never existed. Vol. i., p. 95, Mr. Mathias's edit.

[4] *Capocchio's ghost.*—Capocchio of Sienna, who is said to have been a fellow-student of Dante's in natural philosophy.

CANTO XXX.

ARGUMENT.

In the same gulf, other kinds of impostors, as those who have counterfeited the persons of others, or debased the current coin, or deceived by speech under false pretences, are described as suffering various diseases. Simon of Troy, and Adamo of Brescia, mutually reproach each other with their several impostures.

WHAT time resentment burn'd in Juno's breast
    For Semele against the Theban blood,
As more than once in dire mischance was rued;
Such fatal frenzy seized on Athamas,[1]
That he his spouse beholding with a babe
Laden on either arm, "Spread out," he cried,
"The meshes, that I take the lioness
And the young lions at the pass:" then forth
Stretch'd he his merciless talons, grasping one,
One helpless innocent, Learchus named,
Whom swinging down he dash'd upon a rock;
And with her other burden,[2] self-destroy'd,
The hapless mother plunged. And when the pride
Of all presuming Troy fell from its height,
By fortune overwhelm'd, and the old king
With his realm perish'd; then did Hecuba,[3]
A wretch forlorn and captive, when she saw
Polyxena first slaughter'd, and her son,
Her Polydorus,[4] on the wild sea-beach
Next met the mourner's view, then reft of sense
Did she run, barking even as a dog;
Such mighty power had grief to wrench her soul.

---

[1] *Athamas.*—From Ovid, "Metamorphoses," lib. iv.; "Protinus Æolides," &c.

[2] *With her other burden.*—
  "Seque super pontum nullo tardata timore
  Mittit, onusque suum."
          Ovid, Metamorphoses, lib. iv.

[3] *Hecuba.*—See Euripides, "Hecuba;" and Ovid, "Metamorphoses," lib. xiii.

[4] *Her Polydorus.*—
  "Aspicit ejectum Polydori in littore corpus."
          Ovid, Metamorphoses, lib. iv.

"That sprite of air is Schicchi; in like mood
Of random mischief vents he still his spite."
Canto XXX, lines 33, 34.

" That is the ancient soul
Of wretched Myrrha."
Canto XXX., lines 38, 39.

But ne'er the furies, or of Thebes, or Troy,
With such fell cruelty were seen, their goads
Infixing in the limbs of man or beast,
As now two pale and naked ghosts I saw,
That gnarling wildly scamper'd like the swine
Excluded from his sty. One reach'd Capocchio,
And in the neck-joint sticking deep his fangs,
Dragg'd him, that, o'er the solid pavement rubb'd
His belly stretch'd out prone. The other shape,
He of Arezzo, there left trembling, spake :
"That sprite of air is Schicchi ;[1] in like mood
Of random mischief vents he still his spite."

    To whom I answering : "Oh ! as thou dost hope
The other may not flesh its jaws on thee,
Be patient to inform us, who it is,
Ere it speed hence." "That is the ancient soul
Of wretched Myrrha,"[2] he replied, "who burn'd
With most unholy flame for her own sire,
And a false shape assuming, so perform'd
The deed of sin ; e'en as the other there,
That onward passes, dared to counterfeit
Donati's features, to feign'd testament
The seal affixing, that himself might gain,
For his own share, the lady of the herd."

    When vanish'd the two furious shades, on whom
Mine eye was held, I turn'd it back to view
The other cursed spirits. One I saw
In fashion like a lute, had but the groin
Been sever'd where it meets the forked part.
Swollen dropsy, disproportioning the limbs
With ill-converted moisture, that the paunch
Suits not the visage, open'd wide his lips,
Gasping as in the hectic man for drought,
One towards the chin, the other upward curl'd.

---

[1] *Schicchi.*—Gianni Schicchi, who was of the family of Cavalcanti, possessed such a faculty of moulding his features to the resemblance of others, that he was employed by Simon Donati to personate Buoso Donati, then recently deceased, and to make a will, leaving Simon his heir ; for which service he was remunerated with a mare of extraordinary value, here called " the lady of the herd."

[2] *Myrrha.*—See Ovid, " Metamorphoses," lib. x.

"Oh, ye ! who in this world of misery,
Wherefore I know not, are exempt from pain,"
Thus he began, "Attentively regard
Adamo's woe.[1] When living, full supply
Ne'er lack'd me of what most I coveted;
One drop of water now, alas ! I crave.
The rills, that glitter down the grassy slopes
Of Casentino,[2] making fresh and soft
The banks whereby they glide to Arno's stream,
Stand ever in my view ; and not in vain ;
For more the pictured semblance dries me up,
Much more than the disease, which makes the flesh
Desert these shrivell'd cheeks. So from the place,
Where I transgress'd, stern justice urging me,
Takes means to quicken more my labouring sighs.
There is Romena, where I falsified
The metal with the Baptist's form imprest,
For which on earth I left my body burnt.
But if I here might see the sorrowing soul
Of Guido, Alessandro, or their brother,
For Branda's limpid spring[3] I would not change
The welcome sight. One is e'en now within,
If truly the mad spirits tell, that round
Are wandering. But wherein besteads me that ?
My limbs are fetter'd. Were I but so light,
That I each hundred years might move one inch,
I had set forth already on this path,
Seeking him out amidst the shapeless crew,
Although eleven miles it wind, not less[4]
Than half of one across. They brought me down
Among this tribe ; induced by them, I stamp'd
The florens with three carats of alloy."[5]

---

[1] *Adamo's woe.*—Adamo of Brescia, at the instiga-
tion of Guido, Alessandro, and their brother Aghinulfo,
lords of Romena, counterfeited the coin of Florence ;
for which crime he was burnt. Landino says that in
his time the peasants still pointed out a pile of stones
near Romena as the place of his execution. See
Troya, " Veltro Allegorico," p. 25.

[2] *Casentino.*—Romena is a part of Casentino.

[3] *Branda's limpid spring.*—A fountain in Sienna.

[4] *Less.*—Lombardi justly concludes that as Adamo
wishes to exaggerate the difficulty of finding the spirit
whom he wished to see, "men," and not "più"
("less," and not "more" than the half of a mile), is
probably the true reading ; for there are authorities
for both.

[5] *The florens with three carats of alloy.*—The
floren was a coin that ought to have had twenty-four
carats of pure gold. Villani relates that it was first

"Who are that abject pair," I next inquired,
"That closely bounding thee upon thy right
Lie smoking, like a hand in winter steep'd
In the chill stream?"   "When to this gulf I dropp'd,"
He answer'd, "here I found them; since that hour
They have not turn'd, nor ever shall, I ween,
Till Time hath run his course. One is that dame,
The false accuser[1] of the Hebrew youth;
Sinon the other, that false Greek from Troy.
Sharp fever drains the reeky moistness out,
In such a cloud upsteam'd."   When that he heard,
One, gall'd perchance to be so darkly named,
With clench'd hand smote him on the braced paunch,
That like a drum resounded: but forthwith
Adamo smote him on the face, the blow
Returning with his arm, that seem'd as hard.

"Though my o'erweighty limbs have ta'en from me
The power to move," said he, "I have an arm
At liberty for such employ."   To whom
Was answer'd: "When thou wentest to the fire,
Thou hadst it not so ready at command,
Then readier when it coin'd the impostor gold."

And thus the dropsied: "Ay, now speak'st thou true:
But there thou gavest not such true testimony,
When thou was question'd of the truth, at Troy."

"If I spake false, thou falsely stamp'dst the coin,"
Said Sinon; "I am here for but one fault,
And thou for more than any imp beside."

"Remember," he replied, "oh, perjured one!
The horse remember, that did teem with death;
And all the world be witness to thy guilt."

---

used at Florence in 1252, an era of great prosperity in
the annals of the republic: before which time their
most valuable coinage was of silver.—" Hist.," lib. vi.,
c. liv. Fazio degli Uberti uses the word to denote
the purest gold.

    " Pura era come l'oro del fiorino."
           Dittamondo, l. ii., cap. xiv.

" Among the ruins of Chaucer's house at Woodstock

they found an ancient coin of Florence; I think, a
florein, anciently common in England."—*Chaucer*,
Pardon.   Tale. v., 2200.

    " For that the Floraines been so fair and bright."
" Edward III., in 1344, altered it from a lower value
to 6s. 8d. The particular piece I have mentioned
seems about that value."—*Warton. History of
English Poetry*. v. ii., § ii., p. 44.
   [1] *The false accuser.*—Potiphar's wife.

"To thine," return'd the Greek, "witness the thirst
Whence thy tongue cracks, witness the fluid mound
Rear'd by thy belly up before thine eyes,
A mass corrupt." To whom the coiner thus :
"Thy mouth gapes wide as ever to let pass
Its evil saying. Me if thirst assails,
Yet I am stuft with moisture. Thou art parch'd :
Pains rack thy head : no urging wouldst thou need
To make thee lap Narcissus' mirror up."

I was all fix'd to listen, when my guide
Admonish'd : "Now beware. A little more,
And I do quarrel with thee." I perceived
How angrily he spake, and towards him turn'd
With shame so poignant, as remember'd yet
Confounds me. As a man that dreams of harm
Befallen him, dreaming wishes it a dream,
And that which is, desires as if it were not ;
Such then was I, who, wanting power to speak,
Wish'd to excuse myself, and all the while
Excused me, though unweeting that I did.

"More grievous fault than thine has been, less shame,"
My master cried, "might expiate. Therefore cast
All sorrow from thy soul ; and if again
Chance bring thee where like conference is held,
Think I am ever at thy side. To hear
Such wrangling is a joy for vulgar minds."

CANTO XXXI.

ARGUMENT.

The poets, following the sound of a loud horn, are led by it to the ninth circle, in which there are four rounds, one enclosed within the other, and containing as many sorts of traitors; but the present canto shows only that the circle is encompassed with giants, one of whom, Antæus, takes them both in his arms and places them at the bottom of the circle.

THE very tongue,[1] whose keen reproof before
  Had wounded me, that either cheek was stain'd,
Now minister'd my cure. So have I heard,
Achilles' and his father's javelin caused
Pain first, and then the boon of health restored.

  Turning our back upon the vale of woe,
We cross'd the encircled mound in silence. There
Was less than day and less than night, that far
Mine eye advanced not: but I heard a horn
Sounded so loud, the peal it rang had made
The thunder feeble. Following its course
The adverse way, my strained eyes were bent
On that one spot. So terrible a blast
Orlando[2] blew not, when that dismal rout
O'erthrew the host of Charlemain, and quench'd
His saintly warfare. Thitherward not long

---

[1] *The very tongue.—*
"Vulnus in Herculeo quæ quondam fecerat hoste
  Vulneris auxilium Pelias hasta fuit."
                Ovid, Remedia Amoris. 47.
The same allusion was made by Bernard de Ventadour, a Provençal poet in the middle of the twelfth century; and Millot observes that "it was a singular instance of erudition in a Troubadour." But it is not impossible, as Warton remarks ("Hist. of English Poetry," vol. ii., § x., p. 215) but that he might have been indebted for it to some of the early romances. In Chaucer's "Squier's Tale," a sword of similar quality is introduced:
"And other folk have wondred on the sweard,
  That could so piercen through everything;
  And fell in spech of Telephus the king,
  And of Achilles for his queint spere,
  For he couth with it both heale and dere."
So Shakespeare, "2 Henry VI.," Act v., sc. 1:
  "Whose smile and frown like to Achilles' spear
    Is able with the change to kill and cure."
[2] *Orlando.—*
  "When Charlemain with all his peerage fell
    At Fontarabia."
            Milton, Paradise Lost. b. i. 586.
See Warton's "History of English Poetry," vol. i., § iii., p. 132: This is the horn which Orlando won from the giant Jatmund, and which, as Turpin and the Islandic bards report, was endued with magical power, and might be heard at the distance of twenty miles." Charlemain and Orlando are introduced in the "Paradise," canto xviii.

T

My head was raised, when many a lofty tower
Methought I spied. "Master," said I, "what land
Is this?" He answer'd straight: "Too long a space
Of intervening darkness has thine eye
To traverse: thou hast therefore widely err'd
In thy imagining. Thither arrived
Thou well shalt see how distance can delude
The sense. A little therefore urge thee on."
    Then tenderly he caught me by the hand;
"Yet know," said he, "ere further we advance,
That it less strange may seem, these are not towers,
But giants. In the pit they stand immersed,
Each from his navel downward, round the bank."
    As when a fog disperseth gradually,
Our vision traces what the mist involves
Condensed in air; so piercing through the gross
And gloomy atmosphere, as more and more
We near'd toward the brink, mine error fled
And fear came o'er me. As with circling round
Of turrets, Montereggion[1] crowns his walls,
E'en thus the shore, encompassing the abyss,
Was turreted with giants,[2] half their length
Uprearing, horrible, whom Jove from heaven
Yet threatens, when his muttering thunder rolls.
    Of one already I descried the face,
Shoulders, and breast, and of the belly huge
Great part, and both arms down along his ribs.
    All-teeming Nature, when her plastic hand
Left framing of these monsters, did display
Past doubt her wisdom, taking from mad War
Such slaves to do his bidding; and if she
Repent her not of the elephant and whale,
Who ponders well confesses her therein
Wiser and more discreet; for when brute force
And evil will are back'd with subtlety,
Resistance none avails. His visage seem'd

[1] *Montereggion.*—A castle near Sienna.
[2] *Giants.*—The giants round the pit, it is remarked by Warton, are in the Arabian vein of fabling. See D'Herbelot, "Bibliothèque Orientale," V. Rocail., p. 717, A.

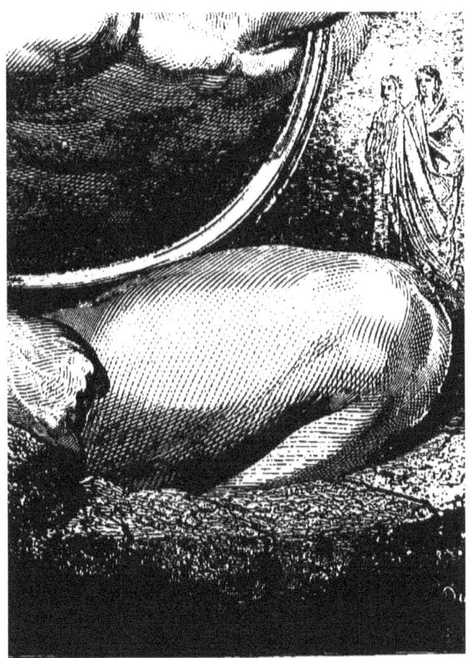

"Oh, senseless spirit! let thy horn for thee
Interpret: therewith vent thy rage, if rage
Or other passion wring thee."
                                    Canto XXXI, lines 64—66.

"This proud one
Would of his strength against almighty Jove
Make trial."   *Canto XXXI., lines 82—84*

In length and bulk as doth the pine[1] that tops
Saint Peter's Roman fane; and the other bones
Of like proportion, so that from above
The bank, which girdled him below, such height
Arose his stature, that three Friezelanders
Had striven in vain to reach but to his hair
Full thirty ample palms was he exposed
Downward from whence a man his garment loops.
" Raphel[2] baï ameth, sabi almì :"
So shouted his fierce lips, which sweeter hymns
Became not; and my guide address'd him thus :
"Oh, senseless spirit ! let thy horn for thee
Interpret : therewith vent thy rage, if rage
Or other passion wring thee. Search thy neck,
There shalt thou find the belt that binds it on.
Spirit confused ![3] lo, on thy mighty breast
Where hangs the baldrick !" Then to me he spake :
" He doth accuse himself. Nimrod is this,
Through whose ill counsel in the world no more
One tongue prevails. But pass we on, nor waste
Our words; for so each language is to him,
As his to others, understood by none."

Then to the leftward turning, sped we forth
And at a sling's throw found another shade
Far fiercer and more huge. I cannot say
What master hand had girt him; but he held
Behind the right arm fetter'd, and before,
The other, with a chain, that fasten'd him
From the neck down; and five times round his form
Apparent met the wreathed links. "This proud one
Would of his strength against almighty Jove
Make trial," said my guide : " whence he is thus

---

[1] *The pine.*—" The large pine of bronze, which
once ornamented the top of the mole of Adrian, was
afterwards employed to decorate the top of the belfry
of St. Peter; and having (according to Buti) been
thrown down by lightning, it was, after lying some
time on the steps of this palace, transferred to the
place where it now is, in the Pope's garden, by the
side of the great corridor of Belvedere."—*Lombardi.*

[2] *Raphel, &c.*—These unmeaning sounds, it is
supposed, are meant to express the confusion of
languages at the building of the tower of Babel.

[3] *Spirit confused !*—I had before translated " Wild
spirit !" and have altered it at the suggestion of Mr.
Darley, who well observes that " anima confusa " is
peculiarly appropriate to Nimrod, the author of the
confusion at Babel.

Requited : Ephialtes him they call.
Great was his prowess, when the giants brought
Fear on the gods : those arms, which then he plied,
Now moves he never." Forthwith I return'd :
"Fain would I, if 'twere possible, mine eyes,
Of Briareus immeasurable, gain'd
Experience next." He answer'd : "Thou shalt see
Not far from hence Antæus, who both speaks
And is unfetter'd, who shall place us there
Where guilt is at its depth. Far onward stands
Whom thou wouldst fain behold, in chains, and made
Like to this spirit, save that in his looks
More fell he seems." By violent earthquake rock'd
Ne'er shook a tower, so reeling to its base,
As Ephialtes. More than ever then
I dreaded death ; nor than the terror more
Had needed, if I had not seen the cords
That held him fast. We, straightway journeying on,
Came to Antæus, who, five ells complete
Without the head, forth issued from the cave.

    "Oh, thou, who in the fortunate vale,[1] that made
Great Scipio heir of glory, when his sword
Drove back the troop of Hannibal in flight,
Who thence of old didst carry for thy spoil
An hundred lions ; and if thou hadst fought
In the high conflict on thy brethren's side,
Seems as men yet believed, that through thine arm
The sons of earth had conquer'd ; now vouchsafe
To place us down beneath, where numbing cold
Locks up Cocytus. Force not that we crave
Or Tityus' help or Typhon's. Here is one
Can give what in this realm ye covet. Stoop
Therefore, nor scornfully distort thy lip.
He in the upper world can yet bestow
Renown on thee ; for he doth live, and looks
For life yet longer, if before the time

---

[1] *The fortunate vale.*—The country near Carthage.   iv. 500, &c. Dante has kept the latter of these writers
See Livy, "Hist.," l. xxx., and Lucan, "Pharsalia," l.   in his eye throughout all this passage.

Yet in the abyss,
That Lucifer with Judas low ingulfs,
Lightly he placed us.

Canto XXXI. lines 133—135.

Grace call him not unto herself." Thus spake
The teacher. He in haste forth stretch'd his hands
And caught my guide. Alcides[1] whilom felt
That grapple, straiten'd sore. Soon as my guide
Had felt it, he bespake me thus : " This way,
That I may clasp thee ; " then so caught me up,
That we were both one burden. As appears
The tower of Carisenda,[2] from beneath
Where it doth lean, if chance a passing cloud
So sail across, that opposite it hangs ;
Such then Antæus seem'd, as at mine ease
I mark'd him stooping. I were fain at times
To have past another way. Yet in the abyss,
That Lucifer with Judas low ingulfs,
Lightly he placed us ; nor, there leaning, stay'd ;
But rose, as in a barque the stately mast.

---

[1] *Alcides.*—The combat between Hercules and Antæus is adduced by the poet in his treatise " De Monarchiâ," lib. ii., as a proof of the judgment of God displayed in the *duel*, according to the singular superstition of those times. " Certamine vero dupliciter Dei judicium aperitur vel ex collisione virium, sicut fit per duellum pugilum, qui duelliones etiam vocantur ; vel ex contentione plurium ad aliquod signum prævalere conantium, sicut fit per pugnam athletarum currentium ad bravium. Primus istorum modorum apud gentiles figuratus fuit in illo duello Herculis et Antæi, cujus Lucanus meminit in quarto Pharsaliæ, et Ovidius in nono de rerum transmutatione."

[2] *Tower of Carisenda.*—The leaning tower at Bologna.

CANTO XXXII.

This canto treats of the first, and, in part, of the second of those rounds, into which the ninth and last, or frozen circle, is divided. In the former, called Caïna, Dante finds Camiccione de' Pazzi, who gives him an account of other sinners who are there punished; and in the next, named Antenora, he hears in like manner from Bocca degli Abbati who his fellow-sufferers are.

COULD I command rough rhymes and hoarse, to suit
    That hole of sorrow o'er which every rock
His firm abutment rears, then might the vein
Of fancy rise full springing; but not mine
Such measures, and with faltering awe I touch
The mighty theme; for to describe the depth
Of all the universe, is no emprise
To jest with, and demands a tongue not used
To infant babbling.[1] But let them assist
My song, the tuneful maidens, by whose aid
Amphion wall'd in Thebes; so with the truth
My speech shall best accord. Oh, ill-starr'd folk,
Beyond all others wretched! who abide
In such a mansion, as scarce thought finds words
To speak of, better had ye here on earth
Been flocks, or mountain goats. As down we stood
In the dark pit beneath the giants' feet,
But lower far than they, and I did gaze
Still on the lofty battlement, a voice
Bespake me thus: "Look how thou walkest. Take
Good heed, thy soles do tread not on the heads
Of thy poor brethren." Thereupon I turn'd,
And saw before and underneath my feet

---

[1] *A tongue not used to infant babbling.*—

  "Ne da lingua, che chiami mamma, o babbo."

Dante, in his treatise "De Vulgari Eloquentia," speaking of words not admissible in the loftier, or, as he calls it, tragic style of poetry, says: "In quorum numero nec puerilia propter suam simplicitatem ut mamma et babbo," lib. ii., c. vii.

"Look how thou walkest. Take
Good heed, thy soles do tread not on the heads
Of thy poor brethren."   *Canto XXXII., lines 20—22.*

A lake,[1] whose frozen surface liker seem'd
To glass than water. Not so thick a veil
In winter e'er hath Austrian Danube spread
O'er his still course, nor Tanais far remote
Under the chilling sky. Roll'd o'er that mass
Had Tabernich or Pietrapana[2] fallen,
Not e'en its rim had creak'd. As peeps the frog
Croaking above the wave, what time in dreams
The village gleaner oft pursues her toil,
So, to where modest shame appears,[3] thus low
Blue pinch'd and shrined in ice the spirits stood,
Moving their teeth in shrill note like the stork.[4]
His face each downward held; their mouth the cold,
Their eyes express'd the dolour of their heart.

A space I look'd around, then at my feet
Saw two so strictly join'd, that of their head
The very hairs were mingled. "Tell me ye,
Whose bosoms thus together press," said I,
"Who are ye?" At that sound their necks they bent;
And when their looks were lifted up to me,
Straightway their eyes, before all moist within,
Distill'd upon their lips, and the frost bound
The tears betwixt those orbs, and held them there.
Plank unto plank hath never cramp closed up
So stoutly. Whence, like two enraged goats,
They clash'd together: them such fury seized.

And one, from whom the cold both ears had reft,
Exclaim'd, still looking downward: "Why on us
Dost speculate so long? If thou wouldst know

---

1 *A lake.*—The same torment is introduced into the
" Edda," compiled in the eleventh and twelfth centuries. See the "Song of the Sun," translated by the
Rev. James Beresford, London, 1805; and compare
Warton's "History of English Poetry," v. i., dissert.
i., and Gray's Posthumous Works, edited by Mr.
Mathias, v. ii., p. 106. Indeed, as an escape from
" the penalty of Adam, the season's difference," forms
one of the most natural topics of consolation for the
loss of life, so does a renewal of that suffering in its
fiercest extremes of heat and cold bring before the
imagination of men in general (except, indeed, the
terrors of a self-accusing conscience) the liveliest idea

of future punishment. Refer to Shakespeare and
Milton in the Notes to canto iii. 82; and see Douce's
" Illustrations of Shakespeare," 8vo, 1807, v. i., p. 182.

2 *Tabernich or Pietrapana.*—The one a mountain
in Sclavonia, the other in that tract of country called
the Garfagnana, not far from Lucca.

3 *To where modest shame appears.*—" As high as
to the face."

4 *Moving their teeth in shrill note like the stork.*—

" Mettendo i denti in nota di cicogna."

So Boccaccio, Giorn. viii., Nov. 7 : " Lo scolar cattiv-
ello quasi cicogna divenuto si forte batteva i denti."

Who are these two,[1] the valley, whence his wave
Bisenzio slopes, did for its master own
Their sire Alberto, and next him themselves.
They from one body issued : and throughout
Caïna thou mayst search, nor find a shade
More worthy in congealment to be fix'd ;
Not him,[2] whose breast and shadow Arthur's hand
At that one blow dissever'd ; not Focaccia ;[3]
No, not this spirit, whose o'erjutting head
Obstructs my onward view : he bore the name
Of Mascheroni :[4] Tuscan if thou be,
Well knowest who he was. And to cut short
All further question, in my form behold
What once was Camiccione.[5] I await
Carlino[6] here my kinsman, whose deep guilt
Shall wash out mine." A thousand visages
Then mark'd I, which the keen and eager cold
Had shaped into a doggish grin ; whence creeps
A shivering horror o'er me, at the thought
Of those frore shallows. While we journey'd on
Toward the middle, at whose point unites
All heavy substance, and I trembling went
Through that eternal chillness, I know not
If will[7] it were, or destiny, or chance,
But, passing 'midst the heads, my foot did strike
With violent blow against the face of one.

   "Wherefore dost bruise me ? " weeping he exclaim'd.

---

[1] *Who are these two.*—Alessandro and Napoleone, sons of Alberto Alberti, who murdered each other. They were proprietors of the valley of Falterona, where the Bisenzio has its source, a river that falls into the Arno, about six miles from Florence.

[2] *Not him.*—Mordree, son of King Arthur. In the romance of "Lancelot of the Lake," Arthur, having discovered the traitorous intentions of his son, pierces him through with the stroke of his lance, so that the sunbeam passes through the body of Mordrec ; and this disruption of the shadow is no doubt what our poet alludes to in the text.

[3] *Focaccia.*—Focaccia of Cancellieri (the Pistoian family), whose atrocious act of revenge against his uncle is said to have given rise to the parties of the Bianchi and Neri, in the year 1300. See G. Villani, "Hist.," lib. viii., c. xxxvii., and Macchiavelli, "Hist.,"

lib. ii. The account of the latter writer differs much from that given by Landino in his " Commentary."

[4] *Mascheroni.*—Sassol Mascheroni, a Florentine, who also murdered his uncle.

[5] *Camiccione.*—Camiccione de' Pazzi of Valdarno, by whom his kinsman Ubertino was treacherously put to death.

[6] *Carlino.*—One of the same family. He betrayed the Castel di Piano Travigne, in Valdarno, to the Florentines, after the refugees of the Bianca and Ghibelline party had defended it against a siege for twenty-nine days, in the summer of 1302. See G. Villani, lib. viii., c. lii., and Dino Compagni, lib. ii.

[7] *If will.*—

" Whether upheld by strength, or chance, or fate."

Milton. Paradise Lost, b. i. 133.

Then seizing on his hinder scalp I cried:
" Name thee, or not a hair shall tarry here!"
Canto XXXII., lines 97, 98

"Unless thy errand be some fresh revenge
For Montaperto,[1] wherefore troublest me?"

I thus: "Instructor, now await me here,
That I through him may rid me of my doubt:
Thenceforth what haste thou wilt." The teacher paused;
And to that shade I spake, who bitterly
Still cursed me in his wrath. "What art thou? speak,
That railest thus on others?" He replied:
"Now who art thou, that smiting others' cheeks,
Through Antenora[2] roamest, with such force
As were past sufferance, wert thou living still?"

"And I am living, to thy joy perchance,"
Was my reply, "if fame be dear to thee,
That with the rest I may thy name enrol."

"The contrary of what I covet most,"
Said he, "thou tender'st: hence! nor vex me more.
Ill knowest thou to flatter in this vale."

Then seizing on his hinder scalp I cried:
"Name thee, or not a hair shall tarry here."

"Rend all away," he answer'd, "yet for that
I will not tell, nor show thee, who I am,
Though at my head thou pluck a thousand times."

Now I had grasp'd his tresses, and stript off
More than one tuft, he barking, with his eyes
Drawn in and downward, when another cried,
"What ails thee, Bocca? Sound not loud enough
Thy chattering teeth, but thou must bark outright?
What devil wrings thee?" "Now," said I, "be dumb,
Accursed traitor! To thy shame, of thee
True tidings will I bear." "Off!" he replied;
"Tell what thou list: but, as thou 'scape from hence,
To speak of him whose tongue hath been so glib,
Forget not: here he wails the Frenchman's gold.

---

[1] *Montaperto.*—The defeat of the Guelfi at Montaperto, occasioned by the treachery of Bocca degli Abbati, who, during the engagement, cut off the hand of Giacopo del Vacca de' Pazzi, bearer of the Florentine standard. G. Villani, lib. vi., c. lxxx., and Notes to canto x. This event happened in 1260.

[2] *Antenora.*—"So called from Antenor, who, according to Dictys Cretensis ("De Bello Troj.," lib. v.) and Dares Phrygius ("De Excidio Trojæ") betrayed Troy his country."—*Lombardi.* Antenor acts this part in Boccaccio's "Filostrato," and in Chaucer's "Troilus and Creseide."

'Him of Duera,'[1] thou canst say, 'I mark'd,
Where the starved sinners pine.' If thou be ask'd
What other shade was with them, at thy side
Is Beccaria,[2] whose red gorge distain'd
The biting axe of Florence. Further on,
If I misdeem not, Soldanieri[3] bides,
With Ganellon,[4] and Tribaldello,[5] him
Who ope'd Faenza when the people slept."

   We now had left him, passing on our way,
When I beheld two spirits by the ice
Pent in one hollow, that the head of one
Was cowl unto the other; and as bread
Is raven'd up through hunger, the uppermost
Did so apply his fangs to the other's brain,
Where the spine joins it. Not more furiously
On Menalippus' temples Tydeus[6] gnawed,
Than on that skull and on its garbage he.

   "Oh, thou! who show'st so beastly sign of hate
'Gainst him thou prey'st on, let me hear," said I,
"The cause, on such condition, that if right
Warrant thy grievance, knowing who ye are,
And what the colour of his sinning was,
I may repay thee in the world above,
If that, wherewith I speak, be moist so long."

---

[1] *Him of Duera.*—Buoso of Cremona, of the family of Duera, who was bribed by Guy de Montfort to leave a pass between Piedmont and Parma, with the defence of which he had been entrusted by the Ghibellines, open to the army of Charles of Anjou, A.D. 1265, at which the people of Cremona were so enraged, that they extirpated the whole family. G. Villani, lib. vii., c. iv.

[2] *Beccaria.*—Abbot of Vallombrosa, who was the Pope's legate at Florence, where his intrigues in favour of the Ghibellines being discovered, he was beheaded. I do not find the occurrence in Villani, nor do the commentators say to what Pope he was legate. By Landino he is reported to have been from Parma; by Vellutello, from Pavia.

[3] *Soldanieri.*—"Gianni Soldanieri," says Villani ("Hist.," lib. vii., c. xiv.), "put himself at the head of the people, in the hopes of rising into power, not aware that the result would be mischief to the Ghibelline party, and his own ruin; an event which seems ever to have befallen him who has headed the populace in Florence."—A.D. 1266.

[4] *Ganellon.*—The betrayer of Charlemain, mentioned by Archbishop Turpin. He is a common instance of treachery with the poets of the middle ages.

   " Trop son fol e mal pensant,
   Pis Valent que Guenelon."
                         Thibaut, Roi de Navarre.

   " Oh, new Scariot and new Ganilion,
   Oh, false dissembler," &c.
                 Chaucer, Nonne's Prieste's Tale.

And in the " Monke's Tale, Peter of Spaine."

[5] *Tribaldello.*—Tribaldello de' Manfredi, who was bribed to betray the city of Faenza, A.D. 1282. G. Villani, lib. vii., c. lxxx.

[6] *Tydeus.*—See Statius, " Thebais," lib. viii. *ad finem.*

Not more furiously
On Menalippus' temples Tydeus gnawed,
Than on that skull and on its garbage he
(Canto XXXII, lines 17–19)

The poet is told by Count Ugolino de' Gherardeschi of the cruel manner in which he and his children were famished in the tower at Pisa, by command of the Archbishop Ruggieri. He next discourses of the third round, called Ptolomea, wherein those are punished who have betrayed others under the semblance of kindness; and among these he finds the Friar Alberigo de' Manfredi, who tells him of one whose soul was already tormented in that place, though his body appeared still to be alive upon the earth, being yielded up to the governance of a fiend.

HIS jaws uplifting from their fell repast
    That sinner wiped them on the hairs o' the head,
Which he behind had mangled, then began :
"Thy will obeying, I call up afresh
Sorrow past cure ; which, but to think of, wrings
My heart, or ere I tell on 't. But if words,
That I may utter, shall prove seed to bear
Fruit of eternal infamy to him,
The traitor whom I gnaw at, thou at once
Shalt see me speak and weep. Who thou mayst be
I know not, nor how here below art come :
But Florentine thou seemest of a truth,
When I do hear thee. Know, I was on earth
Count Ugolino,[1] and the Archbishop he

---

[1] *Count Ugolino.*—" In the year 1288, in the month of July, Pisa was much divided by competitors for the sovereignty ; one party, composed of certain of the Guelfi, being headed by the Judge Nino di Gallura de' Visconti ; another, consisting of others of the same faction, by the Count Ugolino de' Gherardeschi ; and a third by the Archbishop Ruggieri degli Ubaldini, with the Lanfranchi, Sismondi, Gualandi, and other Ghibelline houses. The Count Ugolino, to effect his purpose, united with the Archbishop and his party, and having betrayed Nino, his sister's son, they contrived that he and his followers should either be driven out of Pisa, or their persons seized. Nino hearing this, and not seeing any means of defending himself, retired to Calci, his castle, and formed an alliance with the Florentines and people of Lucca, against the Pisans. The Count, before Nino was gone, in order to cover his treachery, when everything was settled for his expulsion, quitted Pisa, and repaired to a manor of his called Settimo ; whence, as soon as he was in-formed of Nino's departure, he returned to Pisa with great rejoicing and festivity, and was elevated to the supreme power with every demonstration of triumph and honour. But his greatness was not of long continuance. It pleased the Almighty that a total reverse of fortune should ensue, as a punishment for his acts of treachery and guilt ; for he was said to have poisoned the Count Anselmo da Capraia, his sister's son, on account of the envy and fear excited in his mind by the high esteem in which the gracious manners of Anselmo were held by the Pisans. The power of the Guelfi being so much diminished, the Archbishop devised means to betray the Count Ugolino, and caused him to be suddenly attacked in his palace by the fury of the people, whom he had exasperated, by telling them that Ugolino had betrayed Pisa, and given up their castles to the citizens of Florence and of Lucca. He was immediately compelled to surrender ; his bastard son and his grandson fell in the assault : and two of his sons, with their two sons also,

Ruggieri. Why I neighbour him so close,
Now list. That through effect of his ill thoughts
In him my trust reposing, I was ta'en
And after murder'd, need is not I tell.
What therefore thou canst not have heard, that is,
How cruel was the murder, shalt thou hear,
And know if he have wrong'd me. A small grate
Within that mew, which for my sake the name
Of famine bears, where others yet must pine,
Already through its opening several moons[1]
Had shown me, when I slept the evil sleep
That from the future tore the curtain off.
This one, methought, as master of the sport,
Rode forth to chase the gaunt wolf, and his whelps
Unto the mountain[2] which forbids the sight
Of Lucca to the Pisan. With lean braches
Inquisitive and keen, before him ranged
Lanfranchi with Sismondi and Gualandi.
After short course the father and the sons
Seem'd tired and lagging, and methought I saw
The sharp tusks gore their sides. When I awoke,
Before the dawn, amid their sleep I heard
My sons (for they were with me) weep and ask
For bread. Right cruel art thou, if no pang
Thou feel at thinking what my heart foretold;
And if not now, why use thy tears to flow?
Now had they waken'd; and the hour drew near
When they were wont to bring us food; the mind

were conveyed to prison."—*G. Villani*, lib. vii., c. cxx. "In the following March, the Pisans, who had imprisoned the Count Ugolino, with two of his sons and two of his grandchildren, the offspring of his son the Count Guelfo, in a tower on the Piazza of the Anziani, caused the tower to be locked, the key thrown into the Arno, and all food to be withheld from them. In a few days they died of hunger; but the Count first with loud cries declared his penitence, and yet neither priest nor friar was allowed to shrive him. All the five, when dead, were dragged out of the prison and meanly interred; and from thenceforward the tower was called the Tower of Famine, and so shall ever be."—*Ibid.*, c. cxxvii. Troya asserts that Dante, for the sake of poetical effect, has much misrepresented the real facts. See his "Veltro Allegorico di Dante," ed. 1826, p. 28, 29. This would render a conjecture, which the same writer elsewhere hazards, still more improbable; that the story might have been written by Dante when the facts were yet recent, and afterwards introduced into his poem.—*Ibid.*, p. 96. Chaucer has briefly told Ugolino's story. See "Monke's Tale, Hugeline of Pise."

1 *Several moons.*—Many editions, and the greater part of the MSS., instead of "più lune," read "più lume;" according to which reading Ugolino would say, that the day had broke, and shone through the grated window of the prison, before he fell asleep.

2 *Unto the mountain.*—The mountain S. Giuliano, between Pisa and Lucca.

Then, fasting got
The mastery of grief.   Canto XXXIII., lines 73, 74.

Of each misgave him through his dream, and I
Heard, at its outlet underneath lock'd up
The horrible tower : whence, uttering not a word,
I look'd upon the visage of my sons.
I wept not : so all stone I felt within,[1]
They wept : and one, my little Anselm, cried,
'Thou lookest so ! Father, what ails thee ?' Yet
I shed no tear, nor answer'd all that day
Nor the next night, until another sun
Came out upon the world. When a faint beam
Had to our doleful prison made its way,
And in four countenances I descried
The image of my own, on either hand
Through agony I bit ; and they, who thought
I did it through desire of feeding, rose
O' the sudden, and cried, 'Father, we should grieve
Far less, if thou wouldst eat of us : thou gavest[2]
These weeds of miserable flesh we wear ;
And do thou strip them off from us again.'
Then, not to make them sadder, I kept down
My spirit in stillness. That day and the next
We all were silent. Ah, obdurate earth !
Why open'dst not upon us ? When we came
To the fourth day, then Gaddo at my feet
Outstretch'd did fling him, crying, 'Hast no help
For me, my father ?' There he died ; and e'en
Plainly as thou seest me, saw I the three
Fall one by one 'twixt the fifth day and sixth :
Whence I betook me, now grown blind, to grope
Over them all, and for three days aloud
Call'd on them who were dead. Then, fasting got
The mastery of grief." Thus having spoke,

---

[1] *All stone I felt within.*—

" My heart is turn'd to stone ; I strike it, and it hurts
     my hand."

   Shakespeare, Othello. Act iv., sc. 1.

[2] *Thou gavest.*—

  " Tu ne vestisti
Queste misere carni, e tu le spoglia."

[1] Imitated by Filicaja, canz. iii. :

  " Di questa Imperial caduca spoglia
  Tu, Signor, me vestisti e tu mi spoglia .
  Ben puoi 'l Regno me tor tu che me 'l desti."

And by Maffei in the " Merope : "

    " Tu disciogliesti
  Queste misere membra e tu le annodi."

Once more upon the wretched skull his teeth
He fasten'd like a mastiff's 'gainst the bone,
Firm and unyielding. Oh, thou Pisa ! shame
Of all the people, who their dwelling make
In that fair region,[1] where the Italian voice
Is heard ; since that thy neighbours are so slack
To punish, from their deep foundations rise
Capraia and Gorgona,[2] and dam up
The mouth of Arno; that each soul in thee
May perish in the waters. What if fame
Reported that thy castles were betray'd
By Ugolino, yet no right hadst thou
To stretch his children on the rack. For them,
Brigata, Uguccione, and the pair
Of gentle ones, of whom my song hath told,
Their tender years, thou modern Thebes, did make
Uncapable of guilt. Onward we pass'd,
Where others, scarf'd in rugged folds of ice,
Not on their feet were turn'd, but each reversed.

   There, very weeping suffers not to weep ;[3]
For, at their eyes, grief, seeking passage, finds
Impediment, and rolling inward turns
For increase of sharp anguish : the first tears
Hang cluster'd, and like crystal vizors show,
Under the socket brimming all the cup.

   Now though the cold had from my face dislodged
Each feeling, as 'twere callous, yet me seem'd
Some breath of wind I felt. "Whence cometh this,"
Said I, "my master ? Is not here below
All vapour quench'd ?" "Thou shalt be speedily,"
He answer'd, "where thine eyes shall tell thee whence,
The cause descrying of this airy shower."

---

1 *In that fair region.—*

   " Del bel paese là, dove 'l si suona."
Italy, as explained by Dante himself. in his treatise
" De Vulgari Eloquentia." lib. i., cap. 8 : " Qui autem
Si dicunt a prædictis finibus (Januensium) Orientalem
(Meridionalis Europæ partem) tenent ; videlicet usque
ad promontorium illud Italiæ, qua sinus Adriatici
maris incipit et Siciliam."

2 *Capraia and Gorgona.—*Small islands near the
mouth of the Arno.

3 *There, very weeping suffers not to weep.—*

   " Lo pianto stesso li pianger non lascia."

So Giusto de' Conti, " Bella Mano," son. " Quanto
il ciel : "

   " Che il troppo pianto a me pianger non lassa."

Then cried out one, in the chill crust who mourn'd :
" Oh, souls ! so cruel, that the farthest post
Hath been assign'd you, from this face remove
The harden'd veil ; that I may vent the grief
Impregnate at my heart, some little space,
Ere it congeal again."   I thus replied :
" Say who thou wast, if thou wouldst have mine aid ;
And if I extricate thee not, far down
As to the lowest ice may I descend."

      " The friar Alberigo,"[1] answer'd he,
" Am I, who from the evil garden pluck'd
Its fruitage, and am here repaid, the date[2]
More luscious for my fig."   " Ah !" I exclaim'd,
" Art thou too dead ? "   " How in the world aloft
It fareth with my body," answer'd he,
" I am right ignorant.   Such privilege
Hath Ptolomea,[3] that oft-times the soul[4]
Drops hither, ere by Atropos divorced.
And that thou mayst wipe out more willingly
The glazed tear-drops[5] that o'erlay mine eyes,
Know that the soul, that moment she betrays,
As I did, yields her body to a fiend
Who after moves and governs it at will,
Till all its time be rounded : headlong she
Falls to this cistern.   And perchance above
Doth yet appear the body of a ghost,
Who here behind me winters.   Him thou know'st,

---

[1] *The friar Alberigo.*—Alberigo de' Manfredi of
Faenza, one of the Frati Godenti, Joyous Friars, who
having quarrelled with some of his brotherhood, under
pretence of wishing to be reconciled, invited them to a
banquet, at the conclusion of which he called for the
fruit, a signal for the assassins to rush in and dispatch
those whom he had marked for destruction.   Hence,
adds Landino, it is said proverbially of one who has
been stabbed, that he has had some of the friar Alberigo's fruit.   Thus Pulci, " Morgante Maggiore," c.
xxv. :

        " Le frutte amare di frate Alberico."
  [2] *The date.*—
        " Come Dio rende dataro per fico,"
    Fazio degli Uberti, Dittamondo, l. iv., cap. xix.
  [3] *Ptolomea.*—This circle is named Ptolomea from
Ptolemy, the son of Abubus, by whom Simon and his
sons were murdered, at a great banquet he had made
for them (see 1 Macc. xvi.) ; or from Ptolemy, King
of Egypt, the betrayer of Pompey the Great.
  [4] *The soul.*—Chaucer seems to allude to this in the
" Frere's Tale," where a fiend assumes the person of a
yeoman, and tells the Sompnour that he shall one day
come to a place where he shall understand the mystery
of such possessions—
        " Bet than Virgile, while he was on live,
          Or Dant also."
See Mr. Southey's " Tale of Donica."
  [5] *The glazed tear-drops.*—
      " Sorrow's eye, glazed with blinding tears.
          Shakespeare, Richard II., Act ii., sc. 2.

If thou but newly art arrived below.
The years are many that have past away,
Since to this fastness Branca Doria[1] came."

"Now," answer'd I, "methinks thou mockest me ;
For Branca Doria never yet hath died,
But doth all natural functions of a man,
Eats, drinks, and sleeps,[2] and putteth raiment on."

He thus : "Not yet unto that upper fosse
By th' evil talons guarded, where the pitch
Tenacious boils, had Michel Zanche reach'd,
When this one left a demon in his stead
In his own body, and of one his kin,
Who with him treachery wrought. But now put forth
Thy hand, and ope mine eyes." I oped them not.
Ill manners were best courtesy to him.

Ah, Genoese ! men perverse in every way,
With every foulness stain'd, why from the earth
Are ye not cancell'd ? Such a one of yours
I with Romagna's darkest spirit[3] found,
As for his doings, even now in soul
Is in Cocytus plunged, and yet doth seem
In body still alive upon the earth.

---

[1] *Branca Doria.*—The family of Doria was possessed of great influence in Genoa. Branca is said to have murdered his father-in-law, Michel Zanche, introduced in canto xxii.

[2] *Eats, drinks, and sleeps.*—

"But 'tis a spirit.
Pro. No, wench ; it eats and sleeps, and hath such senses
As we have, such."
Shakespeare, Tempest, Act i., sc. 2.

[3] *Romagna's darkest spirit.*—The friar Alberigo.

"Lo!" he exclaimed, "lo! Dis; and lo! the place
Where thou hast need to arm thy heart with strength."
Canto XXXIV., lines 20, 21

CANTO XXXIV.

ARGUMENT.

In the fourth and last round of the ninth circle, those who have betrayed their benefactors are wholly covered with ice. And in the midst is Lucifer, at whose back Dante and Virgil ascend, till by a secret path they reach the surface of the other hemisphere of the earth, and once more obtain sight of the stars.

"THE banners[1] of Hell's Monarch do come forth
   Toward us; therefore look," so spake my guide,
"If thou discern him." As, when breathes a cloud
Heavy and dense, or when the shades of night
Fall on our hemisphere, seems view'd from far
A windmill,[2] which the blast stirs briskly round;
Such was the fabric then methought I saw.
   To shield me from the wind, forthwith I drew
Behind my guide: no covert else was there.
   Now came I (and with fear I bid my strain
Record the marvel) where the souls were all
Whelm'd underneath, transparent, as through glass
Pellucid the frail stem. Some prone were laid;
Others stood upright, this upon the soles,
That on his head, a third with face to feet
Arch'd like a bow. When to the point we came,
Whereat my guide was pleased that I should see
The creature eminent in beauty once,
He from before me stepp'd and made me pause.
   "Lo!" he exclaim'd, "lo! Dis; and lo! the place
Where thou hast need to arm thy heart with strength."
   How frozen and how faint I then became,

---

[1] *The banners.—*

   "Vexilla regis prodeunt inferni."

A parody of the first verse in a hymn that was sung by the Church in praise of the cross.

[2] *A windmill.*—The author of the "Caliph Vathek," in the notes to that tale, justly observes that it is more than probable that Don Quixote's mistake of the windmills for giants was suggested to Cervantes by this simile.

Ask me not, reader! for I write it not;
Since words would fail to tell thee of my state.
I was not dead nor living.[1] Think thyself,
If quick conception work in thee at all,
How I did feel. That emperor, who sways
The realm of sorrow, at mid breast from the ice
Stood forth : and I in stature am more like
A giant,[2] than the giants are his arms.
Mark now how great that whole must be, which suits
With such a part. If he were beautiful
As he is hideous now, and yet did dare
To scowl upon his Maker, well from him
May all our misery flow. Oh, what a sight!
How passing strange it seem'd, when I did spy
Upon his head three faces :[3] one in front
Of hue vermilion, the other two with this
Midway each shoulder join'd and at the crest;
The right 'twixt wan and yellow seem'd; the left
To look on, such as come from whence old Nile
Stoops to the lowlands. Under each shot forth
Two mighty wings, enormous as became
A bird so vast. Sails[4] never such I saw

[1] *I was not dead nor living.*—
            "οὔτ' ἐν τοῖς φθιμένοις,
        οὔτ' ἐν ζῶσιν ἀριθμουμένη."
    Euripides, Supplices, v. 979, Markland's edit.
        "Tum ibi me nescio quis arripit
Timidam atque pavidam, nec vivam nec mortuam."
            Plautus, Curculio, Act v., sc. 2.

[2] *A giant.*—
    "Nel primo clima sta come signore
        Colli giganti ; ed un delle sue braccie
        Più che nullo di loro è assai maggiore."
            Frezzi, Il Quadriregio, lib. ii., cap. i.

[3] *Three faces.*—It can scarcely be doubted but that
Milton derived his description of Satan in those lines—
        "Each passion dimm'd his face
Thrice changed with pale ire, envy, and despair "—
            Paradise Lost, b. iv. 144—
from this passage, coupled with the remark of Vellutello upon it : " The first of these sins is anger, which
he signifies by the red face ; the second, represented
by that between pale and yellow, is envy, and not, as
others have said, avarice ; and the third, denoted by
the black, is a melancholy humour that causes a man's
thoughts to be dark and evil, and averse from all joy
and tranquillity." Lombardi would understand the

three faces to signify the three parts of the world then
known, in all of which Lucifer had his subjects ; the
red denoting the Europeans, who were in the middle ;
the yellow, the Asiatics, on the right ; and the black
the Africans, who were on the left ; according to the
position of the faces themselves.

[4] *Sails.*—
        " Argo non ebbe mai si grande vela,
            Ne altra nave, come l'ali sue ;
            Ne mai tessuta fù si grande tela."
            Frezzi, Il Quadriregio, lib. ii., cap. xix.
                " His sail-broad vans
            He spreads for flight."
            Milton, Paradise Lost, b. ii. 927.
Compare Spenser, " Faëry Queen," b. i., c. xi., st. 10 ;
Ben Jonson's " Every Man Out of his Humour," v. 7 ;
and Fletcher's " Prophetess," Act ii., sc. 3. In his
description of Satan, Frezzi has departed not less from
Dante than our own poet has done : for he has painted
him on a high throne, with a benignant and glad
countenance, yet full of majesty, a triple crown on his
head, six shining wings on his shoulders, and a court
thronged with giants, centaurs, and mighty captains,
besides youths and damsels, who are disporting in the
neighbouring meadows with song and dance ; but no

Outstretch'd on the wide sea. No plumes had they,
But were in texture like a bat;[1] and these
He flapp'd i' th' air, that from him issued still
Three winds, wherewith Cocytus to its depth
Was frozen. At six eyes he wept : the tears
Adown three chins distill'd with bloody foam.
At every mouth his teeth a sinner champ'd,
Bruised as with ponderous engine ; so that three
Were in this guise tormented. But far more
Than from that gnawing, was the foremost pang'd
By the fierce rending, whence oft-times the back
Was stript of all its skin. "That upper spirit,
Who hath worst punishment," so spake my guide,
"Is Judas, he that hath his head within
And plies the feet without. Of th' other two,
Whose heads are under, from the murky jaw
Who hangs, is Brutus :[2] lo ! how he doth writhe
And speaks not. The other, Cassius, that appears
So large of limb. But night now re-ascends ;
And it is time for parting. All is seen."
I clipp'd him round the neck ; for so he bade :

sooner does Minerva, who is the author's conductress, present her crystal shield, than all this triumph and jollity is seen through it transformed into loathsomeness and horror. There are many touches in this picture that will remind the reader of Milton.

[1] *Like a bat.*—The description of an imaginary being, who is called Typhurgo, in the "Zodiacus Vitæ," has something very like this of Dante's Lucifer :

 "Ingentem vidi regem, ingentique sedentem
  In solio, crines flammanti stemmate cinctum.
 . . . . . . utrinque patentes
 Alæ humeris magnæ, quales vespertilionum
 Membranis contextæ amplis—
 Nudus erat longis sed opertus corpora villis.
   M. Palingenii, Zodiacus Vitæ, lib. ix.

 "A mighty king I might discerne
  Placed high on lofty chaire,
 His haire with fyry garland deckt
  Puft up in fiendish wise.

 . . . . . .

 Large wings on him did grow
 Framde like the wings of flinder mice," &c.
    Googe's Translation.

[2] *Brutus.*—Landino struggles, but, I fear, in vain, to extricate Brutus from the unworthy lot which is here assigned him. He maintains that by Brutus and Cassius are not meant the individuals known by those names, but any who put a lawful monarch to death. Yet if Cæsar was such, the conspirators might be regarded as deserving of their doom. "O uomini eccellenti !" exclaims the commentator, with a spirit becoming one who felt that he lived in a free state, "ed al tutto degni a quali Roma fosse patria, e de' quali resterà sempre eterna memoria ; legginsi tutte le leggi di qualunque republica bene instituta, e troveremo che a nessuno si propose maggior premio che a chi uccide il tiranno." Cowley, as conspicuous for his loyalty as for his genius, in an ode inscribed with the name of this patriot, which, though not free from the usual faults of the poet, is yet a noble one, has placed his character in the right point of view—

 "Excellent Brutus ! of all human race
  The best, till nature was improved by grace."

If Dante, however, believed Brutus to have been actuated by evil motives in putting Cæsar to death, the excellence of the patriot's character in other respects would only have aggravated his guilt in that particular. "Totius autem injustitiæ nulla capitalior est quam eorum, qui cum maxime fallunt id agunt, ut viri boni esse videantur."—*Cicero de Officiis*, lib. i., cap. xiii.

And noting time and place, he, when the wings
Enough were oped, caught fast the shaggy sides,
And down from pile to pile descending stepp'd
Between the thick fell and the jagged ice.

Soon as he reach'd the point, whereat the thigh
Upon the swelling of the haunches turns,
My leader there, with pain and struggling hard,
Turn'd round his head where his feet stood before,
And grappled at the fell as one who mounts;
That into hell methought we turn'd again.

"Expect that by such stairs as these," thus spake
The teacher, panting like a man forespent,
"We must depart from evil so extreme:"
Then at a rocky opening issued forth,
And placed me on the brink to sit, next join'd
With wary step my side. I raised mine eyes,
Believing that I Lucifer should see
Where he was lately left, but saw him now
With legs held upward. Let the grosser sort,
Who see not what the point was I had past,
Bethink them if sore toil oppress'd me then.

"Arise," my master cried, "upon thy feet.
The way is long, and much uncouth the road;
And now within one hour and half of noon[1]
The sun returns." It was no palace hall
Lofty and luminous wherein we stood,
But natural dungeon where ill-footing was
And scant supply of light. "Ere from the abyss
I separate," thus when risen I began:
"My guide! vouchsafe few words to set me free
From error's thraldom. Where is now the ice?
How standeth he in posture thus reversed?
And how from eve to morn in space so brief
Hath the sun made his transit?" He in few
Thus answering spake: "Thou deemest thou art still
On the other side the centre, where I grasp'd

---

[1] *Within one hour and half of noon.*—The poet uses the Hebrew manner of computing the day, according to which the third hour answers to our twelve o'clock at noon.

Thence issuing we again beheld the stars.
Canto XXXIV, line 133.

The abhorred worm that boreth through the world.
Thou wast on the other side, so long as I
Descended ; when I turn'd, thou didst o'erpass
That point,[1] to which from every part is dragg'd
All heavy substance. Thou art now arrived
Under the hemisphere opposed to that,
Which the great continent doth overspread,
And underneath whose canopy expired
The Man, that was born sinless and so lived.
Thy feet are planted on the smallest sphere,
Whose other aspect is Judecca. Morn
Here rises, when there evening sets : and he,
Whose shaggy pile we scaled, yet standeth fix'd,
As at the first. On this part he fell down
From heaven ; and th' earth, here prominent before
Through fear of him did veil her with the sea,
And to our hemisphere retired. Perchance,
To shun him, was the vacant space left here,
By what of firm land on this side appears,[2]
That sprang aloof." There is a place beneath,
From Beelzebub as distant, as extends
The vaulted tomb ;[3] discover'd not by sight,
But by the sound of brooklet, that descends
This way along the hollow of a rock,
Which, as it winds with no precipitous course,
The wave hath eaten. By that hidden way
My guide and I did enter, to return
To the fair world : and heedless of repose
We climb'd, he first, I following his steps,
Till on our view the beautiful lights of heaven
Dawn'd through a circular opening in the cave ;
Thence issuing we again beheld the stars.

---

[1] *That point.*—Monti observes that if this passage
had chanced to meet the eye of Newton, it might
better have awakened his thought to conceive the
system of attraction, than the accidental falling of an
apple.—*Proposta*, v. iii., part 2, p. lxxviii., 8vo, 1824.

[2] *By what of firm land on this side appears.*—The
mountain of Purgatory.

[3] *As extends the vaulted tomb.*—"La tomba."
This word is used to express the whole depth of the
infernal region.

London:
Printed by Cassell & Company, Limited, La Belle Sauvage,
Ludgate Hill, E.C.